EVIL LURKS IN THE DARKNESS!

There a new dread assailed him. The sense of undesirable company, already reaching fearsome heights, mounted spectacularly moments before he glimpsed the dim, distorted human figure on the stairs. Vorchek shied back, aimed his bright beam, saw nothing and forthwith charged to the lower floor. The figure appeared again, and again, at every corner, in each alcove insufficiently bathed in light, always an insubstantial image of a man, strangely shapeless at the extremities, always dreadfully close to him, and by the time the professor bulled through into the big hall he thought the crazy shape strove to detain him. Oddly amorphous, shadowy arms reached for him—in his feverish haste Vorchek imagined more than two—and he felt the ghost of an impression of pressure, a retarding influence acting weakly at first, yet building strength at each delirious meeting. At the front door of the church the thing lunged bodily at him, wrapping its damp, clinging appendages around him in a loathsome embrace, exerting considerable power to bear him down to the floor. Vorchek lashed out with his big flashlight, seemed to beat against a swathe of thick, clinging mist, pressed forward with eyes tightly closed to stagger through a foul wet stench into the bracing outside air.

From "The Mystery of the Old Church"

Science and Sorcery II: Fifteen original stories of unabashed weirdness that test the farthest boundaries of the fantastic.

SCIENCE AND SORCERY II
More Tales of the Fantastic and the Strange

by Jeffery Scott Sims

Published by the Press of Dyrezan
Copyright 2014 by Jeffery Scott Sims
ISBN: 978-0-9899322-1-9

CONTENTS

A BRISK HIKE THROUGH THE IMAGINATION

Rather more than a stroll through scenic wonders fantastical I call this one, requiring as it does scaling sheer peaks of weirdness, steeply descending into dark canyons of morbidity, crossing raging rivers of cosmic menace. This new collection of fifteen stories endeavors to reach the heights and plumb the depths of macabre strangeness, with the following pieces ranging from quirky science fiction, through grotesque horror, to the grandest of heroic fantasy. The tales selected for this outing fall naturally into three broad categories, each intended as a laudable destination for the determined, hard-bitten seeker after the unknown.

Reader, I advise warming up for the grand march by attempting the one-off stories considerately placed at the beginning of the book. I try to make it relatively effortless at first: why, before leaving the comforts of town one may stop for provisions in "A Late Night Errand," a simple task unless, as happens to the protagonist, you drive out of the real world into a gloomy realm of nightmare. Accomplishing that much, all it takes is a bicycle—so easy—to reach "The Old House on the Hill," one of the lesser known attractions of renowned Sedona, Arizona. Only, who occupies the house, where do they come from, and is that more than just a basement below? Quite complicated to be sure, but take heart, for "The Palace in the Land of Ice" lies merely a sleep-walk away, even if it does reside on another planet. There's a pleasant goal for you, a place of dreamy serenity, no cares there, no worries; oh, other than the possibility of death and destruction and the loss of everything that matters. Okay, there is that. If this foray proves too immediately harrowing, step back a bit and join the troubled hero of "Jansen's Hypothesis," who prefers sticking closer to home. Of course that doesn't do him any good, guessing as he does

i

that the entire universe is out to get him. No fool this Jansen, who may be on to something profound, if profoundly awful. Feeling prepared for a more adventuresome trek? Give "The Cave of Ceratos" a shot, where you venture into the monster-haunted bowels of the earth with the artful and obsessive wizard Jacob Bleek as your guide. Bleek, the star of numerous published short stories and the monumental novel *The Journey of Jacob Bleek*, knows how to get you to the good stuff. Deal wisely with him however, for once you've served his purpose he may not be so interested in bringing you back.

Having thoroughly limbered up, commence a series of spooky tramps with the eminent scientist Professor Anton Vorchek, my most popular continuing character, a really smart guy, some would say too clever by half. Giving credit where it's due, I grant he always knows where he's going, always manages to come through safe and sound. Those he takes in tow, on the other hand, had better watch themselves. In "The Mystery of the Old Church" historic horror creeps from the past to torment the present. It requires iron nerves to camp out, as does Vorchek, in that creepy edifice. In "The Willing of the Man" Vorchek diligently examines the power of pure imagination, with hideous results. Travel with him as he seeks evidence to confirm his odd theories; eerie tidings along the way I admit, but the professor's lovely assistant Theresa Delaney is there to keep you company as well. Analyzing "The Flaw in the Image" will lead you on a photo shoot to some pretty Arizona locales. That should be fun. As a bonus, Vorchek gets mixed up in this one too. Fear not, he'll deduce the truth from the facts at hand, although whether that can save you from a horror lurking beyond time and space is another matter. Along with Vorchek and Theresa pick up "The Old Camera" once again for still more shots that don't come out quite as they should. Indeed, you snap them at the peril of your life. You needn't blame your own skills, though it's curious how certain pictures inevitably possess artful indications of cosmic madness.

Ready at last for the long haul, the epic journey into the untrammeled wilds of weirdness? With staff in hand and bag of magical supplies slung over shoulder stoutly proceed into the amazing world of ancient Dyrezan, a glorious land ruled and fought over by brilliant mages powerful and wise, greedy and cruel. I offer a half dozen odysseys of different styles and themes illustrating the wonder, mystery, and terror of that strange era. "Nantrech of Dyrezan," a lurid fable, recounts that famous explorer's exploits among the ruins of a still older civilization, and the horror he uncovers there. "The

Charming of Carmeline" takes a rare detour, for me, into mirth, as a foolish magician's hopeless romantic longing stirs the pot of Dyrezanian politics and threatens to rock the empire. In "The Tale of Nantrech" that well-traveled worthy tells of the fateful military expedition across the unknown sea against the evil Rhexellites. In his action-packed report Nantrech especially dotes on deeds of daring performed by the heroic Lord Morca, Captain of the Royal Guard. This pair has previously appeared in a number of published stories, none perhaps as harrowing as this one. It spawned a sequel, "The Adventure of Captain Morca," in which the great wizard warrior desperately makes his way through haunted lands, imperiled at every turn, as he seeks to escape the shocking disaster that annihilated his army. Pushing on, the reader meets Morca again in "The Voice Out of Dyrezan," when the ever questing Jacob Bleek journeys to the ends of the earth, with sorcerial bravado attempts to wring secrets from his long departed colleague's ghost! Even Bleek ought to know better. And in this collection's grand climax, once more guided by Morca, clamber to the pinnacle that is "Skyrax, Lord of Dyrezan," a fantastic novella-length romp through the palaces, avenues, and back alleys of the olden kingdom. The vile mage Lord Albragon, lusting for total domination, would yank the throne out from under the legitimate but weak King Skyrax. Fiercely loyal Lord Morca will do anything to prevent this, and to save the beloved Lady Riena. Sparks fly and the heavens reel when clash the supreme wizards of the world.

It is my fondest wish, brave reader, that you will both enjoy and survive your hike through the aforementioned exotic locales. Enjoyment I would hope to guarantee; as to the other, well, I am not a magician like Bleek or Nantrech, nor a first class brain like Vorchek, so on the issue of survival don't rely on me overmuch. The path is long, the obstacles tremendous, the dangers inconceivable. I've done what I can to prepare you. Before you set out pray to Xenophor, and then take your chances.

Jeffery Scott Sims
September 11, 2014, composed by the shores of Lynx Lake, near Prescott, Arizona

A LATE NIGHT ERRAND

I'm going to tell you what happened to me. This is for real, or at least as real as my memory and its reconstruction of events allows. First, however, I want to ask you a question. Have you ever experienced one of those curious moods or phases when you suddenly feel disconnected from normal life, as if you were a degree out of sync with the rest of the world, or—maybe this is the right way to look at it—the world had shifted a degree away from you? I know I have, and I'll bet everyone has at some time or another. I've gone through those little periods when the face of reality seemed distanced from me, as if it had withdrawn, leaving me behind in a special place of my own, sensing the oddness of my condition, wondering what it meant. At such times I've felt my forehead for fever, or tried to slap a tingling chill from my arms, or struggled to focus my eyes upon everyday objects which, for a while, appeared grotesque. Does that sound familiar? Of course it does. It must, because there's nothing inherently wrong with me, so such spells necessarily afflict us all. I accept that as a premise. I believe you do too. I've heard in conversation, or even referenced in reading, technical terms which seem to be approaching what I describe—"disassociation," for one—but I don't think they cover this business very well. It isn't just a matter of being out of touch with one's surroundings; there's that ineffable sense of *otherness* involved.

Here's my story. Make of it what you will. One night, not very long ago, I could not sleep (neither the first time nor the last), and had stayed up and awake, far past my usual hour, feeling a little groggy, when one of these spells came upon me. I was alone at the time. The visitation of sensation followed what I may call my typical pattern: I

1

felt hot and cold, light and heavy, airless and oppressed, fleeting states of shifting being. I seemed to view my cheap apartment and its drab accouterments from behind my eyeballs, as if the physical aspects around me had inched slightly away, or as if my vision had receded into a short tunnel. All this made me out of sorts, though it caused no physical distress of any kind. In my uneasiness I began to realize that sleep would be wholly denied me that night, and I cast about for something to keep me occupied. Television was particularly inane right then, and the symbols buried within my reading materials resembled cuneiform, by which I only mean that there was no way I could concentrate on the printed page. It occurred to me that I had failed to go shopping that day to pick up some trivial but useful household supplies. I decided, despite my weariness, to make a late night run to the all night store.

I descended the outside stairs to the parking lot, hopped into my compact and trundled into the gloom. I had to watch myself, just a little bit, while walking the stairs and then driving, because my attention tended to wander somewhat, though it looked to me as if the world ran vaguely out of kilter. I got out onto the main street and bore on a straight course to the east, zipping down a road I had long traveled, but which now seemed strange to me. I met no other traffic at all, not a single vehicle or far glimpse of head or taillights. I had thought the thoroughfare better lighted than it now appeared, with more visible indications of houses and businesses at a short remove. Just then I could make out very little, and what I did spy at a glance as I flashed by seemed rather different from what I recalled from previous nocturnal excursions. I wondered if fog lay on the landscape, hiding or transforming what I knew to be out there.

I reached my goal, one of those big, sprawling department stores that carry everything, with an emphasis on quantity and economy rather than quality. For day to day consumables that suited me fine. I drove across the gargantuan lot, passing a thin sprinkling of stationary cars, parked close to the main doors—such was my distinct impression, and how does one mistake that?—exited my vehicle. It was very dark out there, much more so than usual, and the illumination from the huge plate-glass windows seemed muted as well. The air felt densely warm, unseasonably so.

The electric door swung open for me, and I entered. There were no staff about the registers at the time, not too unusual in the middle of the night. What did surprise me was the murky gloom and silence reigning in the place. I wondered if, for some special reason, the store was closed after all. Previous visits accustomed me, at all hours, to harsh glare and trite, tinny music. There was enough light now to get around, but little more, with most of the feeble signs of radiance seeming to emanate from the back, at a far distance, nor did the ubiquitous ceiling speakers squawk their canned pop tunes. I thought I should consider myself thankful. I could collect my required goods in peace, round up a checker and get out of there fast.

Nothing of the sort transpired. I wandered into the tomb-quiet interior, past displays and shelves full of assorted wares, deep into the bowels of the store. I remembered the things I sought being somewhere off to the right, past the clothing department. I found that, but further progress led me farther into a twilight gloom so intense that I couldn't believe I was supposed to be there. Surely that section, at least, was meant to be off limits for some purpose. I backed out the way I'd come, toward a lighter patch, found myself in an altogether different, narrower aisle closely surrounded by shelves bearing an unsorted jumble of pants, skirts, and shoes. Here I met someone, a saleswoman, who came sauntering listlessly down the aisle tapping goods with a metal ruler. She was well dressed, middle-aged, silent save for her mechanical tapping—the first sound I'd heard since arriving, except for the annoying slapping of my own shoes—and she spoke not a word until she tried to squeeze past me, at which moment I addressed her. "Could you direct me to the household department?" I asked. "Keep going around," said she, in a voice harsh with what oddly impressed me as controlled hysteria, "and you can't miss it." "I hardly know which way is which," I pointed out, to which she nodded glumly, replying, "Nor do I. Just keep going." She said this as she passed and strode off at a faster clip into the enveloping darkness. I heard her nutty tapping until she turned a corner, at which moment the sound ceased abruptly. Silence again pressed from all sides.

I endeavored to follow her advice, such as it was, but my course only led to the back wall of the sales floor, a region illuminated solely by a garish collection of old-fashioned lamps for sale. Three of them were on, otherwise I couldn't have seen to walk. To the left I spied leaping shadows on the wall, impressions of moving human figures just beyond my line of sight. My attempt to approach them failed. Advancing to the scene, I beheld the shifting shadows still at a remove, associated with dim sounds like cries or catcalls. Thinking these were lesser employees acting up or otherwise misbehaving, I felt a revulsion for the locale and my predicament. I didn't want to be there anymore. It was a mistake, I decided, to go out on this night when I wasn't at my best. Purchases could wait until daylight. I turned to leave.

A hint of motion startled me. Someone, someone quite close, had just dived, at that second, behind a bank of shelves. I stepped forward, peered down the aisle, saw no one, went briskly on my way. The apparition hadn't registered well, but so much as I puzzled over it, I could not call up in my brain a human shape. Nor did my mind fabricate a substitute. That troubled me a lot. I wanted out.

Vacating the premises should have been easy enough, but I wandered for what seemed ages, meeting no one else, nor happening across any area recognizable to me. It was like I had stumbled into a different store, yet again altered from what I remembered. After a dreadful spell of aimless search I entered a region of total darkness, a shroud of blackness which suddenly descended as from the paneled ceiling. I gasped for breath, swung round violently, staring desperately in all directions. How had I come to this state? But wait; hope beckoned, for a bright light source sparked on, as I watched, directly ahead. I made for it, reaching that position after a longish march (how big was that place, anyway?), finding myself once more confronting a solid wall, only this one sporting a barred fire door with a hot, dangling wall lamp beaming yellowly upon it. I didn't hesitate; though, in normal circumstances, I would never have acted this way, I forthrightly pushed the bar and opened the door, thinking to run for it when the alarm sounded. It didn't, and I emerged into the outer night.

I had clearly come out behind the store, stepping onto unclean, squalid asphalt by a large, untended metal trash bin. It stank uproariously. Rotted shreds of discarded matter hung from the top. I had a little light back there, just enough to notice what I deduced to be a display dummy among the wreckage. It looked awfully decrepit and diseased, with horrid amputations and a strange, naturalistic corrosion of the plastic flesh which I found most unwholesome. I walked around the rancid bin and saw stretching to the close horizon the edge of a parking lot, which must necessarily lead toward the front where I had parked.

Either the lamp posts of the lot were inadequately spaced or few functioned, for I walked a long time before I stood under one, surveying the bleak and bare landscape. That plain of pavement appeared to stretch into infinity in all directions except behind me, where the grim bulk of the store loomed, an anonymous mass of

4

dingy brick and concrete. I had trekked far enough into the emptiness that I could see the next corner of the structure and somewhat around it, and there I noted a stationary vehicle. The angle seemed wrong, but I nevertheless hoped it was my car. I tramped towards it, soon detecting a dark figure hovering nearby. The lighting there wasn't effective, yet I could see sufficiently to tell he appeared a normal fellow, reasonably dressed in coat and tie and hat. I might have thought him old-fashioned to a degree, but certainly not a night time thug haunting the darkness, lying in wait.

It wasn't my car. The exterior resembled what I sought, but the interior, when I pressed my face to the windshield, looked remarkably trashy and dilapidated. In that morbid gloom I imagined that the upholstery was charred. The man stood about ten feet away, slouching, his features obscured. He said in a low, pathetic voice, "Better not get in until you're sure. You never know where it'll take you." A weird thing to say, as I thought even at the time, yet the words contained a frightful significance I could not, must not, ignore. He came my way, asking, "Will the time ever come?" and unaccountably I backed away, not wishing him close to me. A stray ray of light crossed his face; he looked older than he sounded, with slack mouth and wild eyes. There was something about him suggestive of decay, something which sickened me then, though it's hard for me to picture it now. I fled from him a few steps, feeling foolish, not desiring his or anyone's company until I got away from there, where everything seemed incontinent and awry. He stopped, and I made to apologize, perhaps to explain myself, when curious events distracted me.

The sky had gone crazy. Until that moment I hadn't noticed the stars, had taken the sky for overcast, but I did so then, for they visibly moved. As I watched a scattering of bright stars, the only ones apparent to me, crept upward from the indeterminate horizon. I think one was the planet Saturn, which I knew to be up that morning. Regardless, I saw them move, and unless I had gotten myself hopelessly turned around—a distinct possibility, to be sure—they rose from the west, followed by a faint trace of creeping luminosity like a false dawn. Then there came a reddish burst in that sky, like a distant firework. "It's too late now," croaked the man. "You never had a chance." This time I fled in earnest, dashing off into the darkness, away from him, across the illimitable lot.

I ran, making for the front of the store, which took its time appearing. When I came to it at last all was dark there, the doors locked, the interior totally blank, by which I mean that literally nothing could be viewed through those big windows. There may as well have been nothing but void on the other side of those panes. Scraps of paper and other minor debris were strewn across the walk. I banged on a door, shouted frantically, got no answer, thought better of it—I didn't really want to go in there again—rushed back into the lot, running aimlessly, forever, underneath a terrifying dark sky that revolved madly.

And I found my car! It wasn't anywhere near where it should have been, and when I first spotted it, far off, framed by the uncertain lights in a box of faint radiance, I wasn't sure if I recognized it. It might have been another vehicle; I doubted even when I strode up and touched it, for the coloration looked altered, the lines and planes askew. It was incongruously parked diagonally across two spaces. Within, however, I spied the furry toy monkey (an old personal joke) dangling from the rear view mirror, and I knew. Key produced, inserted, twisted—the door opened—I was in. The engine cranked and I sped away, hurtling pell-mell over the endless lot. As I drove, gripping the wheel painfully with claw-like hands, I felt a distinct physical pressure from the darkness closing in upon me, fastening itself around me, a suffocating embrace of unimaginable horror. The only light now visible was that of the dashboard and the headlamps, and the latter appeared to stop short close forward, as if cut off by a wall of opacity. I felt despair, convinced that I had lost the world, that nothing remained to me but the featureless fragment upon which I blindly drove.

By degrees I grew aware that I zoomed along a definite road. Lights in plenty dazzled my eyes, lights of houses and gas stations, lights of cars coming at me or inching past. In no time I came to an intersection I knew, and in very little time after that I was home, shaken, shaking, but relieved by a complete absence of the unusual impressions which had dogged me since my unsuccessful stab at sleep so many hours or eternities before. I had come to safety in my own little personal port, the ordeal over.

Such was my experience, which I now faithfully record, though I carried away not so much as a tube of toothpaste to make my case. I call it an ordeal, despite the fact that nothing tragic happened to me, for I suspect that the possibilities of that night were considerably more horrendous than they turned out to be. You may doubt, you may invoke psychology, you may theorize a kind of waking nightmare, but you won't convince me. I lived it, and I've given it a deal of thought

6

since.

I've often heard these stories about exotic disappearances, cases in which people casually walk out of their homes and vanish from the earth without a trace. I think I now understand some of those stories. I know, with utter certainty, that I transgressed a barrier that night; that a kind of door opened, and I passed through it, to find myself on the other side, in a place not of our maps, one retaining some features of the world on this side, but otherwise incomprehensibly different. I entered that realm, moved about within it, and during my short sojourn observed its superficial aspects. I don't know what belonged there and what didn't; I wonder about those people I briefly met or whose presence I glimpsed; natives, or visitors like myself? I deduce that one can remain there too long, overstay one's welcome, with results incalculable. I believe that almost happened to me. Toward the end I felt an awakening of the power of that realm, felt its force directed against me. This time I sensed a door closing, and I think I barely got out before that barrier slammed shut again. If I hadn't made it in time, would I have wandered in that otherness forever? Would I have missed my only chance?

I escaped, and am here. Others, I suppose, have crossed over... and are where?

THE OLD HOUSE ON THE HILL

You never know what's going to happen, or what you're going to find. They say the world is getting smaller, that modernity brings horizons closer, but I disagree. I do not think it so, for the world is a bigger place than ever, with more people, more buildings, more roads, more information—more stuff in general—of which we must keep track if we intend to make any sense of it. I think the world has gotten so big that we can't handle it any more. Once upon a time we knew, or thought we knew, our place in the scheme of things, but now all is mystery and confusion and surprise. Venture from your accustomed sphere and what will you find? You predict more of the same, but you can't count on it. There are places where different rules govern, where common human experience doesn't apply. There are things going on out there you can't suspect until you stumble over them, and can't understand when you do. Scratch the surface of normality and uncover the weird and the terrifying; there's a possibility one must accept. I know, for I've done it.

I had long fancied undertaking a lengthy cross-country bicycle tour of this our great land, and when, after many years of diligent service at a pedestrian job, I attained the prized goal of three weeks vacation with pay, I set my plan in motion. I had all the right equipment, piles of maps, and a desire to wander aimlessly whither the road would take me. I would keep going, seeing the sights and meeting the people, until time ran out. Careful budgeting guaranteed that I should not be forced back to routine early due to exhausted funds.

I traveled alone, which has ever been my way, willing or no. That certainly made for speed and freedom, both irreproachable boons. I rode across the plains, up and down mountains, through one city after another, through fair weather and foul. I stayed in cheap motels when I felt like it, parked in pleasant campgrounds when climate permitted. Always I was prepared for whatever I faced, and overall I enjoyed myself as I had vowed that I would.

The incident which I now describe took place in Sedona, Arizona, although I've wondered since whether it could just as well have occurred elsewhere. I hope I never know. I intended only passing through the city, not expecting much from such a new, tourist-built locale. I meant to devote my time in the vicinity to hitting the biking trails among the glorious red rock buttes and time-sculptured geological formations surrounding the town. As events developed, I didn't get to see much of those.

Pedaling down the main drag that afternoon, into a busy, dense, retail complex thronging with transient shoppers seeking expensive knickknacks and message tee-shirts, I chose to detour from the highway onto the back ways, the little turning and twisting streets that branched off and led God knows where. I huffed up a rise, then coasted down through nondescript urbanism, eventually arriving at the foot of a high rounded hill crowned with many houses, a hill surrounded at a fair distance on three sides by majestically colorful cliffs and ridges. A kind of haze hung over that hill. No, that isn't right, for the statement suggests fog or mist which obscured vision. It wasn't like that. I refer rather to a sort of vagueness, an indistinctness to that landscape, which gave it a strangely unreal aspect. Daylight seemed altered, the sun difficult to locate in the sky. I only noticed it somewhat at the time, with memory causing the point to loom larger in retrospect. What I noticed fully then, without understanding, when I pedaled onto the slope, was the odd sense of unearthliness that seized me forcefully so soon as I entered that realm. I felt deep in my soul that I had passed from one region to another, from the known to the unknown; felt this before a single definite happenstance suggested it.

It looked an old neighborhood, perhaps the residue of the town's historical center. I guessed, based on practical knowledge and casual study of such matters, that few homes were less than eighty years old, some closer to a hundred. Most were large two-story structures with peaked roofs, well painted and maintained, set amidst wide lawns with several interspersed trees, ancient oak and elm transplants. The place resembled a community of yesteryear, of the type recorded for posterity on yellowing postcards, yet there were improper indications. Having dismounted in order to walk my bicycle up the hill, I was able to observe closely the troublesome elements. I spotted minor signs hinting at recent laxity in the otherwise well-ordered scene: here a car parked crookedly by the curb, there mail spilling out of an untended box; a front door hanging open, a cracked window, a smashed bottle on the sidewalk, even a dead dog in a yard. The animal appeared to have been decaying or desiccating for weeks. I garnered the impression that, just recently, these folks had stopped, of a sudden, caring for their little bit of the world. While I'm not a demonstrative fellow I might have chosen to ask about the situation, only it didn't seem there was anyone to ask. There weren't any people about, neither walking, passing through, lounging nor watering their obviously drying lawns. I didn't see anyone, nor did I hear anything. Dead silence reigned there, save for the metallic squeaking of my machine.

I trudged to the top of the hill, a broad rounded knob upon which stood one house larger than all the rest within an expansive square lot contained by a picket fence. From that vantage I could gaze out over much of Sedona and the magnificent terrain beyond, only I couldn't, and this was another funny thing. The view didn't deliver on its promise. That haziness of vision, that vagueness I previously mentioned, lay more pronounced here, and I realized I couldn't see much of anything off the hill. What had been clear-cut down in town now seemed distant, blurred, in some cases wholly obscured. Much of the vast primordial landscape which I had found so endearing appeared to have vanished as if a cloud had passed between it and me. Something of Sedona was out there—I could make out the line of the highway stretching to the south, with hints of structure nestled by it—but vision failed me to an extent, rendering it hard to focus or concentrate on specifics. I saw more from the corner of my eye, if you can understand this, than direct gaze afforded.

The front door of the big house stood partly open, the gate in the fence loose on its latch. I conceived that an occupant might have just passed by, without really believing it. Tall, fat oaks framed the house, fallen leaves lying unswept on the flagged walk leading to the raised porch. This building rose three stories, was painted blue-gray, sported many multi-paned windows. A weather vane perched atop the highest attic peak. I thought it a pretty place, the oldest of the bunch I figured, but it looked empty. I glanced back down the hill, took in all the other quiet houses, decided to investigate.

No wild or foolish resolve this; I would serve curiosity, and if anyone answered I could gamely ask for directions that I already knew. I leaned my bicycle on the fence, pushed open the gate which swung easily, walked briskly up to the porch, mounted creaking steps to knock at the open door. No one responded. I peeked inside. The interior beyond the small hall suggested a well lived in house, with much antique furniture, although gloomy, for no lights burned within. I hesitated—perhaps out of decorum—then trod upon the white tiles of the entrance hall and put my head into the living room or den, ostentatiously calling out. That was a fine room, filled with valuable antiques, redolent of quaint, homey comfort. It didn't look lived in, however. When I'd entered fully I beheld dust on the surfaces and modest disorder, the telling sort which indicates lack of housekeeping. So it was now, but I presumed it hadn't been this way so long ago. I began to think the house recently abandoned.

I stepped back into the hall, calling out several times, each hail louder than the one before. No one replied, no one appeared. Perhaps, I mused, the owner had died, and his heirs hadn't gotten around to disposing of his effects. It could be, although I doubted it. There was something eerie about the entire neighborhood. Had everyone packed up (or forgone packing up, I should say) and moved out? That was ridiculous. Making the most of a grand opportunity, I chose to explore the stately, historic old house. There were three main floors, containing artifacts of genteel living: family quarters on the first, bedrooms on the second and third; all lushly carpeted, with ornate wooden paneling and the accumulated possessions of tasteful generations; a spacious, triangular attic, heaped with discarded stuff that, with restoration, would have graced a museum; and the cellar or basement, a large but low-ceiled brick room. The living areas were dusty, even unclean, with cumulative signs of forsaken untidiness; the attic was about what one would expect; the basement something else again. The electricity didn't work in that house, another disturbing feature, which counted for a lot down below. I carried a pocket flash which illuminated my way across that trashy space. I saw evidence of hasty or careless rearrangement, storage crates and chests shoved aside, debris—discarded rags of clothing and other personal items—strewn haphazardly or messily piled by the walls. It was very dirty, with shoe prints outlined in dried mud caking the poured concrete floor, many prints which tended to lead to and from the farthest or northern wall. I followed them, came to something strange. I found a door in the wall, a shiny metal door with a handle rather than a knob. I pulled it, opened the door, peered into pitch darkness, as I presumed.

I was wrong. When I clicked off my light for a moment I noted a subtle radiance emanating from that cavity. I entered, found myself within a narrow metal corridor sloping downward into the earth. All very strange; in fact, everything from this point on was horribly so, so I won't keep writing that, but just tell what I saw and what happened. Puzzled, spooked, yet plagued by unbearable curiosity, I descended the passage. It went on straight, at a considerable slope, for quite a spell, then turned upon itself at a sharp angle, still descending. And I could see without my flashlight, despite the lack of overt light sources; something in the silvery metal around me gave off enough illumination to ward off utter blackness. It was weird, and that by itself scared me already, for that tunnel had no business existing, but I went on, like a sleep walker, like a hypnotic subject, ever into the bowels of the earth.

Two more turns, and I began to hear sounds far below, the faint, far noises of machinery, other muted sounds I couldn't yet identify. I marched on, moving slowly, until I spied brighter light ahead. Then the walls of the metal tunnel dropped away and I stood on a railed metal balcony, gazing out over an enormous area of dizzying depth. From the railing the surface dropped like a cliff, and I could see everything clearly.

This I saw: a vast room of shiny metal and crystal, like an artificial cavern chamber, resembling the undivided interior of a gigantic warehouse. The ceiling rose high above me, and it was that which radiated the brighter light. Many men, some in regular clothing, most wearing featureless silver uniforms, moved purposefully about the mighty space, trooping about the floor way down there or driving small motorized transport vehicles of peculiar design loaded with metal boxes. On foot or wheels they disappeared into or emerged from gaps in the walls, dark round openings which I supposed were more tunnels to elsewhere. The size of the place amazed, the suggestion of still more extensions to the complex staggered. It seemed a world within the world. Other than the men and their conveyances everything was clean and bare. No, there was something more: an odd room or machine built into the far wall, a cubical alcove of glass and metal which gave an illusion of small size, but couldn't have been. By this I mean that I thought I could see right to the back of it, and it didn't look big, yet a steady stream of uniformed men filed from it, as if appearing from nowhere, and having done so they immediately joined their busy comrades. There were instruments and devices in there, which made me think of a machine, but I didn't really know what I was looking at.

While I examined that mystery I detected sounds behind me,

turned and spied a trio in casual attire coming down the passage. It's funny, but I hadn't thought of that before. Of course they must go out and about, or why the tunnel? It turned on itself again at the balcony, descended the cliff-like wall to the floor below. I hurried down the ramp, against my better instincts, not seeing much choice in the matter. Having gained the cavern floor I did my best to mingle, pretending that I belonged, observing as I might. Quick glances into the other tunnel mouths revealed nothing but semi-darkness. I loafed briefly across the wide floor from that special chamber, concluded that it was a machine bank rather than a passageway, despite the evident fact that men continued to appear from it. I can only say that they seemed to fade into existence within that recess, coming into being out of nothingness, an observation that thrilled and perturbed. I wondered where they originally came from.

I wondered still more as I rubbed shoulders with those earnest, busy fellows, all active, none speaking. There weren't any women among the whole bunch, but of course I don't know who was at the end of those other tunnels. Never a word did I hear from them, nor note any trace of emotion. They behaved like drones, like human appliances, mechanisms in the shape of men. I grew convinced that they weren't men at all, but things alien, mockeries of humanity. I guess that subtleties, subconscious impressions, gave them away, for they were very like. My conviction received shocking confirmation. I got close enough to the machine chamber to see clearly what was going on in the back. It wasn't men appearing there from the void, but monsters; sickening things without any attributes of the humanoid; tending rather toward the insect, with far too many moving parts. As I watched one, then another, metamorphosed into passable, if not wholly convincing, human beings. I started back, gulping back a shriek.

Apparently that was enough to give me away, for I began to attract unwanted attention. I received cold, blank stares which lingered, saw them looking to one another and grotesquely twitching their hitherto immobile facial muscles. With firm haste, but without exhibiting the panic bubbling within, I edged back to the ascending passage and began to climb. Some of them came toward me—there was a bustle of movement my way—but I continued upward nonchalantly, until I reached the turn into the tunnel, at which point I ran madly. My lungs wheezed, my knees screamed, but I kept running up that cruel slope, slowing once in deadly fear when two men passed me coming down. They stared, I stared back, sidled by and soon took off again. I don't believe they followed me, but if they did I outran them.

When I returned to the cellar I felt like a home comer from a dreadful foreign land, but I didn't tarry, for I couldn't feel safe anywhere on that creepy hill. I dashed through the house, out the front door, into what now was starry night. The air was chill, the houses on the hill all dark. I vaguely observed hints of twinkling lights far below and beyond, the lights—I hoped—of the sane world. I didn't count on guarantees at that stage. Nothing was right in that place, not even the stars in the sky, which I fancied disordered or shifted into new positions. There were more of them, I imagined, than there should be, and they were brighter. I ran down the walk to the gate in the picket fence. My bike had been moved, brought within the fence, perhaps by those who had descended the tunnel after me. Where had they been out here, and what had they been about?

The most awful aspect of an experience like mine is the inability to truly know anything. I deduced that these men or not-men were visitors from another place—don't think of asking me where—and that they were involved in something nasty, but that's all I could guess, and I give warning now there aren't any great revelations along those lines to come. I had stepped into weirdness, wallowed in it, fled from it. That was basically it, and if I'd had my way that would have been the end of it.

While I paused, catching my breath before moving on, another thing happened. Suddenly a black form, a definite human figure, flashed by me in the night, racing across the wide lawn, under the trees, vanishing around the back of the old house. It was all a matter of startling seconds. Chasing, chased, or something else? I didn't linger to ponder this fresh dilemma, but hopped on my bicycle, wheeled it through the gate and zoomed down the hill at top speed. I saw no one, no one or nothing molested me. It was so dark in the street that I could have been pursued by legions without realizing it. After much frantic pedaling I eventually grew aware of street lights burning around me, and pale yellow glows radiating from house windows. I knew, with profound, agonizing relief, that I had returned to the real world, the one that made some kind of sense to me. In no time I was back on the main strip of Sedona, and a few minutes more saw me happily and wearily checked into what passed for an inexpensive motel in that town.

I slept badly, but I did sleep. I know this because there came a period, shortly after dawn, when I realized that time had passed without awareness, and I struggled momentarily to think where I was and how I came to be there. Then I remembered, and I lunged upright, quaking in my bed. Had it really happened? Surely it did—everything came back to me in horrid detail—only how could it have done? There are logical conventions to this our world (I still believed that, you see, to a degree), and my remembrances didn't fit the approved pattern. I remained open to other explanations, would have been grateful for one, so it's a shame that none I could cook up really satisfied.

My plan was to be on my way out of Sedona within the hour: breakfast, pack up my gear, clear out. A sound, tidy plan, only it didn't develop that way, which may be the biggest mystery of all. Pesky, fateful curiosity intervened again. This is how it went. I left the motel in the full light of a sweet, healthy day, turned south on the highway and set out on what I intended as a leisurely cruise to Jerome, the next attractive stop on my itinerary. The route took me past the detour of the previous afternoon. I shyly glanced to the right as I passed, brooding about the specter of that silent hill which was so burned into my mind. Now get this: I couldn't see it. I hadn't paid that much attention the day before, but I know my cardinal points, and I was certain that I looked in the requisite direction, and I saw plenty—there's something fabulous to see in every direction in enchanted Sedona—except the hill wasn't there. Hadn't it been framed between Thunder Mountain and the formations above Soldier Pass? Hadn't it been right there? Was my angle of view wrong, perspective askew? Something was, and it galled me. I doubted once more the reality of my experience, shook that off, pondered the matter. I had stopped in place while I thought. Scarcely knowing what I was doing, I turned onto that side road.

I wandered, riding through various generic modern communities, mounting little rises and coasting through dips. This street didn't seem to lead anywhere special today. I turned onto one petty street after another, followed them to the end, retraced my route, followed another. I thought I had misplaced my unique hill which, if it actually existed, must do so in its own microcosm of space and time. I tried laughing to myself, making a game of the search. I questioned a few passersby. Most didn't know what I was talking about, but I received two intriguing responses. One guy nodded eagerly, placing a hand on my shoulder, then drew back, frowning and shaking his head as he walked away. An elderly woman supposed I meant the Old Town, which she recalled from years back. She'd visited folks there, but she thought the area was gone now, maybe redeveloped.

Then I found it again. I sped around a corner screened by scrubby juniper and there it was, looming dead ahead. My angle of view was radically different; I may have been seeing it from the other side. The old house on top was unmistakable, however, as was the antique nature of that whole vista, and the immediate sense of foreboding which gripped me. Okay, so it was still there, or there once more; whatever the case, I knew, with curiosity sufficiently sated I could go. Then the police car pulled up.

Believe me when I tell you I had no intention, not the maddest desire, to climb that hill again. Here is how I came to do it. The police officer, a solid, beefy fellow who looked born for his role in life, got out and accosted me. He stared for a moment up the hill with a strange expression, then zeroed in on me saying, "I don't know you. What are you doing here?" I explained about my bike tour, but he cut me short. "I mean here," he said. "How do you come to be *here?*" He stared up the hill again, looked puzzled, even worried. "Have you been up there?" he asked. I told him yes; the story tumbled out of me, the story I hadn't thought to tell anyone until that moment. What could I have said? Such experiences don't lend themselves to authority and officialdom. I told him, though, hedging only on a few of the wilder points relating to my explorations under the house. When I'd finished I asked him about the hill. He seemed to strain to think, as if memory served him ill. "I've seen it before," he replied. "It's there, now and again." He paused, groping for words. "I've been there. Sure I have, I know the people. Old man Jackson lives in the house on top. I remember him. Once upon a time he complained about loud music, wanted me to do something about the kids. Sure, I remember that." I realized I'd found a kindred spirit, a man who had felt what I felt. This officer (and isn't it a joke that, if he ever gave me his name, I don't recall it) had been touched by the same weirdness, grappled with incomprehension.

Excitedly I admitted to entering the Jackson house. That irked him. His demeanor grew surly. "Shouldn't have done that," he muttered. He popped his trunk. "Throw you bike in back," he commanded, "and let's take a drive up there. I need to verify that old man Jackson is all right." I blanched, tried to argue, was curtly ordered into the patrol car. I climbed in unhappily. We drove up the hill. It shouldn't have been the same street, or not the same stretch, but I saw houses that I remembered, a fact which gave me shudders. I noted aloud the silence of the neighborhood, the insidious creeping shabbiness, the absence of people. I spoke of the gradually developing haziness of view as applied to scenery beyond the closest vicinity. The officer grunted and drove.

We halted in front of the old house on top of the house. "Jackson's place," he said, and I nodded dumbly. We got out, he briskly, I most unwillingly. I offered to wait; he snapped his fingers, pointed with a thumb, passed through the gate with me in tow. At the door, now closed, he pulled out his pistol. "You say nobody's home?" he asked. "I hear movement." God help me, so did I. As we'd approached there emanated detectable, if furtive, noises from within. The officer knocked. I thought how stupid I'd feel if this Jackson answered, decided I'd live with that and hoped he did. No one came to the door. The officer opened it, we entered, stood in that gloomy, familiar interior. It was quiet now. My companion, holstering his weapon, insisted on a full search. We went upstairs first, although I kept trying to drag him toward the basement, assuring him that the center of mystery lay down there. He ignored me, handled the situation his way. Do they call that by the book? That's how he did it. He looked in every room, poked into every closet. It seemed forever before he finally announced that we should check the lowest level.

We descended those ghastly stairs, he carrying a flashlight as big and hard as a mace. A noise jolted us both, the definite noise of stirring directly ahead. I whispered (my words a deafening racket) something about the crazy tunnel I'd found, what was at the end of it. I thought it useful information. He shrugged and kept going. We reached the bottom of the house. He scanned the morbid space with his flash, revealing nothing of consequence, and here I took the lead, warily pulling him toward the door in the wall. It opened, he peered in, carefully examined the gently glowing metallic interior. He didn't speak, and after a moment he closed the door. The officer stood there a long time. After a while he said simply, "Could be anything; a junk room, or a fruit cellar. None of my concern." I asked him if he ought to check it out. He chuckled grimly, replied, "Not on my watch." His attitude infuriated me, but I felt relieved at the same time. Had I gone down there again into that tunnel, would I have been forced to accept the totality of my previous vision?

A noise from behind whirled us around. The bright light pierced the darkness, focused on a form dodging behind a stack of boxes. "Come out of there right now," barked the officer, hefting his flash like a club. The form emerged into the light, a man of common appearance, standing there unblinking. "Who are you?" demanded the officer, drawing his gun. "What are you up to?" The man replied woodenly, "I am Jackson." With this announcement the lawman seemed contented, began to engage the fellow in chat, throwing out idle questions or observations.

I was astounded and terrified by what was going on. It was another unsettling, unbelievable moment in my weird odyssey. My companion, accepting this guy as "old man Jackson?" This obvious stranger was about thirty, and his responses on basic points were bland, meaningless assurances or noncommittal monosyllables. Also, I knew the signs, which may have been more apparent to me. This man wasn't a proper human being at all, even if he could speak, but one of them, one from below, deep down and wherever the hell they came from.

I was on the verge of screaming in anger and dismay, when the officer changed tactics and attitude. A shadow seemed to fall from his face, and he shook his head as if shaking off a drug. Now he asked for identification; now he asked about the missing Jackson; now, finally, he insisted on an explanation for the impossible status of everything and everyone on the hill. The false Jackson stood mute under the verbal assault, until my companion paused for breath, at which time the stranger, in lieu of answer, began to *change*. Before my eyes he shifted, flowed, seeped from his clothing, his flesh bulging and distorting. There was nothing haphazard about this transformation; the creature was clearly reverting to a definite shape, its native form; a form unspeakable.

The officer bellowed a wild cry and blasted away with his gun. The reverberating shots sounded like thunder in that space. The horror collapsed and crumpled into a rancid, gooey mess, still feebly moving. Once it was down the two of us standing took off, stampeding up the stairs and out of the old house, as I had done less than twenty-four hours before. We piled into the car, the officer spun us around and sent us hurtling down the hill. We sped past the silent houses along the descending street, while I quietly prayed that we escape the monstrous influence of that blighted region. I had gotten out of there once, but I couldn't convince myself that I'd be so lucky twice.

I was, though. We drove a long time down that dead street, far longer than could be justified by the time span of our drive into the strange zone, yet of a sudden, turning a corner, we cruised back into a modern landscape, with people about and sounds of life. Here the officer halted, staring through his windshield for a breathless eternity. Presently he said, almost in a whisper, "I guess it's all under control. I can't treat everything in the world as official business." Without facing me he added, in a firmer voice, "Collect your bike and get out. There's nothing for you here."

I took his advice. What more could I do? I rolled away after fastening my helmet, he passed me without a wave, and after a minute I looked back from a rise in the lane. I didn't see the hill crowned with the big house, nor did I want to do so. I pedaled back to the highway, and this time nothing could turn me from my course.

That's it really, not altogether satisfactory, but it's the best I can do. It's a big world, and there's a lot we don't know about it, maybe much we can't know. There are places not found on maps which you can wander into unawares, and if you're very fortunate you can wander out. Those places are real enough, and I wonder what kind of effect they can have on those parts of the world we deem normal. That hill and those houses belonged, in some sense, to this world, at some time or another. There were real people there once, although they've dropped out of existence without a whimper or more than passing notice. They entered a peculiar zone of influence, or it swallowed them. Somebody else dwells in there, and they're busy at something, although I don't know what it is. I trust I don't live long enough to find out.

I cut short my cycling tour, as it happened, went back to my dull job. Those events stifled my wanderlust. I'm not so sure any more about what lies around the next bend, or on the next hill, and I can get by without that surety. I'd rather not know, and in my ignorance pretend there's nothing to know.

THE PALACE IN THE LAND OF ICE

The vision came to me, or the experience befell me, on that dreadful night when I could not sleep, when I tossed and wrestled with weariness and doubts and forebodings; when the world as it is seemed finally so empty, so inane and dubious, that I came at last to doubt its reality, at least to question its significance. Then, without warning, I found myself in another place, a different land where other than common concerns held sway.

Mark this: suddenly I raised myself from the prone off cold ground, hard packed earth and sparse grass. I gazed up into the fading gloom of what I shortly knew to be the dawn, beheld myself at the bottom of a deep V-shaped valley surrounded by lofty, ice-capped mountains. The high peaks caught the first rays of the sun, reflecting them gloriously. It was not the sun I knew, but similar in size and color, and quite bright. In the better light I saw ice and snow everywhere save in the narrow plain where I stood, which itself bore a dusting of frost. The cold clawed at me. I was, I think, differently dressed than I remembered, but my new attire did little to keep off the chill. Hugging myself helplessly, I scanned the high horizon, saw an amazing sight.

Far above, on a vast ledge in the side of a vaster mountain, loomed a great castle—no, a palace—a fantastic palace of gleaming white as if built of ice, hanging there amidst the ice. This was no such palace as men in our world construct with fleshy hands and harsh tools, but a creation from the minds and endeavors of fairies, that which few men could imagine, none fabricate. It could not be, those ethereal pinnacles and towers, the sweeping balconies, the mighty, seamless walls; yet they rose in their inconceivable glory, with a remarkably gentle ridge of ice appearing to slope upward to the base of the mighty edifice. I could not stay where I was, and I wanted to be

21

there, so I determined to scale that ridge, heedless of hazard, and attain the palace. Even at that moment I thought of it as mine.

So, after marching through the valley, and making my way over an icy stream on convenient rocks, I climbed. Difficult was the journey up that ridge, more so than appearances suggested, but I undertook it with whole heart, and I made it. There came a moment when I reached frozen fingers for yet another protrusion of freezing rock, pulled myself up one more desperate step and found myself crouching before the titanic gleaming walls, with a massive door directly to my front. I staggered and slipped across the flat, glazed ice to the door, which like the walls, I discovered, was composed of a material resembling the fairest marble, yet too like milky glass. That tremendous door might have resisted an army, yet in swung inward easily at my touch.

Inside all was lovely warmth and incredible sights. Devoid of life though it seemed, the palace was filled with every conceivable accoutrement of fine and joyous living. I passed through room after cavernous room, beholding furnishings of a splendid bygone era, or an era that never was: ornate artistic productions, paintings and hangings on the lofty walls, frescoes gracing the distant ceilings, heroic statues among the furniture, and everywhere glowing lamps which never died and fires crackling in their places with replenishment of sawn logs ever at hand. I wandered happily throughout the palace, into great halls with tables laid, and foodstuffs aplenty in big larders. I fed myself, eating ravenously of a meal that combined the merits of nectar and ambrosia, then proceeded upward, pausing to clothe myself fittingly from the numerous closets, so it was attired as a king that I ascended to the higher balconies and climbed the highest tower to an ultimate level with many sealed windows. From there I gazed down upon my domain, the far valley and the shining mountains and the palace spread below me. All this I saw, and knew to be good. Here I could stay and live and prosper in eternal contentment... if I could but share it.

Nor was that boon denied me. I found her there. I discovered her in the monumental library of the ages, a lofty chamber filled with records, literature, poetry of masters familiar, unknown, or impossible. Poetry she read while waiting for me. I had always known, or imagined, or hoped, that she existed, that somewhere or somewhen there must be That One, and so it proved. I learned that she hailed from another time and place, that only here could we be together. I will not describe her. She was everything she need be. Now my joy was complete. She had come to that place as I had come, bearing similar tales and longings, dreaming that I would appear as I did. It happened, it satisfied; we were content.

We established to our satisfaction that the palace belonged to us, with all its properties and features. Certain aspects of our realm we did not try to understand: how the lights steadily burned, how the wood for the fires was always laid on, how food supplies seemed inexhaustible, how and why each necessity and desire had been foreseen and granted. We found all this to be so, accepted it. Must we question bliss?

It would be foolish to ask how we lived and amused ourselves. Not for us the hectic hurly-burly of life as we had known it. We talked, we mused, we strolled, we laughed. We had peace, and—so we both felt—an eternal peace, as we would have it.

We knew, from records and an inner sense, that a great world existed beyond our domain of mountains and ice, a peopled, wonderful world of pristine splendor far without the chill valley. It was out there, which pleased us, but we had no need for it, no desire to go forth. On an upper landing of the great palace we found large crystal globes which we could enter, and in these magical conveyances we soared into the air and sailed about the flanks of the sky-flung peaks, yet we never chose to venture upward and beyond the ringing mountains to view or visit the larger world. All we desired resided within the palace, and it suited us that our heavenly isolation be forever maintained.

Yet that would not be. One day the old man appeared. Dreadful in age yet seeming wise; fearful of visage yet wholly benevolent, rasping of voice yet kind in word, he stood before us one evening while we gazed from a balcony upon the strange constellations in a cloudless sky, and he pronounced prophecies of danger and doom. An ill wind, he informed us, howled throughout the outer civilization, beating down from a remote point in space. Frightful peril had intruded from the stars, one which might destroy this mystical planet, even to our forgotten corner of it. Steps must be taken, he said, deeds be done, lest all be lost. Then he went away. We noted nothing spectacular about his going, any more than to his coming; having had his say, he was gone, and we asked whether he had ever been. His words carried a latent chill more severe than all that land of ice, but we shrugged at the warning, pretended that his dire utterances remained unsaid. Whatever he meant, whatever would happen, surely our paradise was safe.

SCIENCE AND SORCERY II

Fresh news came to us. We learned of it in the great library, however that might be: hitherto unseen books told of invaders from the skies, terrible machines that swarmed and dove and struck without mercy. Fabulous cities that we knew of only from fanciful documents were blasted out of existence. Desperate heroism motivated populations whom we knew solely by report. The fate of the world hung in the balance. We mourned, kept quiet, prayed the storm would pass.

Then sleek, gleaming needles of black metal shot across the blue dome of sky above us, flashing faster than the eye could follow, the harbingers of unspeakable fate. We brooded, she and I, pondering the meaning, scarce daring to speak of it. Came the day we hoped should never come, when the nasty needles plunged down from the void into the valley, engines screaming as they darted for the palace. Hurtling quickly, before we could react, they plummeted, steadied, rocketed upward, and as they passed from sight horrid explosions rocked our citadel, with a lovely minaret, the highest of our fabulous towers, toppling into debris and clouds of dust. A jagged chunk of glassy stone thrown up by the catastrophe ripped past and scarred my arm. After that everything changed. The ceaseless lamps went out, cruel cold invaded the palace, the fireplaces expired as the wood ran out, the supplies of foodstuffs perished or dwindled. Ugly reality had desecrated our heaven, and on that instant our belief in eternal happiness began to die.

We held out so long as we could, praying that the outer world would triumph and that the palace would live again. Our prayers failed us, as grim news multiplied of horrors without, gradually encroaching horrors. One morning I decided: forth I must go, to make common cause with our distant friends, to seek means of salvaging what was ours. Thus the old man had cautioned, and I accepted now his words. I would go alone, daring those dangers for her sake. She remonstrated, I was adamant. I could not act unless she stayed in safety, though the safety be merely relative. With her hidden from evil in the palace, I would brave all foes.

I departed, having prepared for a long, cold ordeal of endless hardship. I exited the vast door of the palace, through which I had never set foot since arriving, and plumbed the frigid depths of the valley, down the rugged, dizzying slopes to the flat lands below. I crossed the icy stream, making my way at last to the enchanted spot from which I first beheld that world and gazed joyously upon my palace. There, on casual whim, I made my camp, settling under furs for the night, planning to march down and out of the valley on the morrow. I slept then.

Slept, plagued by insidious visions, and awoke here, in my stale bed in my stale apartment in this stale world, with a lengthy scar healing on my arm yet no time having passed save that of a single short night, and with all the cares and miseries of this my old life beckoning and demanding as they will. Here I remain, here I survive as best I can, living this empty life which is no more than tepid nightmare.

I live only to sleep, holding body and soul together from one day to the next, fearing death should come before I return. For return I must, and return I will, when so ever the unknowable influences are right again, and I may step lightly from this world to that other which is mine by right. It is there still, and she is there still, waiting for me. I do not know how or when it will come, but I shall cross over again, and she and I shall reestablish our perpetual paradise. There is nothing else left to me.

JANSEN'S HYPOTHESIS

There had never been a time, since intelligent awareness came to him, that Morton Jansen had not felt that he occupied a special place in the cosmos. As a child the wonder of all things amazed him, the bigness and richness of a world that seemed to revolve around him and exist solely to cater to his needs. As a youth his sunny outlook wavered, for there were eventualities and happenstance that pained him along with the joyous boons and grants, but his basic view held firm, that a unique link tied him, in some manner unfathomable, to all the rest of creation, a creation ordered in some curious way with him in mind. By the time he attained his majority these conceptions had both hardened and darkened under the blows and apparently common sorrows of life. That he was the key to everything he did not doubt, but he grew uneasily cognizant that it was not his happiness that the universe had in mind.

Jansen conceived the notion that he constituted the sole objective reality of the world, with everything else in it being a degree—perhaps a very large degree—of illusion. In short, he stopped believing entirely in what he saw, heard, and felt outside of himself. This specific idea first came to him in high school, where he found himself unexpectedly unpopular for no reason that he could ever understand. Suddenly it was so, as if someone had flicked a switch, and one day he found himself under torment by a group of incomprehensibly hostile classmates who proceeded with little effort to make a fool of him. He expressed himself publicly about a girl he liked, as did so many other young men, only in his case the saccharine comment drew catcalls and strange, harsh laughter. He always remembered thereafter the odd sensation of the moment, that he receded within his hot, smarting eyes and looked out onto an alien landscape or (and this was what got to him) an artificial image such as a movie, the characters within the scene behaving as actors portraying antagonistic roles according to cue.

This happened to him countless times in the years to come, each episode strengthening his belief that the world out there was a fraud, built up around him via mechanisms unknown and, probably, unknowable, all of this being done, he regretfully deduced, with deliberately hateful or callously unkind intent. He was, guessed Jansen, a kind of rat in a cage, to which hurtful measures were applied to test him, if not merely for malicious amusement. The why might be forever beyond him; the how hopeless enough; only the what gradually became clear.

So many of the minor tragedies and disappointments which plagued him along the way just did not make sense without recourse to his private hypothesis. He entered college, expecting to maintain his former academic excellence (his only legitimate source of pride), but his grades collapsed. Straightforward exams he aced, but more subjective tests, those requiring the input or approval of other minds, invariably went against him. Nothing he could do would change that. He barely limped to a useless degree. He met a girl with whom he was deliriously happy, the sort of girl for whom he dreamed, and she was completely devoted to him; and then she was not, and without warning or foreshadowing of any kind she chose another, a casual acquaintance, disappearing from his life forever. That was not supposed to happen, not if there was logic to apparent existence. Jansen met another woman after he left the university, a temporary associate at the tiresome office where he worked. She promised that which he had lost, so this time he married, but after that nothing was right. This wife presented a different mind to him, a cold and sterile mental entity which did not really convince. Came three children, but one of them drowned in the pool; he had nothing to do with it, but she made as if he did, and there were others, outsiders, who inconceivably supported her against him. What was bad before turned intolerable, but he hung on because he thought he should, thought he should behave as if he believed, for there was no other way to live. The remaining two kids grew up rotten, too.

Promotions on the job came late, or he missed them when passed over by obvious idiots. Friendships soured without proper cause. Finances utterly flummoxed him; whenever he felt himself getting ahead, some pecuniary foolishness surely arose to knock him back.

And the wide world made less sense by the day. Television and newspapers blasted him with horrors. People, as individuals and as masses, acted weirdly, lurching madly from one disconnected craving or demand, speaking nonsense in spouts of words that signified much to them and those he knew, meaning rubbish to him. Out there he beheld annoying or terrifying chaos, close by stupid, petty miseries and disagreeable insinuations.

By the time he reached middle age, with decades of observation behind him, Morton Jansen had attained certainty: he was the subject of a vast, calculated conspiracy which encompassed all of the world with which he came into contact, and perhaps the totality of the universe as known to him. The great task of his life became that of unraveling the mystery surrounding him and uncovering direct evidence of the forces arrayed against him, striving to peer up through the microscope and observe his observers. To be sure, the task daunted. No book or document or repository of same (at least none to which he had access) could provide definitive proof. There was no one with whom he could talk about the problem, for so many of them must be in on the charade that he must assume they all were; besides, his very infrequent attempts to raise the issue with supposed friends, discussions initiated in a casual, joking manner with those out there—meaning those outside of his mind—elicited nought but blank stares and wry smiles. So his research he kept to himself, the job undertaken merely that he might preserve sanity by knowing the truth.

That Jansen might collect and collate the evidence uncovered he started a journal, a sort of diary dedicated to the one topic. He grandly titled it *Morton Jansen: Episodes from His Life, Concerning His Endeavors to Penetrate the Ultimate Unknown*. It consisted mainly of revealing or telltale anecdotes, interspersed with philosophical interludes, plaintive stabs at comprehension. Through the pages held in this loose-leaf binder he struggled to compile weighty facts and unmask the monstrous deception.

Initial entries tended to deal with those conventional matters that troubled him so in his regular struggles with life. He wrote, for instance: "Mary [his wife] today suddenly disapproved of our long planned vacation to the mountains, saying it were best that we remain in the city this summer. This is inexplicable, in accordance neither with previous expressed desires nor past behavior. She chose to handle the arrangements herself, picking and choosing the items of the itinerary with diligence, so why back out now? There is no logic to her

29

explanations, that the kids are getting too old for such outings, the possible cold, etc. None of that counted with her yesterday, although the children support her position now in unison. Where is the logic? I glean an attempt at frustrating me."

Or this: "Harris [his boss] announces an immediate shift in goals for the forthcoming quarter, one that, quite by chance, cuts across the six month's long development of my program, one designated for implementation soon. Orders from the home office, he claims. I don't buy it. Everybody else expresses eagerness for the new way, seeking opportunities to rub salt in the wound. Of course none of them admit the intention."

He noted: "Bobby [his eldest child, adolescent] blurts at table that his pals consider me moody and reclusive. Offers no reason for bringing up the claim, which causes Tabitha [his youngest by a year] to giggle. It's a pathetic lie, naturally, designed to irritate." Later on that summer, one spent in frustration at home, he found occasion to add to an earlier entry: "Mary seen about town with that dentist fellow? Is that meant to reassure me that causes are commonplace, the hint of a tedious affair (at her age!) to justify staying here? It is to laugh. Even should they orchestrate it that way, I am not fooled. Their scheme proceeds, only they think I'm falling for it. Maybe I'm not the only one who can be fooled."

So Jansen began with his journal, but he was after bigger game, having long ago seen through the staged tableaux enacted for him. He mused, "What I crave now is cohesive, decisive evidence of the validity of my hypothesis, that the whole fabric of faux reality woven around me is fraudulent. If all of these people are fakes, playing at life to irk and confound me, then it reasonably follows that every material aspect is a put-on as well. There is so much they tell me that I'm supposed to accept without question. There is a great big peak in India or somewhere called Everest. Is there really, is that a fact because they say it and show me pretty pictures? Are the stars and planets other worlds as they assure, or just artificial lights for the ceiling of my prison? What about the walls of my house, the layout of the streets, the day to day functioning of this city? They can trick me so easily. I can't believe anything on faith. I must watch, discern, analyze. A focused view will illuminate mistakes on their part." As a rule the "they" to whom he referred in his writings signified the actual inhabitants of all, the masters and technicians and personalities behind the cryptic masks who worked ceaselessly against him, or with him ever in mind.

So he sought flaws in their staging. Easy it was not to catch them in error, for their resources were gigantic, their acumen profound. With amazing foresight had they erected their props, with strenuous determination maintained them. Jansen countered by trying to overcome their cleverness with speed. He understood the difficulties before him. "They have arranged my life that I normally operate within patterns laid down for me, much simplifying their hoax. On a typical day I rise, dress and feed in my house, go forth to my car, drive down the same unvarying route to work, remain there the majority of the day, come home via the same route, save for minor shopping detours. That consumes ninety per cent of my existence, thereby rendering the necessity of a single large standing set kept up permanently for my benefit. They have to keep the wiring in order, paint the facades, clean the streets and stock the shelves. This I have seen them do time and again, activities of feigned naturalness. From a practical standpoint, however, I don't believe they can support an endless landscape, a whole world, of constant false fronts. If I'm right it follows that they raise those to delude me only when my wanderings demand such. Therein lies their weakness. Never will I catch them within the main set-up, for it is established, fully and ornately conceived; yet these other locations must be structured from scratch, often at a moment's notice. There, if they be not gods infallible, I may discover the folds and tears of the magic curtain."

As never before in his life Jansen went rambling, striking out at whim into untrammeled precincts of the city and other places. He altered without warning the path of his commute, made side trips to grocery stores inconveniently located, undertook impromptu evening drives into the outer rural regions where he had no real business going after a hectic day. To his delegated family one Sunday afternoon he proposed an enjoyable excursion to a pretty lake popular for its wooded shores and boating. Mary demurred, pleading chores that required her presence elsewhere, while the children begged off, expressing distaste and disinterest; but of course they would, for their designated task was to restrain him, to hem him in, to keep him to the straight and narrow of the central set. The masters of the game, he reasoned, might be wizards at cost-benefit analysis. He went by himself.

He learned directly very little from these treks into the outlands of his fabricated world. Distress, even shock, afflicted his mind when he thought of how fast they were capable of ordering scenes to confound him. On his lunch hour he set off for dreary blocks harboring nothing of amusement for him, except that of investigating areas not previously charted. Surely those sets were new, built for the moment, perhaps removed immediately after his passage that the materials could be re-used. He envisioned an army of dedicated workmen, obeying orders from unseen entities, slapping up the structures and laying out the lanes at near infinite speed, then pulling them down or rolling them up once the brief aim was served. It dazzled him to imagine the kind and quality of technology required for such incredible efforts, efforts bespeaking intention profound and unutterably weird. Sometimes he spied workmen, maybe the very agents of strange change, lounging or standing idly as he passed, eyeing him suspiciously when he stared at him. He wondered what they had been up to just before he turned the corner.

No single finding laid bare the scheme, but Jansen accumulated a mass of observations which seemed to provide a mounting basis for philosophical satisfaction. He explored urban and suburban districts which appeared, on occasion, hastily thrown together, dirty and strewn with odd bits of debris, as if he had been almost too quick for them, his sudden lunge into an unpredicted avenue forcing them to improvise a tolerable stage which scarcely passed muster. With his increasingly critical eye Jansen found certain nature scenes exceedingly provoking of mirth. Trees bent at senseless angles, curiously scattered shrubs, a sagging wooden fence; what construction had he interrupted, who had been punished for lack of alacrity? He chuckled to himself to imagine them suffering, in a small way, as they made him suffer.

It became impossible for him to take other people seriously, for he could not accept them as real beyond a certain level, and at times he disputed such grants as he was willing to make in order to survive among them. That they were fakes he knew, but to what extent? How far did managed illusion extend? Their fleshy bodies might be expensive projections placed about him through the mechanism of awesome special effects. If so, he need not regard them as fellows in any way. He grew bolder at revealing his views to them. He relished hinting at his knowledge of the truth, rubbing his achieved wisdom in their plastic faces.

Shortly signs emerged that his minor revolts against their snares displeased the powers glaring at him from all sides. "Harris accuses me of inappropriately extending my break. He would, since his chief duty is to restrict my radius of movement. What else is he good for?"

Claimed maintenance projects closed off streets he wished to investigate, indicating that he was on the verge, right then, of getting ahead of them. The antics of his counterfeit family harmed him more, for he made heroic efforts still to penetrate the wall of illusion and treat them as genuine beings, creatures with honest hearts rather than hired actors or—and this notion thrilled him at odd moments with near hysterical terror—complex, programmed automata.

Mary came out of her voluntary shell to confront him with insinuations relating to what she affected to deem his increasingly unusual behavior. She suggested, then stated outright, that he suffered from burgeoning mental imbalance, that obscure sources of unhappiness were marching him toward insanity. "She says I'd better get help before it's too late. She says that! What's the idea now, pack me off to an 'expert' who will diagnose me and dope me? That will keep me quiet, I guess, on a tight tether. Perhaps the trick is to lock me up for a while, save on costs of staging. What's the matter, running over budget?" The children, especially the boy, now openly sniggered at him at table or when he urged them to cease the alarmingly ill expenditure of their time. Indeed, since he had given up bribing them with gifts ("Where is the point, as their greedy, ephemeral joy is only a derivation of their memorized script?") they had reached the point of expressing no filial respect for him whatsoever.

Eventually Jansen sensed that matters were coming to a head, that he approached a crisis of extremis. The invisible powers came at him now with blatant hostility. "Whether I be a guinea pig for their experiments, or unwitting prisoner under duress, I have transgressed, it appears, an unperceived line of demarcation. I don't know if they actually hate me, but they feel no love for me, and my antics are starting to infuriate. There is no limit to their potential nastiness. What will be the end of this? What do they intend for the end? Oh God—if You be more than another instrument of theirs—tell me what is the point of this horribly cruel and contrived lunacy."

His mock family had turned against him. The neighbors whispered vile things about his public deportment and what they called his crazy talk. Continued employment became a concern, the boss sneering at his faltering abilities, advising medical leave. Under pressure he behaved badly, losing control in public places, gesticulating and talking to himself, while designated strangers stared and muttered, only they were doing that already, his involuntary actions being the effect rather than the cause. "The gloves come off," he wrote, "the iron fists exposed. They're trying to break me down once and for all. It's the culmination of their psychic torture, their experiment in induced madness. I must get out, but how, and to where? How does the sole inmate escape from the concentration camp of the cosmos?"

So read the final entry in the journal of Morton Jansen. A policeman stopped him on the street, demanded an accounting. This was a Tuesday morning, following a despairing evening at home (the wife blurted something about her infidelities), when midway through a tedious round at work he reached the breaking point, shrieked unintelligible accusations at Harris and stormed from the office, rushing into the road and staggering down the way through weaving traffic, hissing and cursing at all who came within earshot. The policeman approached from nowhere on cue, demanded of him his business, advised him to straighten himself out. Jansen flinched, backed away, shaking with terror. He feared cops more than the rest of the servitors, for his deductions told him that they were more than actors, rather true enforcers, answerable directly to the masters, of the true laws of the asylum called the world. They knew better than anyone what it was all about, were empowered to enforce secret decrees on the spot, were unimaginably dangerous. Despite Jansen's long standing policy to avoid them at all costs, this one now came at him without worthy reason. He screamed, whirled, fled, dashing onto the sidewalk and running as fast as human legs would move. At the corner he turned, saw the policeman coming quickly, incredibly quickly, speaking into a hand-held device. The trap closed!

Jansen ran. People everywhere, lurching into his path, blocking or retarding his progress, laughing or snarling at him, he their victim pushing them aside, beating at them when they would not move. A frowzy woman wheeled up a baby carriage, its debatable contents wreathed in shadow. He kicked at it, she feigned a scream. The policeman shouted behind him, sounding very close. Jansen elbowed aside the woman, charged into the street again, seeking safety in a dark alley beyond. He heard a metallic screech, a wonderfully ear-splitting sound, and then immediately something very large and massive hit him broadside. He did not see what it was. He went down, staring weakly, painfully at the sky framed by overarching buildings.

Faces hove into view above him, pale images lacking in contrast, fading into eddies of darkness. The visage of the policeman appeared, the communication device to his mouth. He spoke crisply into it. He kept talking as the lights went out in the eyes of Morton Jansen.

JANSEN'S HYPOTHESIS

Sinking into darkness Jansen heard these words, and he smiled to himself at last as his hypothesis was confirmed: "Reporting critical error—subject irretrievably damaged—project terminated."

THE CAVE OF CERATOS

Jacob Bleek, the canny wizard, viewed the painting in the halls of the Duke of Trentino, his wealthy and generous host, one with bizarre tastes who appreciated and enjoyed entertaining strange guests. Long had Bleek sojourned with him before the Duke chose to grant a tour of this outré collection, secreted in spacious chambers in a high tower of his castle in the valley of the Po. Many learned men had heard rumors of that peculiar gathering of artistic pieces, described by the uninitiated as vast, remarkable and costly. A description correct if somewhat vague, the collection was extensive, with much upon which to remark, and the price of acquisition had been exorbitant, sufficient to beggar the Duke's estates and tenants, rendering him a seriously unpopular ruler. Of those who had heard of the collection, many fewer had actually beheld even a portion of it, and those spoke in whispers of awe of its hoary, arcane, and terrible nature. The Duke, it seemed, craved the antique and the lurid in his art—informed gossips dared hint at the paganistic and sacrilegious—sparing no expense to make his own those weird and obscure works from which the pious poseurs of the land recoiled. So it was said, and so Bleek found for himself.

The grant of a minor sorceric favor earned Jacob Bleek admittance into the highest circular level of that castle tower, where six galleries faced in dull gray granite formed a ring of chambers, each offering a unique type of artwork. The first contained life-sized statues, many of Classical make, others still older, Babylonian and Egyptian, all dealing with offensive themes of death and pain; the second contained sculptures on a smaller scale, of intricately detailed workmanship, often presenting entire miniature tableaux of outrageous vileness; the third bore frescoes and mosaics lifted from the plundered walls and floors of forgotten, unhallowed temples and tombs; the fourth an array of primitive items derived from savage tribes at the ends of the earth, grotesque masks of mahogany, oddly etched stones, and fabulous animalistic carvings of green jade; the fifth a series of wall hangings, rare fabrics cleverly dyed to suggest tragic and abysmal scenes of torture and mayhem; and the sixth and last, the largest chamber, containing those paintings which the good Duke thought must necessarily be shielded from unprepared eyes. Many a fine work was presented there, creations of masters modern as well as ancient, affording a variety of styles and themes, though the latter were ever of a dubious nature. Here hung a lovingly preserved production of Apollonius the infamous Tyrian renegade, there a fairly fresh piece by the martyred, or justly punished, Vespasi of Taranto. Much there was to see, all of it daring, imaginative, and rather horrible.

By the light of his host's flickering torch Jacob Bleek beheld the painting. Even in this gallery of the weird it seemed formidably unique. "You admire it, my dear friend," observed the Duke with condescending pride. "Is it not magnificent? Note the precision, the degree of expert realism which envelops this image of apparently pure imagination. A great hand, backed by a discerning mind, painted this. 'Tis a pity that the author is unknown. Neither savant's history nor madman's tale records his name, yet a story lies behind the fruits of his genius. According to tradition, the work is entitled *Beyond the Black Door*." Bleek scarcely heard the man's words, so enraptured was he by the insidious brilliance of the composition. Verbal description could not do it justice, yet for the nonce such must serve. *Beyond the Black Door* presented a curious landscape, grim and foreboding, a fearsome vista in long, rectangular canvas of dark and rocky terrain. At the limits of the picture rough, jagged walls of living stone rose up to meet a domed ceiling of native rock, framing what must be a gigantic underground cavern chamber of unguessable extent, for it continued into the far distance until lost to the sight of the beholder. The nearer portions of the cavern floor, the stage of the scene, so to speak, were strangely lighted from an indefinable source. There was illumination of a kind, a sickly greenish-yellow glow radiating from all directions sufficient to reveal all, without palliating the unbearable air of gloom. The glow revealed a number of impressively detailed forms and figures. Bleek discerned what appeared to be an antique caravan, a line of heavily laden and accoutered wagons of foreign make, with tethered horses rearing and plunging, drivers lashing frantically, the wild gesticulations of passengers frozen in lush, stark oils. The cause of their distress appeared appallingly evident. The caravan was under attack by a throng of hideously manlike beings, hideous because they retained the general outlines of humanity while exhibiting freakish deviations from the norm. Those pale, naked bodies, white as the grave worm, the sloping, hairless foreheads, the curved claws, and the spiky teeth in the gaping maws of those noseless faces never arose from the loins of wholesome woman. Other things hovered in the dimly lit background, a hint of large, complicated shapes suggestive of the insect, with a glimpse of whip-like feelers snaking from behind one overturning wagon. Whatever those things might be, the anonymous artist had chosen reticence in their portrayal.

"You like it?" asked the Duke, chuckling knowingly. "I see by your face that you do, Master Bleek. Gone is your languid, meaningless smile. I see fire in your eyes, animation in your demeanor. No, I would not sell you this painting, not for a pot of pixy's gold. I will tell you the story, however, which lies behind it. As I said, the name of the painter is forever lost in the ashes of the ages, but legend claims that he spoke with the sole survivor of the final expedition of Ceratos; indeed, a variant refers to him as the survivor himself. Perhaps, although tales grow embroideries with time. Yet you care not, for it is the name of Ceratos that thrills, ah my quiet friend? Yes, Ceratos the mage, Ceratos the seer, despised and honored scholar of the olden days. If my sources be not fanciful lies, this beautiful panorama reproduces his moment of doom.

"It is said that the great Ceratos learned of a cave, far to the south across the sea, a cave in which were concealed the imperishable records containing all the wisdom and lore of a lost race and civilization that dominated the world before the Romans, before the prophets and the pharaohs, before known history began. Ceratos went forth in search of these, discovered the cave—a shunned place in a forsaken valley, its mouth locked away behind a thick iron door erected in a heathen era the church fathers refuse to recognize—and he delved into its benighted fastness, and having located the records attempted returning with them to the surface. Instead he met death on that outward trek. At least one should hope so; one can conceive worse alternatives.

"One more thing I recall. Among my manuscripts I possess what purports to be a map defining the true geographical position of Ceratos' cave, with landmark references and guiding notations on how to reach it." Thus spake the Duke, and with that the subject of

39

discourse between host and guest focused exclusively on the map, which Bleek would acquire for his own possession and use. For the Duke knew that the sorcerer craved the wisdom of the world and the cosmos, having devoted his life to seeking great arcane truths, that he might master them and make himself all wise and powerful. Bleek would not rest until he owned the map and was on his way to find the cave and the valuable records of obscure antiquity that must still reside there. During the course of days he cajoled, wheedled, and flattered, yet the Duke remained obdurate. Finally a bargain they struck: the magician received the map, the nobleman gaining temporary access to a harrowing spell which he could employ, only the once, as pleased him. Bleek, with crumbling parchment safely secured on his person, forthwith rode away on swift horse to the south, toward parts unknown, leaving the cunning Duke to contrive a magic which quite distressed and demoralized—nay, largely obliterated—his currently teeming crop of enemies. One may dispute whether the Duke materially benefited from this act, for there can be unforeseen consequences to such a lethal necromantic sending when wielded by an amateur. History brusquely states that, not long after, the proud Duke of Trentino died screaming one night in his bed chamber, to be laid to rest in the family vaults, at the insistence of the authorities, without the customary formalities of public display.

Whatever Jacob Bleek may have suspected or calculated, he neither knew nor cared of this outcome. His journey led him down through the dukedoms, principalities, and kingdoms of Italy, and beyond in strange travels by stranger means to far places across the Roman sea. Many a mile fled by under his horse's hooves, many a league on foot, and seasons came and went unharkened by him, but there came an epoch when, guided by his trustworthy map, Bleek arrived in a distant land of people hitherto foreign to him, and there he ventured into the forbidden valley and espied the mouth of the cave of Ceratos.

Tall, lean, swarthy folk dwelt without the valley, in the miserable village of thatch and mud brick they styled Antokis. They knew nothing of the name and fame of Ceratos, but of the valley and the cave they had much to relate, in a general fashion. The valley was a dead place of harsh, jagged rocks and steaming, noxious vapors where nothing grew or lived, not even by the thin, oddly colored stream which arose from smoking springs and was declared poisonous. The cave surely existed, they told him, for its entrance could be discerned far up one dangerous slope, or rather the great black, iron door which had sealed it since time immemorial. Many legends clustered about that door. Beyond it, according to old and cherished report, lay a fabulous treasure gathered when the world was young by ancient kings. The traditional certainty of a vast fortune residing within the cave had, in former, more audacious times, led many an adventurer to enter the valley and mount the slopes to that door, in order to penetrate the cave and carry off its desirable contents. The folk even retained a hazy tale of a wise man from the unknown north who had resolved to seize the treasure for himself, and had plumbed that spooky land with a great party. All informants agreed, however, that no one had ever gained the prize after which they lusted. Indeed, no account survived to prove that anyone had contrived to open the door, much less peer into the wonders and mysteries beyond. Had any man actually returned from that unhallowed kingdom under the ground, his story had been lost in the mists of time.

Bleek's impatient questioning could educe no further particulars. He scoffed at the tales of gold and jewels, for his knowledge and hopes posited superior marvels of an intellectual nature. Arcane wisdom and cosmic truth lay behind the door, and it only remained for a man of determination and iron will to unlock that iron barrier and make his what the great ones of the far past had left among their moldering bones. So he repaired to the market place and called for guides, porters, and guards to accompany him and his effects into the cave, scattering whatever promises needed to excite their curiosity and avarice. Takers there were none, until one man of hard features and dress of dilapidated finery stepped up and said, "I am Jadeso, of once honored family. My fortunes have failed, yet would I regain them. I laugh to scorn the childish shudders of my countrymen. These feeble free men of failing Antokis will risk nothing, for they forget the meaning of glory, but I remember, and I have slaves still, human beasts who will obey. Let us journey to the Black Door, seize what lies within, and make ourselves, you and I, kings over the land."

Jacob Bleek agreed to this and aught else that would advance his enterprise. The slaves of Jadeso proved unusually obstinate when informed of the tasks for which they had been volunteered. Some ran away, a few submitted to being flogged to death rather than enter the valley, while a mere few only were tamed by suggestions of marginal loot for themselves. The rest Bleek awed with his magic, for he was a true wizard, capable of astounding the layman with his arcane wonders. He stood before them in his black cloak and broad black hat, calling forth fireballs and great winds from the heavens, which so unsettled his captive audience that they, at least for the moment, came to fear him more than they quailed at his dread destination. A cowed team of twelve accompanied Jadeso, who bore with him a wickedly curved sword, and the master mage.

Over the ridges and sere brown mountains passed the party, into the dead, fuming valley, along the rancid stream and up the pathless slope to the forbidding iron door. An arm's span higher than a tall man's head it rose, and looked a solid enough impediment, yet the rounded mass of metal moved at Bleek's touch, and swung outward when grasped and pulled with deliberation. It was not this obstacle that defeated earlier attempts. Within lay horrid blackness, nothing visible to the sorcerer's keen eye beyond where the hapless rays of the sun revealed the irregular entrance to a rocky tunnel. The group began to file in under Bleek's stern gaze and Jadeso's cruel lash. One man broke and ran, scrambling hysterically down the crumbly slope. Bleek uttered a mystic word, flinging powder from his fingers which flashed and smoked. The slave fell dead on his back, his face ugly to see. Jadeso laughed, Bleek turned to the others. Torches were lighted, the servants marched on, one by one, into the subterranean gloom with heads bent.

The tunnel descended gradually at first, then sharply downward, broadening at the sides as it went. Here and there large, dark openings in the walls hinted at an infernal honeycomb of passageways. The main tunnel, fortunately, ran true, never deviating, so there was no sound concern about taking a false turn by mistake. Soon one could no longer speak of a passage, but rather a chamber, a low-ceiled room of indefinite extent. The men were terrified, Jadeso plainly perturbed by this dark, sunless environment, which merely intrigued Bleek. He had known caves, had in his time partaken of strange ceremonies within the natural grottoes which form the pores of Earth, but this was quite different. He noted odd elements of regularity in the surfaces of living rock, hints of unexpected artifice. The tunnel had been too angular, the stone ceiling just above his hat too smooth, bearing occasional marks of chiseling. This pleased him. More pleased was he, if none other, when further descent led to a greater chamber from which the ceiling rose and disappeared. He deduced that they had entered a larger realm, one worthy of exploration, in which wonders might be sought.

"A man may lose himself in this ancient crypt," warned Jadeso, "and torches burn not inexhaustible." The hand-borne flames, indeed, began to flicker and grow dim, the slaves muttering and slowing. Jacob Bleek strode to the fore, removed from his cloak a glittering globe of glass, which he held above him in one hand to the accompaniment of a laconic chant. The crystal ball glowed pale, then flared into bright, cold white light. Bleek marched forward, his men following with brisker step.

They came to the ruins in the floor of the chamber. A cavity yawned before them, a wide square pit containing remnants of structure in coarse wood and jumbled stones. Bleek insisted on exploring the pit. What the party found resembled a primitive dwelling of three stories, only sunk into the ground, with ledges and paths for walking and vestiges of ladders. Hovels of curious wood, dissimilar to that found on the surface, with stone foundations nestled against the plunging walls. The site had clearly been abandoned for ages. Jadeso gave vent to what Bleek had already quietly observed: "Truly, by the scars upon the rock, this opening into the depths can not be natural, but must have been fashioned by hand, a mighty labor, and if the direction of the marks tell the tale, dug from below." Scattered about underfoot lay a few old bones, splintered and gnawed, remains of beasts mainly, though a fragment of femur, among items of less certain value, gave rise to the most antagonistic speculations. The lowest level was filled with dense, rocky debris, which the wizard opined could conceal a trap door. He regretted lacking the means to uncover and open it. He acknowledged, however, that this did not provide evidence of a powerful civilization, and that what he had journeyed there to seek was unlikely to be found among such crude trappings.

Returning to the main chamber they trudged anew along the gently declining slope. In time a fresh marvel attracted Bleek's scrutiny. For a moment he doubted his senses, then called a halt and gazed about him. Convinced at last, he extinguished his magic fire globe, the consequences of which act drew gasps, for though the vital light dimmed and faded into nothingness, still the men could see. A vague luminescence, difficult to place, yellow with an underlying taint of green, suffused that underground world.

World it was, for only now did those men of the sun realize the extent of that realm. The ceiling of tortured, variegated stone loomed a hundred rods or more above them, while they now understood themselves to stand amidst a vast, featureless plain, stretching infinitely ahead and to both sides, its farther reaches eventually lost to view due to distance rather than lack of illumination. In the absence of landmarks Bleek led them straight on, trusting that previous investigators would have done the same.

Lost to natural cycles of sun and stars, they kept no track of time, yet in the end weariness determined chronology, and the party camped on the abysmal plain. During their trek they learned that a rare species of fungus, clinging thinly to occasional boulders and outcroppings, emitted the ghostly radiance, a fungus which must also drape the far walls and roof of the titanic chamber. They halted at the edge of a slight declivity through which sluggishly coursed a feeble stream. The slaves were advised to sample the water, proclaiming it brackish but healthful. During the period of the encampment small swinish creatures with large eyes approached the stream to drink and snuffle hungrily among the sparse, weedy vegetation rooted in the mud. At Jadeso's instigation his people slaughtered one. Its meat proved nutritious, though slightly unpleasant to the taste.

After a period of rest the party resumed their march. That morning—if morning it was—they began to detect interesting shapes in the pallid gloom before them. Far in the distance, at the very edge of visibility, they descried those regular forms. The march of an hour disclosed more detail. Away in the back of the cavern, somewhat downhill, so that the vista gradually rose into view, there loomed the copious outlines of a fantastic city. Whitely gleamed its stark, cubic walls, proudly rose those spires which survived intact the ravages of unknown eons, though others lacked their fluted tops or lay entire in dimly spied heaps of elongated rubble. Jacob Bleek inquired of Jadeso, but no local legend made mention of such a place. The sorcerer concluded that they approached a lost city of that mystic elder race of which he had heard in conversation with the Duke of Trentino, the race of great minds whose relics great Ceratos had sought. He judged it half a day's journey at most, perhaps much less, from their present position. Fired by intellectual rapacity, Bleek demanded that Jadeso apply the lash warmly, and drive their human chattel with all speed.

The span of an hour, as it could be reckoned, brought something nearer to their attention. On the murky plain ahead there appeared an odd grouping of discordant shapes, not high, but spread about the grim landscape. Though somewhat off the direct path to the city, Bleek urged an examination of this find. Within minutes they knew it for the wreckage of an antique caravan, a ragged line of scattered, broken, or overturned wagons, far gone in decay. This discovery excited Bleek as had no other. Could the old story have retained such precise information? Did he stand on the verge of an acquisition that would make him mighty and immortal? He, with his partner and slaves, entered the zone of devastation.

Bleek told off one despairing servant to proceed onward to the city, to go there and report back promptly on what he found. Then the wizard organized a careful search among the debris, the refuse of machines, the skeletal remnants of horses, the mortal remains of their masters. The men, putting aside their terror, avidly tore into the wrecked wagons, with Jadeso leading the pack, questing for abandoned treasure. Jacob Bleek found what he craved in the largest, most ornate vehicle, one which lay on its side with shreds of canvas still concealing the collapsed interior. Within he found a haphazard mess of disarticulated bones, heavily gnawed, including the cracked skullcap which once encompassed a very large brain, and a finger ring bearing a primeval signet which meant much to one schooled in magical lore. There could be no doubt that this pitiful scene marked the final resting place of Ceratos, one of the grandest mages in the annals of the human race. More, too, Bleek uncovered. Inside a crushed wooden box he spied a tied sack of canvas which, upon unraveling the disintegrating string, revealed a stack of seven oblong golden plates heavily engraved with indecipherable writing.

The expedition had succeeded. Jacob Bleek had come to the designated place, where glorious Ceratos had fallen, and found there the fabulous records of that civilization hailing from an age forgotten by modern scribes. These wise Ceratos had chosen to bear away with him, nor would Bleek dispute the adequacy of the selection. The former giant of magic had met doom—most likely at the hands and claws of the vile ones that inhabited the cave in those long ago times—but his devoted acolyte would benefit, make good where the other had failed. Those plates must contain well nigh universal knowledge, a kind only to be acquired through millennia of systematic delving. So Bleek reckoned.

Bleek's account of this moment survives in a fragment from his legendary *Black Book*, in which he waxes poetic as he broods on the tragic end of honored Ceratos. What follows is a fair translation:

Ceratos, mighty magician of old
Into the dark caverns adventured bold
He sought what would make him king among men
Wise with wisdom arcane beyond their ken.

SCIENCE AND SORCERY II

Granted him the Gods the sight of his prize
The joy of beholding with his own eyes
The ultimate secrets of great ones gone
The taste of marvels over which he'd fawn.
Perhaps from caprice They chose to deny
His triumphant return to the fair sky
Whether noble or cruel Their reasons be
Never glory or power would he see.
'Tis a pathetic end for one so great
Yet such are the jocund traps of fate.

The men, disappointed in their search, ate at last, grumbling and cursing over their paltry meal of stale bread and plain water. Jadeso swigged from a flask of cheap wine and muttered darkly to Bleek, "Naught but trash we find among this squalid scene. I fear that the doers of this evil deed bore away the promised treasure. These plates of yours, however, be solid gold, and melted down will fetch a lovely price. Then, too, yon city lies ripe for looting. Let us get on, that I may recoup my fortunes, and emerge from this dungeon of filthy stone a man to be feared." Bleek replied primly that the plates belonged to him alone, constituting his share of the loot. Jadeso asked with a snap in his voice, "Where, then, be my share?" Bleek smiled and shrugged.

The scouting slave did not return within a time frame deemed reasonable by Bleek. Rather cavalierly he deduced aloud an unpredicted cause for delay, which he did not consider to apply to himself. The safe recovery of the mystic plates, he averred, was vital to the success of the expedition, and for the nonce all matters else must wait. In due time they would return to explore the wonderful city, and Jadeso might gather what baubles he would, but now scholarly duty required backward departure. Jadeso sputtered and seethed, until the wizard made clear, in unfeigned honesty, that another journey into the horrid cave formed his next priority. So, most unwillingly, the sunken nobleman gave the orders, and the men rose angrily, gathering their burdens to commence the homeward march. Bleek retained the plates in the tattered bag, not being willing to let them out of his sight.

Before long concerns for personal safety came to the fore. The men were seized by the disturbing notion that they were being followed, that there were others within the cave pursuing them quietly or paralleling their course across the weirdly litten plain. At first Bleek, wrapped in his esoteric thoughts, would not credit their whispers, judging them the product of ignorant imaginations shaped by grandam's tales of olden times. When Jadeso, however, claimed to have spied furtive shapes creeping closer through the gloom, Bleek paid heed, pondering the hitherto unimportant fate of the missing slave, brooding over the possibility that the sweep of vast ages might not have laid to rest all that once dwelt there. From his studies he knew of obscure and horrible survivals, admitting that the cave of Ceratos might not be the least likely of hiding places for ancient menaces. He wished that his slender funds had provided him with a horse, that he might gallop away and leave his now unnecessary companions to carry on as they could.

Then the shapes came into definite view, and mindless terror grasped the minds of the surly bearers. Out of the darkness into the vague, fungoid light their crept a throng of hideous things that should have been men—that may have been men once, in their own day—but surely were not. Pale and unclean they looked, as they raced toward the terrestrial party, hairless and naked, glistening oily, with claws on their hands and feet, and large, dark eyes in their noseless faces, and wicked spiky teeth gleaming in their dark mouths. Bleek had seen their portraits in a far away gallery of ghoulish art, and well the artist of old had drawn them, but no picture could have prepared him for the ghastly reality.

What were they? Even in those heart-stopping moments Bleek's scintillating brain puzzled over the mystery. Such lowly creatures had not raised the great subterrane city—now impossibly far behind them—but they might have built lairs in its presumed vacancy, having once dwelt in rude pit houses like that found higher in the cave. What was their relationship to the fabled heroes of the lost civilization? They might have been the destroyers of those ancients, or their goblin children, that which resulted when fair men hid themselves forever within darkness and solitude. Bleek feared that he would never know the answer.

Most of the slaves died quickly. They fought for their lives, and man to man they were more than a match for those things, but sheer numbers overwhelmed them. The clash—a ragged wall of bodies, armed with tools and rocks—then swirling knots of flesh, those hopeless souls, shouting and screaming, surrounded by the pale, fishy, stinking ones. Jadeso swept his sword from its sheath and, bellowing with rage, hacked about him with gusto, lopping off misshapen heads and skinny, rubbery limbs. Jacob Bleek employed more original tactics. He produced a fire globe, willing it into brilliance, at which the attackers gave back, staggering and shielding their huge lidless eyes with their claws. The few that still endeavored to grab for him he thought down; that is to say, he made a magic, simple enough for him, that rotted their slimy, reeking flesh to the bone. So it was that Jadeso and Bleek won clear, the latter still clutching the crucial plates, scrambling madly away from the humanoid creatures which did not follow. Both men guessed the reason, and saw enough in their flight to confirm suspicion. The loathsome troglodytes were content with the victims at hand, preferring to indulge their discreditable culinary tastes.

The pair fled across the seemingly endless plain, past the ominous, primitive ruins, into a region at last where the softly glowing fungus was left behind and total darkness reigned. Bleek lighted another glass globe and by its radiance they passed easily into the narrowing tunnel leading to the surface. "Now we be safe," cried Jadeso. "Almost we are home, and none may take us unawares in this constricted passage." Bleek was not so sure. He remembered the numerous side tunnels, and he recalled something else as well, a final facet of that hateful painting which now he prayed, to the dour Olden Gods, was mere artistic license.

The first deliriously delightful gleam of honest sunlight had bathed their eyes when the monstrous others struck. They lunged from the side passages with lightning speed, the massive mandibled heads emerging waving frantic feelers, then the long, lithe, segmented bodies scuttling on many legs. Bleek had no opportunity to count the number of their limbs. The things resembled ants of incredible size, insects as big as bears, but he could not have said then or later whether they possessed six legs or a dozen. He did observe, in that instant of pure panic, that they lacked eyes altogether, being true denizens of the nethermost pits. The lack neither fazed nor hindered them. Jadeso shrieked like a woman and ran for the cave mouth, flinging aside his useless sword, with Bleek pressing closely behind, the horrors closing fast and snapping chitinously at his back. The two men gained the exit, Jadeso being like to run on, but Bleek roared at him to stay, to aid him in shutting the heavy black door. Encumbered as he was with his precious golden plates, the wizard could not manage the task on his own. A flash of sanity flickered in the eyes of Jadeso, who dashed back and threw his weight against the iron mass. Together they had almost sealed it when a soul-sickening force began to build on the other side. Irresistible pressure checked their supreme efforts, then reversed them. The black door creaked open. Whip-like antennae lashed out into the open air. The crack widened as the men's feet slid uselessly in the dirt. Loathsome, jagged mandibles thrust into view. The canny Bleek realized it was hopeless. He sprang away from the door, hurtling himself down the valley slope and, in an act of pure desperation—one that would long haunt him—he frantically hurled from him the magical plates for which he had been willing to risk all, or almost all. As he fled he begged forgiveness of the glorious shade of Ceratos, whose achievements Bleek had thought to exceed. There was a cold logic to his decision. He did not believe he could outrun those insect monstrosities, but—in this lay his only hope—he reckoned he could outrun Jadeso.

So it proved. The man of Antokis stumbled when the door swung wide, but such was his agility that he leapt up as he fell and hit the ground running, screaming curses at his departing companion, and made a valiant effort to evade his pursuers. In this endeavor he failed, his warm red curses at the wizard's betrayal shortly transforming themselves into bright crimson shrieks and gurgles of agony. Bleek never looked back, choosing to achieve distance rather than acquire clarity. His imagination, as well as certain queer sounds that continued long to meet his ears, nicely filled the gaps in his knowledge.

The happy sun had hung low in the west when he regained the surface, though he had scarcely thought of it at the time. By the time he left the wretched valley night had descended, a night that spitefully reminded him of his dreadful underground odyssey, save that the beautiful stars appeared to cheer him. He made his way to Antokis, where he might receive food and shelter, but he chose not to enter. Explanations would be in order, yet he had no desire to answer to or for the doom of Jadeso. Then, too, it suited him not at all to slink back into town as a failure and refugee from perils he could not master. Finally—a thought that gave him a modicum of cruel, morbid pleasure—he knew that the legendary black door gaped wide now, its horrors exposed to the world, and it occurred to him that Antokis might not prove the safest haven for a comfortable night's lodgings.

THE MYSTERY OF THE OLD CHURCH

Professor Anton Vorchek, piloting his private plane, banked over the amber plains and brown hills of Verde Valley and swooped low toward the dark green highlands rising above the starkly vivid gash of Oak Creek Canyon. He circled back and within minutes landed atop Airport Mesa, where a hired automobile awaited him. After a natural pause to admire the astonishingly vivid red and white hues of the complex and spectacular geological formations spread across the landscape all around him, he drove his car down into picturesque Sedona, where he checked into reserved lodgings at a very fine resort famed for comfortable accommodations and a marvelous command of striking scenery. It was a wonderful place from which to work if one could swing it, and Professor Vorchek could. When embarked upon an historical or antiquarian expedition money was for him no object, and such was his purpose now.

He came to this lovely land to study relics of prehistoric Indians, an old subject for him, but one which continued to fascinate, for the story which he and others had gleaned from the ancient crumbling monuments and broken shards of those lost civilizations revealed much of oddity and strangeness, conjured a picture of life ways and beliefs and knowledge forgotten by the modern world, yet still, in some furtive sense, living. Many a time had he led professional digs into the lurid catacombs beneath the tottering walls and sprawling foundations of a weathered site from the Sinaguan or some still earlier period, and he would soon do so again, heading a hand-picked team once he completed solo his initial survey. All had been arranged, all would proceed according to plan once he set the machinery in motion.

51

SCIENCE AND SORCERY II

Yet a puzzle distracted him, as puzzles were ever wont to do to him. So it went with Vorchek; a line of investigation would suggest itself, and without ado he must drop all else and delve. Something of the sort happened now, and for the most trivial of causes. While making his aerial turn above the forested plateau beyond the canyon he had spied below him, ever so briefly as he flashed past, that which he did not expect to see, an incongruous glimpse that intrigued. Surely he had beheld, in that remote and largely trackless expanse of seemingly pristine wilderness, the spire of an old church, of a style commonly toppled by time or, where men could afford to care, converted into museums. It had appeared to rise up from one of the infrequent clearings or meadows, and he had noticed nearby a hint of track or narrow dirt road.

This he saw, and this he pondered as he arrived at the resort, settled his belongings, personal effects, books and papers; on this he ruminated as he lounged luxuriously in the spa, and while he ate alone his sumptuous dinner. In the privacy of his room he poked through his assembled literature, seeking enlightenment. Vorchek knew a deal about the history of the area—was considered an expert by those who forgave his interest in topics thought by some to be morbid or sensationalist—so it surprised and irked him that this rather impressive specimen of olden reliquary fell beyond his academic purview. Once upon a time someone had erected a church in the middle of nowhere. How could he not know of the existence of such a place? He felt that he had failed himself. Either the story behind the site was truly obscure, even by his standards (which he doubted, for he gloried in the obscure and the strange), or it might be that the location lay far enough from the center of his chief investigations, many miles away from his primary stomping ground, as to have never received reference in the accumulated local lore. For the moment he assumed the latter explanation most likely correct.

Whichever the case, he must know. Vorchek determined to look into this puzzle, and tasked himself on the morrow with seeking the mysterious church on the ground. So he did. Putting aside immediate responsibilities (which were, to be fair, largely self-delegated) he set out at dawn by car for the north, armed only with an unneeded road atlas and a topographical map prepared by the Forest Service. He drove leisurely along the charming road through majestic Oak Creek Canyon, then up onto the densely forested plateau beyond, where he grew serious in his exploration. At a pretty overlook he stopped to consult

52

his map, gain ideas as to how he should proceed. A couple of very bad dirt roads left the highway and ran west, in the desired direction, just ahead. One circled back to the south behind the canyon, which did not seem appropriate. The other continued west, twisting around wooded hills and breaking into secondary and tertiary paths of problematic surface condition. Nevertheless, that appeared to be the way he should go.

He found the turnoff, bumped and rattled his way west into the wild. The surface, as predicted, proved difficult, became more so as he advanced, with protruding rocks and deep narrow ruts, the kind easy enough to avoid, yet dangerously awkward if they snagged an oil pan or trapped a tire. Vorchek kept his eye on the road, not wishing to make of himself a statistic. He regretted not acquiring a better vehicle for the outing, which more properly demanded high clearance or even four-wheel drive. Live and learn, he told himself.

He had only the haziest idea of the location he sought, thinking it to be far out and lost among the dense pines and spruce of the interminable forest. This turned out not to be the case, for as he approached the general area he began to see signs of civilized encroachment other than the ubiquitous rusting barbed wire paralleling the lane. He came to an intersection crossed by a recently graded road, turned south onto that, followed it past parked construction vehicles. He supposed that this byway was being leveled and smoothed, perhaps paved, from the north, from Flagstaff or maybe Williams. That suggested greater concern for tourism, or even some isolated suburban development, an occasional feature within the National Forest where pockets of private land held out. He came to a detour which turned back to the west, also graded, followed that until it reverted to little more than a jeep path, continued shaking and bouncing in nerve-wracking fashion to the edge of a wide highland meadow thick with tall grasses and speckled with brightly colored flowers. He skirted the clearing, passed through a thin stand of pines, spied the bulk of a structure looming beyond. A little further and he saw the spire, knew he had attained his goal. He pulled up in front, where he found himself again on graded road, this time coming from the south, and got out.

The place was everything his antiquarian tastes relished. There rose before him a great large church, a peaked wooden monstrosity of the faux Gothic style popular around a century or more ago, with a high vault, two-story living residence adjoined in back, and the sky-piercing steeple from the slender pinnacle of which sprouted a greenish-encrusted bronze cross. It had once stood in a little park, naturally, but the trees had long ago overrun the lawn and now pressed thickly against the walls on both sides. It surely seemed abandoned to the ages, with its bleak two-by-four panels barren of whitewash and the lower tier of windows broken or crudely boarded, but for all that the structure looked sound and whole, denoting the sturdiness and care of its construction.

Vorchek wondered why the church stood out there, forlorn and solitary. No one ever built a church by itself. His practical mind conceived possibilities, scanned the near terrain for evidences, found them. Across the wide clearing he discerned low mounds and hillocks, barely perceptible in the high grass. Foundations, of course, foundations of simple, ephemeral dwellings where families once lived. There had been a town or village here in that fading era, whose pious denizens raised a temple to God in this place they had made their own, where they expected their descendants to live for all time. Naught remained of their dreams and labors but the forgotten church.

In out of the way places outposts of civilization come and go for many reasons, but Professor Vorchek had a strange feeling about this case, one that raised his hackles. He removed his big floppy hat and fidgeted at his itchy scalp, asking himself what troubled him so. He thought he knew the answer, one derived from decades of study in this peculiar region, where certain aspects of weirdness fed his inordinate fondness for arcane lore and outré possibilities. The church, and the former village, had been constructed on the site of a vortex, one of those unusual upwellings of conventionally unexplainable power which dotted the forbidding and complex landscape of the Verde Valley and the surrounding terrain. They were found from the mountains above Jerome, far to the south, across the valley and among the awesome sandstone and limestone buttes of Sedona, through the great canyon and apparently, in at least one instance, on the highlands above.

The existence of the vortices was generally known to experts, but few of them chose to speculate on what they might connote. The popular mind, as Vorchek knew only too well, had eagerly fastened upon the concept, polluting it with sentimental New Age maunderings fit only for the mindless tabloids. They imagined these peculiar forces to be beneficent expressions of a fabulous cosmic mind, any association with which must be inherently fruitful and rewarding.

Vorchek knew better. Cosmic the forces might be—probably were—but nothing benevolent lay behind them. The professor knew the dreadful history of the ancient Indians of those parts: first the Anasazi, who had embraced the vortices and made them the focus of their dark kingdom, only to collapse into madness, cannibalism and death; then those who came after, the Sinagua, who learned from the abysmal fate of their predecessors and strove to avoid the toxic centers of influence, with indifferent success, judging from their present absence from the region and the planet. With the later white settlers the process varied, for their *Weltschung* did not allow for such potentialities. In their case luck of the draw reigned, and communities prospered or withered by chance. This one had died.

Vorchek's studies of old history and modern science had taught him the locations, had trained himself to sense the presence of these sites, and he knew he stood within or near such a vortex now. The citizens of the dead village had not known, had brought their families here, had endeavored to make lives for themselves, and... what? Guess only he could at the details, but he knew the patterns, suspecting that past events here had not been pleasant.

He pushed open the double doors, one panel sagging, hingeless at the top. Within the inner chamber lay the wreckage of decades, overturned or broken pews, a sunken dais, smashed glass and thick dust. Cobwebs draped the damp-stained walls. He slogged through the debris, hoisted himself up by the podium—the steps looked too dangerous—walked gingerly around a creaking patch where the cracked floorboards inclined steeply, tried the door leading into the private offices and quarters of the bygone minister. It did not give. He noticed, not far away in a sheltered alcove, a trapdoor missing its iron band. Contrived to open the trap, Vorchek peered into the darkness below. A stout step ladder descended, as did he armed with a pocket flashlight. He entered the low-ceiled basement or crawl space of the church. He spied oaken chests which might once have contained historical treasures, only they were all plundered and empty, their lids yawning or removed by force. A pity, but all too typical, this wanton pillaging of the past. He did discover something fascinating about the foundations of the edifice. They were of limestone, native rock, and cut according to an architectural style never adopted by the pioneers. These were remnants of an earlier, darker, harsher age. The church had been raised, he deduced, atop the ruins of a primordial Anasazi structure.

Now, in quick and startling order, Vorchek heard the following: the sound of a growling vehicle driving near, stopping, the slamming of metal on metal, footsteps in the hall overhead, an angry voice proclaiming "I've got you this time!" and the crash of the trapdoor into place. The professor crouched stunned for a moment in the greater darkness, then called out, "Excuse me, but I think there is some mistake." "You kids will learn to stay away from here, the hard way," shot back the voice. Replied the prisoner, "I am not a kid, sir. I am Professor Anton Vorchek, carrying out historical research. I beg you to release me, now be a good fellow."

After a short, pensive period the trapdoor creaked upright. A puzzled face appeared in the illuminated square. "You aren't exactly what I expected," it said. "Come out of there, professor." Vorchek did so gratefully. "My card, sir," he said in his well-modulated, slightly accented tones, "and who do I address?"

"Jason Roebeck," said the swarthy, middle-aged man with the hard, grizzled face, "foreman of the crew laying this road. We're driving it about a mile south, where some fancy cabins are going up. We've had problems with punks and their vandalism. They sneak down from Flagstaff at night and tinker with the machines." "Regrettable," said Vorchek. "Are you responsible also for cultural landmarks?" Roebeck scowled, explained, "It isn't safe. We had a young fellow, a stupid thrill seeker, break his neck here last month. The floor we're standing on won't support a kitten much longer. Let's get back into the sunlight."

They exited the church, idling in conversation before the foreman's mammoth SUV. Vorchek admitted that he knew little about the place, which surprised him, given his research. Roebeck told him, "You're standing on what's left of Parkersville, founded around 1890. These folks came down from the Williams area, never had anything to do with Sedona or the valley. When I was a boy the town was already abandoned, but there were still a few houses standing then, barely. You can't tell it now. They built the church to last, I guess." Vorchek mused that the location seemed prime real estate, wondering pointedly why the inhabitants gave it up. "Drought, maybe," Roebeck muttered, then grimaced, as if he had bitten into something sour, adding, "I always heard the place was haunted. Silly, you say, but it's better for people to stay away. Funny things do happen here." "Such as broken necks?" Vorchek asked innocently. He received an earful in return. "That poor joker was found lying in the vestibule," exclaimed Roebeck, "nothing around him, no big drop nearby, but his neck bones were snapped clean off each other. Go figure that. There's stories from the olden days even worse. If half of them are true, this place is a slaughter house. Maybe it'll be okay once the church falls down. Nothing lasts forever. Until then, I tell you it's wisest just to take your pictures, hop in your car and clear out."

"My work requires rather more," Vorchek replied coolly. "I have given thought to spending a night here." Roebeck warmly remonstrated against this, though there was very little he could say by way of substantive argument, nor did he possess any authority to enforce his opinions. Vorchek had conceived the notion on the spur of the moment, but of a sudden he knew he must do that thing. They talked earnestly for a while, then the professor drove away, leaving Roebeck gazing unhappily after him.

Vorchek returned not that day, but the one following. That afternoon he occupied himself in Williams, sifting the yellowing records of a respected private museum devoted to local lore, records which contained curious tidings of the past. The next morning he spent several amiable hours in Flagstaff, absorbing certain unusual nuggets of wisdom stored safely in the files of the Pioneer Museum. He learned something from these sources, enough to convince him of the existence of a phenomenon worthy of investigation, not quite enough to frighten him away. He had spent one more relaxing night at his Sedona resort; now, in the late afternoon of the second day, he once more approached his destination over those rugged roads, in a more rugged vehicle, with plans for a different kind of evening.

He pulled up before the church, unloaded his meager supplies: bedroll and sleeping bag, kerosene cook stove, simple foodstuffs and thermos of water, a bottle of wine (must he do without all niceties?), a hefty high candlepower flashlight, and writing materials. That would keep him for a single evening. He again entered the church, made his way to the rear and up the wrecked dais, confronted the locked door beyond. This time he forced it, applying a determined shoulder. The door gave with a squeak, and he trod warily into the long sealed, disused quarters.

Here he found much dust, less damage, more signs of organized vacancy. Once the offices of the minister surely contained desks, bureaus, filing cabinets full of papers critical to the congregation and the community. All were gone now, furniture and contents. The boarded windows allowed no light, so he employed his big flash as he carefully mounted the groaning stairs. The aging supports held; he reached the landing, entered the private quarters. Here unbroken, unshuttered windows provided sufficient light. These quarters consisted of four rooms: a respectable dining room retaining a large rough-hewn table, a tiny sitting room with remnants of quaint furnishings, another small room which, he guessed, might have belonged to children, and a spacious master bedroom which contained the intact, though stripped, wooden bed frame. All the bed slats remained in the frame, and Vorchek thought he could comfortably spread his sleeping gear upon it, thus keeping himself off the dirty floor.

He descended, ate his light meal on the porch while evening gathered, as gloom closed in and the first stars appeared, then prepared for business. He returned to the large bedroom and entered, leaving the door open, settled his effects, sat on the bed jotting inconsequential notes. Having finished these, he ate a simple meal, sipped a plastic cup of wine and undertook the next step of his operations, which was to crawl, fully dressed, into his sleeping bag on the bed and go to sleep. Slumber eluded him for a time—as well it might—as he expected. He lay in darkness, listening to the furtive sounds customary in such a place: the creaking of wood, the breathing of wind against the outer walls, the rustling and scrabbling of branches. These he heard, knew them to be natural, put them from his mind.

Vorchek awoke, disoriented at first by the inky blackness all around. He remembered his situation, realized that he had slept, wondered what had roused him so suddenly. Truly, his nerves tingled under the impact or at the instigation of something. What had he sensed? That something had touched him, or that someone had joined him in the dark? He suffered from the most uncanny feeling that he was not alone, that somewhat more than pitch night enveloped him. He stared, saw nothing. He listened, heard nothing, not even the moaning of wind or the other predictable sounds. He lay, in fact, embedded within immense, dead, hollow silence of a kind painful to his ears, wholly unnatural. That by itself stimulated his interest. He keenly strained his hearing, slowly rotating his head to grasp at any aural impulse. He thought he heard one—then he believed it his imagination—then he heard it again, a faint scratching, not that of branches outside the walls, but something within. Vorchek abruptly sat up, clicked on his light. Sweeping the room with his flash, he saw only the familiar realm within his limited view. Another scratching, toward which he focused the light, led his rapt attention to a long, fat cockroach on the wall. Disagreeable, but he could live with that. The insect scuttled under a hanging strip of wall paper, and Vorchek turned off the light and lay back down.

In seconds he detected the scratching or scuttling again, presumed its source, endeavored to ignore it. This he managed successfully for a spell, until the irritating noise began to multiply itself. A flick of a switch pasted a circle of brilliant light on the moldering wall, where three nasty pests darted toward their favored darkness. This displeased Vorchek, but he could accept such company in small doses, in the name of his peculiar research. Light out, once more reclined, struggling to relax, he heard the noises immediately burst out afresh, with redoubled volume and intensity. He questioned now his scheme to inhabit such a filthy hovel, thought longingly of the warm, clean, soft bed at the resort he had forsaken this night. He rose again, eased out of his bag, sat rigidly. The sounds, those damned sounds were all about him, seeming especially heavy toward where he guessed the door to be. He snapped on the flashlight, and gasped.

The room crawled with them, every exposed surface glistening with particulate movement. Vorchek choked back a scream as he spied the scurrying swarms of roaches clustering on the walls in their hundreds, their multiplicity of tiny legs scrabbling for purchase as they jostled and crept over one another, their feelers waving insidiously. More still scuttled across the high ceiling, and when he looked to the gaping doorway he beheld an army of the chitinous monsters surging through it in his direction. Hundreds? Nay, thousands of the vile little horrors were coming at him. Already they were creeping up onto the foot of the bed frame, and as he watched a couple dropped down onto his sleeping bag from above. The shock of this weird circumstance was more than he could stand. With a hoarse shout of terror Vorchek sprang from the bed, crunched his way to the door, somehow managing in his wild alarm to maintain a firm grasp on his light. The process of getting out of the room, though nearly instantaneous, almost maddened him. He felt himself wading through a sea of living disgust, out of which the individual components, with horrifying deliberation, flung themselves at his legs and leapt onto the hand he thoughtlessly rested on the door knob. Then he was through into the corridor, but the walls still shifted and seethed with repugnant life as he stamped toward the stairs.

There a new dread assailed him. The sense of undesirable

company, already reaching fearsome heights, mounted spectacularly moments before he glimpsed the dim, distorted human figure on the stairs. Vorchek shied back, aimed his bright beam, saw nothing and forthwith charged to the lower floor. The figure appeared again, and again, at every corner, in each alcove insufficiently bathed in light, always an insubstantial image of a man, strangely shapeless at the extremities, always dreadfully close to him, and by the time the professor bulled through into the big hall he thought the crazy shape strove to detain him. Oddly amorphous, shadowy arms reached for him—in his feverish haste Vorchek imagined more than two—and he felt the ghost of an impression of pressure, a retarding influence acting weakly at first, yet building strength at each delirious meeting. At the front door of the church the thing lunged bodily at him, wrapping its damp, clinging appendages around him in a loathsome embrace, exerting considerable power to bear him down to the floor. Vorchek lashed out with his big flashlight, seemed to beat against a swathe of thick, clinging mist, pressed forward with eyes tightly closed to stagger through a foul wet stench into the bracing outside air.

He made it to his car, pausing only to beat a few pernicious vermin from his clothing. Here nothing extraordinary intervened to assault his conventional senses, but the eddies of vast and baleful force still swirled about him. He got into the car, cranked the engine and took off on the instant, scarcely heeding the route until he had put space between himself and the ancient church. As it happened he did drive the wrong way, spending the better part of an hour negotiating wretched roads in the middle of the night, circling and turning aimlessly to no purpose, save that he did gradually distance himself from the cause of distress. In time the tenacious pall of evil fell from his soul, which told him more certainly than any compass might that he had left the awful vicinity of the church behind him. So it proved, for eventually he came to a backwoods intersection that he recognized, with a crude sign indicating the way, and from there to the highway consumed just a few more minutes of his life.

Unappealing though his experience in the ruin of the old church had been, some kind of inordinate consequences stemming from his brief sojourn there came not unexpected, for Professor Vorchek had diligently studied the materials of the two museums prior to his odyssey, knew something of what once had lurked at the site and, obviously, still did. He knew that the town of Parkersville had suffered unbearably, since its inception, from an unknown, debilitating ailment which plagued its weaker members and led to a frightening incidence of child mortality. Old diaries stored in the Flagstaff archives told of this, with many a curse at fate or pleas to God. They also wrote of the recurring cases of nasty and unheard of birth defects which crippled the youth, or rendered them insane or vegetative, or made them nightmarish to their folk, who shunned the poor wretches. He read accounts of disease, wholly unknown sicknesses which weakened or destroyed the livestock. These stories he had found in Flagstaff, and more like them in Williams, but the museum of the latter city contained in addition a copy of an official transcript prepared by worthies of the Missouri Synod, a team headed by Reverend Jonathan Mellow, who had journeyed to Parkersville in 1904 to investigate the sequence of events which resulted in the death of Morris Hill, the local minister. Selected extracts follow.

From page 2: "They aver it has never been a healthy place. The land fails to produce its bounty as it should, the domesticated animals prove listless and sickly, the old and young of the congregation linger poorly, wan and dispirited. The beasts of the forest, so protest my informants, behave strangely, exhibiting an evil degree of aggressiveness."

From page 7: "Joshua Martin, farmer, a godly man, revealed to us the thing he keeps imprisoned in a locked chamber beneath his house. He assures us that the misshapen monstrosity is indeed his second son. We have seen with our own eyes. Death would be a blessing for the wretch."

From page 9: "Truly noxious pests swarm in this village to a disturbing degree. They are prone to creeping in the shadows of night, and there are areas where one can not step without crushing them underfoot. Despite constant endeavor on the part of the populace, Parkersville is the most unclean human habitation any of us have ever encountered, including Reverend Lee, who spent his missionary years in the Belgian Congo."

And this, from page 24, after a relation of testimonials and other anecdotal findings: "In sum, the tale they tell of Reverend Hill stands confirmed by the facts at hand and living witness. Early on that wise and learned man (for whom we held such high hopes) began to imagine, or discover, that evil forces reigned in Parkersville. His sermons increasingly focused on tribulations sent by an angry God, or visited by night-walking demons. The folk were saddened by his mounting wildness of manner and speech, yet most admit that he spoke for them, and that they do not consider his behavior any sign of mental or spiritual feebleness. The death of his good wife in child-bed pained him, as did the ultimate taking of his daughter, but he bore manfully these trials as he must, until others of a more mysterious nature oppressed his resolve. That the temple should groan under a despoiling infestation of noxious insects (a thoroughly attested phenomenon) caused him agonies, an abhorrent happenstance which he connected with his growing fear that other, rather more formidable, intruders conspired to introduce themselves within the holy precinct. Such appearances were proclaimed chiefly on the nights after public meetings, as if the very presence of gathered humanity could instigate the haunting. These beings, or illusions—we allow for the latter, though reports from fine gentlemen are remarkably consistent—the folk describe not as men, but as grotesque travesties or caricatures of same, veritable monsters from the normally unseen world, intangible as a rule, yet possessing the power to exert physical force against the brethren on occasion. Toward the end Reverend Hill expressed the belief that the visitations were directed mainly against himself, and that it behooved him to abdicate his position and withdraw from Parkersville, for his own sake, and perhaps for that of his flock.

"The facts concerning his death, outlined in the previous section, stand confirmed. All of us have viewed the body. We refuse to enter a judgment of unlawful self-destruction. While we agree that it is conceivably possible for a man to kill himself in such a manner, it is thought by all that the attendant physical suffering would necessarily stop short such a vile scheme midway through its progression to demise. We gratefully incline to accept the conclusion of Mr. Parker himself, that rabid or otherwise maddened creatures did the deed, and that Reverend Hill should be held morally blameless. Reverend Totter has also noted (what not all of our party will credit) that the action of a multitude of insects could account for a portion of the corporeal damage."

Vorchek had read this, as well as the rest of the report, which detailed in dry terms the state of Reverend Hill's corpse. The professor could only agree that the late churchman was unlikely to have made off with himself in such a manner, despite evidence that the deceased had been alone at the tragic moment. Vorchek also deduced that the morbid spell which shrouded the locale had not died in those olden days. His own experience assured him that something unpleasant and dangerous remained, had persisted beyond the eventual, gradual evacuation or dying off of the town itself. The site of abandoned Parkersville, he thought, might well constitute a fine venue for continued study by men like himself, but it was no fit place for future habitation. He thought of the new commercial cabins going up nearby, and he wondered—mere speculation only at this point—whether the time would come when he would have occasion to investigate them.

THE WILLING OF THE MAN

Professor Anton Vorchek and his lovely, youthful assistant Theresa Delaney relaxed after dinner over glasses of wine. She had provided the meal (one of her French concoctions known to appeal to his Old World palate) in her fashionable Scottsdale apartment; he provided the conversation. "I embark upon a major line of study," said he, pausing to puff his pipe to life, "one on which I require your aid." "What might this be?" Theresa asked dolefully: "Deciphering weird prophecies from an Aztec stele, or searching for secret codes in medieval manuscripts?" For she knew his interests, and the kind of work in which he indulged, usually somewhat lurid and disreputable to her tastes. "Nothing of the sort," he replied in his well-modulated, slightly accented voice, adding grandiosely, "rather, think of it as a foray into the exciting world of public relations."

"I don't get that at all. Since when have you cared about PR?"

"Never," Vorchek admitted, "but I have conceived a special variant, an outgrowth of a previous endeavor of mine, from before your time. Ever have I described to you the experiment of the sealed box?"

"No. It sounds horrid."

"It is not. I tell you now, what will intrigue you." Theresa snorted. Said Vorchek patiently, "Listen, my dear, for the principals embodied in this tale shall count later. Several years ago, early in my career, when I carried considerably more clout at the university, I arranged a curious test of matters psychological. For this I requisitioned the largest auditorium on campus, which I packed with precisely one thousand graduate psychology students from that and nearby colleges. I took position center stage, with a simple wooden table before me, and on that table I placed a small cube of lead, three inches to the side, a

65

hollow, thick-walled box of metal with a tightly fitting hinged door on the front, facing the audience. To them I proposed the following as fact: that within the box I had, moments before my appearance, secreted a live spider—a modest-sized tarantula to be precise—and shut it up. I stated the creature's exact dimensions, showed them a large, crisp photograph, projected on a screen at the back of the stage, which purported to present a picture of the very spider in the box. Then I got to the ostensible point. For a mumbo-jumbo of reasons, with which I do not bore you, for they served merely to draw in these eager students (oh, it was something about quality of observation, ability to mentally conceive detail, something along those lines), I asked them to concentrate on the box, to focus every ounce of their minds upon its eight-legged contents, to think of that spider and nothing but, for the entirety of a ten minute span. This they dutifully commenced to do, and an amusing sight they were, most of them, those thousand scientific acolytes with their rapt faces, closed eyes, and furrowed brows. I kept track of the time, most scientifically, with my expensive, ever reliable gold stop-watch, the same that I still possess and keep always on this expensive chain in my pocket. When the stated time period concluded I thanked them and, much to their surprise, instead of opening the door to the box dismissed them forthwith, falsely promising to get back to them with my findings at a later date. Falsely, I say, as I had tricked them. Actually I was putting to the test, in a clinically framed fashion, the age-old question of the power of belief. For you see, there was no spider in the box. That was a pretty lie. They, however, *knew* it to be true. When they were all gone, and I was quite alone, I opened the box and, Miss Delaney, what do you think I found?"

"Nothing, of course." "Why say you that?" "For the very reason," cried the girl, "that you've pounded into my skull a hundred times: belief doesn't determine truth. Lots of people believe in all kinds of crazy things—flying saucers, Loch Ness monsters, ESP—but the belief never, it never—"

"Transmutes?"

"I guess; never transmutes into reality. Belief doesn't directly affect the material world."

"Very good, my dear, logical so far as it goes." The professor nodded approvingly, benignly patted her hand. "I have devoted much of my life, after all, to investigating bizarre claims of all types, striving to separate the actual from the spurious. Far be it from me to collapse into mindless acceptance now. However, there can be degrees of truth, special factors, controlling circumstances. Among the great unwashed, belief tends to be unfocused, haphazard. There are very few hard core 'true believers,' who know all with crystal certainty, lock-step with one another. Most people, after all, belief in God, yet think of the many theological representations and viewpoints existing out there, conflicting, overriding, clashing. What, though, of focused belief: concentrated, directed toward a specific, absolutely defined end? Might not the result differ from the norm in that case?"

"How should I know?" Theresa squirmed uncomfortably in her chair. She hated discussions like this with the professor, for she could invariably predict that he was up to something unusual and utterly weird.

"You would know," he replied crushingly, "by heeding the results of my prior experiment. Bear in mind that my test group were highly intelligent, educated, focused, and mastered by me. As I say, I opened the box, and I did find something within it. It was not a spider—there was surely nothing alive in there—but it might have been the bare beginnings of one in the process of formation, or the withered, desiccated remains of one that had been. I found a clump of black, sooty residue, possessing the minimal essentials of a spidery form. There was a tiny bulk of a body, from which sprouted fine, crumbly appendages like legs. The thing lacked detail; the number of legs was inaccurate; the material, under analysis, proved to be unremarkable organic compounds, polarized improperly and lacking biological enzymes; but something vaguely spidery had come into existence where it had not been, willed into existence by the scientifically controlled belief of special subjects. This, Miss Delaney, that much from a ten minute test."

"It's amazing," she granted with a shake of her blonde head, "if you aren't pulling my leg."

"That I would never do," he insisted with a sly grin, perhaps recalling infrequent episodes when he had actually committed such an atrocity. He grew sober again, said, "I am entirely serious. I intend, at last, to test the theory on a major scale, via fresh experiment." At Theresa's unhappy but requisite prompting he continued, "I shall make a man. Not, as the fabled Doctor Frankenstein did, through the stitching together of dead flesh, but solely through the power of the human mind, by the concentration of utter belief, will I build up my man from scratch. Already the wheels of industry turn. My fee from

Applied Physics Processing has arrived (you remember that knotty problem I solved for them), and as a result of their inordinate generosity I find myself with a surfeit of funds. Contacted have I the three most prominent public relations firms in this country, offering them a massive price for their services. Through them I shall create my man."

"All right, Professor," demanded the girl, "give. What are they going to do for you?" And Professor Vorchek told her.

This is how it came to the attention of the public. All of a sudden anyone with a television, a radio, an Internet connection, or a newspaper subscription began to see, hear, and read of a remarkable man, the dashing international financier Arthur J. Mandrake, a brilliant, staggeringly successful, reclusive globe-trotter. A complacent audience, ever eager for information on entertaining personalities, greedily drank up the tales swirling about this hitherto unknown gentleman. Last week, they were informed, he cleaned up once again in the stock market, driving a hard bargain which gave him a dominant interest in the pharmaceuticals industry. Yesterday he had personally sealed an oil deal with the prince of a minuscule Middle Eastern country which no one had taken seriously before. The prince had little to say to this, though his spokesmen immediately denied the story, regretting that his joyous, enlightened land, unlike most of his neighbors, lacked the precious fluid. A follow-up story hinted at strong reasons for the prince's reticence. Tomorrow, it was then reported, Mandrake would be testifying as a consulting authority before an obscure but critical government panel.

Who was Arthur J. Mandrake? No one could say—no one—but they learned. His biography, necessarily shadowy and vague, yet provided a firm picture of a young man, hailing from fine stock, who had set out upon attaining maturity to conquer the world. His rise over the subsequent ten years had been quiet yet meteoric, and by the present day he had made himself the lone king of a vast commercial empire, dabbling in anything lucrative, along the way living life on a grand scale.

For what drew most the fascination of a receptive populace were the flashes of revelation concerning the magnificent private life of this elusive man. Most of the time he lived as a hermit, but when he deigned to enter public view he moved in rarefied circles, hobnobbing with captains of industry, powerful politicians, trend-setting socialites and glamorous movie stars. He bounced brashly from one worthy or entertaining companion to another, shuttling between popular adventures to stay, perhaps to rest, at his private penthouse apartments in New York City and Los Angeles, and his big house—his mansion—located, the stories indicated, in a secluded district somewhere far out on the north side of Phoenix.

Those who cared (and they were legion) saw as much of this as they could be expected to see, and maybe a bit more. Apparently an army of photographers and video teams lived for the sole purpose of chasing after glimpses of this man, for the image of Arthur J. Mandrake became a common household item in short order. Here was a snap of him taken at moderate distance, in sober conversation with a group of earnest, important-looking, middle-aged gentlemen. There was his amiable smile and royal wave of the hand, in close-up with a beautiful, well-dressed red-head, a perky young girl clinging devotedly to his arm. He was filmed exiting a fashionable Hollywood restaurant escorting an up and coming starlet, viewed briskly mounting the steps of the Capitol building in Washington. Whenever he went anywhere notable, it seemed, or appeared with anyone whom the public fancied, someone was likely to be nearby with camera or TV crew.

And a fine specimen of a man he appeared. Tall, lean, and long-legged, with a youthful Gary Cooper mien, spiced with a James Dean boldness, he always went about immaculately dressed and tailored, a walking fashion statement to a world that felt, upon beholding him, its cultural lack. The one time the paparazzi caught him out of coat and tie, during a seaside frolic aboard his sleek yacht, his casual attire still screamed expensive elegance. Woman were particularly fascinated by his evident charms. Ratings of entertainment and pop news programs zoomed whenever he made a showing.

His features were striking rather than handsome. A high forehead, surmounted by a shock of perfectly groomed light brown hair; piercing, bright blue eyes; a strong, aquiline nose that twitched when he laughed; a firm mouth, determined yet ever ready for a disarming grin; from these elements were constructed the face that beamed via every media outlet to a hungry audience.

The whereabouts of his apartments could not be established—only close-ups of the entrances and photographs of the interiors were released—but there developed a frenzy of speculation concerning the location of his main home near Phoenix. Full particulars were presented of its features, all save its address. Three stories—forty rooms—five hundred acres of tended estate, complete with golf course, Olympic pool and tennis court—a garage bigger than a house, crammed with dangerous foreign sports cars scarcely road legal in this country—all these, and the majestic interior, furnished in an Art Deco variation of Louis XIV, became well known. Television tours revealed all, yet people wanted more. Uninvited camera crews scoured the countryside seeking the place, while sight-seers rambled the likely avenues and by-ways, hoping for a distant glimpse.

Throughout this period Theresa Delaney, at the behest of Professor Vorchek, busied herself with coordinating the efforts of the three high-powered PR firms, feeding them suggestions, orders, fresh particulars from her mentor. "It's amazing," she said. "This PR stuff really works. People will believe anything if it's sold to them properly. In no time at all we've got them all by the tail. Of course," she added, "it doesn't mean anything. Nothing's really going to happen."

For all of the preceding developments were part of Vorchek's carefully orchestrated, incredibly expensive experiment. There was no Arthur J. Mandrake; he was merely a creation of the professor's vivid imagination. Vorchek, during many a stimulating work session with Theresa, had conceived the character, built up the bare bones of a personality, clothed him with the flesh of intriguing detail, and then let the big boys loose to peddle him. The campaign mystified the advertising men, since never was the source of ultimate profit clarified, but they were professionals, engaging in their chosen and rewarding labors with gusto. They did the job, succeeding as they were wont to do.

"The parameters are complete," said Vorchek. "Millions, tens, perhaps hundreds of millions know for certainty of my Mandrake. They know his face: that of a dinner theater actor, gratefully accepting anonymity in return for bankable currency. They know his associates, as rumored by us or bribed to cooperate, and there was that dazzling red-head who caught every eye; well done, Miss Delaney, a splendid performance, and a fetching wig. Through the eye of the lens they have been inside and all around his house: stage sets, genuine interiors from various places, computer imagery, the fabrication of location. They know his tastes, his hobbies, his goals. They know, and they believe. I have focused their mental energies, made them intellectually concrete. There is no weakness of portrayal, no softness at the margins. All of my subjects, that mighty herd, are thinking and accepting in identical unison."

"So they are," admitted Theresa. "You accomplished that much. We could've taken a fancy trip around the world on the money you've shelled out. You've got your belief. That's as far as it goes, though. Now it ends. Nothing's going to happen."

Something did.

Diligent seekers at last discovered Mandrake's palatial estate. One determined couple, on the roam north of Phoenix in the vicinity of Cave Creek, took a snap with their family camera of an impressive dwelling located on a mesa below the foot of Elephant Mountain. It was a very long shot, enhanced by only a modest zoom, and the hazy atmosphere of the hot desert hindered seeing conditions, but the edifice fuzzily pictured in their photograph could be readily identified as the place in question. This intrigued Professor Vorchek, whose first-rate investigative skills soon established, via county records, that no house of any kind was known to exist in that remote wilderness area. With Theresa in tow he set out, in his four-wheel drive van, to check out the spot for himself.

They found the approximate location from which the picture had been taken, at a turn-off by a bend on a forlorn Forest Service road. There before them loomed Elephant Mountain, its steep slopes of boulders and saguaro cacti capped by its colossal namesake formation; there beneath its east flank the mesa, and on that, appearing very small in the distance, the dim outlines of a house, seemingly tiny, but surely monumental in size to be noticed at all at such far remove. At Vorchek's command Theresa produced binoculars, a powerful 16X pair which she trained upon the designated object. "It's there, all right," said the girl, turning the knob to sharpen the image. "Professor, it looks just like those fake pictures we made. No, wait, something's wrong. I do believe... Oh, these things are so heavy. Here, look for yourself."

Vorchek did so, removing his glasses and adjusting the binoculars to suit himself. "That is very strange," he said pensively. "I do not know. Let us go closer." They drove farther, until the horrid dirt road turned away from the site, at which point they parked and proceeded on foot, carrying cameras, notebooks, and canteens. Quite some time before they arrived Theresa was laughing at her crestfallen companion.

"It's just a rock formation," she announced at last, "like the one on top of the mountain. From a long ways off it looks a little like a house, but you can see it's nothing of the kind." "The resemblance is uncanny," Vorchek noted. "Those broad planar surfaces produce the appearance of white-washed walls, and those odd cavities mimic windows, while that fringe of scrubby junipers above creates an illusion of a roof. Other details—those cracks and folds of stony terrain—enhance the effect. That depression in the foreground could be the foundations for a big swimming pool. Truly a unique formation, yet hardly decisive evidence of what I am testing."

Said Theresa, "Told you so."

The mystery deepened, however. Later that day, examining documents related to the site at the courthouse in downtown Phoenix, Vorchek uncovered an interesting find. "Cast your eyes on that!" he crowed. "It is a photograph of the exact location, taken by Federal surveyors in the 1940s. The image quality is perfect. Miss Delaney, tell me what you see." Theresa studied the large black and white picture. "There's the slope of the mountain," she said, "and the line of the mesa, and I remember that volcanic outcropping on the left. But Professor, this obviously isn't the place. We must have the angle wrong. The house formation isn't here." "The angle is correct," Vorchek sighed happily, "yet the formation is not there. It was not there, then; it has come into being since. In a strange, out of kilter fashion, something has developed there, a mockery of our fantasy house. This accords, my dear; this accords, somewhat, with my parameters."

"I don't believe it," said Theresa.

Vorchek verified his findings, added the data to his files. When informed, geologists scratched their heads and lamely pointed out the wildness of that country, the possibility of having missed relatively minor features. The professor inclined to another explanation.

There was more. Sightings of Arthur J. Mandrake accumulated. Eye witnesses spoke of him as appearing at assorted glamorous locales, commonly in company with uncommon public figures. Vorchek avidly took notes on these claims. "So what?" queried Theresa. "It's like flying saucers. People see what they expect to see." Vorchek sagely granted this, but the next twist on the story bulked larger in his mind. A fashion photographer for an esteemed national magazine videotaped a beautiful movie star and her gentleman escort leaving a ritzy Paris hotel and hailing a passing taxi. Publicists of the actress subsequently placed her at the scene, although they could not officially identify her companion, who was said to be a casual acquaintance. The man, however, was the spitting image of Arthur J. Mandrake. Theresa, who kept track of all details relating to Vorchek's weird scientific campaign, was forced to admit that their PR men were not involved in this stunt, and that their covert actor impersonating Mandrake had been operating in Milwaukee at the time. Also, the professor proved to his satisfaction that the tape had not been doctored.

"It makes me think," said he. Said Theresa, "I don't know what to think. Maybe this time someone's playing a gag on us." That might have constituted the preferred explanation as well when a textile firm received a shipment of soft-line goods invoiced from a holding company averred to be solely owned by Mandrake. The return address proved a fiction, leading back to a long abandoned warehouse in San Diego that once housed imported textiles, and the contents of the crates turned out to be nothing but rotted junk, yet the receiving company held in its files papers documenting this and other transactions, papers the existence of which puzzled the corporate managers. Vorchek interviewed them all, came away wondering.

Then, at the height of what Theresa styled "the Mandrake hysteria," came the curious mystery and, probably, tragedy of Donald Nelson. Nelson was none other than the fairly unknown actor who had portrayed Mandrake in his many fleeting, carefully packaged public appearances. He had done extremely well for himself lately, being highly paid for his services, looking forward to the ultimate revelation that would make him, in his own persona, a household name and establish a genuine career. It was not to be. As the weeks passed it transpired (this Vorchek learned after the fact) that he began to complain of feelings of ill health, listlessness, a loss of vitality. For no reason that he ever stated, Nelson was overheard to exclaim that his lucrative assignment had been a mistake, that he feared the consequences of his activities. He did, too, say something about a plague of tormenting dreams, which he refused to describe. At a Hollywood party where he appeared incognito—meaning not playing his role—he came over gravely sick, scurrying into the bathroom before he made a mess of himself. He did not emerge from the compartment in what his solicitous hostess deemed due time, so she sent two other male guests were to check on his welfare. They found him not there. That was passing strange. He could only have come out the one way, nor had the party been so lively that comings and goings could be unanimously ignored. Nelson vanished from the bathroom that night, never to be seen again. Friends were contacted, the police called in, a missing persons file opened; all for naught. It was as if he had disappeared from the planet.

Vorchek offered a curious comment on the unpleasant matter. "I sincerely hope that I am not at fault," he said. "Look here, Miss Delaney, at my graph of the Mandrake Index. As you can see from this chart, the belief quotient verges on one hundred percent. Under these circumstances Mandrake counts for everything, the impostor nothing. Could it be? I ask you, my dear, could it be that I have, with all good intentions, rendered our Mr. Nelson superfluous, literally immaterial?"

Despite absolute belief in his actuality, the esteemed and envied Arthur J. Mandrake could be no more than what is termed a "nine day wonder," though he lasted a little longer than that. In time, despite all of the cunningly generated hoopla, public interest in the fake character faded, dwindled, and died. There came a day when, although no one doubted, no one any longer really cared. When these reports arrived Professor Vorchek declared the experiment concluded, paid off his hired guns, took stock with his charming assistant in the den of his old, lonely house. There they lounged after a festive night on the town, seated among documents, photographs, charts, heaps of scribbled notes.

Said Vorchek, "We obtained results. I consider that established. Highly impressive results, if I may say so, even if not wholly on the mark. You must accept now, Miss Delaney, that by scientifically focusing the mental powers of millions and tens of millions of ordinary human beings, we garnered genuine additions to the world corpus, aspects of reality which did not exist before our campaign commenced. Think of the faux mansion, the spurious shipments, the verified appearances beyond our efforts, even, I must allow, the apparent loss of Mr. Nelson. Something truly happened."

"Something happened," replied Theresa, nonchalantly puffing on her cigarette one more time, then flicking it into the tray, "but not hardly what you predicted. It's kind of like the spider all over again. You got bits and pieces, Professor, fair enough, without ever getting close to what you sought. You're the man who would be the 'Frankenstein of Thought,' willing a man into existence, but where is he?"

"This business of creation *ex nihilo*," admitted Vorchek, "is not all it is cracked up to be. I am prepared to grant, on a provisional basis, that in order to achieve my end I would require considerably more god-like powers for that. I am but a simple man; I attain what I can, absorb, learn, move on."

"You almost had me believing in Mandrake," said the girl. "That's quite a feat. Wouldn't it be a scream if he showed up to set us straight?"

The door knocker thudded, once, a startling sound in the quiet night. "I expect no one," said Vorchek, with irritation. "See who it is, my dear, and send him away if you can. I would not wish us disturbed tonight." Theresa rose languidly, sauntered across the room into the hall. Vorchek heard the sounds of tumblers and chains, the creaking of the old oaken door. He heard a piercing shriek of absolute terror. He sprang to his feet, making for the hall, collided with the frantic girl backing into him. They both fell back, and something horrible entered after them.

It was not a man, had never been a man; it was too crudely unfinished, too monstrously, loathsomely incomplete, yet there appeared in its lumpish, corroded outlines, its repellent insinuations of feature and misshapen fragments of clothing, something resembling a man, akin to the first vague form fashioned by a cruel and callous sculptor. The thing shuffled forward, sagged onto the carpet, a quivering pile of impossible life. Theresa, face blanched ghastly white, cringed against the professor and turned away her head in disgust.

Vorchek the brilliant, Vorchek the rational thinker, even through his exhilaration of abhorrence knew the thing for what it was. "Get out of here, Mandrake!" he shouted shrilly. "You must go away!"

And the putrid mass raised its viscous, muddied travesty of a face, lifted two miserable stumps in an imploring stance, and somehow, incredibly, croaked in a dreadful, rasping voice, "Please, Vorchek, make me go away."

THE FLAW IN THE IMAGE

Josh Crundt had reached a point, of some disquieting duration, at which every aspect of his life repelled him. The senselessness, the aimlessness of it all wearied him. He helplessly despised his dead-end clerking job, felt an aching emptiness over his latest sputtering relationship, meekly deplored his unchanging material circumstances; hated his name, although that was nothing new. Then again, none of it was new. Since his earliest memories he had staggered under a heavy pall of menacing oppression. Even his hobby, that life-saver, filled him now with deteriorative ennui. A hobby was supposed to add spark to life, and once his had done so, but lately it had come to seem of a piece with the other broken links of the Crundt chain.

Photography was that hobby, one dating back to his teenage days, a period rather distressingly far away. Every spare penny of his meager income had dropped into that bottomless pit over the years, going for the latest cameras, increasingly fancy gear, rolls of film once upon a time, later memory cards, the allure of will-o'-the-wisp achievement driving him on. Crundt spent a cumulative fortune replacing his previous 35 millimeter kit with the best all-digital system, grabbing every high-tech lens he could afford and a bit more. His current outfit could do just about anything except, so it transpired, satisfy him.

The problem was (to a degree; being no fool, he knew the root cause went much deeper) that his digital output lacked the living fire produced by his earlier film kits, the color and dynamic range that had drawn him into photography on an enhanced amateur basis in the first place. His grossly expensive digital SLR, with its shockingly pricey lenses, gave him clear, crisp pictures every time, pictures which his computer monitor displayed big and bright; that, and soulless. They were glossy, they were plastic, they were, somehow, despite all their unbeatable detail, fake. Crundt disliked that, had come to see it as too akin to the rest of his existence.

On yet another typical Friday night he squatted alone in his cramped apartment, poring over his camera equipment, musing on the possibilities of a time-gobbling expedition on the morrow. Then he rebelled, casting aside his professional gear as so much junk. It would not do any longer. The realization opened a dreadful hole into which he dreaded to peer, chiefly because he feared that nothing would emerge from it. Instead he opened the hall closet, probed the clutter for a spell, extracted at last the monumental leather bag containing all of his surviving 35mm stuff. Plenty of that had been sold to pay for the digital items, and he'd occasionally gotten good prices for what were now deemed collectibles, but a heaping residue remained. This he shortly strewed on the little kitchen table.

Possessed he still his original film SLR—single lens reflex that meant, meaning in fact a battery of supporting lenses—in fine condition from its elaborate cleaning a few years back. It was his trusty Minolta SRT-102, purchased by him in 1972 for six months' savings. How proud he had felt then to own such a thing! A big camera it was, hefty metal and black enamel, all its functions operated manually save for the light meter, which he had trained himself not to use. For years he'd bragged to whoever would listen that he owned a top of the line camera that didn't require batteries, a feature which often amazed the next generation. Everything worked by hand: focusing, setting of shutter speed, opening and closing of the lens aperture, regulation of the clumsy but serviceable flash attachment, feeding, winding, and rewinding of film. Built like a tank, the machine was rock solid, as numerous harrowing accidents established.

Crundt had kept a pile of lenses, a sampling of the manual focus selection he used to carry in two cumbersome bags. Now he fondled them lovingly, one by one: the super-wide 18mm which bent everything at the sides of the picture, as if the world were falling in on itself; the 24mm wide-angle, a superfluous lens he seldom used, which only functioned adequately if stopped down all the way; the 28mm wide, good and sharp; the 50mm, his brightest and sharpest, though it was the standard that came with the camera; two telephotos, the sharp 90mm macro with which he'd snapped a thousand bugs, and the slow 135mm which nevertheless rivaled the 50 in overall quality; the 70-300 zoom, a bulky thing which he only employed for its full reach; and that great dinosaur, the behemoth 600mm mirror lens, a beastly thing like a stubby telescope, which he mated, with problematic results, to a 2X teleconverter attachment.

Somewhat to Crundt's surprise he also discovered a crumbling card-stock package containing six antique rolls of film. He placed them at as many years old as their number, at a minimum, which suggested to him that the film was far past its prime, perhaps beyond usability. He checked the "develop by" date, snickered at that, also noted the presence of a powdery substance, probably a fungoid growth, on and in the carton. He threw away the ruined container, wiped the fine grayish-green particles from the ends of the film strips where they protruded from the canisters, and pondered. In its day this had been the finest, costliest 100 speed film he could buy. He harbored no desire to spend any money on a questionable lark, beyond the necessary; therefore, why not try the stuff, see if it retained its olden virtues?

The next morning, which proved enjoyably fair, Crundt drove the few miles to the solitude of a nondescript nature park, managed by the county on the outskirts of encroaching urbanization, there broke out his obsolete apparatus. Just off the looping park road, within the confines of an unfrequented picnic ground, he set up his heavy professional grade tripod, quite a load to carry on a hike but a statue's pedestal for steady photography. He sat at the concrete bench of a concrete table, where he inserted a cartridge into the back of the camera and, drawing out a length of film, fed the material onto the take-up spool, made sure it was snug, closed the back and mounted the machine on the tripod, screwing it securely to avoid wobble. For his test shots he began with the attached 50mm, his old reliable.

The scene before him was common enough for the area: a level plain of desert scrub and cacti stretching into the moderate distance, where piles of dark, weathered volcanic hills met the intense blue sky. To his right front loomed a high blunt peak; ahead a jumble of rises possessing interesting rock formations; to the left canyon-cut mounds of boulders interspersed with isolated but eye-catching saguaros. Crundt took a test series with the one lens, utilizing mirror lock-up and a remote release to avoid shutter shake. He thoughtfully clicked down through the various f-stops, from 1.7 to 16, then released the lens, removed it, attached the 28 and worked through its range. After that he took an assortment of odd shots with several lenses, the result being, after almost two hours of surprisingly delightful labor, a spent roll of film. This he carefully rewound, removed, placed in a plastic bag. He appreciated the effort required to produce the pictures, so much more inconvenient than his modern digital, so much more evocative of an earlier period of life when—at least the pretense of—wonderful possibilities throve.

Never, however, had film development sufficiently appealed, nor did it now. Crundt did not possess, never had possessed, a private darkroom, so having reached this point he packed his gear and drove back to town, dropping off his questionable roll at the drug store nearest home. He ordered prints, negatives, scans on CD, paid for overnight service in order to save a couple of bucks. A far cry, to be sure, from his digital, which he could hook to his computer and view the shots in seconds.

That was that for the day, all until the following morning, Sunday. He devoted the night to eating alone out of a foam microwave cup and solitarily watching an old movie that bored. On Sunday morning, of course, he did absolutely nothing, as always, until he roused himself adequately to go out and visit the photo lab tucked away in the little alcove of the drug store. The clerk, young, gum-chewing, female, unattractive, said, "We don't get many of these any more. We mainly make prints from memory cards." Crundt sniffed, "I only seek quality in my pictures." The clerk shrugged, charged his order in advance.

Crundt waited until he got home to unseal the paper package and examine the ready prints. In most respects the results gratified him highly. Apparently the film had not lost its tone after all, despite the abuse of time, for the color and range of the shots were marvelous. His special care had ensured that each photograph was beautifully crisp, measuring up to what he considered the professional standards of glossy magazines. The subjects interested him little, save that they lent themselves to his test. The film performed as he recalled, pulling out shadow detail, retaining highlights, filling the images with color slightly warmer than reality. Surely that bland county park never looked so good.

One aspect of the prints annoyed and disgusted him. He noticed it in the very first image, detected it again and again as he flipped through the others. Every 4x6 print bore a startling flaw, one so egregious that even a minimum wage drug store clerk should have caught it. A pesky, recurrent black blot marred the whole series. Obviously it did not involve the lenses, for he had used them all, had checked their optics before employing them. Their glass was clear, pristine, facts conveyed by the totality of the images. It seemed unlikely that the film could be the culprit, though he knew the stock to be dubious, and chose to keep an open mind on the point. Most likely the cause was miserable development, perhaps a dirty negative processing machine.

How else to explain the same false spot appearing in each picture? It was a small black oval, impenetrably dark, sporting no inner detail in the prints, which appeared at the exact location relative to the aspect of the frame, meaning that it did not correspond or relate to anything in the scene, but rather moved with the field of view, always maintaining a position up and left of center. It was a terrible eyesore, entirely unprecedented, increasingly frustrating. That flaw went a long way toward blowing his tests out of the water.

Maybe it was only a problem with the prints. Crundt slipped the CD of store scans from its sleeve, popped the disc into his computer in order to analyze the results. The scans were bargain basement stuff, as predicted, but gave him decent images that filled the monitor screen. Everything looked okay, except for the flaw, which was still more apparent amidst the glow of electronic pixels, and still utterly sharp at the edges and dark inside. Crundt hated the sight of it.

That afternoon he ventured back to the store, waving his sheaf of debauched prints at the same bored, disinterested clerk. "These won't do," declared Crundt. "You screwed them up. See this? It's on all of them, the scans too." Said the clerk, "I did everything like always." Crabbed Crundt, "Not good enough. I want my money back, or I want them fixed." "All right," drawled the clerk. "I'll run the negatives through again. Give me twenty minutes." Crundt chose to wait, radiating impatience throughout the unbearably tiresome ordeal.

The girl attempted to engage him in conversation as she operated the mini-lab. "I saw that thing, you know. We're supposed to check for obvious mistakes. I ran the software to get rid of blemishes, dirt and such. That works pretty good. It didn't make any difference here, so I figured those blobs were on your end, that's all."

After what the irate customer considered an interminable period the girl produced a fresh batch of prints, identical to the original set. More processing had not eradicated the flaw. "I want my money," demanded Crundt. He got it, and a free roll of cheap store brand film to boot. "I don't use such garbage," he muttered as he left, but he kept the roll, for it crossed his mind that he could utilize it for cross-checking tests of the old film stock.

SCIENCE AND SORCERY II

So much for the moment. Despite his characteristic sense of woebegone harassment, Crundt realized that his first foray into reclaiming the world of film photography had gone rather well, in the main. The processing error, or film weakness, whatever it might be, was certainly highly unusual and distressing, but with next to no chance of it happening again he could be content with the general quality of the photographs, try for more when opportunity arose the following weekend. Just to play it safe he would get his artistic productions developed elsewhere. Josh Crundt cheered himself with these thoughts as best he could, then commenced the routine Sunday night exercise of steeling himself to return to his wretched job.

The ensuing five days were, as he regularly felt, a complete waste of a chunk of his life. He amused himself through the inescapable tedium by planning his upcoming photography project for the weekend. Friday afternoon arrived, not a moment too soon, and after wolfing a TV dinner Crundt set in motion once more his latest onslaught against wearied unease and indifference. That night he lovingly organized his film kit, preparing for bold deeds behind the camera.

As matters fell together he felt sluggish come the morning, so he decided quickly against any long range ramblings for the day, concluding instead that another foray into the local park would serve his purpose. There he went, setting up shop right where he had last week, taking essentially the same pictures under similarly bright conditions. This time he ran through two rolls, one the old good stuff of twenty-four frames, the other the free store roll of twenty-seven. He sniffed at the latter—"400 speed, grainy and lacking vibrancy, I bet"—but it was free, he did not wish to spend cash foolishly, and he wondered how it would perform. He began with it. When most of the old roll was exhausted he left the park, snapping the final three shots in the parking lot of a grocery store which still offered development service. There he turned in both cartridges for pick-up next day.

On Sunday morning the elderly photo clerk (who also handled DVD rentals) politely handed him the goods, which Crundt whisked away after paying. This time he tore open the thin packages in the car, starting with the prints made from the drug store roll. He had to admit that they were more than passable, rendering landscapes, paloverde trees and cacti with reasonable crispness. Only the color balance was off, the shots degraded by a faint but tell-tale yellow-orange cast that could never pass muster with the big boys. Good to fair, he designated them. He opened the second package.

Crundt hissed his impotent fury through clenched teeth. Then he swore aloud to himself. The very first print from the second batch revealed the black spot. It was there, and on each succeeding picture, those colorful, gorgeous images stained by that flaw, that hideous blemish of defiling blackness. He saw it in the parking lot pictures, too. No question, then, that the antique film was to blame. Curious, he thought—downright weird—that improper storage and subtle contamination should have affected two rolls in precisely the same fashion, and only that way. What could it be? Had water trickled onto the rolls from a forgotten ceiling leak in the closet, or something filthy grown through them with amazing regularity? Not much by way of explanations, but something like that must answer for the effect. It bugged Crundt, a photographer with knowledge sound enough to rule out the conventional hazards. This resembled nothing in his experience.

At home he studied the pictures in earnest, blowing up on his computer the listless scans to the maximum from the supermarket CD. One thing he had already noticed: the flaws were not exactly the same as in the first roll after all. This time the black horizontal ovals obtruded closer to the center of the frames, and were visibly larger. In this set of 4x6s the flaw, no bigger than a BB in the first, was now the size of a dime, rounded at the tips in the shape of an eye. Yes, it looked like a black, vacant eye staring at him. Oddly, it did not quite come across as a film flaw. The horrid mark possessed no quality of transparency as was normal, but entirely obscured the bit of scenery or sky underneath, as if it were a real thing, an actual presence at the site, which just happened to interpose itself between artist and subject. Crundt paid careful attention to the scanned blow-ups, struggling to decipher feature within the spot. He could not. The interior was pitch darkness, without any hint of structure or form. It appeared more a hole in space than anything else, an absence of rather than an overlay on reality. This peculiar estimation did not prevent him from stupidly picking at the flaw, as if he might scrape it from the screen and dispense with it.

Software cloning wiped away the spots pretty well, filling in the offending field of black with surrounding color, but did not answer the question that tantalized: what the source of the flaw? What was it, what made it happen? Of course Crundt could junk the old film—for a moment he had the firm intention of doing so—only the mystery intrigued him. He wished, he realized, to delve to the explanation. It would be a learning experience. Besides, he had little else with which to entertain himself.

During the drab work week he thought much of the flaw, pondering its significance, pondering why he should deem it significant. He told himself that was the aura of the budding professional, one who cared deeply about all aspects of his art. Problems arose: they must be confronted; they must be understood; they must be resolved. That was the correct view of the matter. At his desk he doodled black ovals on scraps of paper. During one coffee break he broached the issue to a pretty girl who had just started working in the office. Her reaction of contemptuous amusement hit him like a sledge hammer, and he did not mention the business again, to anyone there.

Crundt did not return to the grocery store to fuel a fuss, lamely accepting that the trouble lay on his doorstep. It did cross his mind that photographic technicians possessing more in-depth knowledge than drug store or grocery clerks might be in a better position to clarify the murky situation. He knew of an old, esteemed camera shop way downtown, many miles away, where the best of everything was to be had. Several years before he had occasionally journeyed there, could do so again if it mattered enough to him.

For no coherent reason it did. He called from the office at lunch, verified their inconvenient hours. There was nothing to do but ask for the afternoon off. Raising the issue with the boss caused needless and aggravating stress. The callous fellow blandly objected, vaguely hinting at unspecified consequences for this shocking evidence of lack of workplace zeal. Crundt got the afternoon, but he had to put up with the nonsense first, and he brooded reproachfully at the thought that other, far less reliable employees, got their way on a greater scale, more often, with little or no difficulty. It seemed to him that it had always been like that there.

He swooped by the apartment, picked up his negatives along with the prints and a roll of unused film, and set out on the long, hazardous drive into the busy urban center, a place he avoided assiduously if he could. In recent years he had only been downtown twice, both times for tiresome jury duty. The shop, located in a declining business district within a deteriorating strip mall, boasted a tiny store front of garish posters and tripods displayed behind glass windows.

The interior was much as he remembered it, though mainly given over to digital items since his last visit. He enjoyed perusing the stock for a while, then homed in on the much shrunk film development counter, where a vacuous female clerk awaited him. He guessed that she was not the final word on any subject there, a feeling confirmed when she responded blankly to his questions and called into the air for "Tim." He emerged from the back room, an elderly man with little hair but an intelligent, earnest face. After listening to a brief summary of the conundrum Tim replied in the following manner:

"Now that really is odd. As you describe it, Josh, I don't know of a case quite like it. There are so many ways film can go wrong, but they tend to leave obvious signs. If the colors were off kilter, or the crispness cocked up, or you picked up ghosting or light flares, I could zero in on the problem fast. This is good film, the prints look otherwise sound. The negatives..." Here Tim held a strip to the light, staring through a magnifying glass. "I can just make out the spot in the image. It's in the negative, all right. There's some kind of flaw there."

"I know that," Crundt replied, "but what causes it? It's the same, more or less, on each roll."

"Yeah, that's odd. I have no answer, Josh. I don't see how it could be. My advice is to buy new film and forget about it. Well, Josh—" Tim scratched his bare scalp at Crundt's expostulation and shook his head—"I don't know what to say. Tell you what I'll do, though. If you like, I'll keep the negatives for now, and this roll of film. Does that bother you? Okay, I'll open the cartridge in the darkroom, examine the contents for visible damage, get back to you tomorrow. In fact, if this won't cramp your style, I'll shoot the roll, put it to the test. I'm glad for a chance to break out my old gear. Of course I only shoot digital these days. Who needs this kind of headache?"

Crundt felt uplifted at having a caring professional investigating the mystery for him. Predicting great results on the morrow, he allowed high spirits and heightened interest to sail him through the twenty-four hours and more before he arrived at the apartment next evening and found his answering machine beckoningly blinking. However, the message from Tim (for such it was, along with two others promoting life insurance) took him down a bit.

"Josh, I did what I said," rasped the homey voice. "Couldn't see anything on the emulsion itself, except for some scattered particles that wiped off, definitely not what we were seeing. I shot the roll. It came out great—nothing wrong with it—the pictures are perfect. Looks like you got hold of a couple of bum rolls, that's all. I wouldn't worry about it any more. You might should pick up some fresh film, anyway.

"You got me puzzled, Josh. I'd like to know how that happens. If you don't mind, I've contacted a buddy of mine who works at the university. He's a physicist who does work with optics. He knows all that kind of stuff. I'll bet you he comes up with the answer. I'll have him get in touch with you when he finds something." The message trailed off into a pitch for new camera accessories.

Crundt did not feel overly enlightened. It galled him slightly that the third roll had performed flawlessly, that he had derived no benefit from the fact. He assured himself that the remaining three should function similarly well, that he could utilize them for a properly enjoyable outing when he chose. He did wonder at the interest the case generated, at the amount of mystery it seemed to invoke. He would have thought the business concluded long before now. Even a university physicist was getting into the act! Apparently somebody out there considered his personal concerns to be of some minimal importance.

That night Crundt, who never dreamed, did so. In the dream he drifted in a dark, featureless limbo, the only sense of presence other than his own awareness of his state being a sort of muffled shouting that bombarded him from all sides, unintelligible gibberish that seemed directed at him with hostile intent. Nothing actually happened during the vision, yet the mounting tension and specter of danger so unnerved him that he burst awake with a moan of fear. The particular meaning, if any, eluded him. Sometimes in real life he felt like that. Lots of times he did.

The week ground on. Two days later—this was Friday—Crundt came home to find another message on his machine. A pleasantly engaging voice identified itself as Doctor Harrold of the physics department. In a breezy manner he told Crundt a few things. ""It's pretty mystifying, Josh," said the voice. "In my spare time I've been tinkering with your stuff Tim gave me. No big deal, just kicking around ideas. I ran the negatives from all three rolls under a microscope, looking for anything out of line in the emulsion base. I found quite a lot, actually. The chemical composition isn't entirely right—I mean it's way off specs—it's undergone alteration to a surprising degree. Something changed the material, distorted its optical qualities in a manner I can't yet classify. The only visual indication of the change is the spots on the two rolls. Don't ask me why the third doesn't exhibit them. Seems to me it should have.

THE FLAW IN THE IMAGE

"I scanned the flaws with an opacity meter. I don't know what to make of this. They come out true, inherent in the base image, as if they belong in the scenes you snapped. Good pictures, by the way. I'm tempted to tell you they're just blurry shots of birds, but I admit that can't be right. It's a wacky situation. I know there's a simple solution, but I don't have it yet. You've caught my attention. Give me the weekend to mess with it some more."

Now a big brain, Crundt mused, was puzzled by his aged film and its properties. He jollied himself thinking that it was not so silly of him to spend time on the matter as he had occasionally supposed. Crundt need not see himself as a dopey guy wasting days and weeks in trivialities; he was, instead, an intrepid seeker engaged in scientific enterprise, a part of something beyond the drearily commonplace. That sure sounded a whole lot better. He encouraged himself with the hope that Dr. Harrold would produce decisive results soon, deliver knowledge of a technically thrilling character.

On Saturday Crundt took off on a real photographic expedition, driving north on a frigid dawn toward regions worthy of good film. No more tests for him; this was the real thing. He made his way via interstate and secondary highway to majestic Oak Creek Canyon, arriving at the southern reaches just as the sun peaked over the lip of the rim. There he entered a glorious realm of startling red sandstone formations, rugged white bluffs, sheer stone walls, extensive pine forests and swiftly moving, rock-splashing water. He had been there a hundred times over the years, would gladly go a hundred more. It was his favorite place on earth, affording him a fleeting feeling of peace.

It was, too, a photographer's paradise. Crundt made his way to the high north end and began his series at the overlook, which offered him a view ten miles down the canyon. He loaded his old roll, the fourth, into the camera, then worked by the numbers—tripod, mirror lockup, remote release—seeking the classic pictures he knew he was capable of taking. Four shots down (wide angles with his 28mm lens), he walked back to the car and pulled back down into the canyon, halting by the creek full and wild after recent rains and melting snowfall in the higher elevations of the mountains. He snapped two of the rocky, foaming stream (rather dark in there under the thick stands of trees, so he opened up his 50mm all the way), moved south to the area of the most picturesque red rock spires, even drove up the decrepit back-country dirt road for a view of the formations from above. Amongst those wonders he blew the roll, quickly switching lenses with practiced hands as the shots demanded. A dark brown, white-bellied hawk brooded sullenly on a distant limb, tarrying motionless as if posing for posterity; Crundt caught it with his clunky 600mm mirror lens, teleconverter affixed.

It was a marvelous day. He ate a late lunch at a little one-off restaurant that specialized in pork chop sandwiches, then cruised pleasantly back to civilization, reaching town as evening fell. Having spent more on gas than he cared to admit, Crundt stopped off at the drug store to deposit his film. He accepted that they had done nothing to wreck his pictures, desired to give them another chance and save a few bucks on their cheap rates.

He slept like a log. It was not until late Sunday afternoon that he sufficiently roused himself to leave his drab abode to collect his treasures. This he did, taking them all the way home and settling in, changing back into his robe, before viewing the results. He truly screamed when he beheld the first print. Repeated flipping of glossy photographic paper told the same story. That damnable flaw had returned.

At once the insane conjecture struck him, a thought unbidden, unwelcome, unacceptable—that the source of the traumatic spots lay within him, was an upwelling of something reserved wholly unto himself—a thought then dismissed as too crazy, incomprehensible, and frightening to be borne for a moment. The flaws were back, behaving according to now sickeningly familiar pattern, a rule of imagery no one could explain for him. There were definite differences this time. The black, eye-shaped ovals were now placed dead center in each picture. They were much larger, occupying a territory on the 4x6s the size of a quarter. Even on the small photographs he could now barely make out a hint of lighter substance inside the harshly black circumferences.

To the computer then, where he studied the CD scans in a morose frenzy. There he blew up the flaws as big as baseballs. Each one appeared the same on this roll, which accorded to form, and what he saw so contrived to give him the creeps that he half desired to close out the screen and throw the disk away, along with the prints and negatives. There were now soft but definite objects within the black ovals, many of them, a crowded myriad of faint yellowish subsets of strangeness. Their shape was like that of the encompassing darkness, creating the unsettling illusion of an array of eyes packed densely and haphazardly into a small space, disembodied eyes peering out of nighted gloom.

Crundt fancied that each minuscule eye sported a near microscopic pupil, a vanishingly small circle slit like the eye of a cat, only sideways.

The limitations of the inexpensive drug store scans frustrated him. He wanted to see more, to see all. On the instant Crundt decided to do that which he had never done in his later film career, when opportunity had once presented itself. He charged out to the nearest big electronics store and purchased his own film scanner.

It was a cheap machine, of course, one than even the salesman pointed out was insufferably slow, but it offered 4800 dots per inch of image resolution, which was twice what he got from any standard commercial service. He bundled out the big, awkward box, after slapping down his one hundred and sixty dollars (including a suspiciously generous discount), rushed it home and set it up, spending the remainder of the evening, save for a short meal break, connecting the bulky beast to his computer and learning to operate it.

He stayed up way past midnight fooling with the thing. The machine chirped, whirred, and growled interminably as it recorded and magnified the data from the little images. Scanning negatives proved, as he had always heard, a chore, and the initial results dismayed him with their softness and dirtiness, the latter bane due to dust and other household debris which drifted onto the cut strips and, when enlarged, revealed grubby specks and filaments of hair. For the time being Crundt ignored those, which could be laboriously dealt with by software. Having spent what seemed an eternity to scan four frames, he had eyes only for the genuinely offensive flaw that so bedeviled him.

He stared into one for long minutes, the repellent image expanded the size of a plump grapefruit. It was ugly, hateful to him, curiously nasty in its subjective effects. He was not sure that he could see any more detail inside the loathsome blot, though seeing it bigger still caused him queasy sensations. The impression of evilly watchful eyes remained. Crundt tried to convince himself that the giant scan better illuminated the interior structure of the yellow orbs, then strove to convince himself otherwise.

He felt a wreck at work next day. The boss maliciously opined that Crundt might be due for more time off, perhaps an extended leave. "I don't expect much of you," he said, "but I want what I'm paying you for." At home Crundt found another message from Dr. Harrold. The muted voice muttered from the answering machine, "I regret to say I didn't come up with anything. If there's any possibility of the images being true I could help you, Josh, because that's how it checks. Failing that, I surrender. Not to worry, though. I'm passing your materials to a colleague—a colleague of sorts—an interesting fellow, who's specialty, if he has one, is weird mysteries. I'm stumped, but he's been known to come up with explanations when everyone else throws in the towel. He might just pull something out of his hat—maybe nothing will come of it—but it's worth a try. Professor Vorchek will see your stuff, and contact you if he wishes. Sorry about this, Josh."

Crundt no longer cared that Harrold, like those before him, confessed defeat. Furthermore, he had no desire to suffer through the attentions of this Vorchek character, whoever he was. Crundt now revolted against the entire experience, the complete, miserable sequence of events. How had he gotten himself to such a state? Last night he had squandered real money on the mess, and for what? He derived no joy from it, nor from his resurgent film photography. Best to forget the whole thing, go back to his easy digital gear and put aside nostalgic daydreams.

This Crundt resolved to do. He held to his resolution for two days, until he came home Wednesday to a blinking answering machine. Two sales pitches, then three silent pauses during which someone had waited for him to pick up the telephone and, not receiving a response, had hung up. While he munched on a ham sandwich the phone rang. Crundt picked it up, announced himself, heard this in turn:

"This is Miss Delaney, calling on behalf of Professor Anton Vorchek. I believe Dr. Harrold referenced him. The professor has agreed to look into the case, citing matters of mildly intriguing interest. He wonders if something quite out of the ordinary may be occurring. He asks you to extend your full cooperation."

Crundt was petrified by the voice and what it said. It was a young, sultry, self-engrossed voice, a voice of intensely feminine allure that surmounted the veneer of brusque officiousness. No one with a voice like that ever spoke to him. He rather detested the subject at the moment, yet wished to continue the conversation. He explained, as charmingly as he might, that he thought the film oddities overblown, maybe not really worthy of such grand attention. He regretted troubling the professor, who must be a busy man. "No one else can make anything of it," Crundt pointed out.

"We have the prints and the negatives," said Miss Delaney with a mysterious, covert air, as if about to launch into blackmail demands. "Those passed on by Dr. Harrold, I mean. If you have more, the professor requires them at once, along with one unused roll of the pertinent film. Here is the address." She rattled off a mail drop at the university. "Professor Vorchek will make report when he is ready. A pleasant evening to you." Miss Delaney disconnected.

Crundt was like to laugh, without very much bitterness. These people would not leave him alone! Well, it was no skin off his nose. He packaged the latest prints and negatives, along with one of the two remaining rolls and a couple of scans printed at 8x10, mailed them in the morning before he headed for work. Then he tried his dead level best to forget the arduous matter forever.

That week, and the weekend, he largely succeeded in putting aside fretful questions of archaic photography. The surviving old roll he ostentatiously ignored. Something else arose to plague him cruelly, however: this unfortunate spate of dreaming. It began Friday night, hitting him every time he slept or dozed throughout the weekend. The visions were much like that last dream, he assuming consciousness in sleep within a black condition of terrifying limbo, out of which a grumbling, inhuman voice bellowed or raged. With each session of slumber (and there were several, for none brought him rest) the murky virulence of the dream taxed him more. By Monday morning, when he started awake with a plaintive yelp, the dreams had assumed a definitely noxious cast. The horrid voice shouted louder in its unknown tongue, nothing remotely similar to any language he knew, only he felt, in the dream and for a span of rapid heartbeats thereafter, that he could decipher the meaning of the harshly barked words. They clearly addressed him; they called to him, demanded of him something; ordered him to come, to submit, to face and accept an unspeakable fate. That was what the hideous voice wanted. The mere realization sufficed to jolt Crundt out of his dreams. However, what propelled him to feverish wakefulness the last time was an insidious glimpse of something emerging from the surrounding darkness: an impression beyond common sight, even as conventionally expressed in dreams, a visual sensation of an entity vast, all encompassing, implacably hostile, closing in on him. Crundt actually wondered what would have happened if he had not awakened when he did.

He went to work that day. That was a different kind of nightmare. The boss, sensing weakness, proved incorrigible, insufferable to a degree encouraging of violence. Crundt held his frayed temper, restraining his words, replacing them with noncommittal grunts or saying nothing. He simply wished to get through the day in one piece. He did, drove inattentively, stumbled home, collapsed on the sagging sofa. He would not dine, though he had not eaten since breakfast; he would not exert himself at all, for he lacked a single erg of energy; he would not sleep. On this latter issue he took a stand, determined to fight. He craved one full day without the incredibly agonizing ordeal fostered by those horrendous dreams.

He stayed up all night. Exhaustion plucked at him. He asked aloud, into the stifling air of the apartment, why the dreams frightened him so. Was there an answer? Equally disturbing were the stray thoughts that connected his dream visions to the stupid blots in his photographs. The equation made no sense; what he saw in the dreams, the little he had gleaned so far, did not really correspond. Somehow, though, he suspected—a nagging inner voice, a spiteful whisper assured him—the correspondence would come. Why did he think that? Why expect the worst in this, as in all else? Perhaps, he reasoned, because he had felt all his life that someone or something had set up the world that way with him, specifically, in mind. He loathed the suggestion, as ever, nor could he shake it, as ever.

Crundt went to work. He survived half a day before he gave in, left for lunch without returning, called in from home, slammed down the receiver while the boss sneered. So be it. He disintegrated into sleep. The dream recommenced. The thing, the object, the raging being of his nightmares approached more closely, revealing more of itself. Very large now, it seemed to fill the dream universe, blacker than the shrouding darkness, an opaque shadow emerging from curtains of shadow. There was something more...

Ringing woke him. Deep dusk had fallen. Miss Delaney announced herself from the answering machine. Crundt morosely replied. The pretty and arrogant young voice said crisply, "Professor Vorchek has completed his initial calculations. As a result of his observations and deductions he thinks he has arrived at a fair summary of the situation. By way of confirmation he wishes you to shoot the final roll and send the negatives to him at once. He is convinced that these pictures will tell all to his satisfaction. Also, he recommends that you, Mr. Crundt, settle your affairs while time remains.

"The Professor reports, for the moment, a remarkable alteration of the film emulsion, one which radically enhances certain light gathering properties of the stock." Here Miss Delaney spoke precisely and slow, as if reading from notes. "This means... hmm, let me see... yes, this means the film is capable of generally normal exposures, but also may detect presences usually imperceptible save when bidden by psychic influences. In short, what is seen possesses validity, but solely to the mind receiving and accepting the data. Since he saw nothing unusual in the roll he developed, Professor Vorchek infers that the mind in question is your own. Do you, sir, consider that the case?"

"I don't know what you're talking about," cried Crundt. "What do you mean, settle my affairs?"

"The professor," went on the girl, heedless of his testy ignorance, "desires explicit information relating to your mental condition. Allow me to go down the list." There came a sound of ruffled papers. "Are you prone to psychic visitations or paranormal disturbances? Do you suffer from an intimation that life is a deck stacked against you? Do you intimate the existence of unknown enemies, deducing them from life experience rather than objective evidence? Are you prey to exotic episodes of dreaming, or has such a condition recently arisen?" At the end of each sentence Miss Delaney paused for the reply, which Crundt helplessly, if waspishly, provided. After several more odd queries she said, "Very good. Expect a written summary of his findings shortly in the mail. Don't forget to take the pictures. That is all. Good day to you."

Crundt slept for two hours that night, in one hour bursts interrupted by his set alarm. The dream began in each case, mercifully never developing far before the siren whining of his clock rescued him. Both times his dream assailant started to reveal itself fully. Afterward Crundt debated with himself whether it resembled the latest appearances in his pictures. He did not go to work, did not call in. With the passage of dawn he mechanically loaded his trusty old Minolta with the last old roll, set it up on the tripod in a weedy vacant lot behind his apartment building and snapped away every frame. Utilizing the self-timer he inserted himself into the twenty-fourth shot. He would not ponder why the idea came to him; seldom did he photograph himself. A strange urgency commanded him. He removed the film, abandoned the camera and its mount, scarcely caring any longer. He took the roll to the drug store, paid for overnight service, saved on costs. Crundt surmised that money might be tight in the near future, and that only if he was lucky. Weirder thoughts rose to mind. The boss called once, bayed to the recording.

Crundt allowed himself three short snatches of measured slumber that day and night, which just barely held the dreams at bay. He prayed that he was merely suffering a nervous breakdown. He guessed that his problem was quite a bit more serious. At first light he forced himself to run an errand. With the morning mail arrived a large envelope addressed in an elegant hand from Professor Anton Vorchek. Crundt sank into his sofa, at the end where the table lamp offered good light, tore open the packet and read the typed sheets it contained. The critical portion ran as follows:

"My research into esoteric matters—a lifelong quest—has revealed evidence of peculiar influences and powers beyond those adjudged as aspects of the material world. I have found, via study of anthropology, folklore, and scientifically attested modern cases, impressively cogent evidence that certain individuals of the human race are especially prone to the effects of the insidious actions of these powers, seldom if ever benign, often lethal. The individuals in question typically lead miserable lives, at a subconscious level aware that baleful designs have been woven against them. Needless to say this induces chronic unhappiness, occasionally outright insanity, which may be misdiagnosed as cause rather than symptom.

"No such error need be applied in your case. The remarkable coincidence of the distorted photographs (if coincidence it be; for under the conditions I describe, all events and consequences may arise due to arcane manifestations of Will) establishes beyond doubt the occurrence of a true, objective phenomenon. This fact, the relation of your dreams, and statements concerning long-standing life issues paint, or shall I say snap, a clear-cut picture, complete in its essentials. It only remains to identify the root source of the encroaching disturbance.

"I think I have done this. Many years before I heard of your woes I acquainted myself with the oddly pervasive, worldwide legends of Xenophor, referred to in myth as the 'Ultimate Cosmic Lord,' the 'Creator and the Destroyer,' who unites attributes of god and devil, an invincibly powerful and malicious being. He is commonly called by his acolytes—a few of whom still walk the earth, in surprising places—as 'He of the Million Eyes,' understood to mean his (His?) omniscient capacity to know all, see all, dominate all. Very old artistic representations, however, depict him as a formless mass of glowing eyes extruding from unnatural darkness. I ask you, sir, is not that the very likeness of the supposed flaw emanating from your images, especially in the most recent batch I have examined? If so, the results of your final 'enhanced' roll should prove illustrative and, to you I infer, rather disconcerting.

"I conclude, tentatively, that the wonderful apparitions in your photographs are not flaws at all. Quite the contrary, I deduce that someone—something—sees *you* as a flaw in the image of the universe, someone now bent on rectifying that situation in, I dare say, an irrevocable manner. I realize that this is not an altogether joyous conclusion for you. I hope I am wrong. I think I am not.

"Thus my report. I would appreciate it, as a favor to me and for the advancement of knowledge, if you would, without delay, shoot the final roll and mail me the product. I much desire (am most boyishly eager!) to see them. Thank you, Mr. Crundt, for presenting me with a wholly stimulating, even entertaining, mystery.

—Vorchek"

Crundt lingered on the hand-inscribed surname for a time, then let the sheets fall from nerveless fingers. He sat at his dining table with the latest pictures, those he had picked up that morning, spread haphazardly before him. He had to hand it to this Professor Vorchek, who surely came across as knowing an awful lot about weird stuff. Crundt figured he had nailed it pretty good this time. The photographs showed a massive black blot, with several inky streamers or tendrils of darkness thrusting at the camera in a warped fashion like that induced by a fisheye lens. From within the black field there bulked a still darker shape, an incomparable form studded with countless gleaming yellow-green protuberances readily identifiable as glowering eyes. It was simply the last clear vision from his dreams imprinted on photographic paper, and a dead reckoning for the professor's judging. The photograph in which he had inserted himself stunned him with its apparent implication. For once he beheld in the image an indication of relationship between a known physical object and the black, outreaching thing.

Crundt would not send the pictures. He had not the strength, probably not, he assumed, the time. Vorchek would have to collect them himself.

THE OLD CAMERA

"It's just an old camera," said Theresa Delaney, looking over the stooped shoulder of Professor Anton Vorchek, "and not in the best of condition. I don't see what the big deal is. Camera repair is hardly your line."

"Thank you, my dear," Vorchek replied crisply, in his well modulated, slightly accented voice, "for pointing out the obvious on all counts. It is an old camera; that, in and of itself, is of no consequence; and so far from being a camera repairman, this machine has been loaned to me, supposedly already fixed. Yet it comes my way, and I accept it. What deductions do you derive from that?"

His lovely young assistant knew her mentor well. She snorted, tossed her blonde curls and said, "There must, I suppose, be a horrid mystery associated with it."

"Certainly an intriguing one." Vorchek raised up from his laboratory work table arching his back with a groan. "Behold the item, catalogue these basic facts. I have here a Minolta SRT-102, a single lens reflex, or SLR, film camera, manufactured circa 1972-73. Attached is the standard kit lens, 50mm focal length, maximum aperture ratio 1.7. The camera is purely mechanical in its functions, save for an optional battery-powered light meter, and possesses a handy mirror lock-up feature which, besides minimizing shakiness, also confirms the date of creation, for that feature was dropped in later editions. Once upon a time this served as an extraordinarily popular device for taking all kinds of photographs, from family snapshots to professional studies and portraits.

"So much for technical background. This particular machine is the property of one Franklyn Jones, who finds himself seriously troubled at this juncture. His Minolta suffered a problem, a pinpoint hole in the shutter curtain, a failing arising no doubt from the cruelties of age, which I know too well, which you will learn at your own pace. There are not many shops that still work on these antiques—digital is all the rage now, I believe—but Mr. Jones, after diligent search, tracked down an ancient fellow on the far east side of town who boasted of experience and emotional ties to the good old days. This man, a Waldo Murgatroy, undertook the repair of the shutter, in exchange for a tidy sum. Do you follow thus far, Miss Delaney?"

The pair had removed from the cluttered laboratory, located in the back of the Professor's big, isolated house on the outskirts of Phoenix, to his cozy den, where the discourse continued over drinks, with the camera before them on the coffee table. Vorchek, pausing to puff alight his pipe, had doffed his white smock, lounging in his natty suit, while Theresa, ever dressed to stun, drew absently on her cigarette and nodded, an action shaded with annoyance. "My previous summation stands," she said.

"Not for long," cautioned Vorchek. He stroked his short, iron-gray beard and continued. "You see, while Mr. Murgatroy did repair the minor damage, he introduced a fresh and peculiar factor, one which has quite excited and disturbed Mr. Jones. He, learning through inquiries at the university of my interest in the outré, contacted me, explained his dilemma, begged for help. After examining samples of his recent productions from that camera, I agreed."

"So what's the matter?" Theresa demanded, after the professor had paused for an irritating period with an expectant smile.

"Since you are so keen," he said, "I will give you the low-down. Mr. Jones' repaired camera is taking what he calls 'funny' pictures. Strange, that designation, for he does not laugh. He strikes me as rather a nervous gentleman. Perhaps I would be too, in his shoes, if every photograph I had developed from my trusty old camera exhibited images of hideous monsters."

"Monsters!" cried Theresa. "Oh, Professor, that sounds like a bad joke. What sort of monsters?"

Said Vorchek casually, "See for yourself. Look in that envelope on the table, next to the camera. Indulge me with your fresh impressions."

Theresa picked up the envelope, lifted the flap, extracted a sheaf of color four by sixes. She stared intently at the top image without speaking, flipped to the next, stared very hard at that one, began to shuffle through the others. Never did she speak. In time she gathered the pictures and placed them back into the envelope, set it down on the table top with an affected manner as of discarding something unclean. Her normally healthy white face blanched sickly, her eyes like cold blue marbles.

This is what she saw. Against a background of commonplace scenes—a suburban house with wide lawn, stands of trees among rocky landscapes, the close-up of a flower, and a series of portrait shots of a sandy-haired, youngish fellow—she beheld, superimposed upon these, hideous phantasms of nightmare. In every picture appeared one or more repellent, shocking, distorted representations of apparently living things such as no one could expect to photograph, nor would attempt to photograph if opportunity arose. Sidling around the corner of the house, for instance, she observed the frozen image of a bulbous, leathery mass, as big as a bear, from which protruded a number of black, spidery eyes. Emerging from trees she saw a towering insectoid thing, like a clutch of spiny sticks, with loathsome serrated jaws jutting from a tiny pale-green head. Even the picture of the flower revealed, blurry in the distance, an abominable humped shape streaming dim suggestions of feelers. In some ways the human photographs were the worst. Each showed, in addition to the obvious subject, lumps of squirming, tentacled organic nastiness in the process, judging from their stilled behavior, of approaching the man with dubious intent.

Theresa rallied. "I said it was a joke. That's what it is. This Murgatroy character—some sort of camera whiz, right?—he's behind it. He did something to the photos, inserted this awful stuff. There are all kinds of tricks one can do with pictures. There's your explanation. Why suspect more?"

Vorchek nodded approvingly. "An excellent hypothesis, my dear. In this day and age, why indeed suspect more? It only remains for me to confront Mr. Murgatroy, take him to task for his disagreeable sense of humor, and establish precisely how he tampered with the negatives." The professor re-fired his pipe, picked up the camera, sank back into his luxurious sofa. "Unfortunately, the explanation will not serve. I have examined this machine, a cursory purview yet, but find nothing altered other than what has ostensibly been repaired. No great surprise that, since the Minolta is merely the mechanism which allows lenses and film to function. Mr. Jones provided those, naturally. As to the negatives, I find myself momentarily stumped. They appear fairly normal, exhibiting a hint of cloudiness, but otherwise no unusual imagery; they show what one expects, nothing like the developed result. The film, by the way, was developed at a typical drug store, by a typical minimum wage girl, using a typical machine called a mini-lab. At present it is difficult to finger the exact moment of grotesque intrusion."

"Talk to Murgatroy," Theresa insisted. "He's the culprit. Hit him with it."

"That I will not do," Vorchek replied. As his assistant began to protest he cut in, saying, "Not, you must believe, from lack of desire. There is nothing I would enjoy more than interrogating that gentleman. Sadly, I learn that he is deceased; that, in fact, he died immediately after working on this very camera, leaving it to an ignorant helper to actually return it to Mr. Jones. The story appeared in yesterday's newspaper. Here, you may read it for yourself. It is a curious tale, written with some hedging, a certain glossing over of strange details. Shortly I shall investigate Mr. Murgatroy's passing in all of its aspects and particulars. For the present, I can sum up the story by telling you he perished of violence, that he was, in some mysterious manner, torn to pieces."

Vorchek emitted a harsh chuckle. "These developments very much worry Mr. Jones. He craves our aid. I am sufficiently interested. What of you, Miss Delaney?"

Professor Vorchek's next endeavors consisted of what he styled "further preliminaries," closing possible loopholes in the case as it had been presented to him, or as he had come to understand it from initial examination. Necessarily he must, accompanied by stalwart (if grumbling) Theresa, bear down on the poor girl who developed the offending roll of film, "analyzing chain of custody" as he put it. He ascertained, to his satisfaction, that she knew nothing whatsoever of even the elemental rudiments of photography, that she simply pushed buttons at odd whiles on the mini-lab when not as excitingly engaged at operating a register or counting vials of nail polish.

"She's a dope," Theresa concluded. "Forget her."

"I have," announced Vorchek. "Now, I would like you to hear Mr. Jones speak."

Franklyn Jones ("Call me Frank"), as Theresa shortly discovered, proved to be the young man appearing in several of the most distressing images, photographs captured with the camera's self-timer. A recent college graduate, he lived in a rented house in a modest neighborhood. He said, "I tell you again, Professor Vorchek, it's none of my doing. I just like to take pictures, and I thought I'd try out my father's old camera. You know what I got for my trouble. I should have stuck to my cheap digital. It does okay. Anyway, I wouldn't know how to concoct that stuff.

"I tell you, Murgatroy's behind it. I knew he was a nasty piece of work the moment I laid eyes on him. Too bad about what happened to him, but I'm telling you what I thought at the time. He was one of those goofy hippie types from the Sixties, straggly long hair and a shaggy beard and dirty clothes. He had weird New Age posters plastered all over the walls of his shop. He talked strangely, like he was high on something. I wrote him off as a goofball, but he did promise to fix my Minolta, and there weren't many others who would, and they charged even more, so I went with him, and that's it. I picked up the camera on Friday—he had it about a week—tried it out on the weekend, saw the sickening results, called him, got no answer, heard on the news he was dead."

Jones at last took a breath. "So, I just want you to find out for me what kind of trick he pulled, and then I'll rest easy."

"What's the problem?" asked Theresa. "If you know it's just a put-on, and Murgatroy's out of the picture permanently, why worry? He won't bother you any more."

Jones stared at her with nervous significance. "Because, Miss Delaney, the pictures don't look fake. I've seen what trick photography can do—I've seen all those computerized special effects in the movies—and these are nothing like. They scare me. I admit it, I'm spooked by this. Professor, I don't even want the camera back until you've figured it out."

Vorchek said, "I intend to keep it for the time being. I shall investigate thoroughly, sir, nor will I stop until I have resolved the mystery. There are answers to every puzzle. I specialize in finding them."

Afterward, as they drove away in Theresa's sporty coupe, she observed to her silently thoughtful passenger, "Jonesy really is afraid, isn't he? What gives? What does he know that we don't?"

Vorchek pondered the question, replied at last, "Mr. Jones operates on intuition and subliminal impressions. He possesses no data, I believe, yet having been immersed in the situation, he carries away from it unreasoned but powerful sensations. That is a sign. Not, perhaps, a sure indicator, but a strong suggestion of true strangeness. I must delve deeply if I am to surpass his intense feelings."

"What next?"

SCIENCE AND SORCERY II

"Tomorrow we pay a visit to Murgatroy's shop."

For the remainder of the day the pair cast aside all outward interest in the case, choosing to explore instead the many intricate possibilities pertaining to an upscale French restaurant on the north side. A good time they had.

In the morning, after Vorchek had called ahead to arrange matters, they produced themselves—Theresa bearing her note pad, the professor his battered briefcase—at the door of "Murgatroy's Cameras and Photographic Supplies", located in a grubby strip mall on the margins of the wrong part of town. Ominous characters lounged in nearby doorways, watching and whispering among themselves. The shop appeared small, with a very narrow front consisting mainly of two windows crossed with security bars. Stenciled lettering on the glass proclaimed various services and products, such as professional wedding photographs, the latest digital cameras and lenses and, of course, complete repair services. At the professor's knock the door opened and they were admitted.

Al Martinez received them, Murgatroy's former assistant with whom Vorchek had previously spoken. He was an affable elderly man, his speech plagued by broken English, a fellow (Theresa opined in a whisper) of doubtful legality. The front room, the sales area of the shop, was as Jones had described. They saw cameras inside glass cases, accessories strewn on counters or hanging from wall pegs. Theresa delivered harsh comments on the lack of taste revealed by the unusual assortment of gaudy posters. These also drew Vorchek's attention, the curious pictures holding his interest in a fashion unfathomable to his associate. He noted something else as well, the evidence of professional law enforcement activities on site.

"That yellow tape across the rear door," he said, "and these traces of black powder, immediately inform me of facts I had not gathered prior to this moment. Apparently Mr. Murgatroy met his sad fate in that back room. I must see it."

Martinez expostulated incomprehensibly, but the professor with relentless resolve brushed him aside with curt command and snapped the tape, entering what proved the work room of the shop. In that gloomy, dusty place he beheld shelves of old books, paperback technical manuals, plastic trays containing screws and bits of wiring, and a large, Spartan wooden table littered with the disassembled corpses of cameras and the tools to revive them. In addition he spotted signs of less necessary disorder: a cracked, overturned chair, a smashed drinking glass, a shattered overhead light bulb, a cheap painting hanging awry, lurid brown stains splashed across surfaces.

"Murgatroy struggled, all right," Vorchek said. "Not, I think, with animals, nor, Miss Delaney, with any common foes. I hesitate to deem this a crime scene in the ordinary sense."

When he had seen enough he drew his companions into the outer room and commenced his questioning of Martinez. The man's statements, liberally translated, went roughly as follows: "Waldo was a funny guy. He made his living from cameras, but he lived for something else. He was into every wacky idea you ever heard of, and a few more. He didn't go to church, but he believed in things, terrible things. When I tell my wife, she calls it devil worship. I asked him about that once, he laughed, told me, 'Nothing so stupid. I believe in the real thing, the real powers. You wouldn't understand.' He was right, I didn't, only I didn't like, only I needed the job, so when he went in back and shooed me away and locked the door and sang or chanted nonsense, I smiled and kept the store for him. What could I do? Who was he hurting?"

Martinez, who found the body—with Jones' freshly repaired camera still on the table—could not imagine anyone desiring to murder his employer, especially not the way it was done. "He wasn't shot, he wasn't beaten, he wasn't stabbed. Waldo was shredded like lettuce in a grater. How does that happen? What's wrong with the world these days?" He also made mention of his impression that his boss had been suffering from ill health for quite some time, and that mounting physical disability had weighed heavily on his mind.

That afternoon Vorchek contacted the police, managed to pump them for pertinent details which added little to his portfolio of acquired knowledge except to learn, from autopsy results, that the deceased was burdened with a failing heart. Still later, over the fine dinner provided by Theresa in her fancy apartment, he said to the girl, "At this juncture I am seriously inclined to consider Mr. Murgatroy the key to the concerns pestering my client. I will accept another helping of that chicken, if you please. For your information, my dear, I have been seeking the focal point at which true weirdness was introduced into the life of Mr. Jones. Surely you may already deduce that we have found it."

"Fair enough," replied Theresa. "Pass me the sauce, will you? Okay, Murgatroy's the culprit. Jones was right, which seemed likely in the first place, only it doesn't get us anywhere. Murgatroy is dead, and we haven't the slightest idea how he played his picture trick on your so-called client, who hasn't offered you a penny, by the way. Professor, I've known you to work cheap, but this is ridiculous."

Vorchek chuckled, said with a grin, "This case may generate its own rewards. Now, Miss Delaney, your terse presentation is accurate as far as it goes, but you stop well short of the totality of our findings, even as they are known to you. Allow me to fill the holes. Mr. Murgatroy is indeed the root source of our Mr. Jones' dilemma, yet I am not convinced that any deliberate trick is involved. Nay, I begin to suspect—have reached the provisional conclusion—that the phenomenon is actual. Mr. Jones faces genuine trouble. It remains for us to establish the degree.

"I have gotten an idea of the kind of man Mr. Murgatroy used to be: one of strange tastes and weird beliefs, beliefs which I now know he accepted with the utmost gravity. He was an adherent of, perhaps a member of, an ominous sect or cult devoted to religious practices of a lurid nature. Some would call it devil worship. That is an inaccurate, absurd, and incomplete view. Nothing so conventional for our dearly departed camera repairman! Oh no, he had bigger fish to fry, at least he did so until such time as, I think, they fried him.

"The only connection between him and Mr. Jones is that camera. There can have been no tampering with the film, because Mr. Murgatroy never possessed it. The Minolta is, ostensibly, just a camera; nothing up its sleeve, no clever insertions, as I can attest. So, all we must do is determine what the dead man did on the last day of his life, how that affected the instrument, why that has come to torment its owner."

"I am hopelessly confused," cried Theresa.

"In you, Miss Delaney, that is ever a charming condition," replied Vorchek.

"No cracks from you. Either you're assuming too much or you aren't playing straight with me. I've picked up enough of the scientific method from you to know you can't possibly figure all that from what we've got. It sounds like you're taking a few stray comments and weaving a hulking great novel out of them. It doesn't fly."

"Does not it?" asked the professor with mock seriousness. Then with a smile he nodded and said, "Quite right, my dear, to that extent it does not. I have acquired further data, in the substance of these revealing books which I purloined from Mr. Murgatroy's back room." He bent down, opened his briefcase, removed three large, crumbling, evidently heavy volumes. He placed them on the table next to the serving dish. "These," he added, "tell a tale."

"Naughty," said Theresa, who picked up the uppermost book, glanced at the inside cover, wrinkled her nose. "This isn't your property, Professor. You ought to know better. Anyway, it looks horrid."

"I assure you that it is," said Vorchek. "You are holding a copy of *The Book of the Second Lazarus*, this edition published in early 19th Century Heidelberg. The 17th Century author, true name unknown, compiled that as a collection of spells and magical terms—the subheading translates as 'Words of Power'—infernal catechisms which could be employed to influence the fortunes of others, often adversely, as well as to contact the shadowy denizens of the less material planes of existence. I am familiar with the book. Its reputation, a most alarming one, precedes it.

"The second volume is a copy of Arthur Halliday's *Preparations For the Future State*, dating from the '40s, a particularly snide and disagreeable disquisition on the true nature of the posited afterlife. This book is not well regarded among devotees of the esoteric, although it had a certain vogue among the college crowd in years past; when, for example, Mr. Murgatroy was an impressionable young man. It provides me with some idea of his mentality, if nothing more.

"The third volume marks our greatest find. Here, let me see it again. I glean a vast magnitude of pernicious evidence from the intrusion of this book into the situation. Behold, Miss Delaney, a privately bound transcription (no date, anytime in the last century) of extracts from what scholars style *The Black Book of Jacob Bleek*, penned by the reputed sorcerer of long, long ago. No complete copy of the work is known to survive, but portions have circulated among dark cultic groups throughout the ages. In my personal collection I cherish a typed copy of several pages, maybe twenty, donated to me years ago by a grateful colleague, and pleased I am to own that much. This is incredibly rare stuff, yet Mr. Murgatroy had on his shelf—if this prove legitimate—a much bigger selection than I have ever seen or read. That induces amazement."

"I guess it's something," Theresa admitted. "So, what's Bleek all about?"

Said Vorchek, leafing through the yellowed pages, "As he would tell it, about everything. You might call Bleek the supreme scientist of the pre-scientific age. Early in life he set out to learn everything that could be learned from history and observation about everything there is. He delved into every mystery ever posed by previous scholars, and quite a number that only he had theorized. Perhaps as a matter of personality his bent inclined toward the morbid and the grotesque. Truly what I have read of him, and more that I have heard, suggests a taste for vile wisdom approaching the scandalous. During prior centuries his writings were routinely banned, which may explain the difficulty in tracking down surviving remnants today. Yet Mr. Murgatroy owned this volume, not a light one, as you see. Again, I discern much from the bare fact of ownership. I needs know more."

"Wow," Theresa sighed. "It sounds like you're on to something, I'm afraid. What now?"

"I study these documents. Therein I shall uncover, mayhap, the extent, if any, of Mr. Jones' peril. We must know what he faces."

During the following days Vorchek withdrew reclusively into his lonely abode, there to absorb the quaint and arcane lore found within the olden books from Murgatroy's library. Franklyn Jones attempted to contact the professor, telephoning Theresa, whose number he had been given, when he received no response from her companion. She could only inform him that the investigation progressed, telling him also not to fret, for without the offending camera, where was the harm to him?

"It's these wretched dreams," cried Jones over the line. "I see those things in sleep, creeping closer to me. I'm tired all the time, can barely function. Whenever I nod off they come." Theresa, trying to be helpful, advised over the counter sedatives. Jones hung up abruptly.

Four days later Vorchek invited Theresa to his home. She left town on the northwest highway, turned off onto the "improved" gravel road which wound precariously up the steep desert hill to Vorchek's outpost, a two-story survival of pioneer times. She let herself in with her own key, discovered him enraptured with papers in the reading nook of his laboratory. The now infamous camera lay on a ledge at his side.

After brusque courtesies he said, "You know, Miss Delaney, I really do think that I have pieced together the puzzle. There is a way to understand everything that has happened." Theresa informed him of Jones' communication, to which he replied, "Excellent, another factor that fits my hypothesis.

"Attend, my dear, and know as I know. What I tell you may be the answer. Firstly, Mr. Murgatroy was far more than an aging malcontent, but rather a cultist extraordinaire, a devotee of doctrines associated with the ferocious deity termed 'Xenophor' in ancient writings. There are scattered references in Bleek, and an entire chapter in Murgatroy's copy, describing the weird behavior and wants of this so-called god. That chapter has been much probed in the past by messy fingers. Would you care to speculate as to whose fingers left those prints? I do not require a police kit to reach my conclusion.

"Halliday, in his relatively trivial work, refers to Xenophor as well. Perhaps I not esteem that author highly enough. From embedded literary clues I can argue that Halliday raided Bleek's writings while forming his own ideas about the blessings bestowed by the god. He makes the case that one may approach Xenophor in order to avoid death or stave off the worst horrors beyond the grave. Mr. Murgatroy was an ill man, probably dying. It would not surprise me if the crude theology of Halliday possessed special meaning for him at that juncture.

"Then we have the revelations of the self-styled Second Lazarus, who wishes to entertain us with knowledge beyond mortal ken. Maybe he has. Mr. Murgatroy had marked a specific page, one involving a complicated spell to be employed only by those in the desperation of final extremis. It makes for, as you say, 'spooky' reading. An immensely convoluted series of incantations—many designed to be spoken aloud in an archaic Babylonian tongue unsupported by formal linguistics—are chanted to the greatest god, 'the Lord of All Things,' the 'Maker and Unmaker, the Creator and the Destroyer;' may we read Xenophor for him? I think so. Granting that, the long chants constitute a hymn to the god's eternal majesty and boundless power, as well as a supplication for his mercy.

"The Second Lazarus posits incredible hazards associated with this spell. Firstly, he notes that the 'Mighty Receiver' is not prone to granting boons; rather, he manages the affairs of the universe for his own unknowable ends. He may refuse requests, even from his most faithful, and it is possible to annoy him with too strident pleas. This accords well with Bleek's analysis of the chancy ways of Xenophor."

"So asking him for a favor is just a crap shoot," Theresa interpreted.

Vorchek shrugged. "That is one way to put it. Attempting to contact Xenophor directly, as Bleek would have it, is a dangerous business, fraught with dire consequences. The god may grant the blessing, or do so in a freakish fashion, or ignore it, or—get this—lash out virulently and without warning. There are no guarantees. Bleek relates a tale concerning a visitation by Xenophor's otherworldly minions which does not make for happy reading."

"And you really think that happened!" cried Theresa. "It's a pretty story, if nothing else. You're saying Murgatroy did just that: tried to talk to his mystical master in order to save himself, got 'no' for the answer, which explains what happened to him. Xenophor's beasties came and did whatever, ate him up or made hash of him. Okay, I'll buy that, just for the sake of talking. Too bad for Murgatroy, and maybe good riddance. That does not, however, begin to explain what has or is happening to Frank Jones."

Vorchek nodded gravely. "Well done, Miss Delaney. As a budding researcher you demand more data, which I shall supply. There is one thing more. Jacob Bleek, several times, mentions cases of mystic contamination, while our Lazarus Secundus devotes an entire discourse to the problem, in relation to the very spell in question. It seems there can be a kind of 'blow-back' of incantation, in which the attempt to channel strange and mighty forces may leave unpleasant subsidiary effects upon items associated with the rites, or even those happening to be nearby. I am convinced that Mr. Murgatroy sought to raise the extra-planar powers in his workroom. They came, reacted in unwholesome manner, then departed, leaving, however, traces of vile influence. The Minolta, resting on the table throughout the affair, suffered esoteric exposure. Perhaps other items in that room were affected as well. I must ponder that. Regardless, the effects on the camera were what we know. It is merely random misfortune for Mr. Jones, who was surely in no way involved."

"But what does that really mean to him?" Theresa asked. "If it's just creepy pictures coming out of the camera, then we can take a hammer to the contraption and be done with it."

"Absolutely not," Vorchek said warmly. "We do not know that. We have not yet isolated the parameters of menace, if any. I require more trials with the camera."

"I get it," Theresa said. "Put the camera to work again, see if it still does what it did. Well, I'm good for that. Give me a roll of film and I'll snap it off."

"Heavens, no!" roared Vorchek, leaping to his feet. He hesitated, then with a forced air of calm replied, "That would not do. You do not possess the necessary qualifications, lack skills with a camera of this type. Mr. Jones, of course, has such experience. He will take the photographs for us."

The girl shrugged, said indifferently, "As you like. It looks simple enough. Anyway, Jonesy seems sort of flaky to me. I wouldn't count on him to handle it properly."

"He suits my purposes adequately," Vorchek said dryly. "I will return the camera, delivering precise instructions, and Mr. Jones will serve my needs."

As matters transpired, that was the last of Theresa's direct involvement in the case. On the subsequent morning the professor, camera in hand, met with Jones, explained the next phase of operations, requested immediate action. As Theresa understood it (based on an off-hand comment of Vorchek's) Jones resisted at first, neither desiring the Minolta's return nor any further part in the investigation, but the professor genially pressed, wheedled, eventually getting what he wanted, a fairly typical result for him. Jones agreed despite his reservations, promised a batch of pictures within forty-eight hours. Theresa heard no more about it until two days later, when she saw the story on the local television news. Franklyn Jones was dead, killed in an untoward fashion the previous day, motive and identity of assailants unknown. Despite the oddly vague description of his death, something in what she derived from the reporter's words filled her with foreboding. She had read similar verbal clumsiness in comments on another heinous crime not long before. In a flash she telephoned Vorchek, hoping to derive clarification from him, could not make contact then or all that day. Late that night, though, the professor stomped into her apartment, waking her with his hasty entrance. Immediately she plied him with questions.

"It is all so terrible," Vorchek began, hunched on the sofa with demanded drink in hand. "My dear, I require, too, my pipe. Give me a light, if you please. Ah, thank you." He continued after a deep puff, "I got the news this morning, early, when I called Mr. Jones to ask for an update. A policeman answered. Within the hour, via friends in official positions, I had the scoop. It was, as you will already have deduced, much as with Mr. Murgatroy. As they told it to me, they found little left of poor Mr. Jones. Something got at him, in his back yard, during broad daylight, and, in your colorful vernacular, 'went to town on him.' No one saw anything, but there were signs of a great ruckus, and latter tales of fearsome cries overheard. Once I suspected the worst I swung into action, pulled every string I could, managed to approach the scene and observe the relics. They did not edify. Also, I spirited away the camera, which was still lying *in situ* close to the debris. Only three frames had been exposed. I rewound the roll, got it developed, learned all. I am pleased to inform you that the camera has been destroyed, and its smashed parts buried. So far as you and I are concerned, the matter is ended. I recommend that you put it from your mind."

"That's not good enough!" Theresa snapped. "Professor, say on. Don't leave me hanging. What did you see in the pictures?"

Vorchek grimaced, sighed. "As you will, Miss Delaney. I would have spared you this. Those few photographs exceeded all bounds. Imagine, if you truly want to do so, that herd of filthy, verminous entities from the nether pits crowding close, thrusting their faces or worse than faces straight into the lens, filling the image with their disgusting enormity. There can be no doubt that these were not, as before, invisible impressions of mystic light printed on film, but—at least in the final shot—material presences beheld by Mr. Jones as he clicked away. He saw them this time in the flesh, and they finished him."

Theresa groaned, sagged against the arm of the sofa. "So it was all for nothing," she said at last. "Jones was in danger, but we couldn't save him. It was good of you, Professor, to get rid of that blasted camera, but you should have done it earlier." She sat bolt upright then, fixed him with an accusing stare. "Why didn't you? You guessed some of the horrid possibilities. What decent reason could you have for holding off? I don't get it. I don't, unless—I don't want to believe this—unless you used Jones as a guinea pig. That would make an ugly kind of sense, but if you knew you were placing him in danger—"

"Certainly not," Vorchek sniffed. He stirred uneasily, looked sidelong at his companion under lowered lids, said, "All before this new outrage was indeed guesswork. I had little to go on save formless theories, of a nature which you will grant were wholly wild; some would deem then insane. Mr. Jones begged me to find the explanation. Only experimentation would serve. I insisted on a further test, never realizing, of course, the immediacy of the peril."

"I suppose that's right," Theresa said after a while, her voice still reeking with doubt.

"And I will have you know," added the professor, "that I have since taken other measures to quell this evil. I went out and about this night. There has been one more development. Mr. Murgatroy's abandoned shop burned to the ground."

"You mean—"

THE OLD CAMERA

"Sharing your concerns, I could not allow it to stand. Other implements within may have been affected. They had to go."

Theresa nodded, her countenance brightening. "That was a wise decision. I'm glad you did it, Professor. What of Jones' pictures?"

"You can be sure that I have eradicated those." He waved his empty glass. "Another round, Miss Delaney, if you please." The girl rose, departed into the kitchen with the glass to refill it. Professor Anton Vorchek relaxed, comfortably stretching out his legs. With satisfaction he muttered to himself, "Eradicated, did I say? Safely hidden in my files, that is. The camera had to go, certainly—there I would be playing with fire—but the photographs are too precious. Much information may still be gained from them, and from those delightful books of lore. It is my duty as a scientist."

NANTRECH OF DYREZAN

Nantrech, wizard warrior of the mighty city of Dyrezan, went forth to explore and conquer worlds unknown, leading his little army of gallant freebooters far beyond the realm of civilization into the trackless wastes and darkly rumored vastness of the unfathomed western lands. Preternaturally wise and grimly determined, he sought wonders beyond the ken of men, craving the glory of eternal mysteries unraveled. Through the green, cultured valley marched he and his following, over the jagged mountains and across the sere plain where wandered the furtive nomadic traders—whom Nantrech laid under tribute—then into dank and gloomy jungles illimitable, tramping without path on the sodden bare turf where sunlight seldom trickled down between the high canopied trees. Endlessly they trekked through the murky stillness unbroken by human voice or artifice, mystified by the wild denizens, the birds and monkeys and slithering or creeping things that lurked there. The wearisome monotony of the lightless days distressed them—they, the inhabitants of a great city brilliant and vibrant, its walls of marble and towers of crystal glistening and shimmering in the sun—and they came to dread the oppressiveness of the savage night, when darkness closed down around them like something alive and questing, greedily reaching shapeless fingers of dark toward the sputtering fires of their camp.

Not all survived that passage, for amidst the living darkness there dwelt unseen beasts or presences bold that encroached upon the patrolled perimeter and snatched the unwary. This happened on occasion, and fell diseases took off others, and still more unfortunates died under the fangs of poisonous serpents or with mouthfuls of untested herbs between their clenched teeth. So those hard swordsmen wavered, accustomed as they were to battling men rather than nature, beseeching their commander in soldiers' council convened that they go back and leave to the jungle its perils from which the strongest and bravest quailed. Insisted Nantrech, "Onward we go. Dangers we truly face, including matters of strangeness which my sorcerial arts would reveal, only a mystery that looms before preoccupies my mind, requiring all attention and skill on my part. Let us win through this nasty wilderness, for ahead I discern, via the inner seeing arcane, a worthy goal to lure us on to storied greatness. This we do." This they did, the men grumbling, yet ever heeding the wisdom of so fine and daring a mage.

Indeed, on the second day after the warriors' deputation the expedition marched up from a stinking swamp and over a densely thicketed rise, pushing on orders through the sucking muck, the clinging vines and tormenting thorns, to behold a relatively clear space of considerable extent framed by stark cliffs of granite on three sides, somewhat overgrown by low fern and creeping bush yet unchoked by the trees of the pressing jungle. Within that wide level space they beheld ancient evidences of the presence of man, the ruins of what might have been either a minor city or a major ceremonial complex. A gray stepped pyramid of cracked limestone rose high from the surrounding carpet of foliage, with the stumps of four broken minarets protruding from the upper platform. Here and about geometrical outlines of stony debris marked the foundations of former edifices, many of goodly size, some square, some rectangular—perhaps houses of a lost era—others round, or serpentine, or oddly angled. No living thing, man or beast, graced the site.

"This I saw in a vision," declared Nantrech, "at the very edge of the baleful jungle, the image of which drew me on when another would have shunned the way and deemed himself rightly wise to forgo the urge. I brought with me books, however, tomes of archaic renown, and from the study of their yellowing parchment I have seen what the fleshy eye can not discern. Beware, my men, and keep a sharp lookout, for there is more here than you reckon, mysteries and curiosities galore, and it is for these that I breathe. Let us descend."

So they trooped in files down the little ridge, the only safe entrance into the spacious hollow, and there they made camp among the ruins. Nantrech told off squads to establish a sound base, more to determine the confines of the realm, and the remainder, an entire company of swordsmen plus a handful of lesser fellow savants, to investigate the time-forsaken ruins. Much there was to observe and record, which the learned ones did with diligence, but ever Nantrech was drawn to the wonderful citadel of the pyramid, which seemed indeed the heart of the complex.

"Attend," said he, "to the inscriptions about its base, weather worn but legible still. They tell a tale, if we can but read them. Chiseled they are in an unknown script, signs no doubt of a foreign tongue, yet possess we keys to unlock such doors, base and arcane. Note the fractured sculptures accompanying the words." He indicated the panels of bas reliefs, garbled by time, still hinting at mighty deeds of yesteryear. "I think these a proud people," he said, "who captured these scenes. Spy here a pageant in honor of a great king; there the triumph of victory in battle; around the corner of this massy block, a configuration signifying a sacred rite, one perhaps of supreme importance to the worshipers. See you, a tiny image of this pyramid, with spires intact, appears in the display. Surely we behold a recorded ceremony unique to this place. The pyramid surely is the focus of their activity. The carven picture shows their priests or similar worthies entering the structure. Magical vibrations inherent to this spot assure me that we must do likewise."

So saying, Nantrech divided his force, setting his graybeard scholars to deciphering the script of the carvings while his brawny lads sought a way into the pyramid. Both endeavors proved the work of many days. Labored they by day, slept they by night as they could, for with the darkness strange portents and visitations oppressed them. Ominous cloaked figures appeared at the camp perimeter, hovering just at the edge of the flickering fire light, or stood upon the cliff tops with arms outspread, beseeching the explorers to leave that shunned and unholy place lest doom befall them. When brave men, prodded by stern commands, approached the figures, they found nought. In the air curious ghostly scenes transpired, visions overlaid upon the material landscape, lifelike moving images of stirring parades, columns of marching warriors in unusual armor, and one appearance after another of robed and bejeweled men bowing obsequiously to something never quite glimpsed. There were other images too, rather more dire, of priests lying dead with glassy eyes and stricken visages, and common folk in flight, stampeding madly from some heinous peril. The soldiers of Nantrech saw these things, and they murmured afresh, but their master silenced them with cold glance and curt dictate, informing them that it was to their own glory that he strove to unravel the secrets of those forgotten folk whose shades lingered so unquiet.

Through their own cunning, supported by Nantrech's mystical insights, the wise men learned in good time to read the words frozen in the casing stones of the pyramid. In those antique etchings they read of wonders. Once had dwelt there a great people who styled themselves the Rhexellites, the founders of marvelous cities and expansive empires, who in their heyday sought all knowledge of the earth and the heavens, and who deduced the existence of other realms also worthy of their regard. Especially fond were the Rhexellites of lore concerning the Gods, who fashioned all that was and would be at the beginning of time, who still determine the ways of fate and men. Most keen of all were they to adduce the identity and properties of the one Ultimate God, He who rules as King of Kings over the lesser deities, instructing Them in Their eternal majesty as They instruct the world of perishing flesh. To reach this One, that they might bow before Him and adore Him, they searched the lands and seas for signs of His presence, and thought they had located a portal opening into His domain in this jungle lair.

At that place the brilliant seekers among the Rhexellites discovered a vortex, one of those fountains of cosmic energy through which pours forth the boundless powers of the Gods. This vortex was especially strong, generating an intensity of force which, believed those olden ones, must bespeak the Most High God who governs the all and the ever when. There they built a temple in the form of a towering stepped pyramid, with copious houses beside for the legion of priests, and other dwellings for favored pilgrims, and there the best minds of their race studied and fawned and placated and queried until such time as they made contact with the God beyond the celestial gate.

They called Him Blug, surely because He told them to do so, for who ever hailed by choice the Master of the universe with such a crude sounding title? Blug He was, and they accepted Him as their Lord, knowing or imagining that all in their lives descended from His goodness. And He sent His own acolytes from beyond the spheres to instruct them in His ways, and those curious beings came unto the Rhexellites and passed among them, teaching truth, and right and wrong, and proper obeisance, as Blug ordained. Certain chosen ones of the people were allowed to enter into the realm of the vortex, to journey far through mystic tunnels in the cosmos, so that Blug might grant audience to them. They returned in time, albeit changed beyond recognition in mind, sometimes in body, to lay upon their folk the sole goodly way. This they accepted, and the human priests of Blug caused to be fashioned a mighty statue of their Lord, its attributes gleaned from those favored with sight of the God.

Said Nantrech, "This is a great wonder, which if it be not fabulous, should constitute a boon to that most pious of nations which is our own. For do not we love the Gods? Do not we ever strive toward Their perfection, though we behold Them not, nor hear Them speak? Given the chance, all decent Dyrezanians would relish the opportunity to converse with the Most High, and to adore Him to His face. Let us read more."

Here the tale inscribed on the pyramid blocks took an odd turn. Despite their favored status the Rhexellites did not prosper. Indeed, that period marked a sudden decline in their fortunes. Public morality decayed, the arts of administration and science failed, so that the people were cast adrift among contending and rancorous ideas and factions. By degrees, in steps so subtle, yet evident within the span of a human lifetime, civil order and the respect for decency collapsed, leaving those folk bereft of hope and possibility. They abandoned their reaching for greatness, gave themselves over instead to curious desires, furtively at first, then more openly as a kind of madness seized them. In the name of Blug they thought and did that which the olden chroniclers scarce dared to set in stony script, formulating and performing deeds of degradation beyond sanity. They conceived, somehow, the abysmal notion that the whole of the universe is a vast cesspool of noxious and toxic squalor, that all life and motion and endeavor are vile, every aspect of existence wholly polluted beyond redemption. This they understood as the teaching of Blug, and their grotesque responses to this revealed wisdom His decree. So they behaved as Blug would have them, and amidst their frantic thrashings of mindless turmoil they brought down their empire upon their heads. The Rhexellites fell, their greatness shattered, their population dwindling through murder and bleak despair. In time their cities lay deserted, burned or forsaken. The mighty pyramid temple of Blug and its priests they maintained to the last, from which continued to spew the poison corrupting the pitiful survivors, until such time as they were all gone, and the glorious race of the Rhexellites departed forever into the unlighted halls of extinction.

Deduced Nantrech, "These Rhexellites were a mighty race indeed, but not a virtuous one. Having received the holy word, they fell shot of its merits, and in frenzy rebelled against the teachings that ought to have liberated their minds and unlocked their hearts. We would not stoop to such foolishness. Let us, therefore, open a passage into the pyramid, that we may behold the statue of the Ultimate God, and let us receive communication, that we may know the final goodness bestowed by the All Mighty. This I command."

At this his soldiers and savants took some cheer, for they craved goodness in that place where so much troubled their hearts. No door could they find, though the inscriptions alluded to one, from which observation clever Nantrech assumed that it had been sealed in those latter days, that the foulness of unimaginable disaster might not sully the inner precinct. Armed with this explanation, the strongest youths of the party commenced to dig into the stepped walls, boring with tools of steel aided by cunning magical influences stirred by their leader. With a hole opened in the hard outer shell, they drove a tunnel into the softer filling, day by day advancing readily through the porous limestone. In due course they struck an interior chamber, one which, as it developed, gave them access to all the rooms and corridors of the secret temple.

They uncovered much to explore, and Nantrech bade his scribes record everything for posterity, but he had thoughts only for the most devout recesses of worship, wherein they should find the statue and the fabled gateway to the God. Within hours of the breakthrough Nantrech and his chosen compatriots stood before the eidolon of Blug, and they marveled in awe at what they saw.

No inscription had prepared them for the sight. Truly, the olden writers had practiced reticence when it came to describing their God. The Dyrezanians stood stupefied at the base of the pedestal upholding the statue of Blug, unable for many minutes to give voice to their disordered thoughts. About them lay the detritus of ages, toppled and smashed columns, splinters of fallen tiles, dirt and dust and, partially buried in the rubble, a single yellowed, fragmentary, brittle skeleton; but on these things they did not at first choose to dwell. This they beheld: rising from the plain silvered base a formless mass of beaten gold towering ten cubits above, near scraping the arched ceiling, a heap of precious metal worked into the amorphous shape of a thing without parallel on earth. Lumpy it was, that frozen image, with loathsome folds of golden flesh from which sprang horrid droplets and rivulets of carven ooze. Within the fabricated substance gleamed thin ovals of what could have been meant for eyes, scattered randomly about the metallic mass, each appearing to drip golden trickles of mucus. Along the base, overhanging the pedestal, depended wormy obtrusions which, though motionless, gave the dreadful appearance by the light of torches, head in nervous hands, of a shadowy, snaky writhing. These terrible appendages were also portrayed as leaking fluid, in considerable quantities, at certain points appearing, as plates of filmy gold, to run down the sides of the pedestal.

Nantrech justified the fell vision in the following manner. "Only in the pretty fables of children must the Gods be fair of form, like unto us; They, dwelling apart from common space and time, may take many curious and intricate shapes, corresponding to nought that is base or perishable. I say to you all that genuine perfection must be diametrically in opposition to those conventional shapes and forms we cherish in our earthly ignorance. Let us gaze upon the visage of Blug, rejoicing in beauty beyond our ken."

This they did, albeit in half-hearted fashion, stooping and kneeling in determined obeisance while Nantrech chanted an earnest prayer. And before he proceeded further Nantrech the wise went aside into a solitary cell with all his books and rare materials, where he made a great magic, by which he peered beyond the mystic gate into the realms unimaginable. When he emerged he said, "I have spoken with He who shall be our Lord. Blug is good and great. I know this, for He tells me so."

Then, "To work," said he. "Where the Rhexellites disappointed their Master, we shall succeed. This God shall know us, as we know Him, and He will favor us with His blessing. The golden statue is an offering to Him, left callously in these miserable surroundings. Come, let us remove it from this dread wasteland and this citadel of folly, and escort it to Dyrezan, where we will enthrone it in a new temple of white marble, and surround it with devoted priests, there we forever to worship at the symbol of this Great Old One. This Blug told me. So long as our faith in Him endures, so shall Dyrezan endure. This I say."

Began the monstrous effort of moving the gigantic statue and extricating it from the pyramid. During this labor of weeks the soldiers suffered a plague of insidious visions, of crying wraiths flying in the night, of withered human shapes begging for mercy from the shadows, of conclaves of vacant-eyed supplicants rising from the earth to beseech in their chimera of agony for release from some encroaching doom. Certain of the hard warriors of Dyrezan lapsed into an enfeebling melancholy and slew themselves, or lost their minds in savage fury and turned murderously upon their fellows. It proved difficult to keep the others at task. Meanwhile the savants of Nantrech, having prized from the fleshless fingers of the statue chamber skeleton the remnant of a slate tablet, undertook the business of translating the faded writing found thereon. The script was like that of the outer pyramid inscriptions, though cruder, evidence of lesser learning on the part of the writer, or a decline in style toward the end. As the tablet was incomplete, the rest having been crushed to powder by the falling of a column, only portions could be read and understood, but what little it still said was not mete to those wise ones.

The writer seemed to be wailing against a wholly unexpected menace, coming at him from a quarter where he least expected it. The clearest intelligible segment began, "...of our pitiful end. Thought we to find everlasting love, joy, fulfillment of the highest longings, but we were betrayed by the true horror lying behind reality... not a God of greatness and magnificence, shining like a beacon of hope over the world, but a God of squalor and decay, a God of filth, of shame, of everything rancid and inglorious. We embraced Him, drank of the foul juices of His substance, and since then our people have died squealing, craving only oblivion. Only I tarry, so long as is necessary to pen this warning, and then I too shall accept the balm of nonexistence. I pray to the true Gods, if there be any in this wretched universe, that I do not go to Him. Have mercy, Blug, if that word has any meaning..."

Said Nantrech, "Confirms this prattle my prior conclusions. With the stink of their own sins filling their nostrils, the Rhexellites accused purity of foulness. Utterly debased were they, unfitted to sit at the feet (had He feet) of Blug and receive His largesse. Not so ignoble am I. The golden image travels with me to Dyrezan, to be emplaced in a temple grandiose, where all of virtue may joyously worship. The labors are completed. Let us move Blug from this dusty tomb, and install Him with pomp at home, that He may forever move our hearts."

Several of Nantrech's warriors thrust their swords into their own bellies rather than touch the peculiar sculpture. Most obeyed, cursing. Three savants quarreled with and rebelled against their leader, attempted to murder him in ambush; failing at this, they killed themselves, in strangely painful, lingering manner. The statue of Blug moved, roped and trestled, grating over the floor of the passage, eventually arriving in the open air. Nantrech directed the fabrication of a massive cart, with wooden wheels hewn from jungle trees, wheels shod with iron forged from the shields of dead men. This done, and the statue loaded by grunting gangs, those who remained of Nantrech's army set forth from the desolate pyramid of the Rhexellites, back through the sinister jungle, where still more men were carried off, and so eventually returned to the bright, teeming world of civilized Dyrezan.

The wisest of the city were wont to bow to Nantrech's judgment in all things, for he was great and learned, so they all embraced eagerly his opinions and lovingly caused a grand new temple to be raised, one that stood higher and bigger than all the temples for all the Gods of Dyrezan. In this temple they situated the marvelous and strange statue of Blug, and they bowed down before Him, and they prayed, and He answered them, as Nantrech had promised He would, and they learned from Him new and better ways. In this fashion was the noble dream of Nantrech made real.

All of this happened a very long time ago. History records no trace of the Rhexellites, save as they are mentioned in this olden tale. Many legends of magnificent Dyrezan survive to this day, yet the wonderful city lives only in legend, for Dyrezan—in that distant epoch called eternal Dyrezan—ceased to be a long time ago, in the generations following that of Nantrech, whose sterling reputation and enlightened views fastened the worship of Blug upon his people. Story and song record that something went very wrong in that elder time, that which brought low the highest of earthly splendor, though they do no more than hint at the cause, hints which many choose to doubt, for they speak of matters wholly fabulous, obscene, and sacrilegious. Dyrezan is gone, a heap of ruins jumbled in a pitiless desert, but among the wreckage of that crumbling pile there still stands, it is said, within the fallen temple of those latter days, a weird statue, frightful to behold, all of gold, that some say is the everlasting eidolon of Blug. There, perhaps, He still reigns, awaiting those who may come after to adore Him.

THE CHARMING OF CARMELINE

The Princess Carmeline of Dyrezan was the happiest of mortals in the happiest of lands. Beauty she had, and enormous wealth, and the glory of standing proudly as daughter to King Skyrax, might he reign unto eternity; and she dwelt imperiously in that noblest city of those olden days, the mighty citadel of marble and crystal and magic that was Dyrezan, rising high into the fair skies above the deep, circular, mountain-girted valley hollowed out by the Gods at the beginning of time so that the chosen ones could live there near to Them. As Dyrezan soared above the valley, above the highest crags, so the abode of Carmeline loomed over Dyrezan, for she lived her days in the Royal Palace, the seat of riches and power and empire, making over the tallest white spire for her own use as a boudoir and tower of pleasure. There she did as she pleased, with whom she pleased, lacking for nothing (for the King was a fearsome fellow with a stern core of iron that melted soft only for her), caring for nothing, save that which pleased her. Truly a grand life for a young girl.

Of course she had admirers, legions of them, with every fine nobleman, every staunch captain, every studious young mage seeking her hand. Carmeline idly felt, when she could bring herself to ponder the matter, that the time approached when she must choose. Certainly those around her thought so, especially her father the King, who wished to ensure that his line and house continued as it had for five hundred generations. He lacked a wife, as she, Carmeline's mother, had been carried off by baleful demons shortly after the girl's birth. He, therefore, craved a marriage proper and fruitful for her.

"Take your pick," he commanded or pleaded, depending on his mood or hers. "These men be yours for the having. Consider Lord Marstow, who I swear hoards more wealth than I, or General Granicas, successful at conquest for my honor, or good Master Albatar, a clever and witty wizard, one who should go far with his unusual research. These, and numerous others like them, wait at your beck. Choose one, and determine on happiness." Replied the Princess at last, "All fine men and bold, brilliant or esteemed they be, but I would stoop to only one, the Lord Jellorn, who combines all these virtues." "Indeed," said Skyrax, "a magnificent specimen is Jellorn: handsome of face, stout in body, a true scholar of the esoteric arts, and a champion warrior to boot; a splendid subject in every way, a great catch for a son-in-law. A prize even for a King's daughter, but he knows it, and hangs aloof. Get him if you can: bat your eyes, smile with white teeth and red lips, laugh and make merry with him. If that fail, however," growled the King, "then I make the selection. I warn you, girl, if I wring not a grandchild from you, then I shall instruct my court sorcerers to conjure one from clammy clay and stinking potions." Carmeline, considering herself chastised, dutifully got about the business of seeking a mate.

Far across Dyrezan—in an ancient quarter of the city builded of weathered obsidian chiseled in the times of the first Kings, beyond the bridges of the river Ceralas, a lovely stream fashioned by magic that ever bubbles up from its artificial spring in a green hill and flows forever into a porcelain sinkhole in a sylvan grove surrounded by statues of forgotten heroes—stood the squat gray castle of the incomparable magician Vexis. Within that castle, in the gloomy onyx library where the mage currently resided, and within the mind of Vexis, other matters loomed large. For years great and renowned Vexis had wrestled with a particularly arcane spell, one involving lucrative communications with the fabled denizens of the seventh celestial plane, beings or creatures who lived but one step below the wonderful Gods Themselves. Long had he dreamed, wise Vexis, of contacting those mighty spirits, that they should instruct him further in his studies or grant to him weird boons. He believed at last that he had found the way, having gathered unto himself a variety of necessary elements and solutions (things like the scrapings from the bones of the antique behemoth Xazafar, or the oil derived from the unquiet vestiges of Vasgarran mummies), and having formulated or deduced the appropriate series of equations and chants, using long forgotten symbols of power and syllables torn from dead, shunned languages. So much he had done, so that he tasted success, save that one peculiar item eluded him, a magical passage of whispered dread from the fearful *Book of Tantellas*, which served as the lock, as well as the key, to the desired spell. This passage would Vexis employ to his satisfaction, only copies of the *Book of Tantellas* were not to be found lying casually about on shelves in Dyrezan, nor anywhere else in the wide world. According to legend all copies of that formidable tome were burned, along with their author, in the early ages of the city. Vexis knew of a rumor, however, that a single, priceless volume survived in the ill-used collection of the lesser wizard Futtabal. To that fellow had flown an invitation to dine that night in the gray squat castle beyond the Ceralas.

Futtabal and his sole retainer arrived early, he being pitifully eager to please the great Lord who condescended to request his company. Vexis smiled to his face, frowned at his back, deeming Futtabal little more than a buffoon or clown in the rarefied circles of the magic artisans. Truly this fellow knew little, had mastered less, and he was an ill-featured, corpulent, silly man to boot, yet by strange fortune or for the mysterious pleasure of the Gods there had descended into his hands the vital *Book of Tantellas*. This Vexis craved, so he must act charming and fulsomely gracious to one he would ordinarily have openly despised. After ostentatiously warm greetings Vexis queried, "Is that the book?" indicating the large rectangular object wrapped in old cracked hide borne by Futtabal's liegeman. "It is," Futtabal cried gaily, bobbing his fat bald head. "May it serve you, great one. Dear me, such difficulties I had finding it in the clutter of my books and scrolls. It was being used as a doorstop. I glanced through it for the first time this very day. Interesting stuff, I am sure." Vexis advised that he dismiss his man to eat in the servant's quarters, while the two mages repaired to the dining hall.

There Futtabal ate well, gorging with innocent gusto on the splendid repast prepared for him by worthy chefs at the instigation of his host. Vexis constrained conversation to general pleasantries until his guest had sated himself, a process which consumed considerable time. Then they withdrew into an elegant chamber furnished with warmly colored velvet hangings, where by the light of a well-stoked fire they came together on a comfortable couch, with the wrapped book on the table before them along with goblets brimming with the purple wine drawn from the famous vaults of Albragon. When the servants had departed at the casual wave of their master's hand Vexis broached the all important topic, explaining simply—as befitted the mental capacities of the listener—his need for that particular passage from Tantellas. Try as he might to present his request in a disarmingly naive manner, Vexis could not conceal his pressing need.

"Of course you may use it," said Futtabal, sipping his wine. "Take it, keep it for as long as you like. It is really rare, is it, that book? Fancy that. When you are finished I must pay more attention to it. I am happy, my Lord, to be of some small benefit to you. I say the deal is done. Of course," he added, pausing and then laughing foolishly, "of course there must be, for the sake of propriety, some degree of reciprocity, a form of compensation. That, after all, is the rule."

"So it is," replied Vexis agreeably. "Great sorcerers—such as you and I—never dispense with the precious fruits of our craft for nothing." That was the rule indeed, and Vexis was quite prepared to pay a price for the loan of the book, whether it be in coin or in services. He was ready to hand over a large sum in metal and polished stone, likewise dole out a helpful spell or swap an arcane treatise from his mammoth collection. Futtabal could have what he pleased, Vexis assuming that it would take relatively little to satisfy the fellow.

"Tantellas' book," mused Futtabal, gulping his wine, "must be incredibly rare, that you would ask of one such as me. Yes, I think so. I wish to profit well, then, since opportunities for gratification seldom arise in my case." "This is your moment," returned Vexis, "so ask, and receive. What may I offer you?" "My life," said Futtabal, draining his glass, "is a compound of dissatisfaction and disappointment. I have failed, oddly, to achieve my due according to my many merits. That rankles. I tell you frankly—just between us, as colleagues and equals—it wounds me. My abilities do not earn favor at court as do yours, for instance. The lords speak not my name with awe and respect, as they do yours, to mention but one example. Nor have I conquered a woman, unlike you, O Vexis, who have known great ladies, and keep a bevy of devoted concubines. I have none of these things, yet I desire, always desire."

"All I can not do," pointed out Vexis, distressed by the bitter tones and the galloping wine consumption. Futtabal had poured himself another goblet full, quaffing it between sentences. He began another. Vexis went on, "Largesse, though, it at my command, therefore yours. Tell me that one thing which will sweep away these unjust injuries."

"Precisely!" cried Futtabal. "You understand. Our minds meet, as should the great to the great. Take the book—use it, keep it for all I care—but grant me that which lies within the reach of your arts. I would be, like you, one with whom men must reckon. The right woman would do the trick. Get her for me, make her mine, and you and I are clear with one another."

Vexis nodded, leaning back in his chair, sipped his wine, grinned easily. "Your will is mine, Futtabal. Choose, my friend, from my stables. Take the loveliest of my girls, make her yours. Whichever you desire, I grant her to you."

Said Futtabal, "I want the Princess Carmeline."

Vexis demurred; he remonstrated, expostulated, pleaded at last, to no avail. To his profound chagrin, amazement, even shock, he realized that his ridiculous guest was absolutely serious. Vexis could not shake him. After sustaining and withstanding a barrage of fruitless argument Futtabal made clear that he had long intended to approach the royal daughter, that only the weakness of his position in life restrained him. Laughing stupidly he said, "But you, O Vexis, can turn the key, if any mage can. Snap your fingers, simmer the oils, whisper the words. Bend her spirit to mine."

Vexis agreed, not without much self reproach and recrimination. After giving to Futtabal the sorcerer's guarantee—which had only been violated once in all of Dyrezanian history, with horrific results—and demanding full secrecy ("Act I will, but I must not appear in this.") he sent the drunken fellow on his way, he remaining long in the chamber, clutching to his bosom the cherished volume of Tantellas. So he had what he needed, the book that would open doors to worlds unseen; right and required, then, that the other should receive his fee. It was, though, a miserable business. Vexis stood high with the court, had delivered many a noble service and garnered great advantage in return. Skyrax had once called him "a marble pillar of the kingdom." He would not gladly risk this lofty connection. Still, a deal was a deal. Vexis, the very next day, went to work.

Meanwhile the courtship between Carmeline and Lord Jellorn advanced apace. Once the Princess made known that she inclined to serious aspirations, that fine man paid her attention as never before, began to refer publicly to his duties to his family, the necessity of establishing a fitting foundation for the forthcoming generation. "I must take a wife," he announced before a coterie of the court, "a young woman of such intrinsic virtues as to bless my house beyond estimation. Is there such, but one, in all of Dyrezan?" He paused, smiled knowingly to his knowing audience, replied to himself, "There is but one." And during those days Carmeline was commonly overheard to speak of her obligations to her father, and to rejoice in the prospect of a mate pleasing to her, gratifying to the people. "I have met the man," said she, "who embodies the epitome of qualities masculine and noble." In no time word spread that the occasion for an important announcement from the throne was in the offing.

So determined Skyrax. Addressing Carmeline he said, "All is arranged. Tomorrow I shall proclaim the bans myself, with the grand ceremony ensuing in a week. Is it agreed?" "It is," said his daughter. The King scowled, asked of her, "Be you certain? Until recently your manner struck me as fey. This I want, above all else, yet I would not force Jellorn upon you, at the risk of unhappiness or scandal. Make clear to me your heart." Said Carmeline, "My father, know I well that this event was written in the book of the Gods at the dawn of time. Destiny calls me. I have toyed with fate and posterity this long because, being your daughter, I could do so, but ever I knew that only Jellorn would stand beside me, if any man did. Rest content, as father and King. Jellorn I will have, and no other, for I love him, and the years will prove how he loves me. Blast me for a villainess if ever I decree otherwise." Skyrax embraced his daughter, his heart at perfect ease.

In the conjuring chamber of the squat gray castle Vexis busied himself. Much he desired to inaugurate his great plumbing of the forbidden spheres, but he must needs render payment first as agreed, thus he restrained himself to fashioning a spell that would turn the head of a pretty girl and bind her to a man. The magic of love was an old and, as he deemed it, trivial enterprise, yet he undertook the task in earnest despite formidable misgivings. In matters of the heart magic served best when the twain were well on the way to rightful connection, requiring merely a powerful push to join them. This case was far otherwise, the intended target being scarcely aware of he who desired and, most likely, loath to receive his caresses. Truly, thought Vexis, what girl of merit could be transported with joy at the touch of Futtabal? And she the Princess no less! He thumbed through his tomes of esoterica and arcana, memorized curious words and phrases, gathered, rendered, purified certain rare elements and strange mineral and vegetable compounds. With his materials before him he chanted the weird passages that initiated furtive chemical reactions. Oily liquids steamed, foul gases puffed and billowed. Through a polyhedral crystal Vexis did a dangerous thing, the shunned act of piercing the magical veil that surrounded the Royal Palace, the barrier raised by court magicians, and peering through into the residence of Carmeline. Only a mighty sorcerer could have done this. Having broken the barrier and focused on his subject, Vexis muttered a line containing the ominous name of Antrodemus, the Primordial Trickster.

THE CHARMING OF CARMELINE

At that moment the Princess Carmeline relaxed easily and happily in her bath, laved by the gentle hands of her maiden thralls. Then she sat upright, splashing warm water and sudsy foam. Demanding a robe she rose, and when shrouded in sheer silk she removed her loveliness from the bath and ordered her women gone. She felt herself alone now, though unseen to her eyes cloudy forms hovered about her in the air of the chamber, patting her face and breasts and limbs. On the instant her mind moved in odd channels. Said she aloud, "All is clear, where murky darkness formerly reigned. Jellorn, the man of my choice? It is laughable. Why should I give myself to such a one, I the daughter of Skyrax, discarded to feed the hubris of that pretty-faced fop? I should not sink to feckless surrender, when my heart beats captive to the one true man in this city, Futtabal the Splendid." A moment later she wondered at this crazed notion, struggled to forget it. During the ensuing days it returned to plague her.

The King announced the betrothal of Carmeline and Jellorn, to great rejoicing. His ministers planned the intricate and expensive ceremony. Skyrax demanded only the best for his beloved daughter, issuing directives for an enormous feast at which all the nobility would attend, insisting on a bridal dress of the finest stuffs looted from faraway conquests, a dress laden with scintillating jewels and creamy pearls. In exquisite detail he menaced with torture and death any who failed him or so much as stumbled in their preparations for the wonderful day. His minions accepted his judgments, knowing him to be a man who chose his words carefully, never forgiving a perceived injury, always following through on his dire and frightful threats. His daughter held aloof during that time, but the devoted father assumed her rapt in anticipatory ecstasy, and worried not.

Came the day. Rampant crowds, entertained and fed by the King's much heralded largesse, mobbed the central plaza about the Royal Palace and the wide avenues leading to it. Singing and merry festivities without, while within, gathered inside the mighty Throne Room, all the nobles of Dyrezan stood in audience before the solemn ceremony. Proud they were, and lordly, those grandees of Dyrezan, accustomed to every pleasure and nicety of life, yet none present could fail to be moved by the majestic coming together of the fair Princess Carmeline and the upright and honorable Lord Jellorn. Surely the twain were destined for greatness. The ceremony commenced at the King's blessing, which he recited from his golden seat. His chief minister, wise old Osthrakkias, having gravely preached on the meaning of the occasion, orchestrated the ancient sacred rites. He intoned the olden phrases to Jellorn, who responded in kind. Turning to Carmeline, Osthrakkias began the final step which would lead her to verbal consummation.

Something went wrong. At the critical moment there burst from the tongue of Carmeline a frenzied shouting, almost a shrieking, in which honored form gave way to speech impromptu. Staring wildly at nothing she ejected the words harshly and loudly, crying, "Enough of this mock show! I reject illusions of devotion, for I can no longer restrain the truth which moves my heart. There is but one man for me in all the world, and it is not this dancing master Jellorn who struts beside me now, but rather the goodly Futtabal, that son of nobility who radiates wisdom and greatness from all his parts. Reveal yourself, O Futtabal! and come forth, to stand at my side and recite the words that shall unite us for ever more."

Commotion erupted in the hall. Amid gasps and mutterings and cries of dismay the eager, starry-eyed Futtabal, that unseemly and ill-favored fellow, jostled past the throng and tramped heavily to the dais where stood Carmeline and her astounded escorts. At the far left of the audience Vexis watched these developments tensely, nervously chewing on a long fingernail. Futtabal came before the Princess, bowed clumsily at her feet, saying breathlessly, "My adoration belongs to thee for all time. Give me your hand, Your Grace, and so make it mine." This she did, at which sight Lord Jellorn roared a mighty oath.

"Betrayal and humiliation!" he screamed. "This supposedly perfect flower, which I prepared to pluck with my own hands, bends into the muck to kiss this foul toad? I brook not this disgrace. And you," he bellowed, turning to the dazed Skyrax, "O Kingly father, who strove to entrap me in mortifying shame, have not heard the last of me. This beastly enterprise shall culminate in your untimely doom." Without more ado Jellorn strode down the dais steps, and in company with his liege-men stormed from the Throne Room.

Raged the King, springing to his feet, "Many will die for this. Clear the hall!" The guests evacuated quickly, pushing and stamping in a wild huddle for the door. Vexis slunk out with them, still fretting his fingers. Second thoughts plagued his mind. He predicted a baneful issue from these events. Would Futtabal keep mum, as he had promised, as to how the sorry business had been concocted?

There remained in the largely deserted chamber the King, Osthrakkias, Futtabal and Carmeline. Groaned Skyrax, "My child,

130

justify your untimely jest to your father. My heart shreds to bloody strips at the enormity of your action. Futtabal, you fell idiot, how dare you insinuate yourself into the bosom of my family? It means your death. Guards, enter and seize him!" Armored men clanked from positions unseen to do their Lord's bidding. Said he sternly, "Here, in my sight, separate his empty head from his worthless body." Futtabal stammered, "But she is mine, fairly so, as agreed. I must have her, or relinquish life." Wailed Carmeline, "If you draw one drop of his blood, O Father, I will make away with myself." The King, red-faced with fury unquenchable, ordered his soldiers to stand down, then made as if to speak again.

At that problematic moment Osthrakkias said hastily, "King Skyrax, just and terrible, do not decree over quick. I divine the employment of arts behind this business. There is much to be discerned. May I investigate, that you should know all?" The King assented with a grunt. Continued Osthrakkias, "Futtabal, to your lodgings, there to await the Royal judgment. Sweet Princess, please if you will, accompany your father's men to your tower, there to calmly reflect while the winds of the tempest die down." Both obeyed, though it were difficult to break them apart, for they had intertwined their fingers in a loving lock.

A quiet, mounting terror gripped the city that night. Dreadful rumors slithered throughout Dyrezan. Jellorn had withdrawn to his castle, there to gather adherents to his standard, declaring that he were a likelier monarch than the current aging dolt. Would there be fratricidal warfare in the city? The King had executed three men he adjudged to have failed him, breaking their bodies with savage instruments of correction before bursting their brains with murderous spells. Would hecatombs of victims follow? It was said that Carmeline had shut herself in her rooms, threatening nevermore to appear again until married to the absurd Futtabal. Was this the end of a great and enduring dynasty? If so, would it end in miserable apathy, or blood-drenched despair?

Late, round about midnight, Skyrax convened a private meeting in his offices of state with his faithful minister and mage Osthrakkias. Already the latter had much to say, relating a few facts and several deductions. "Our finest scholars have examined her, O King," he informed his liege, "and by the fruits of their study they diagnose her as genuinely ensorcelled. A cunning charm has turned her mind toward this fellow, a spell of incredible power and tenacity, the likes of which I have not seen in all my career. Be sure, Lord, that she will not be cajoled from this false passion. Furthermore, if the charm stands, and she be not united with Futtabal, then your daughter will die, if not by her own hand, then by a rupture of the heart, induced by infernal forces. These are the ordained fates we strive against."

"What says Futtabal in his defense?" demanded Skyrax. "Pleads he guilty of artistic calculation? Tell him to reverse the charm, if he relish breath in his nostrils and juice in his veins. Promise him safety. I can still kill him later, slowly, by agonizing degrees."

"So far from confessing to black delvings," came the reply, "he pleads innocence to the charge, and will only admit to an honest longing for your daughter's hand, stating that she returns his love through no potations of his own. The questioners sent by you, O King, were relentless and exacting, yet he would not budge."

"It must be so," snapped Skyrax. "Carmeline, of right mind, would not have him, would not sit down to table with him. I can not bear it."

"Again, there is no doubt of her behavior being dictated by sorcery. It is so. What I can not grasp is how the paltry mind of Futtabal could manage such a feat. There is murk and mystery here." Osthrakkias paused pensively, then exploded with, "On my life, great Lord, I do not reckon Futtabal capable of summoning the gigantic forces necessary to do the deed. Always I deemed him nought but a feckless oaf. Now this transpires. Either an enemy waits in the wings, still to show himself, or Futtabal has acquired, unknown to his peers, a source of vast magical power, and the inspired training needed to use it."

"Discover all," commanded Skyrax, "then report to me."

Osthrakkias and the magicians of the court did, in the days to come, probe and question and study further, without materially adding to their store of helpful information. Meanwhile the love-struck Futtabal cried out for "his lady," ineffectually protesting against their enforced parting, as his dear Carmeline pined forlorn, exhibiting the first symptoms of wasting away. Mighty and furious Jellorn marshaled companies of armed henchmen sworn to his house, holding them in readiness while he formulated spells of destruction. Cried the King, "This can not go on! My daughter languishes, my throne totters. Osthrakkias, do something!"

Admitted the Chief Minister, "I own myself puzzled as formerly. With so much at stake we must not stand on ceremony. I urge you, O

Lord, to call in outside aid. Only one mage of the city is brilliant and learned enough to uncover the minutiae of this sinister scheme, yet discrete enough to serve us. I say to you, bring Vexis here at once."

When Vexis received the Royal Summons, hand delivered by official messenger under cover of darkness and carried in by faithful household servant to his master, he threw himself prostrate upon the tiled floor of his bedroom, bewailed his sorceric greed, almost cursed the Gods in his bitter dismay over what he presumed his approaching immolation. Futtabal must have talked—sheer imbecility, for the truth could never advance his suit (a point Vexis had hammered home when they struck the deal)—and now the King craved retribution upon the author of his misfortunes. Vexis contemplated flight or conflict, rejected both—where could he run, how could he stand against all the arcane might of the empire?—chose instead the honorable tactic of brazen bluff. He accompanied Skyrax's squad of waiting swordsmen to the Palace, striding solemnly through the nighted streets, his countenance gravely composed; saying nothing, thinking at lightning speed.

"So, Vexis, you know the situation as we," the King concluded, after Osthrakkias had recounted the known facts. "Give me your rede, as to how we should proceed."

"O King," said Vexis, striving heroically to mask his relief (they suspected him not!), "I hear a tale of woe indeed, nay a tale of madness, that any should dare insult and invade the sanctity of your family. Surely only a lunatic or a fool could have conceived the crime."

"Well and good," said Osthrakkias testily, "a view to which all the sane incline, but can you bring to bear greater knowledge or skill to the problem before us?"

Vexis nodded. "I think I can. In the course of my esoteric delvings I have sought intercourse with all the mages of our land, be they ever so seemingly humble, that I might miss not a jot of precious lore. I know—very slightly, you understand—this Futtabal, consider him under-appreciated. In his solitary, unprepossessing fashion he has broken the seals of many a strange matter, for which he garners no renown owing to his callous penchant for hoarding his findings. Now, public mutterings tell me he is being held at home incommunicado. Be this so?"

"What of it?" barked Skyrax. "The man is a criminal, or a tool wielded by enemies of the state. By the Gods, I will not stop at house arrest."

"Before I draw broad conclusions," Vexis continued with an air of mystery, "I must speak with him. I pray you grant me admittance to his chambers, that I may inquire of him at the scene." The King gave him leave to do this thing.

Vexis appeared at the door of Futtabal that day, alone, bearing a wrapped parcel of considerable size. "This is nothing," said the visitor in response to his host's query; "other business I transact as a blind. In this manner I eluded the circle of guards and made my way to you, my friend." O Vexis," moaned Futtabal, "great master of the esoteric, you must help me. Knowing that Carmeline loves me, I can not survive this cruel separation. She is mine still, is she not, her heart locked against all others?" "She is truly," soothed Vexis. "This I have from the King's lips. By the way, you said nothing of our bargain?"

"Of course not," Futtabal cried in horror. "Though my tormentors deduce some, they know nothing definite of the magic transaction, which wisdom on their part would sink me forever, as well as you. Until the marriage be done, you and I must keep silence."

"As you say," replied Vexis with an offhand air. "Friend, I crave refreshment. Before I tell you my welcome news, bring me wine and meat." Futtabal waddled away, calling to his meager staff within the inner chambers to prepare repast. With sudden alacrity Vexis sprang into action, unwrapping his parcel and secreting its contents under a pile of papers inside a convenient cabinet. When Futtabal and his people returned with food and drink Vexis was seated comfortably. After the servants were dismissed he announced, "O Futtabal, I come to you as intermediary, a bearer of glad tidings and spokesman for the Princess. She demands of me that I further your passions, by the mechanism of bringing you two together, that you may embark upon a gloriously romantic escape from this prison of a city, to live as one in a far place until such time as our King relents and accepts you as son. Pleases you this plan?"

"Like no other news this world can hold," Futtabal sighed. "Yet how can this be done? Hateful men with swords and spears lurk without, while hostile spells of the court mages restrain my limbs. Struggle as I might, I can not get to her."

"Leave the arrangements to me," assured Vexis. "I shall send to you a guide, armed with charms of protection, who shall pass the barriers unchecked, and lead you through twisting alleys to a secret entrance into Carmeline's private tower. This shall be done." With these transactions concluded, Vexis took leave of Futtabal shortly thereafter.

"What I tell you now be absolute truth," Vexis lied to the King when next they met, "as, all going well, subsequent events shall prove. Futtabal, thinking me a safe colleague, boasted of his exploits, crowing that he alone ensnared the Princess your daughter by means of a hideous tome of his sole possession, which he claims is none other than the shunned and forbidden *Book of Tantellas*." Cried Skyrax, "The *Book of Tantellas*? I have heard mention of its evil. Also, I recollect that a sage predecessor of mine long ago eradicated that vile work from the fair earth. What say you, Osthrakkias?" Replied his advisor, "Futtabal must be imposing on our friend Vexis. Even if Futtabal possessed a stray copy, he is not so keen of mind as to employ it to his will. He spews falsehoods in order to misdirect us." To which Vexis responded quickly, "Yet he vouchsafed me a glimpse of the volume, a big book cased in aged leather, with the name of the dreaded author in antique letters on the spine. This much I saw, though he whisked it away ere I could peer inside, nor did he reveal to me its hiding place. Surely that which I beheld with these eyes is more than imposture."

Osthrakkias still giving vent to reservations, the King exclaimed, "Given what you tell us, Vexis, what do we do?" To which clever Vexis had a ready answer: "For my love of you, great Skyrax, and your ensorcelled daughter, I shall lay a trap for this conniving Futtabal. He must be brought to the Royal Palace, here to meet with Carmeline—" "Never that!" "—and thus to be wrapped and bound by cunning necromancy of my devising. For this I require your daughter's cooperation." "That she will never grant," moaned the King. Said Vexis, "But I tell you she will. Attend to my plan."

Next morning Vexis, after a night long spent on strange labors, climbed the dizzying circular stairs to the top of Carmeline's sky flung tower and produced himself before the Princess, taking her very much unawares, cautioning her to silence for, as he told her, it had been difficult and chancy to reach her without her harsh father's approval. This intrigued Carmeline. Vexis quietly announced, "I speak to you on behalf of your lover Futtabal, who comes to you this very evening that he may arrange your escape from this comfortable cell." "Joyous news!" cried the Princess. "I knew that our love could not be denied. The virtues of Futtabal entrance the Gods Themselves, who fight for us." Vexis bowed, saying with all due grace, "There is nothing I would not do for my dearest friend, and your happiness." Cutting short an outburst of teary panegyric from the girl, he said, "Now, listen to me.

Futtabal, the sun of your heart, will intrude here via the brilliance of his arts one hour after twilight. The two of you will abscond on wings of magic from this very chamber window. No liege-men of your father can prevent flight from so high a perch. Necessarily you must travel light, with but the clothes on your back, and one thing other." Said Carmeline, "If I have this thing to hand, I will provide it."

Said Vexis, "As an accompaniment to the winging spell your lover shall conjure, you must give over to him, freely of your desire, the most precious jewel of your personal collection. Have you one such?"

"I do!" Carmeline rummaged among the ornamental boxes strewn about the vanities of her boudoir. From one she held up a slender gold chain dangling a weighty gem. "This blood red ruby, O Vexis, my most cherished adornment, descends through many generations in my mother's line, brought here from the Vasgarran mines when her people came to unite their fortunes with mighty Dyrezan. There is none like it in this or any land."

"Let me see it," said Vexis. He took the necklace, bent low as if to examine it, turning his back upon the Princess in the process. He murmured odd phrases under his breath, meanwhile wiping from his fingers a clear, iridescent oil, produced from a vial in the folds of his robe, onto the ruby. He held the gleaming stone in his fist and squeezed, feeling the radiation of faint heat. In a second or two it cooled. Facing Carmeline he held out the necklace, saying, "Yes, the gem is flawless. It will do. Be sure to give this to Futtabal as soon as you see him. Only then will his flighty magic work. So he instructs me."

As Vexis advised the King soon after, "Now Futtabal need only play his part, and all will be well with his victim, the Princess." Skyrax grimaced and growled, "I like not your plan. If he be guilty, then I need only send to him my executioner." Osthrakkias frowned, shook his head at this, saying, "His guilt, with all appropriate respect to our friend Vexis, has not been established. I, too, disapprove of this scheme, which is overly complicated and fraught with needless risk. Let us take Futtabal, place him under torture, and ring from him the truth." "So I decree," demanded the King.

"Which leaves the future wanting," Vexis pointed out hurriedly, who for personal reasons dreaded this consequence above all others. "Only he who laid the charm on Carmeline can remove it. If Futtabal dies under questioning, or is forever broken in mind, then the Royal daughter languishes his captive unto eternity. I beseech you, handle the matter my way. At great cost to my being I have conjured a formulation that will induce him, at the precise moment, to restore Carmeline's soul. My plan will lure him into freeing her, O King, at which time he is yours for your sport."

"That I decree," said Skyrax.

And so Vexis raced back to Futtabal's abode, where he announced himself ("Scarcely did I elude the guards," said he.) and, with curious modifications of his tale, explained the situation. "I have strained my powers to the utmost," declared Vexis. "Imps of the outer spheres, mighty beings bound within the gem Carmeline will deliver unto your hand, shall lend you invisible wings, and borne on the aether you and your lady love will soar away to foreign kingdoms, dwelling in joy until your enemies submit to fate."

"O Vexis," cried Futtabal, "you are a friend indeed, true and unbending. I will devote my life to repaying you." Said Vexis, "I believe you utterly."

At the appointed time, not long after full darkness, a slave of Vexis appeared at Futtabal's door to escort him secretly to the Royal Palace. Quite easily they eluded the ring of guards, the slave muttering something concerning the "spells of obscuration" laid down by his master. Futtabal was led on a seemingly random odyssey throughout the dirtiest, most crooked alleys and paths of the lower districts of Dyrezan, finally appearing at a concealed entrance at the base of Carmeline's tower. There the slave departed, leaving Futtabal to creep into the interior (oddly vacant) and scale alone the monumental tower, an undertaking that required desperate exertion on his part, for he dared not pause at the many levels for rest as his sweaty corpulence demanded.

Meanwhile, at the instigation of Vexis, the King's men raided the home of Futtabal and, following a thorough ransacking, discovered the *Book of Tantellas* hidden under a stack of papers in a cabinet. Osthrakkias, who had accompanied the troop, shouted, "At last, the evidence we seek. I doubted erroneously. This clinches the case."

Finally, close to midnight, Futtabal reached the upper tier where lay the chambers of the Princess. "Bliss eternal opens before us!" he cried as they embraced. "Thus so," replied she, "so soon as you take from me this ruby that I freely grant." Carmeline offered the stone, Futtabal greedily and happily received it. On the instant something amazing happened. Suddenly Carmeline screamed, leaping back from Futtabal, squalled fiercely, "Be gone, repellent reptile, that dares soil the flesh and honor of the King's daughter. Think you that I would squander my life writhing in your filthy grip? Guards, guards! I summon you!" She yanked a bell pull, and to the solemn din of iron chimes came the muted thunder of pounding feet on stone steps below. Futtabal, flabbergasted, tried to protest, to urge, to cajole, but the shocking development further stunned his sluggish brain, and the great jewel in his hand burned and blazed with horrid fire. This it did because (although no one present knew this) it reeked with the reverse spell of Vexis who, having first laid the love charm, could easily remove it when he wished. Realizing, though not comprehending, the approach of disaster, Futtabal clumsily sprang to the big open window, brushed aside the curtains, stepped onto the sill and, crying, "All is not lost, O Princess; I shall return on celestial wings to carry you away," he clutched the painfully hot ruby with both hands and jumped. Naturally he fell shrieking to his death.

King Skyrax mollified Lord Jellorn, explaining matters as he understood them, and that nobleman—truly a noble man—accepted what he was told and withdrew his prideful ire, admitting that pernicious sorcery was a disease to which no one, not even a princess, was immune. Once the residue of scandal had subsided the young couple married, and they did indeed live happily ever after, as had surely been ordained by the Gods.

Vexis, honored and rewarded well by the King for his acumen and loyalty, was left somewhat disgruntled by the whole affair. He owned his skin still intact, and quite a bit more, but it rankled that he had been forced to give up the marvelous tome of Tantellas, which the King shortly burned with great ceremony and speeches of righteousness. Vexis had surmised—correctly—that only the finding of the dread book in Futtabal's chambers would satisfy the keen and suspicious mind of Osthrakkias, so he had chosen, most reluctantly, to sacrifice it. Of course he had, before secretly returning the volume, copied those passages he immediately required, but during the brief period of his possession he had noted many more wonderful, exotic, and dangerous spells which simply cried out for further examination and experimentation. To a mighty wizard such as Vexis the loss of such arcane treasures constituted a tragedy for which no amount of life, liberty, and reward could ever wholly compensate.

THE TALE OF NANTRECH

In the olden days great Nantrech of mighty Dyrezan told this tale to the assembled mages and sages of the city, after his return alone from his long journey. Thus spake Nantrech: "My Lords of Dyrezan, masters, scholars, and friends, harken to my words, for I tell thee a strange story of curious lands east-aways, that I beheld in the course of explorations thither in search of mysteries that I might unlock in order to increase our vast store of arcane lore.

"With five hundred men, soldiers armed and armored, and savants bold and keen of mind, I marched forth toward the dawn that morning long ago, seeking to acquaint myself with the dim lands that lie at the fringes of the maps bequeathed to us by our fathers of the Middle Kingdom, which legend or myth inform us was itself so distant in the past as to seem the beginning of creation. So I can attest, for I aver from mine own experience that when we had trekked from this fair city, across the great valley that surrounds the metropolis like a mountainous bowl, across the immense fruitful plains that feed us, and beyond the limits of our present conquests among the lesser civilizations, I came to a realm—somewhere on the far side of peaceful Vasgarra—where maps failed me, their wisdom no longer speaking true. Instead of the boundless forested plateau I expected to find, I stopped short at the edge of a sullen sea wreathed in roiling mists. Think on that, friends, if thou wilt, for such epochs of history have swept down the corridors of time since those maps were fashioned that the very scape of the earth has changed. So I packed away the maps, as they were no more good to me, and gave order that boats should be builded from such stuffs as could be acquired on that bleak shore.

"When all was in readiness, and supplication made to the Gods who determine fate, we set sail on that darkling sea in ten boats, steering east by faith at most times, by the sun and the stars when the mist deigned to lift. Surely no true course could be set under those conditions, so I will not estimate for thee the leagues we bobbed on the little swells, but I say we sailed many a day, many a week, across the unpredicted waters. 'Twas an uneventful voyage in the main, though once a tempest blew up, a gale that tipped and spun us about like so many toys, but I spoke a magic which calmed the elements and turned them from us. Command of the small fleet lay in my hands, the train of scholars my special responsibility, with the warriors taken in charge by noble Morca, that grand Captain of past renown for his daring deeds of valor. He kept all quiet and seemly when the men were apt to mutter, cautioning them of their honor and promising them fine rewards or adventure. Indeed they were like to object to their enforced confinement in frail craft far from firm ground, not knowing—for what man living should advise them?—when they would see land again.

"They did, however, at last, all rejoicing when the clinging fog blew from us and our tiny ships coasted upon a happy breeze to another shore, one quite different from that we had left. Here cliffs and bluffs and spiny mountains rose in huge terraces from the wide beach, and even before we pulled onto the white sand we spied copious evidences of native habitation. Among the orange and white boulders, among the thorny bushes and stunted trees, girdled by belts of orchards gay with colors, loomed the stark, austere limestone dwellings of an unknown race. Certain of their people came timidly down to the beach to meet us, and when I had organized my people to deal with all contingencies I went forward with a select party of swordsmen and scribes. Up the slight slope, where the high tides sculpted the reddish rocks into odd forms, we greeted them, short, swarthy men of a type hitherto unguessed, albeit obscure passages in an ancient testimonial of an early King Skyrax may hint of them. Thus or not, they were new to us, unusual in body and opaque of language. By signs they welcomed us, as I supposed, and by gesture we offered friendship. Peace we made without difficulty. Among that initial group I observed no weapons, which pleased me then, and after this first contact I made bold to declare their land for Dyrezan, hoping in time to add it to our conquests or tributaries, as the case would prove.

"I established our camp, hastily stockaded, on the dry, rocky soil above the line of lapping tides, in the lee of that peculiar stone village clinging to the terraced slopes. The villagers acquiesced in this, as in all things we did. I sent out military parties, flying squads, to reconnoiter. Captain Morca arranged their tactical movements to my satisfaction. When all was done and a food supply negotiated I, with my colleague wizards, set about the interesting task of conjuring knowledge of the native tongue. This, a process of some days, involved the machination of spells overlaid upon the bare essentials we gained by conventional means. Within a reasonable span we could converse with those people, explain to them the might and majesty we invoked as sons of glorious Dyrezan, and learn somewhat of their ways.

"So we discovered that those simple folk, fishers mainly and farmers, were representatives of a race styling themselves the Peoki. Dwelling upon the shores of the great sea for countless leagues both north and south, they retained memories, recounted solely by oral means, of a far gone age when their people had dominated the land well into the interior of that country (which even now I can not tell you if it was big island, continent, or extension of our own terrestrial domain), living in fine cities and knowing all the civilized arts, though from their speech I gathered that the principles of magic had eluded always their best minds. Whatever of archaic history they recalled, the more recent eras concerned them most, for once upon a time—still very long ago as they understood chronology—another power had arisen farther to the east, another race of men who, if the spoken tales be believed, had crept in enormous numbers without warning from holes in the ground, natural caves or cunningly conceived tunnels, and marshaling their forces had waged war with mighty armaments and evil magic, driving the Peoki from their homes, exterminating the majority and reducing the survivors, forced into a pitiful existence at the margin of the sea, to piteous thralldom.

"These conquerors called themselves the Rhexellites, claiming to be descendants of a magical kingdom which once ruled all the world, until it was destroyed in the course of arcane delvings into mysteries of utter horror. The dregs of their empire—which flourished at a period so ancient that Dyrezan seems young by comparison—fled underground, where the remnants of their keenest minds fashioned a new world within the peculiar twilight of frightful caverns of unguessable extent. There they, or elements of their race, built themselves strong again, though others dwindled in physical and mental corruption. The hardiest stock of the ancient ones, after eons incalculable, assayed forth into the world of the sun again, dreaming of retaking their past lands and glories. Thus their war against the Peoki, and the erection in that far place of a dark power, one that boasted even now of insidious designs against all those who had come after them upon the face of the earth. Harsh were they, not fair to gaze upon I gathered, and suborned to hideous practices of vile tortures, inhuman amusements, and—although I did not credit this then—abominable diets.

"This I was told, or came to understand, and this set me thinking of my own designs. Morca, he of unchecked bravery, such that our King favored him with wealth and sought always his counsel, Morca the soldier laughed the story to scorn, saying, 'March I with my five hundred to the seat of this degenerate empire, which having lost the world creeps like termites from the nether pits, and smash them utterly,' a sentiment shared by many a stout warrior. I pondered, I wrestled with ideas; admittedly, I hesitated, for the Rhexellites sounded fearsome enough; I determined, calling into convention every village chief of the Peoki who might in good time attend me. From distant points they came, by the score, intrigued by news of our advent, wondering what I might tell them. When the meeting convened, in the best rude stone hall of the village over the camp (the town being called Rongia, by the way), I stood before their primitive grandees flanked by my sages and soldierly body-guard, addressing them thus:

"'Know you that, whatever the impostures foisted upon you by these cruel tyrants, only one great empire of unchecked steel and unbridled wisdom rules in this world, the unstoppable, eternal empire of Dyrezan, which holds absolute sway wherever it chooses. Our swords are bright and sharp, our shields impenetrable, our hearts august, our magic arcane and devastating. It is not meet to me that these brazen upstarts should torment such peaceful, hapless folk as yourselves. Your deplorable situation I would overturn. Lend me then thine arms, the strength of your youth and such weapons as you possess, and make a pact with me, that under the banner of Dyrezan we shall march together, confront these ogres in their den, and rid you of their stranglehold. This I say. If your minds attain that place in common with me, then swear to me now your fealty.'

"To this grand scheme they offered their full assent. There followed a period devoted to the collecting of volunteers from all the coast thereabouts, and the fashioning of rude weapons that might equip such a makeshift host. Morca saw to their training, as such could be in the time I allowed him. So before the new moon waxed gibbous we set out for the east two thousand and four hundred strong, a motley fabric of warlike material stitched together by the steel cords of my five hundred tried men at arms. East-away we marched (myself and my officers on horses provided) up rising ground onto a level plateau across barren, unpeopled scenes, hewing to a rugged road of loose dirt and sand.

"On the second morning we confronted a small party approaching us from the sunrise. On horseback rode they all, a score of spearmen with their leader, and unpleasant they were to behold. Lithe they appeared, sparse the hair on their heads, and pale their faces, with large dark, round eyes, pointed chins, slits of mouths and no noses to speak of save flaring nostrils and no ears but holes; my poor words but suggest to you their ugliness. They whispered among themselves in a sibilant hiss, then the leader trotted forth and addressed us in a foul travesty of the fishers' speech. Croaked he, 'Why wanders this crowd of rowdies from their appointed place? Gorgras, great King of the Rhexellites, he who rules from his mighty fortress of Tsathgon, master from sea to sea, has not authorized migration from your watery abode. Contrarily, he sends me yet again for levies of fish and corn, and the tribute he truly craves, a selection of youths and maidens. Turn back and march before me, lest distribution give way to retribution.'

"So spake he, to which I rejoined, 'It is thou who must scamper back in fear. Go to your toad king, go to that one and tell him that not tribute comes, but tribulation. Tell him that magic greater than his own enters the land to awe him, and to crush him if he behave wrongly. That he may heed your words in all belief, I give you this token of my esteem.' And, my friends and wizards, I did that cutting trick of which you know to be readily effective against lesser mortals: with the right passes, and words uttered at the correct pitch, I inverted the flesh of his nasty face, rendering him mutilated and uglier than before. He howled in miserable madness and blindly whipped his horse back among his men, who took him in charge and raced away before us. Our advance resumed.

"On the fourth day we entered a misty, damp upland dotted by villages of cubic stone houses, each inhabited part surrounded by broad swaths of marshy field planted with unfamiliar and unappetizing root crops. Through these the eastward road ran straight, here the soft dirt of the lane giving way to massy square blocks, well hewn and tightly fitting to form a solid surface. The villagers proved furtive, unkind folk, like unto those who had accosted us on the march; the type, as our allies had explained, of the Rhexellites. During the night parties from the villages thought to raid among our camp. We killed all we could seize, but for ten chosen captives. From these, at Morca's suggestion, we hacked off the hands and sent them onward to their king, that they might testify to our power and resolve.

"On the fifth day we spied through the drifting fog of the lowering clouds a high, rocky mountain rising from the plain without foothills, flat topped with steep bluffs on all sides we could see, with hints of Cyclopean architecture at the loftiest level. Up the mountain wound the road. As my army approached the base I espied a gigantic host of fell warriors tramping down to meet us. Within the van rode a massive chariot, plated with silver and studded with myriad unpolished gemstones, drawn by six black steeds. They met us at the first upward turn of the road. Within the chariot, in a frontally open traveling chamber behind the driver and his armed, flanking companions, stood up a man dressed in a black robe overlaid with white silken threads resembling a spiders' web. Above his pale, unspeakable face he wore a heavy crown of iron inlaid with bands of gold and a single circular ruby in the forehead. I surmised who he was before he hailed us.

"Said he, 'I, Gorgras, Lord of the Rhexellites, power of life and death in Tsathgon, welcome you, O people from the sea. Enter as guests my castle, where quarters will be provided for your men, princely abodes for you nobles.' I proclaimed myself and assented to his offer, thinking it better to gain admission peacefully than to battle up the mountain. So Gorgras and his army turned about, his chariot passing forward between the armed files, while we followed, winding our way up the long road to the highest bluffs, where Tsathgon stood in the clear air above the clouds. We passed within the high, thick walls of obsidian into the enormous expanse of the courtyard, where all transpired as this king promised. The troops went into barracks, my fine folk into apartments nearby, adjoining to and in the shadow of the keep. Within we found doorways opening into the main structure of the royal residence, which we blocked and barricaded. Morca wisely advised the erection of an earthen rampart stretching from our quarters and around the barracks. This was done.

"I describe Tsathgon to you, fellow mages, as a mathematician's dream and an architect's nightmare. We found ourselves dwelling within an artificial cubistic landscape, every structure blocky, angular, precisely square or rectangular, composed in every case of dark, gleaming volcanic stone native to that singular mountain, which I surmise was once a raging natural cauldron. The king's private tower—the greatest of many—consisted of a simple stack of cubes, each so big as a house, rising ten stories above its own ringing walls, with occasional vertical slits for windows. Truly Tsathgon in its immensity was more city than fort, for it teemed with life, the citizenry who plied their trades in the quarter of drab stone cubes they dwelt in, and the swarms of soldiers, who kept, then, a respectful distance.

"That night Gorgras invited us to an entertainment in the openness of the court. His lackeys raised up a grand rectangular pavilion of polished red wood and many soft, ornate hangings in the yard into which he, his courtiers, and his guards entered from one end, while I, my great ones, and my picked company entered from the other. There the fools of Gorgras pranced and capered for us, and desirable women (captives of other races or tribes, certainly) lasciviously danced, and the king himself regaled us with a show of magic. He first performed a series of minor tricks that would bore any tyro of Dyrezan. The chiefs of the Peoki seemed impressed, but I made a point of ostentatiously yawning. This caused my people to laugh out loud. Seeing this, Gorgras, with some show of anger, called for materials, and shortly he made for us a stronger brew. This time he, after mixing ingredients in a cauldron and hissing unintelligible formulae, opened a hole in the air above the paving of the court, from which plopped a revolting greenish monstrosity as big as a bear, a mass of bulbous eyes and writhing tentacles, which squatted heaving but otherwise motionless until Rhexellite spearmen thrust out from their midst a cringing, weeping captive; a young girl, as pretty in her way as the dancers, only her features naturally distorted with terror. The horrid thing immediately lunged at her, moving quickly and glutinously across the intervening space, then leapt somehow, taking the girl into its substance. She disappeared with a scream within—there was a commotion of slippery, animate surface—and she was gone! The king clapped his hands, and the guardsmen began menacing another captive with their spears.

"Morca whispered to me, 'O Nantrech, wizard beyond compare, conjure us a champion that will slay this denizen of the lower hells.' I would not, choosing to keep our enemies in the dark as to our full powers, and I commanded Morca—himself a grand sorcerer when he wilt—to refrain from displays of esoteric prowess. 'So be it,' cried he, and forthwith he sprang from the gallery into the yard, sword in hand, vowing at the top of his voice to best the hateful beast. My people, Dyrezanians and Peokis all, roared their delight. And Morca fought the monster. Called from unhallowed spheres though it was, the thing was composed of matter, flesh and blood if you will, though it seemed more foe than one man could handle. Save, I tell you, that man be Morca. The thing rushed at him, waving its awful feelers. Morca dodged, spun, circled, and slashed... and slashed, and cut and ripped, until a final thrust into the vitals laid low the monster, leaving it a quivering, subsiding heap of noxious gelatin. My company cheered deliriously. Gorgras sneeringly spat a word, which caused the mound of green ooze to vanish.

"Then the king, feigning graciousness once more, commanded that gourmet viands be served. Morca rejoined me, grinning proudly. Thralls brought among us the food. Quickly arose another cause of contention. Cared not we for the foodstuffs served on those silver trays, for though much was concealed by sauces and complex preparations, the aspect of certain whole joints plainly revealed the nature of the repast. The men grew unruly, murmuring their hostility. Unable to control my disgust I stood and raged, 'Do not dishonor us with the comestibles of fallen savages. As men, we repudiate this filth, and those who offer it, and in no wise will have it.' Thought I that the Rhexellites would fall on us then, but their lord restrained them, though his nasty face was a mask of evil intent, and he offered us dishes of vegetables. This I would have accepted, only I feared the broth, so I rejected the substitute, giving order that we return to our encampment, to partake from our supplies. So ended, sourly, the entertainment.

"Next morning fresh produce, of a healthy sort, was brought to us with the king's blessing, and for the remainder of our sojourn in Tsathgon we ate as men. Now began a period of watchful waiting and tension while my party strove to learn the ways of these reprehensible conquerors. Lord Harmon, scholar of strange folk, led our sages among the inhabitants of Tsathgon and the members of the court to investigate practices and glean history. This Gorgras allowed, though little pretense of friendship endured past that first unpleasantness. His spearmen surrounded us, manning the keep and the walls of the fortress, and with the passing of days their numbers grew. Minor incidents flared—taunts and private combats—which kept all on edge. Morca craved action, counseling a surprise move, while I demanded caution until we had gained what useful knowledge we could.

THE TALE OF NANTRECH

"What can I tell you of these Rhexellites? They were a fearsome race, a curious compound of fallen nobility and wretched barbarism, a people whose fathers may have surpassed us in the great arts of civilization, yet who had sunk low throughout the eons of their exile from the sun. This irruption of their might onto the surface must represent the last gasp of their better elements, as from what they told us I deduced that only the more unwholesome types, scarcely human still, remained in the dreaded caverns beneath that land, living like animals in a weird twilight world lit solely by the glowing emanations of subterranean fungi. Once theirs had been a glorious empire of magic and majesty, one which dreamed itself eternal, until their delvings into cosmic secrets carried them beyond grasping after sane knowledge and into a pursuit of forbidden mysteries. The ancient ones went too far—their brutal children of our day had forgotten how—and it was to escape some pitiless horror dredged up from the limits of the universe that they fled into the underworld. Now they had returned, to a small degree, changed in body by long isolation from the human stream, refashioning a pathetic mockery of former greatness, bringing with them the abysmal practices fostered by the extreme conditions in the bowels of the earth. From such grand heights of pride, fallen to such pitiful depths; pray to the good Gods, my learned friends, that in the fullness of time our fate be not theirs!

"It was their cannibalism, rather than their too common cruelty, that made them loathly in our eyes. Proper food they would eat, but only to supplement their desired diet. I had occasion to behold the sumptuous feasts of the nobility, the simple meals of the poor, ever the same main course. The king and his cronies preferred fresh meat, red with blood, lightly cooked after being slaughtered for amusement before their eyes. Oft times they would boil their victims whole and aware, as we do lobsters, casting them shrieking into vast, bubbling pots; or they would roast them living over coals inside bags of canvas. They did not inflict this degradation on their own folk, at least not before us, although one may presume that in the lengthy centuries underground they must first have learned to prey on their kind. On the surface, perhaps, they had too great choice of foreign morsels to plague their own.

"The explosion of violence that shattered the uneasy truce came following our sojourn there of well nigh a month. The winds of destiny blew but one way during the interim, with the lesser officers of their surrounding, ever growing army shouting at us vile insinuations

147

pertaining to our ultimate fate, while many of my people, despite my remonstrations, taunted back what we proposed to do with the Rhexellites once we subjugated them. My findings of fact were nearly complete—we knew much of their language, relevant portions of their history, something of the sinister cast of their minds—and I had reached agreement with the Peoki chiefs on the necessity of a quick and relatively bloodless coup, when suddenly all plans were thrown over by the outbreak of crimson war.

"It was valiant and reckless Morca who did the deed, on the evening of an exotic Rhexellite religious ceremony. The folk swarmed into a high, massy cube of a black temple, far across the open yard of the court, maybe a quarter league from our position. Priests dressed in gaudy scarlet robes (one of the few splashes of color in that dismal realm) led the way bearing torches and silver staffs of office, along with what appeared the majority of the Tsathgon nobles. Amidst the wildly shouting and inharmonious singing throng numerous guards herded hundreds of miserable chained captives, evidently being taken into that place for sacrifice, feasting, or both. As the cavalcade passed by and beyond us hostile soldiers on the fortress walls above us called down evil jests, snickering loudly among themselves as to the identity of the next guests chosen for the ceremony. The mob of Rhexellites disappeared into the temple, cramming themselves within the building, from which ominously regular chanting presently arose, punctuated by distantly heard, lingering screams of unendurable agony.

"Morca reached the breaking point, a situation in which he had much company. He feared, as he told me later, that the rites of the black temple were a disguise for an onslaught against us; that there were too many people, too many natural leaders, too many spearmen pressing close. That is as may be. He claimed to have sought me to offer his rede, but could not find me—I was, indeed, away from my chambers, walking the perimeter discoursing science with fellow savants—and, in what he considered a moment of extremis, decided to initiate swift action in order to forestall what he deduced or imagined as a cleverly laid scheme of attack upon us.

"He threw open the makeshift gates of our rampart, charging across the gloom of the flagged yard at the temple with almost half my military complement. Two hundred men of Dyrezan advanced in phalanx with shields interlocked, first at stride, then at trot, finally at a run, backed by many hundreds, perhaps a thousand of vengeful Peokis, as they rushed the three large doors facing them in the temple wall. The Rhexellite guards went down with barely time for a warning cry, and then our men burst inside, to behold a ghastly sight within the single large, multi-tiered hall that comprised the temple interior. In a flash of disbelieving insight they took in the incredible scene. The thousands of celebrants sat or stood on a sloping floor ringed with circular benches, gesticulating and chanting crazily as scores of victims were being butchered at a stroke in the arena or central dais. Those unfortunates were killed with spears, or burned by magic spells of the priests, or fed to creatures not unlike the one I had witnessed, spawned of sorcery. The Rhexellite troops within turned and dashed at our soldiers, who mad with righteous blood-lust began a massacre of all Rhexellites within, both those who opposed us and those who, stricken with fear, endeavored to flee. The crude martial virulence of the enemy combatants proved no match for the exquisite tactical training of our men, backed by the many Peoki. With Morca leading the way, swinging his sword and reciting cunning charms of confusion against the foe, the warriors of Dyrezan swept all before them, hewing down the enemy and trampling their bodies in red ruin underfoot. A few Rhexellites only escaped through doors in the other three walls. Their priests were slain with enormous satisfaction. When the ground level had been cleared of life—except for a handful of rescued captives—Morca led his ferocious host up the stairs to the upper levels. No Rhexellite escaped alive from there.

"Morca returned triumphantly with his men and, when confronted by me, boasted of his exploits and his slight loss. I upbraided him for his hot-headed audacity, but I was in no position to argue the merits of the case. As we spoke a tocsin boomed, clanged, and reverberated over the fortress. Hundreds of torches flared from the battlements above us, and from a high perch in the royal keep a familiar commanding voice sibilantly bawled, 'Death to the interlopers! Kill them all!'

"The Rhexellites charged madly in their thousands. Thank the eternal benevolence of watchful Xenophor, Lord of All Creation, that we stood awake and aware, under arms to meet the onslaught. I buckled on my armor and, with weapon in hand, joined the fight. The stampede of bloodthirsty retribution stormed across the dark court, our bowmen among the Peoki raining arrows into the packed ranks. The Rhexellite wave crashed in a foam of blood against the rocks of our fortitude. They clambered up the ramparts to meet death at our hands. Steel swords bit into their mercifully thin armor, those that wore any, and slashed at their flesh; bronze shields pounded purple their pasty white skins. They retreated, leaving scores of the slain behind... and came on again! Over and over throughout the interminable hours their immense numbers broke against our thin but hard line. Then lights, weird colors and ethereal radiances, flickered from the slit windows of the keep. I knew those signs; Gorgras conjured battle magic to smash us down. Leaving Morca in full command of my forces, I repaired to my chambers where, with the aid of my scholarly colleagues, I commenced a counter enchantment. Meanwhile blazing fireballs rained down on our camp, with hideously unnerving specters wheeling among the stars through the night sky, calling on the men to cower or flee lest they face doom.

"I brewed from the unseen spheres the corrosive rain that eats flesh and pocks stone and metal. Quickly the spell consumed the bulk of my arcane substances at hand, but faced by such oppressive numbers I could but hazard the utmost on a single roll of the dice. I cried out, 'Xenophor the Mighty, and the Gods who serve You, protect your devoted children, and smite these wicked ones.' And a mysterious gust of hot wind burst forth from nowhere, and about the ramparts black sheets of acidic droplets pelted down from the clear sky, and the Rhexellite soldiers howled and squalled in their pain and rage. They fell back, and with the break of dawn it seemed they would come at us no more.

"I took rapid stock of the situation. We had suffered casualties, more from the fires of Gorgras than the spears of his army, but our ranks were largely intact, the greatest losses being absorbed by the Peokis, who fought unarmored like the majority of our foes. Before me loomed the immediate question: what to do now? We were, at first reckoning, trapped within the citadel of Rhexellite power, cut off by a wall of hatred propped by the formidable arts of the king. What to do? Morca said, 'Carry the war to the enemy. Each man of Dyrezan is worth ten of them, and we have the Peoki warriors at our side. Let us extend our strength, as the cornered tiger leaps from his lair.' I agreed without reservation. I had come to suppress the Rhexellites, and any chance for subtle diplomacies was past. So with the ranks reformed, a small company being tasked with holding the camp, flying columns surged forth to take the castle and pierce the heart of the enemy empire.

"Two columns stormed to the left and right, bashed their way up the steps on the inner wall and in a brutal fight cleared that portion overlooking the encampment. The main column advanced squarely against the keep, where Gorgras lurked with huge forces and unguessable secret powers. The gate we threw down with charmed rams, the potent force being supplied by Morca and I in unison. The barrier gave, but with significant resistance, indicating a counter spell applied from the other side. The king, and whatever mages he supported, were still active in the fray. Then we entered the human beehive. The soldiers hacked and thrust their way through a dense wall of Rhexellite bodies. We attained the door of the keep, crushing our enemies beneath us, forced passage into that perfectly square portal, where a conjured monstrosity splashed to the floor and scrabbled toward us. I say this king of theirs relied too much on fear. Frightful was that thing, but we readily sliced it to shreds. The subsequent clash cleared the barbaric throne room on the ground floor, where a gilded seat stood empty among the reeking refuse of those who fought to defend it.

"Up the harshly diagonal stairs we climbed, destroying opposition on one floor, then the next. Many a worthy man fell on our side, for the enemy were bold and, quite rightly, expectant of no mercy, so they fought and slew like devils. The Peokis, when they advanced to the fore, suffered horrendous casualties, yet they battled on cheerily, ever eager for a go at the foe. The thirst for revenge of miseries inflicted drove them on. Came we at last to the topmost level of the royal tower, where we grimly hurled ourselves against the final barrier of men and fortifications. A spasm of killing led us into a great gloomy chamber of shelves bearing arrays of scrolls and instruments of magic, the walls of the chamber adorned atrociously with the hanging bones of royal victims. There stood the king, Gorgras, amidst the last of his guard, hissing vicious commands and intoning desperate spells. From a steaming cloud of yellow mist rose up a black spirit champion, armed with knobbed mace and loathsomely curved hook to protect the royal person. Morca thrust through his fellows and, laughing heartily, strode forth to do battle with the entity. He would not use his arts, insisting as he passed that I not interfere. I gave him his head, and he made the most of the opportunity. What a duel that was! Morca's lust for combat flamed as he fought. Steel rang on steel, and once I thought the hook would tear out my companion's vitals. The spirit champion could not be killed as readily as men perish, but it could be rendered into fragments, and this Morca laboriously performed. When that strange one was entirely chopped up Morca stumbled away and fell gasping against the wall, utterly spent. Then I gave the order, that all within be exterminated. So ended the life of Gorgras, king of the Rhexellites.

"Tsathgon was ours, the terror of the dark kingdom forever broken. The fortress we secured in short order, for the common folk—all who remained alive in that place—had no fight in them. The men spent much of the day in merriment and drinking. The Rhexellites boasted a potent sauce that, of all their wonders, most impressed the troops, and under those joyous circumstances restraint could not be thought of. I commanded, to the few remaining under arms, that the keep be ransacked for secrets and marvels, and this was done. I hoped to carry back much illustrious booty to Dyrezan, to startle the multitudes and increase the lore of the wise. I was to be tragically disappointed.

"Came that baleful night when unkind fate shockingly dashed all my fond dreams of glory and wisdom. Exactly how the events transpired I may never know. I have since suspected that a few Rhexellite survivors of the battle, priests or noblemen maybe, knew of one weapon remaining to them, a power to be unleashed solely when all hope was gone; a weapon of suicide. Possibly they hid themselves within underground chambers of the keep—there were such, which I intended to explore at leisure—or utilized tunnels within Tsathgon that we never had time to locate. However it happened, I first became aware that something was horribly wrong when a single Dyrezanian warrior, one of the garrison squad guarding the keep, dashed breathlessly into the encampment, unarmed and bleeding from odd wounds, babbling a morbid tale.

"He told us that from corridors in the lowest level of the keep had come an irresistible tide of barely glimpsed beings, a mass of squirming shapes surging out of the darkness, taking the men unawares as most of them drunkenly slept. He could not describe them, though he had seen, for a moment, and gazed upon them by feeble fire light. These things clawed and bit a path through the soldiers, slaying silently, chewing on the bodies of living and dead. The man shrieked that they were already eating of him when he broke away and ran for his life.

"Scarcely had he choked out this wild story when the bitter truth presented itself. There burst from the broken gate of the keep a raging river, a tempest, an avalanche of forms that only in the murk of night, at far remove, could be mistaken for human. Akin to the defeated Rhexellites they were, but it was a distant kinship, one that even the beaten foe had tried to disown. And more came, a teeming horde gushing from the black temple, then from all points. I and Morca marshaled the men for renewed battle as we could.

"This is not a period that I wish to recollect. The creatures of the ultimate darkness stalked abroad! Thou art all wise and brave, my friends and fellows, but who among thee would not flinch from the ghastliness I beheld then, nor despair of the memory? These were the true children of the primordial Rhexellites, the most debased and despised specimens that still crept through burrows and caverns beneath the lands smiled upon by the Gods. Down there they fester to this day, in astounding numbers, as I can testify to thee. I doubt not that they had been released or liberated in some fashion, for their murderous appearance at that juncture could not be the work of happenstance. Fast it occurred, terribly fast: the irruption from the keep, then the temple, and from the common folk's quarter, from which some of the less polluted subjects of dead Gorgras ran for their lives, accompanied by those Peoki—stationed only that afternoon among the little cubic houses—who were sober enough to seek safety. Came a torrent of mindless bestiality! Naked they clawed toward us, with hairless, corpse-white bodies, lean and hungry looking, with repulsive spidery limbs sporting curved claws on the wiry fingers of their misshapen paws. Below their low-domed pates gleamed monstrous eyes, big as saucers. I see now as then their noseless nostrils, mere holes in those evil masks, and the filthy red mouths filled with long needle-like fangs.

"As the outliers among my troops were swept up and torn apart in that verminous maelstrom, Morca barked furious commands. He did not deign to consult me, and I admit it was better he did not so tarry. 'Form up, all ye who hear me!' he roared. 'On the double, secure the castle wall.' He realized immediately what I understood critical seconds later: that this was not an enemy to be opposed, but a menace to elude at all costs. The men fell in; how many I wonder—perhaps a couple hundred sons of Dyrezan, maybe five hundred of the Peoki—the rest already cut off, dead or doomed. We carved a path through blood and gristle to the main gate which opened upon the road of salvation. Most of us reached it. We could hack the things down, but unless firmly dead they would not stay down, still biting at us as the severed heads of ants are wont to do. Many a man who could have stood against five civilized opponents went down screaming, stricken in terror when enmeshed by those skinny, clawed limbs that wrapped around their prey like binding web. Nevertheless we opened the gate, struggling frenziedly to hold our position while our people passed through. Behind us a living carpet of insanity, stretching to the limits of vision, pressed closely at our heels.

"Said Morca to me, 'Give me one hundred of our best, that I may hold the gate until thou and the others escape the mountain via the road.' It saddened my heart, but I agreed to his plan. As my larger party ran down the royal avenue toward the far away plain, unseen in benighted mist, Morca held his ground. With my last glimpse I saw him conjuring thunderbolts in the darkness.

"His sacrifice—thus I say, for never I saw him again—was valiant but fruitless, for we others fleeing in the dark were scarcely halfway down the steep slope when the pale troglodytes appeared from all sides. I blame the mountain, which could not have been solid, but rather honeycombed by the dwellers down under. At this moment all organization, any semblance of order vanished, replaced by a pell-mell scramble for life. We ran like scared children! It was the last I saw of Harmon the wise, and Nemedas the philosopher, and many another worthy man. I know they perished on that cursed mountain. I fell in with a band of Peoki, scant protection against the peril, but companions at a time when I dreaded being alone. The cavern horrors closed in, slinking over the stones to get at us. Out of my nightmare delirium I remembered Morca's thunderbolts. I thought as he must have thought, that the denizens of darkness emerged in darkness, for true light was anathema to them. Within the folds of my robe, tucked under armor, I carried a handful of fire globes, useful for producing light and fire by night. I cast one to the heavens and spoke it alight... and the vile creatures gave back, cringing from the glare! While the globe hovered above I used the miraculous chance to gather my handful of allied warriors and descend the slope. A few furlongs more and the horrors came on again. Another globe repelled them. We advanced, slicing them into steaks as we barreled through. What I would have given for my cache of magical supplies, or the abandoned potions of Gorgras, that I might have conjured a wall of flame. I used the last globe near the base of the mountain. A relative few of the filthy ones still leapt from the deepening shadows to bar our way. Against them we steeled ourselves and charged, I calling on the great Gods of the universe, the Peoki crying out to their imaginary deities.

"Naught remains of interest to tell. My pathetic band met the dawn as we scurried across the plain, and the troglodytes disappeared from view, nevermore to molest us, and in the days and weeks to come we made our way back to the land of the Peoki. Never did we meet others of the allied army, all of whom I fear gave up their spirits that infernal night. In order to proceed we must needs avoid the scattered villages of the Rhexellites, for though their hateful kingdom was obliterated, our numbers counted so paltry as to render local gangs dangerous to us. After our great ordeal, it would be too awful to yet fall among the leaderless cannibals.

"We did attain the coast, at the village of Rongia, and amidst the weeping of the women for their lost heroes we rejoiced in our continued existence. Merry I was, strangely so, until a stray fever caught me, the result I think of solemn distress and discordant emotions—induced by the loss of so many friends and honored ones—and my brain burned for weeks. When sanity returned I asked of my friends the Peoki that they build me a raft that I might cross the westward sea and rejoin my people far to the sunset. This they did for me, out of gratitude that, despite the fearful cost, their oppressor's hand was off their necks. I sailed alone on that raft for a sad age, and passed over the wild lands beyond, and so in the fullness of time came unto ye again, my Lords of Dyrezan. Thus ends my tale."

THE ADVENTURE OF CAPTAIN MORCA

The struggle over, all that could be done faithfully achieved; in the aftermath of devastating defeat it was all that Morca—Captain of the Royal Guard, nobleman, and mage of renown—could do to save his own skin from the catastrophe. The army of mighty Dyrezan, golden empire of magic and steel, had marched forth to glorious conquest against the dark kingdom of the Rhexellites. Great battles had been won, distant peoples laid under the yoke of Dyrezanian power, feats of valor performed that should live forever in story and song; yet in the end retribution had come, when the warriors of Dyrezan met, on the desolate, misty slopes of a black mountain at night in the heart of enemy territory, hosts of monstrous foes that could not be overcome nor withstood. With the army facing annihilation great Morca was tasked with holding the enemy at bay until the rest could escape. With his tiny rear guard of hard-bitten troops he fiercely fought and cunningly retreated, hacking and slashing and casting grim charms of death at the foe, holding open the lone road to salvation with the blood of his men that others might live. In the end sword and shield and magic staff and arcane spell could no longer repel the irresistible hordes, and Morca's brave band were swept away in the frenzied melee at the foot of the mountain. Come the dawn Morca wandered solitary, skulking amidst the fog shrouded ravines and crevasses and boulders bounding the lowland plains.

Gripped he still sword and shield in hand, his armor intact though battered and rent, bearing yet a pack of sundry items and esoteric materials, the necessaries of a practiced magician, on his back, though his food bag was entirely lost with its contents. With the light Morca could survey the scene, to the extent possible in the murky grayness, and take bearings. What he could see discomfited him. No living trace of the main army met his eye, nor did the many familiar corpses over which he had stumbled during his hectic journey down the mountain give him much hope for succor from that source. If they had made away from the crimsoned grounds, then they had departed in flight to the west hours before. That way, thickly inhabited by the supposedly conquered peoples, was denied him now, for one man could not likely surmount their thirst for revenge. To return up the fateful mountain, to insinuate himself among the wreckage of the despoiled Rhexellite citadel, was madness. At present he crouched under rocky cover to the south of the dimly perceived peak. He must go south then, into unknown lands, before he could negotiate a passage back to his own.

In these circumstances the thought of returning home solely motivated him. Gone forth to glory in strange places, he now cursed himself, cursed fate, gave fleeting thought to cursing the Gods yet wisely refrained. Fearful of Their anger, he rounded again on himself. "Fool I was," he muttered, "to seek wonders and excitement among the fell realms of this nasty domain, surrendering in the act all the happiness and pleasures of my native land. Am I not a noble citizen of great Dyrezan, jewel of the world, seat of all that is joyful and glamorous? Dreadfully do time and space separate me from those sky-flung towers of gleaming marble and glittering crystal, the broad avenues teeming with civilized throngs, the temples and palaces and libraries where work and dwell the inquisitive scholars and studious sorcerers whom I call friends. All that I willingly left; these, and the favor of the King, proud Skyrax who adored me and honored me with his favor; perhaps never more to behold and revel in! O Morca, thou held the world in thy hand; where the benefit of casting it away like a tinsel bauble?"

And he vowed, "Enough of adventure, save that required to get me safely to that good spot. From this moment I do what I must do, and with the goal achieved, I renounce fretful amblings forever. May the Gods hear me." So he spoke in that awful refuge among the austere gullies and piles of glassy obsidian, making special supplication to great Xenophor, He of the Million Eyes, He who sees and knows all things, praying that the Eternal One would grant him strength of spirit and unwavering resolve for the labors ahead.

All that morning he trekked toward the south, keeping to the concealing broken terrain lest the denizens of the unsheltered plains should spy him. Despite his caution he was noticed, though this because he met another refugee sojourning in shadow. Morca rounded a rocky knob to confront a short, swarthy fellow with disordered lank hair and wild eyes. The stranger leaped back, brandishing a dagger his only weapon, then seemed to recollect himself. He smiled, flashing white teeth. "You are Morca," said he. Came the reply, "I am Lord Morca, Captain in the service of King Skyrax of Dyrezan. I know you. Surely you are of the Peoki." The Peoki, barbarians dwelling along the shores of the great sea bounding to the west the kingdom of the detested Rhexellites, had been loyal allies in the late campaign. Said the man, "I am Raspas, son of chief Narga, he who fell in the night's battle." Morca said, "I honor him." Continued Raspas, "With all lost, I sought safety in flight. I wish to reach my own lands to the west." "As do I," Morca told him, "and much farther west is my home, beyond your inviting sea. I take a roundabout course, choosing wisdom over speed. Accompany me, that together we may win through alive, and having accomplished this, forswear adventure forever."

To this Raspas heartily agreed. He fell in behind Morca, together they tramping onward throughout the rest of the day. In the evening they camped by a trickle of stream among low, unpeopled hills, made a supper of hand-caught, untasty lizard, and plucked bitter herbs. Next day they went on, veering west once until they approached an extension of the plain, then south again, where the hills rose higher above the widening creek. In answer to a request Raspas replied, "I know nothing of these lands, which were ever forbidden while the Rhexellites oppressed us. The sea of my people laps far to the south. It may be that this watercourse will turn and flow into it. Let us keep to the water."

What the stream did, over the span of several days' uneventful, if hungry march, was broaden considerably within the spacious confines of a low, desolate valley. No one lived out there, no sign of human artifice greeted the wanderers, except for the curious totems emplaced at the head of the valley. Two of them stood there, tall posts hewn from branches of the scrubby native trees, carved with hideous designs of leering, unearthly faces and decorated with weather worn feathers gummed with tar to the crudely worked wood. "I care not for this," said Raspas. "Someone would warn us away. Let us heed the advice." Said Morca, "Be convinced always, my friend, that I will avoid trouble whenever it raises its head. Henceforth I shun risk. I can not, however, read the meaning of these primitive poles, therefore I need not harken to them. For all I care they may be forgotten boundary markers, of no concern to anyone living. We will go on." Further argument on the part of Raspas availed nought. They went on.

The sprawling stream widened more, and the earth underfoot grew springy with damp, then sodden, and lush green shrubs sprouted along the indeterminate banks, and before the travelers knew it they were driving obstinately forward through a marsh choked with dense foliage. "If this continue," said Morca, "then we camp tonight on the bluffs." The hardy masses of tough, brittle branch and clinging vine closed about them, shutting out the hazy day's sun, shrouding them in murk. It was cooler in there, but the going was hard, the footing difficult and messy in the glutinous mud, and from points uncomfortably near things rustled amidst the undergrowth and, at times, bright little eyes winked at them from dark lairs. Morca took to cutting his way forward with his sword. Late in the afternoon the men began to ponder the lengthy hike up the receding bluffs to the rim of the valley, when they came upon a curious place.

The snarled plants gave way onto a wide lagoon, an apparently shallow pond framed by thick stands of willows. Yellowed reeds clustered about its shore. Within the lagoon they spied the sloping rise of a small island where nothing but scattered weeds grew in the mucky soil; these weeds, and a harshly composed structure of gray limestone, large featureless slabs of living rock cut and fashioned into a big oblong enclosure, capped by a flat black roof of basalt. It looked a wholly uninviting edifice, bereft of windows or other convenient adornments. The long wall to the right bore a square, doorless opening, closed only by a hanging curtain of dirty fabric.

Observed Morca, "If simple folk dwell within, then they may grant us shelter, decent food, and knowledge of the world around. It this hut of rock be untenanted, then at least we sleep here dry tonight. Barring treachery of the waters, it is an easy wade. Come, Raspas."

They sloshed through the foul smelling pool, sinking into greasy ooze to their ankles, attained the island, advanced without pausing to wipe their boots of filth. At the entrance to the stone building, pulling aside the grimy curtain to peer at them, appeared a frightful figure, a withered, shaggy old man with long gray beard and gray matted hair cascading over his bright black eyes. Dressed in scanty rags, he grinned a toothless grin, saying to them in a cracked, screechy voice, "No farther till thy feet be clean. This be a hallowed precinct." Morca and Raspas looked to one another, then squatted to unmire themselves. This task accomplished, the horrid ancient bid them enter, saying, "Welcome to thee, Captain Morca, Lord of Dyrezan, and to thy man,

Raspas the chief's son of the Peoki." The strange elder turned and shuffled within. His visitors followed warily, pushing through the flimsy barrier.

Inside they found a large room which occupied the majority of the interior, save for a tiny alcove to the left, a squalid cubicle littered with shreds of rotting fabric and gnawed bones of small animals, which presumably formed the man's private quarters. The main room they found quite different, being spotlessly clean and mostly barren. In the polished limestone floor there opened an oval pool of oddly deep crystal clear water contained within a chiseled rock basin. Except for the little light coming through the entrance, the only illumination in the chamber stemmed from this pool, which emitted from its depths a faint, ghostly radiance. "Be seated," said the man, "at the edge of the shrine. I am the Tender of the Oracle, who will guide you in the ceremonies."

Asked Morca, "How know you our names, and what is this place, that you speak of shrines and oracles?"

To which the Tender replied, "I know many things, told to me by the Sacred Ones of old who peer through the window of the waters. They told me you came near, but not why you came. You are unaware that this ground be sacred? There are markers up the valley, understood by all for fifty leagues around, and throughout the wide world as I thought. You, however, do not know. Why be you here?"

"Hapless wayfarers," explained Morca, "be all we are. Great deeds and cataclysmic events shake the earth beyond your lonely confines. We journey homeward. Will your Sacred Ones prepare us a map?"

Said the Tender, "They will show you, if They choose, what is to come. Sit, if thou wilt, and behold the future ordained." So Morca sat cross-legged by the glowing basin, and Raspas with somewhat less alacrity did the same, saying in a whisper to his companion, "O wise magician and brave warrior, you may relish such insights, yet I dread these mysteries that lie beyond my ken, and I fear signs and portents, which seldom profit a man, but are inclined to decoy him to doom." Morca grunted, muttered back, "Let us see what there is to see. True knowledge never harms. What we learn we may embrace or ignore at our ease or peril, just so that we know." Raspas sighed, saying, "Spoken like a dedicated mage. I submit myself."

The Tender intoned, "First thee, Raspas, look well into the bottomless waters." With the words he produced from the folds of his rags a fistful of brown, glittering powder which he sprinkled onto the still surface. He croaked meaningless words over the pool, adding at the last, "Grant him vision, grant this to him, this Raspas, as he accepts." And the waters stirred by themselves, as if one unseen had fished in the pool with a stick. Raspas watched as if mesmerized. Morca too paid heed, but he saw nothing but the troubled waters eddying in the basin, and the rough walls of the pool descending in the weird radiance like an unfathomably deep well litten from below. From the starkly rapt look on his fellow's face, he gathered that one saw more.

Suddenly Raspas sprang to his feet, and uttering a low cry rushed from the room and out of the stone enclosure. The Tender cackled to himself, a high harsh sound, and said, "Thy turn, Morca. Gaze deeply, focusing thy eyes as upon a far mountain or unreachable star." He cast again the handful of powder, recited once more the ceremonial formula. Morca stared intently into the shimmering pool. The waters swirled, flowing round and round and frothing and foaming. Eddies clashed and droplets seemed to spring at his eyes, so that he involuntarily blinked though he felt nothing. The glow intensified, and then it was as if he gazed through a window into a scene far away at a distant horizon. The scene expanded to fill his range of vision. Morca saw himself, struggling in an anonymous chamber against a multitude of anonymous foes, not apparently strangers but men such as himself, his own kind coming at him with sword and dagger, striving to kill him. He beheld his heroic defense against their onslaught, his great deeds of laughing insolence and grim violence as they crowded close, stabbing and hacking and wearing him down. Finally with a snarling oath he bowed before their attack and sank down to the anonymous floor, as the scene grew dark and passed from sight. Now he looked unto nothing, vision and reality gone from him. Out of the darkness roared a voice, or a chorus of voices, full-throated like the raging of giants, the voice of gale fury and fiery upheaval. It said: "This, Morca, be thy destiny, if thou shalt hew to thy chosen path."

The darkness receded. He stared with tired eyes into the still, warmly glowing basin. He turned to the Tender, wanly smiled. Screeched that one, "Hast thou chosen?" and Morca replied simply, "I have," and the Tender said, "Then go, Captain. I have finished with thee." Morca strode forth from the gloomy chamber without further word.

Said he to Raspas, who stood forlorn at the muddy shore of the island, "Come. There is no more for us here." They crossed the island, splashed through the rank water of the lagoon and went on their way downstream through the overgrown marsh. When the sun threatened to dip below the rim of the valley they clambered up the slope to a dry, level place where they camped for the night. They ate of the squalid game slain on the march, roasting it in a sputtering fire of green branches and shavings. Throughout Raspas chewed morosely, silently.

Asked Morca presently, "Wilt tell me of thy vision?" Raspas said, "I can not. To think on it is horror, to speak of it madness." Morca said, "The oracle has not laid secrecy on me. I saw my end, that which is ordained should I keep my way. It was nought but what I would have expected, sooner or later. I died in combat with my enemies. I have ever been a fighter, have lived my life with sword in hand and charmed curse at my lips. So one day will come the last fight. What of it? How do I desire the Noseless One to greet me? Should I shake hands with him in bed, coughing out my vitals between silk sheets? Never more will I seek trouble, but I do not fear this pictured death."

Said Raspas, "'Twas the end, and not the one I would have chosen. That grisly fate should set such in store for me; it is unbearable; I can not bear it! Better anything than what I saw!"

Morca spoke, sedate, as if not hearing. "What does it mean, for that matter? You were right, Raspas, to shun oracles. What do they reveal to thee? Such and so will be, if other things be, not if not. When I think on it, I realize no enlightenment. Do I go to a miserable homecoming? Do enemies lie in wait? Will a long laid plot hatch when I return? Or did I view an incident in years to come, a stroke of misfortune long down the road? The details of the image grow misty. I can not say sure. Therefore, my position in the grand scheme alters not one whit. I go onward, as one must in life, and I take what comes. Understand you this logic?"

Raspas whispered, "Anything but that revealed. I will not chance the risk."

In the morning they descended again into the swampy valley, that they might keep to ready water, and continued their journey many more days without variation. In time the valley broadened more and the sluggish stream, fed by springs trickling from the rocks above, transformed into a nice, sparkling river that turned happily to the west. This the two men eagerly followed, for its new course was likely to lead them both to the great sea where they wished to go, Raspas to his own people, Morca among friends who would aid him in furthering his journey.

SCIENCE AND SORCERY II

Throughout the span of a weary, airless day of gathering dusty haze they tramped up rising ground among peaked hills and rugged bluffs. The sparse, sere vegetation of the broken landscape gave way to a starkly barren scene of cracked, blackened rocks and crumbly dirt that clung to their feet and retarded their steps like sand. Through this ran the river, even its banks devoid of life. The men tightened their already pitiful rations, trusting to hope to carry them beyond the dreary wastes to more fecund regions. When the faded sun balanced on a rocky point they beheld below it the shadowed scape of a sprawling city, the ornate outlines of a metropolis shrouded in gloom. No lights as yet burned in there, and as they closer approached they hazarded the guess that any lights must be furnished by them.

It was a dead place. While traces of Cyclopean cubic architecture remained, what they had deduced as exotic in silhouette revealed itself to be disintegrating ruin. The place looked old and worn and weathered, and more: it looked devastated, bleak and blasted as the immediate countryside. An obsidian totem, looming at the outskirts of the shattered pile, bore barely visible carven patterns.

"This be Rhexellite writing," observed Morca, "like enough to what I learned to read during the campaign against them, but unfamiliar in style. This, I think, is an elder form, possibly very older. From what little I can decipher the words proclaim the everlasting greatness of the city and its people, defying any to tread here unbidden. Know you, Raspas, of the Rhexellite legends?" The other replied, "Too often have their tales been dinned into my ears during their more boastful days, before we shook their power. The Rhexellites, to hear them tell it, once owned the world, until recourse to evil magic brought doom upon them and sent them scurrying into the interior caverns of the earth." And Morca continued for him, "There they decayed, until the few better elements, less changed than their dregs, emerged once more to plague your people and seek to regain their mastery. A foolish and vainglorious dream, as it happens." "Aye," agreed Raspas, "but it was the fabled dregs—the inhuman denizens of the earth's bowels—we need fear most, for surely it was they that crept from black burrows that night on the mountain to slay us all at the moment when our victory was well nigh complete, and the Rhexellites wholly overthrown. Thus did fate tragically confirm the worst of the olden stories."

"It seems so," said Morca, "and now, a dead city, blighted by time, a funereal monument, perhaps, to an age of glory lost forevermore.

Let us enter, my friend, that we may behold the residue of ancient marvels."

"That I will not," cried Raspas. And when Morca remonstrated, arguing that their path lay forward, and only thus, his companion said tearfully, "Now the wisdom tendered by the Tender comes clearly. I understand, all too well, the fearsome vision vouchsafed to me. There within lies my abysmal fate, there or elsewhere in this benighted land, the fate inescapable and unendurable. I shall not face it. There is a way, despite what I have said, one way that leads to an end otherwise. I dreaded it before, yet now, seeing and recognizing this hateful spot, I gladly embrace the alternative I shunned." Raspas drew his dagger, at which Morca stood back in surprise, but Raspas turned the knife and held it to his own throat, saying with solemn formality, "'Tis a better way, O friend. May the Gods have mercy on thee, Captain Morca, and spare thee from what thou most fear." So saying, he smiled sadly and slit his throat, stood frozen for an instant, then collapsed to the ground, his dagger clattering on the stones by his dead hand.

Morca wept to see yet another companion in adventure lost to him. Before he marched on he spent time to honor the Peoki warrior, son of a chief, with what decent burial the terrain and the tools at hand would allow. This task complete, Morca went on, into the heart of the forgotten city of the antique Rhexellites.

By now shadows had lengthened to merge into twilight. Morca fabricated a simple torch from the scanty supplies in his bag, using this to better view the shattered or corroded walls about him. Here and there he spied traces of old writing, never enough to tell him much save that the Rhexellites had dwelt there, and occasionally he happened upon surviving remnants of worn frescoes that once illustrated an age of supreme might and pride. He discerned glimpses of great armies on the march, feats of stern magic by powerful sorcerers. It intrigued him and sparked his fancy that the olden Rhexellites portrayed in these pictures were not the degenerate physical specimens against whom he had made war, but fair men like himself, untarnished by ages of wretched existence in sunless holes. About him the night closed in, and with his progress new shapes of ruin and wreckage rose up from the darkness, furtively presenting themselves to the feeble flicker of his torch.

Exploration in the night being profitless and fruitless, he sought for himself some form of secure shelter among the massy basalt blocks of that place. Morca peered into several square or rectangular buildings, but within he either found heaps of stony rubbish from fallen ceilings or, more ominous, mouths of burrows in the earthen floors which indicated egress, at least in the past, from beneath. Dismay at the possibility of once again confronting subterranean terrors turned him aside. He became aware in his wandering of an edifice larger than the rest, a vast low cube of walls surmounted by the debris of a toppled tower. A circuit of the walls revealed a single intact entrance (with two others sealed by rubble) which he could guard if the interior be safe; that proved solid, unbroken stone, with floors of granite flags that had never yielded to burrowers. This satisfied him, and he set up a solitary camp inside a cramped, cloistered cell adjoining a big inner court or plaza, the dissimilar enclosures connected solely via a defensible crawl space. Morca guessed, from his knowledge of recent Rhexellite manners, that the greater structure had constituted a temple in their heyday.

There he lay in full harness, hunched in a corner, striving to snatch a few hours of requisite slumber. The actuality eluded him, however, when the sounds of creeping and slithering at a remove in the darkness assailed his acute hearing. Surely unwelcome company moved about there at night, and it required no effort of imagination to conclude that foul creatures from beneath his feet roused themselves and went abroad when the upper world periodically feigned, as it will, the black underground world of the most debased sons of the olden Rhexellites. He heard the pattering of clammy feet invading the precincts of the supposed temple, noted the insidious noise of what could be claws scraping on corridor walls. He got up, posting himself at the opening of the cell. Then by a hint of rising crescent moon he saw them, white and spidery, naked, dead fish bodies lean and bony, with hairless heads and bulging wet eyes and slit mouths glistening with toothy needles. A surging horde of these, erupting from nowhere in the dark, had massacred a victorious but unaware army in the open. Here they were few, but he was only one.

One aware, that is, one ready, thoughtful and prepared. From out of his bag of arcane supplies he produced a cunningly devised nodule of strange elements which, when spoken to as friend, and massaged and blown upon with vigor, ignited with a flash and sent forth a blazing bolt like an electric arc, a handful of lightning ripped from the heavens and brought to earth. This way had shepherded him through the night of chaos and disaster when many a good man perished, and it availed him now. Morca's blast released cruel light, of an intensity that blinded him momentarily, and which sent the monsters reeling in agony amidst howls of animalistic rage and distress. They withdrew as fast as their lean limbs would carry them, and after the noise of their frantic retreat subsided, he heard them not again.

Morca laughed heartily and easily. He relaxed into his cubbyhole, saying to himself, "Why had I cause to fear? Raspas, I can reckon, saw these vermin tearing him, a morbid vision fit to quail the heart of even a brave man. Mine differed. It was not these filthy foes that the Tender showed me, that would end my days by the will of the Gods or whatever devils he serves. Those were true men who did me in, as he would have it. It follows, maybe, that I have not yet deviated from the path set for me. If that be the case, then the ancient loon's dire vision makes up a boon of the most sterling quality, for it assures me that no final peril can conceivably overtake me here. Men of sound race, enemies or otherwise, pass scarce in these parts."

Reasoning thus, and accepting thus to a major degree, Morca contented himself with the dreamful hope of a needful rest, unmolested further by craven hobgoblins marauding senselessly in the murk. He held to it as he reclined in an approximation of comfort, came to believe it as drowsiness bore him under its gentle weight. The jarring, reverberating notes of a solemnly tolling bell fostered renewed concern. Awake and clear headed on the instant, he listened breathlessly, upright and immobile, to the mournful chimes. Six times they rang, gave way to ominous stillness and silence. Morca would not forebear, but must learn the meaning of this thing. He got up and re-lighted his torch, and with that in one hand, sword in the other, ventured forth.

In the big hall he espied moving pinpoints of light, motes of twinkling illumination that seemed to hover and dart and spin in the air. Careful scrutiny disclosed no material source for these lost stars. "I like not that," he muttered. "It has a magical look. By the Gods, I would seek my sleep in the seat of elder sorcery! Here, once upon a time in eons best forgotten, the Rhexellites practiced mysterious rites and unhallowed enchanteries, through ages without number. I should know best that such accumulations of fearsome arcana leave indelible stains. Great Xenophor preserve me, but what have I stirred up by the paltry use of my arts?"

Now Morca would depart from that place and find safety in distance. His path out of the temple took him along one extended wall of the open court, then through a battered corridor leading to the exit.

Hardly had he gotten himself into motion when he discerned vague presences moving among the lights. He thought of shadows, only these stood out from the pitch darkness of the wide chamber, lesser shadows among the greater, and they moved like men. He beheld ethereal shapes of definitely human form, robed figures clustering together and waving oddly their arms and shifting their shod feet in unison, all of this occurring without sound, as in a dream. It appeared a ritual of a sort.

"Ghosts of the Rhexellite priests," thought Morca, "still practicing their trade, shades of mages miming the arts that brought them down. May their magic be also shade, without true substance."

He completed his wary walk along the wall and dashed into the corridor, making for the opening in the outer casement of the structure. When he emerged into the starry night the mystic bells tolled again six times. Then he realized that neither stars nor moon burned overhead—haze or cloud obscuring them—but that witch-fires danced in the air. They floated and swirled, tossed and driven by wind his senses denied. Morca took bearings, as best he remembered the lie of the place, making off through the ruins of the city to the west.

Immediately he happened upon a trio of those degenerate foul ones from the nether pits. A bolt of artificial lightning dispersed them. The next obstacle demanded considerably more ingenuity. Racing down a rubble-strewn avenue he again beheld wispy presences, shimmering shapes of faux humanity coalescing out of empty air. They appeared in disquieting numbers before him, and when he turned to double back on his trail he noted others behind. As the mirages assumed a deepening clarity he thought they differed from those within the temple. Indeed, he marked two distinct differences: these seemed to be men of war, accoutered in mail and beweaponed with sharp blades, wicked swords and daggers; and they appeared to take as great a notice of him as he of them.

Morca slipped between two cubic piles and ran, seeking escape. For a moment fear seized the stout Captain. He saw them clearly before he fled. These were not eidolons of the unworthy Rhexellites of a later era, but fine, hard men of a former hard age, spirits or strange survivals from a time when that race were fair to look upon like other noble peoples. What unmanned him, however fleetingly, was the nagging revelation that such as these might well be the furious opponents who mastered him in the vision of the Tender's oracle. It occurred to him that he was about to die, there, at that time and place, his fate ordained.

He entered into another avenue where the mystic warriors appeared before him. A full score of them closed in. He rushed into a narrow alley, stumbling over jagged chunks of masonry, came to face a blank wall that rose twice a man's height. He had no hope of scaling it so, with his pursuers at his heels Morca turned and, dropping his torch in his haste, thrust his way into a rubble choked opening leading into the nearest structure. There, within a small bare room of unadorned, polished stone surfaces, those others caught up with him. Then Morca knew no fear, for the Gods had cast Their dice, and what would be would. By the feeble light of the torch without the door he readied himself, seeing his enemies as black shapes pushing through the gap at him. That he might know them better he wrenched the pack from his back, retrieving and hurling down a fire globe that, with his prayer-like chant, burst into brilliance when the crystalline shell broke and flamed steadily. Morca saw hawk-faced soldiers grinning eagerly for the kill, appearing not as ghosts but as men of bone and sinew and healthy flesh wrapped in gleaming armor, hard metal that must ring under the blows of his sword.

Morca saw, and then Morca fought for his life. With a joyous cry of battle he tore into them, sword high and shield close, seeking death for all who would stand against him. If they be apparitions then no weapon of earthly material would suffice, but then, mere mists of former lives could not have harmed him. The evil magic of the ancient Rhexellites, still haunting this dead city with astounding potency, made its warriors substantial; therefore, Morca reasoned between rasps of hot breath, they could be destroyed, so he went at the task with a vengeance, slashing at them as they slashed at him. Forgotten as irrelevant was the vision of the Tender. What use for theories and abstruse calculations of fate when fighting need be done?

For this he lived, and if it be written so should he die. Until then rivers of fiery blood burned in his veins, more streams splashed the floor about him. The great sword of Captain Morca, Lord of Dyrezan, struck as a lunging snake that uncoils and brings terror to anything in range of its venomous fangs. He chopped into the living dead Rhexellites, cut them down, sent their limbs flopping to the floor and their heads spinning through the air, grimaces of startled dismay etched into those helmed faces. Their swords darted ever at him, piercing his shield, scraping his mail with a metallic clang, probing for his flesh. The stray point cut him, but he took the pain with laughter, ripped into them again. Quivering bodies stacked up in a semicircle at his feet, more staggered back with crippling wounds, yet never did they utter a word nor make any sound at all, not so much as a grunt of pain.

Morca fought until his arms were lead and his blade massy as an anvil in his weary right hand. His helmet spun away under a dazing stroke, his shield cracked and shivered to fragments at a bold blow. Three Rhexellite warriors still stood, battling like automata, their swords rising and falling and swinging as if choreographed to hellish music unheard. It seemed nigh the end. Morca, bereft of his finest arcane defenses, shouted or croaked any spell of power that came to mind, groping for one that would aid him in this moment of extremis. His opponents fought on, unchecked, that he could tell, even for the fraction of a second. Could he discover no limits to the baleful power of old that animated them?

He did, but not by his doing. Of a sudden the Rhexellites paused, then backed away and stood looking to themselves. Morca, driven to a wall, spied through the entrance of the chamber a faint radiance of a wholesome sort he well knew. Dawn had come. Now the Rhexellites turned to him, bowed gravely and saluted with their swords. They vanished, the seemingly living and the seemingly dead, departing without fanfare, simply ceasing to be, as if they had never been.

Morca said, sitting down heavily on the floor, "What, is it a game for them, that they fight only so long, testing the metal of their prey, and releasing him at the appointed hour, should he survive to see it? Maybe the noble Rhexellites were jesters, comics after their own fashion. It will not be my way today to tarry for them further, that I may confirm the hypothesis. Let me go from here while there is good getting."

So he rose, pain speaking from every tired joint and each crimson flesh wound, and he departed that edifice and went out into the dead city, where he aligned his steps by the sun and strode toward his shadow, quickly as his burdened body would bear him, to the west. Once the last ruins lay behind him, and a ridge of shelving stone peaks separated him from all sign of that place and its powers, then did he grant time to nursing the injuries of his mortal self. Against a boulder he sprawled, with his meager medicines about him while he practiced physic. Sleep he craved, but that he would forestall until he put leagues behind him.

Said Morca, "I guess it was not my time after all. I acted as I ever would, yet life remains to me, sweet and dear. Who knows when my time will come, or where that shall transpire? The Tender told me nothing of estimation, however valid his vision. A journey of unknown length stretches before me, as it does for all men. Raspas, thou wouldst have done better to stay and fight. Even now we might be boasting of our exploits together, spinning them wilder with the telling."

With that Morca braced himself for the long trek ahead. Home, splendid Dyrezan, lay somewhere to the west, across uncounted and uncharted leagues of desert and sea and wilderness, with possible enemies lurking past every milestone. As far as he had thus far traveled, his journey had barely begun. He dared not deny the chance of further adventures on the march.

That pleased him. Captain Morca set off, one step at a time, blessing with a grin whatever came before his eyes.

THE VOICE OUT OF DYREZAN

The wizard Jacob Bleek, since notorious in whispered report, once went traveling in his youth, striding to the ends of the earth (and beyond, as it was known in his day) seeking the totality of esoteric wisdom and power that would make him the greatest mage of the ages. Especially would he know of Dyrezan, the fabulous lost city of the ancients, about which so many odd stories were told: that it had been the capitol of an empire of sorcerers back in the misty dawn of civilization; that it had flourished for what, by mortal man's reckoning, seemed well nigh an eternity; that its great lords of might and magic had, through their incredible mastery of the arts arcane, raised their glorious metropolis from the earth and sent it soaring into the sky, there to hover majestically as a portal to heaven. All this Bleek had heard, so he would go there, in his pride of prowess, to where whatever remained of Dyrezan was said to be, and there plumb as he could its hitherto unfathomable secrets.

This he did, after a journey marvelous for its adventures and perils. Came a darkling afternoon in a far barren land, where nothing living moved and scarce a weed clung tenaciously to the rocks, and there within a curiously round valley guarded by a ring of jagged peaks he found the olden site of Dyrezan. Much later he wrote of what he beheld and learned in that place, and what follows, very freely translated, makes up the core of his account.

"Nought survived to the eye but a chaotic jumble of stony wreckage scattered across the enclosed level plain. Nowhere did I espy evidence of coherent ruin, as one would expect from an antique city that had crumbled under time and the elements. Truly I could believe this finely strewn rubble had toppled from a great height, in accord with the wilder legends. I passed within the radius of the devastation, hoping that I could discern revealing traces of writing on the shattered blocks. This I found not, but within I felt a presence, an emanation from the spoiled terrain and the sour air which bespoke of lingering magical influences. Something unseen yet vaguely felt dwelt there, a fading power that tarried long after its physical ornamentation had ceased. I would know what it was, that I might learn, so with the advent of pure night I cleared a circle and laid out the materials of my trade, there drew a figure of unearthly geometry on the gritty ground, and by the wavering light of a fashioned torch I brought forth my priceless books of strange matters, deriving of them through careful consultation the proper gestures and recitations that would brew a calling from beyond. This I did, and of a sudden the still air roiled with surging wind, and a blot of black cloud appeared which spread and obscured the stars, and witch-fires danced on the rocks around, bathing me in cold radiance. Up from the earth appeared a semblance of form, a patch of softly glowing mist that mimicked the shape of a man, and this eidolon coalesced into a definite image, and I gazed upon a tall and strong gentleman, fair of face and hard in muscle, clothed in robes of white.

"Out of this form came a voice saying, 'I awake, who thought not to awake, yet feel to have slept the world away. What truth explains this?' I told him of my coming, of my purpose and my actions, and inquired of him his name and station. He said, 'I be Morca, exemplar of wizards, skilled in the arts and ways of the universe and the Gods, faithful minister as well to Skyrax, who rules eternally as king in everlasting Dyrezan. This I know, and much else besides, only I confront mystery now. Last I recall beauteous sights and the wonders of Dyrezan my home, then awaken here amidst this murky scene of desolation. How and why have you carried me to this miserable land?'

"I laughed, and chuckling with my knowing mirth made clear to him the reality of the situation. He cared not for what he heard. 'Dyrezan fallen?' he cried. 'Then it is so, as the philosophers tell, that with infinite time even impossibilities must come to pass. I, too, merely a feeble specter of my invincible glory? I would not credit this, yet when I crack my brain I do remember a day of death; a good death it was, too, one I would have chosen had the decision been mine; and here I be again, whole but not entire. So you speak truth. What, then, will you have?'

"Advising this Morca of my great and baleful power, I insisted that he deliver over to me all the knowledge of the ancients, that I

174

might use it for my purposes. I demanded a detailed catalogue of the spells and enchanteries that open the celestial doors of the cosmos, that grant audience to the most high Gods, that master the will of men. From this boon I should glean, I told him, the wisdom that would gain for me eternal life and strength and lordship over all. At my statement he laughed.

"'O Jacob Bleek, it is with amusement that I consider your request, or your command, as you would have it. Fear for you I feel not, I who have been tested in my time by the mighty and overcome them all; I who am dead, and dread not the loss of life. How will you harm me, should I cross you? Send me back into the shade from which you plucked me? Surely there lies my destiny once you have your fill of me. Would you call to the great Gods to curse me? I, who was always favored of Them, who groveled especially before Xenophor, the ultimate King of time and creation, need not concern myself with Their displeasure. Never needst I seek Them, for ever was I close to Them. Rather it is you who must fear Them, you who are far from Them, weakly striving to unmask Their secrets.

"'Yet with light heart I choose cooperation. Harken, Bleek, that you may know of the wonders in store for you, if you should pursue them to the end.' And this Morca told me:

"'We men of Dyrezan, the children of the Gods, rose above our barbarous fellows through our quest for the magical properties that animate all matter and energy in the universe. In remote eons, ages distant even to me, my noble fathers conceived the principles underlying the esoteric arts and mastered them as had none before nor, I suspect, since. They deduced the spells of attraction and repulsion, the charms that sway the unwary mind, the enchantments that deliver contact with the ethereal powers that infest the cosmos. As their skills increased they dared more, and came the time when they built for themselves a city of magic, the holy citadel of Dyrezan, and that it might not be fouled by the muck of the world they united their brains for a great task, and with spells supreme lifted Dyrezan from the earth and hurled it into the sky, ever to hover like a cloud of bright marble and strong granite and gleaming crystal. Nor did they stop there, but grew greater in wisdom and power and knowledge by the year, so that in my time, five hundred generations after the founding, Dyrezan had attained complete mastery over the earth, and insights into the mysterious spheres which can not be sought in geography.

"'You wish to know, Bleek, as we knew? Let me tell you of these things in sample. In my library I possessed a book, penned by a dead hand, that disclosed to me the whereabouts of the portal into the ninth plane, the realm of the Hidden Feasters, beings that exist to suck at the souls of men, yet which can be dealt with for a price, and turned to fearsome allies. Have you heard of them, Bleek? Would you accept these adversaries as friends, that you may slaughter your enemies at your beck? I can tell you how to do it, what you will gain, what it will cost you. Believe that I know.

"'There is a spell so powerful that the only copy, inscribed in the flayed skin of a foreign queen, was kept under guard in the lowest vaults of the dungeons of King Skyrax. Beloved of him as I was, he granted me access to that frightful document that I might employ it should his enemies forget themselves. I had to learn it by heart, memorizing the weird words of a lost tongue, and I know it still. Would you have me recite it to you, Bleek?

"'There is an enchantment of vibrating flame, a destructive agency unleashed from within the very fabric of the universe, that may be used to annihilate whole armies at a stroke. We of Dyrezan considered it beneath us to wield such a weapon, for we conquered all without it and feared becoming soft if our martial skills were lain aside; but I know the enchantment, Bleek, and am qualified to teach.

"'Speak I only of power? Yet you also crave knowledge. Turn this in the window of your mind and behold it. There are ancient fains of forbidden lore, cities lying already in legendary ruins during my life, where all the chronicles of history, human and pre-human, are inscribed on walls of imperishable metal that neither wears nor corrodes. Many of these places, lost in remote fastnesses, must linger yet to this day. I can speak to you maps, Jacob Bleek, maps that will carry your feet to repositories of elder lore unknown to your people. Does the possibility of reading the ages excite you?

"'Do the hateful bonds of time fill you with detestation? O Bleek, I realize you are skillful, one who may call up the misty souls of the ancient departed and converse, but would not you do more? Let me tantalize you with the prospect of casting your mind through time, so that you may, however dimly, perceive directly not just that which has been, but to some degree what will be. If I explain the method, you will, as you like, taste pragmatic glimpses of the future. Has that not a sweet savor?

"'But if you be so big a man as you claim, you shall not rest at this, but require more, much more; the ultimate attainment, the approach to

the Gods, Lords of all things. This grim and mighty task I have
shunned, as have all who revere the Gods. Enough for us that we are
Their playthings, to use and abuse as They will, for Their ends, for
Their sport or amusement. That is the way of flesh, of space, of
eternity, as They decree. Why should I argue, who have been, for
whatever inscrutable reasons, blessed? In your case, however, that
must not satisfy. You would gaze into the million unblinking eyes of
great Xenophor, the Creator and the Destroyer, and you would treat
with Him. So be it. There is a way, a means so secret and so dangerous
that I hesitate to think on it. As a kindness, Bleek—call it that!—I can
grant it to you. Does that stoke your hunger?

"'All this I can provide, and will, Jacob Bleek, as you crave, only
pay heed to what I tell you now. By the standards of my race, the
nobles and mages of departed Dyrezan, you are but an insect, Bleek, a
pathetic, pitiful creeping thing, wallowing in the foetid mire of your
unjustified hubris and flimsy dreams bordering on craven madness.
Seek you the marvels and powers of Dyrezan? I tell you that the
magical strength that made us a wonder in the land and throughout the
ages was bred in our bones, part of our natural substance. I take it as a
jest that an upstart like you, with your handful of books and bag of
potions, could dare scale the airless heights we considered tame
foothills, much less climb the crags we deemed best left alone. Your
greedy quest is for nought, Bleek, for a thousand years of study would
not make you what I was at birth, certainly not what I came to be.
Worm, you lack the necessary essence. Go back to your herd and
dazzle them with your childish tricks. Leave off groping for morsels
too rich for your tongue; give up this grasping for knowledge broader
than your brain; forget the Gods, who, should you annoy Them, are
like to spit your existence away amidst mocking laughter!'

"Seized by anger" (so wrote Bleek) "so intense that it tore with
teeth at my soul, I shrieked my hatred of this dead Morca and, without
wise deliberation, uttered the olden words that reversed my spell and
cast him back into the everlasting gloom. He disappeared, he and that
monstrous voice of his out of the doomed past, the terrible sounds
trailing away in a mirthless chuckle as they ceased their assault on my
ears. Not long thereafter I recollected myself, realizing that for all of
his sneering promises I had learned nothing, and I made to raise him
again, he or another like, but this task I could not accomplish. I had
drawn so upon the magic of the place that it had weakened, would not
obey my desires. So ended this hopeful episode. I would find what I

sought elsewhere than among the rubbish, discarded by time, of Dyrezan."

His writings, as they have come down to us, record that the wizard Jacob Bleek continued his eerie quest, yet fail to establish how it concluded. Surely he refrained from surrendering his goals, but history provides no evidence that he ever succeeded. History, of course, plays pranks on its scholars, and far be it from us to assume that Bleek settled for the common lot, nor that he would quit his titanic endeavors this side of death.

SKYRAX, LORD OF DYREZAN

In eons past mighty Dyrezan, that great citadel of civilization fashioned by powerful magicians through strange arts at the dawn of time, dominated the earth. Cunning were those men, masters of incredible secrets wrested from nature and the Gods, wise and noble too, and having conceived their fabulous city they thought it proper that it should rule all and outshine all, so they made themselves an empire of sword and mind, and they builded themselves a city of gold and crystal towers and walls of living granite willed from the bedrock of a fertile valley where it was believed that the Olden Gods once dwelt, and where some of Their essence still lingered. Glorious was the city, yet not sufficiently befitting the pride of its masters, so in their hubris they delved further into the arcana of cosmic lore, amassing learning and wisdom, and in one incredible day they raised up Dyrezan from the surface of the world and sent it hovering in the air above the valley, to be forever known in story and song as the Sky City; forever, that is, so long as the remnant forces of the Gods prevailed, and so long as Their favor endured. For even in Dyrezan forever is a long time.

Greatest of those wizards who established the empire and set soaring the city was Skyrax, fierce warrior and supreme sorcerer, whom his fellows honored with the title of King and granted to him ruler-ship for life. A truly awesome man, they considered it nice and agreeable to his honor that his son, also an eminent worthy, should succeed him, and so it proved, and his son after him, and so forth, as they imagined it, throughout eternity, one Skyrax following another, each taken for the image of his sire, each treated as the eidolon of the original Skyrax. So those brilliant magicians would have it, and thus it must be. There came a time, after five hundred generations (and quite

179

long generations at that), when the latest Skyrax assumed the throne, robed in purple with collar of gold and stripes of crimson, and all praised him to his face.

Appearances have been known to belie reality. Despite the protestations of tradition, the more recent descendants of the gigantic Skyrax of old could not fill the prints of his feet, nor did they try. Born to ultimate power, assured—as if by law of nature—of their ascendancy, they knew no testing hardship, but basked in soft living, whiling away their years in aimless splendor. An easy and comfortable life they led, none more so than the latest Skyrax, he of the five hundredth or so generation of Kings. His kingdom soared and it throve, or failed to thrive as the case might be, while he cavorted and taxed himself with amusement. He was Skyrax, and that should be good enough for all the world.

One man disagreed.

Albragon, that grim, jaded old nobleman, adept of the black arts, ostensibly loved for his smiles, genuinely feared for his frowns, said to his courtiers, "Surely we deem the first Skyrax a great man, for it is recorded in the treasured annals of misty antiquity that he was stern in command, unsurpassed in magical skills, a genius of dynamic dreams and bold desires, therefore innately suited to lording over the Earth and over us all. Who of our day, I ask you, emulates him best? Surely not the pusillanimous toad that squats on the throne now, but I, Albragon, who embodies those olden traits of virtue, who justly dreams of attaining power to shape destiny." His lackeys agreed fulsomely, clustering before him where he stately sat, heavyset and dark, in the marble hall of his fathers, shouting their approval of his ideas. Replied in a thin, high voice his chief servant, the clever Thocratis, with a nod of his elderly bald head, "I perceive signs that big change comes. These many nights I have experienced a recurrent dream, a valid dream hailing from the black pits of the Other-world, in which I beheld a mountain crumble away from its weak foundations, and a vaster mountain still rise up in its place, thrust up amidst rampant earthquakes and eruptions of pure gold. This dream I could interpret for you, Albragon, if you wish." Said his master, "Necessity lacks, O Thocratis, for honest dreams sent from strange and far places are meat for my table. I read it as do you, my friend, and ask if others among your high body would see as we." For Thocratis, though in thrall to Albragon, was himself a member of the Council of Twenty, the score of the prestigious august who decided the administrative affairs of

Dyrezan, "by favor of Skyrax and the Gods."

Thocratis frowned, said pensively, "I fear that many hold to stale notions, bound in chains of rigid formality and cumbersome etiquette. It is not to such that you must look for support. Instigation is not their suit, nor will they heed the fitting and natural blowing of the wind. On the other hand, once the wind blows, many there are who will lean with it. Create, O great one, the conditions that satisfy, and surely they will fall into accord with you."

"So be it," said Albragon. He pondered darkly, grand thoughts chasing across his formidable features, then dismissed all save Thocratis, whose views he currently esteemed. "Good man, sit at table with me. Later you may accompany me into the dungeons, where by way of gratitude I will allow you to join me in delicious amusements at the expense of certain new captives, unfortunate and forsaken guests from the valley. Truly, I tire of a regime that requires me to conceal my peculiar pleasures. I would have openness in all things, including genial ferocity. Yes, you and I will make merry, laughing at the misery we cunningly induce. Screams are heartier to the ear than songs, I say. Meantime, let us formulate gigantic designs. The portents are right, the goal worthy. This weakling of a Skyrax must go, for fate decrees that I shall rule as next king of Dyrezan."

Meanwhile Skyrax, in name eternal King of the eternal city, whiled away the morn in games with his attendants. Slight of stature he was, and feeble of manner, judged silly (in their private thoughts) by those who served him daily. "A six and a nine!" he cried, squatting among his trinkets on the flagged marble floor of his palace chamber of crystal and gold, with rare gems laid in silver settings on the walls, and a multi-colored painting of exotic heavenly scenes on the ceiling. There he gamed long with his people, until a messenger appeared to annoy him.

"An ambassador enters the city," announced the fellow, "on behalf of the Princess Riena. He seeks audience." Skyrax idly waved a hand, saying abruptly, "Tell him I bow busily before matters of state. Tell him I tour the fields of the valley below. Tell him I am deceased, but keep him from me for now. Make an official appointment. I will see him by the by, after I have transacted"—the King laughed—"after I have transacted important business." His game resumed.

The account of this seemingly trivial incident sat not well with Morca, Captain Most High of the Royal Guard, and a respected lord and mage in his own right. Strong of arm he was, and quick with sword, as well as keen with magic, even by the lofty standards of Dyrezan. Well-formed youth gave him strength and vigor, harsh practice and harsher experience skill at arms, relentless study wisdom and vibrant knowledge. He passed for a cheerful, easy gentleman as a rule, but not now. "In Vasgarra they will take this for an intolerable slight," he pointed out to his subordinate officers, "and verily so. The King must marry—the royal line must go onward—and no woman is better fashioned by birth and education for the station of Queen of Dyrezan than Riena, famed noblewoman of our loyal and enlightened province of Vasgarra. This union would transfer the vitality of her race to future sons of Skyrax, a connubial formulation most necessary at this juncture. Our Skyraxes grow thin and peaked. That we can not allow, nor abide."

"It will be," casually replied Portian, a High Guardsman and bosom companion of Morca, scarcely less fine a man than his friend. "The King frolics as he will, yet he too shall eventually bow to the will of the city. It is ever the way."

"I should greet the ambassador," said Morca, "in order to salve the wounds to decorum. I gather that Riena follows swiftly, and no ill report must inflame her ears." "Aye, her opinion counts enormously," observed Portian. "Her folk are not so under our thumb that they readily endure slights. Also, she owns popularity in our city, having made good impression during last year's ceremonial visit. Come, let us speak with her mouthpiece and soothe him before he scalds." So they did.

Where cleverness and wisdom reign unchecked, few secrets are kept. Shortly Albragon knew all these developments, which he folded into his schemes. After midnight he toiled in speculative thought with Thocratis, snacking late on bread and cheese and wine while they discoursed. "This Riena is the key," intoned the great nobleman. "She is loved, she will be followed. Bring her into my orbit, and she will cement my position. I calculate the ramifications, find cheer in what they foretell, am inclined to act swiftly. All come together in this instant of time: the affront to the ambassador from Vasgarra, the immediate appearance of this fair lady, the foolishness of the King, and my boundless desires. You and I shall tie these factors with unbreakable cords. Around whose neck will those cords form a noose?"

"Yours, my lord," cautioned Thocratis, adding hastily, "yours, that is, if you make one misstep. As I understand it, your plan requires the benevolent glances of Riena's countenance beaming upon you, to the exclusion of the current simpleton."

"So it does," admitted Albragon. He smiled, a hideous leer dredged from the bottoms of foul pits. "Yet doubtless you will observe that, based on our previous short acquaintance, she extended to me no great regard. I see that as a trifling matter. Her people (mere cattle, fit only for slaves) know little of our arts and acumen, nothing of mine. I can bend her to my will, against her own. A shabby trick I grant, one not likely to endure, but sufficient to complete the immediate task. She will serve her purpose, however temporary, and my destiny shall be fulfilled. King Albragon; it has a ring, think you, Thocratis?"

"In the interests of policy—" began the councilor.

"I know, I know. Should I style myself the new Skyrax, tradition will be obeyed, quite enough to please the mob. I accept that—" Albragon chuckled—"in the name of compromise."

Morca mollified the ambassador, gently implored the King to bestow audience. "Truly he will bask in your graciousness," said the Captain, "and speak glowingly to the lady, who is all charm, and already eager to fawn at your feet, Your Highness." "Out of condescension to you, my friend," sighed Skyrax, "I concede." Indeed the King did, when he thought of it, love Morca, and pay homage to his fine qualities. So it was settled, and Skyrax admitted the Vasgarran ambassador with his train, delighting them with honeyed words in the majestic Hall of Receival, an octagonal room with walls composed of varying shades of rose and amber quartz. There important deeds were discussed, protocols arranged, the timing of the Princess's grand entrance into Dyrezan affirmed.

This gave Morca great joy, for he dearly wished once more to behold the lovely Riena, his inmost reasons having nothing to do with the aggrandizement of Skyrax or the monumental city of the sky. When first she had come out of deference and common policy, the Captain had conceived a fierce passion for the woman, a flame which had not begun to die, but had rather flared forth into an inferno during the many months since. Then he had acted as her escort, reveling in her closeness, and had before she departed imagined (while doubting himself, of course) that she covertly returned his regard.

The Princess arrived, she and her retinue rising from the circular plain far below, soaring into the airy void within columns of humming ethereal force, the mental emanations of a battery of chosen magicians. Like it was to standing on solid ground, and like it was to drifting within a cloud; a pale mist closed around them, lifted them from the vulgar clay, propelled them by degrees into the sky. Came an odd moment when disembodied voices beckoned them forth, and the young woman and her people stepped forward onto a dais of orichalc. "Welcome, most beloved Princess Riena," cried Morca, "welcome to glorious Dyrezan, which we pray you shall ever regard as your home." He spoke those trite and formal words from the heart, speaking more as a man than as instrument of state. Whatever Skyrax or the Gods might deign, Morca wanted her there. Said the Princess, with little formality, "My happiness radiates as the sun when greeted by my faithful friend of the heavens. All will be well, if I have you again by my side." Morca was required by law and custom to pronounce other words gay and fey, but surely certain of his companions felt that he botched the job after the lady spoke, for the man came across as tongue-tied and verbally inept thereafter. To be fair to him, any young man of high-born tastes might stutter in the presence of so perfect and regal a representative of femininity. Though the proportions of Riena were wholly human, she managed to outshine, some said, the many-bosomed and multi-eyed Goddess of Love Erinaellas, who grants to each female a dollop of Her sensual allure. Riena, it seemed—with her flowing golden hair, healthy white skin, gentle and minutely sculpted features, exuberant smile and attractive curves—had gained at birth far more than her share of the Goddess's blessing, while good living and carefully nurtured tastes had granted her still more.

Morca led the Princess and her party from the Eyrie, as the magical entrance platform into Dyrezan was styled, and along the Avenue of the Ages, that great roadway lined with life-sized statues of legendary heroes and colossal monuments to each cherished God, which passed between mansions of nobility and past barracks and across the wide green belt of the Gardens of the King, a splendid park enfolding the center of the city, where amid lovingly fashioned woods and the joys of sylvan scenery the populace were encouraged to play. From there they progressed to the Central Plaza, a large circular pavement centering on the Spire of Xenophor, an obelisk dedicated to the chief God of the Dyrezanians, raised in half-forgotten epochs and capped with a dazzling clear diamond bigger than a man's head, a jewel the likes of which the world had never seen elsewhere, both for its size and the fact that it twinkled of its own light even by darkest night. Over all loomed the mighty towers of Dyrezan, great pinnacles of stone and colored glass faced with pure lustrous gold, radiating a brilliance that, caught by the clear rays of the sun, gave to the metropolis its other cherished title of the City of Burning Gold. There, in the Plaza, the crowds thronged in their thousands. "Hail the Princess Riena," they cried. "Hail the new Queen!" The object of their affection curtseyed, rose and threw back her arms as if to embrace them all, ruffling the many veils of her exotically foreign dress. The masses roared their approval. The Plaza fronted the Royal Palace, that grand and formidable castle where, from a distant window in an upper tier, the King made an appearance, bowing and waving gracefully, then dodging back into the shadows of his intricate edifice, his minimal duty done for the nonce.

Morca conducted his charge to her temporary quarters in a small but stylish building adjoining the palace. Arrangements settled, they found themselves alone for a brief passage. Riena's brow darkened and she said with petulant asperity, "Born I was to do what I must do, so it shall be done, yet it seems that even your great King might stoop to the occasion and greet me before his people in person, as a man, rather than as a demi-god from on high." Morca, chagrined by the justice of her remarks, his loyalty to his monarch, and his unquenchable longing, merely replied lamely, "Perhaps Skyrax tends to the overly formal before his lessers, but rest assured that in private, when that moment quickly comes, he shall favor you as his rarest treasure. No man of sense and breeding could do otherwise." "Speak you from authority?" asked Riena.

"It must be," muttered her escort.

Riena laughed lightly, a series of musical tones strummed on a celestial lyre. "I would know your mind, O Morca," said she. "Of my previous adventure to your astounding city, I remember your companionship the most. Hard you strove to please and to win me to your people. Often I thought—deny this if you will—that you acted from the heart rather than duty. A curious fancy, I suppose, yet one that appealed. Of all the grandees of Dyrezan, you struck me as he most innately kingly."

Morca reddened and, just perceptibly, shuddered. "Not as a jest may I claim that," he said with evident embarrassment. "Skyrax reigns here, now, forever, and always. It is the way of things, the way in which I place all my trust. None can change that, even if he would." They gazed into one another's eyes for a space, until the Princess blushed and turned away. Whispered she, as if to herself, "I rebel against the 'mustness' of this world. With all its bountiful fascinations, why should there not be scope for 'want'?"

Albragon and his retainers lurked at the edge of the Plaza, observing the continuing pageantry of songs and music, ignoring the speeches of minor dignitaries. Said the nobleman to Thocratis, "Mark you, she lodges in the guest hall. Her sojourn there will be fleeting, I presume, yet the location is ideal." "Aye, my Lord, once whisked into the palace we could scarcely approach her." "Then the time is right," decided Albragon, "and critical. Before another day dawns the iron-shod wheels of my destiny shall begin to roll, grinding down everything in their path. Let us strike." "Indeed we shall," agreed Thocratis, "as you determine in your magnificence. However—"

"You disapprove?" growled Albragon.

"Impossible," gasped Thocratis. "It does occur to me, however, that Morca sticks close. He is a brave fellow, arcanely wise, of foolish fealties, hot-tempered to boot, and he keeps a close eye out for irregularities. His presence at or near the scene might prove awkward."

"I will remove him," said Albragon darkly.

To Morca's astonishment he received in his chambers that evening an invitation to dine and treat with no less than the great and terrible Albragon, the most powerful nobleman of the city. It was an honor of sorts, though the Captain cared not for the man, would rather have kept himself about the Royal Palace and its precincts that night; the messenger, however, alluded blandly to "pressing matters of public interest at this momentous occasion," hinting that revelations were in store concerning issues vital to the King and his chosen wife. The furtive nature of the business intrigued and disturbed Morca, who doubted the good nature of his offered host, but he would know more, deeming it a dutiful requirement, so he agreed to heed the apparently friendly summons. Before setting out he retired to his conjuring room, closeting himself alone to cast crystals and magic powders in order to analyze the signs. They did not read well. Wondering what the portents foretold, he embarked warily on his mission to Albragon.

"Yes, I marry," said the King to his ministers, licking from his thin lips the sweet wine he had imbibed in lieu of a wholesome meal. "Settle it as you wish, but plague me not with the details. I will keep about the house a decent woman with a pretty face to amuse my underlings and impress my foreign subjects, only I will never tolerate any abrogation of my life and pleasures. I am Skyrax, so these rules and niceties do not apply."

Morca arrived at the onyx castle, heavily fortified (both materially and psychically), of Albragon, where he was immediately inducted by thralls through gloomy passages to the immense dining hall illuminated by blue arcs of light hanging in curtains from the concave ceiling. At the big table which could seat fifty the resident Lord sat alone awaiting him, a heavy bear of a man wrapped in gold-laced black cloak, with fleshy features and grizzled hair. Albragon greeted him expansively as if they were old friends, actually rising to honor him, then dismissed the servants once the food was served. It was an excellent repast of unusual meats and delicate accompanying sauces, graced with an assortment of old wines. Morca relished the cuisine, not so much the conversation, which he thought did not live up to its promise. "It is uncommon," began Albragon, "for the Eternal Monarch of Dyrezan to select an outlander for mate. I have consulted the annals, studied the historical developments of prior occurrences. We must be alive to cultural difficulties." This he said, and much more to the same and little purpose, all of it rather conventional talk of a sort heard in the city during previous months. Of revelations he broached none, nor fresh ideas. As the hours—yes, hours—passed Morca squirmed and fidgeted in his silver chair, for he found the meeting increasingly pointless. He replied at intervals, casually and evenly, to every point the great man put forth, but truly there seemed no pressing justification to the drift of their chatter. Nevertheless, midnight came and went before Morca could appropriately escape.

The Princess Riena having completed her bath, her women dried her naked loveliness with soft towels before wrapping her in a filmy gown of sheer silk and leaving her to herself. It was Riena's custom in her comfortable palace in Vasgarra to repair to her bed chamber and read a while—mainly olden poems of fanciful romance—before retiring. This evening, however, in this strange place in a strange city, where interior lights burned by themselves without fire, set ablaze by the primordial power of the Gods, she found her accustomed program radically altered, nor with her consent. Indeed, she did not even leave the room of baths before her progression was interrupted by a weird appearance. Suddenly an old man stood opposed to her at the far end of the room, where no ingress was possible; an old man with scanty hair and wreathed in the robes of nobility. Riena started, glanced about wildly, felt a thrill of supernatural fear, then recollected where she was, in a city where strangeness was commonplace. Therefore she summoned her courage and her ire, demanding with the coldness of offended regal pride, "Who are you? How come you here? What require you of me?"

The apparition grinned, responding in a high, cracked voice, "O Riena, angel of Vasgarra, your Lord and Master Skyrax of Dyrezan grants you this gift, the first of many." The unbidden figure did not approach, but laid on a marble bench built into the marble wall a small box of ebony, sealed and unadorned. "Treasure to treasure," said he, before he vanished forthwith, leaving no trace that he had been save the alluring presence of the little package.

Riena remained frozen in place for long moments, stunned by the alarming nature of the apparition's coming and going. Then she bethought herself that Skyrax might well be the sort of disagreeably affable man to pull a stunt like this one—it accorded with her opinion of him as fey and unreliable—thus she advanced at last with light, hesitant steps toward the box. She picked it up with both hands, held it at arm's length, examined it closely. It was not a heavy burden. She raised the box in one hand, brushing aside her long tresses with the other, brought the thing to her ear and shook it gently. Nothing inside rattled. Curiosity and eagerness overcame her. She sat on the bench by the tiled bath pool, popped open the box.

A bright flash of searing white light blinded her. A gush of thick, oily, acrid smoke burst forth from the container, coursing into her open mouth and nostrils, choking her. Her brain went numb, her mind and thoughts softening and running like heated honey. A harsh, guttural voice noxious with hatred and disdain bellowed and sneered, barking stern and cruel commands, pounding its vicious message into her skull. Riena sagged against the wall, oblivious to the room about her, but still she could not help but hear and listen to every word.

With the dawn Morca arose to resume his duties, to be met at the Royal Palace by Portian, ever the bearer of the latest news. He did not fall down on the job this day. "The King has come round," said he. "His best advisors talked him into line, and he wishes the ceremony to proceed immediately. The fair lady is also in tune with these developments. 'No need for delay,' says she. You know, Morca, I get the feeling that Riena is driving matters, which is more than I understood to be the case only yesterday. Then I imagined her distracted."

The Captain ignored the mocking leer and conspiratorial wink of his companion, shrugged somberly and replied, "Of course it had to be. So much has been publicly proclaimed that even our great King could not tarry. The people grow restless, both for the connubial festivities and for an heir of quality. Let it be done and over." Morca went to the King, found that all was as he had been told, began the process of appointing guardsmen to their stations within and about the palace.

In the bowels of his castle Albragon said, "My skill at high arts has been honed and perfected through years of experimentation, openly where advisable, secretly when circumstances demand. I doubt not the efficacy of my potion, but of your hand in these activities, Thocratis, I require surety. All must go as planned, or we are dead before we draw another breath. Merely approaching the Princess, at my behest, without royal permission is crime." "None shall learn," averred Thocratis, "of your part in this day or last evening from my mouth. I pledge my faith." "And well rewarded you shall be," snapped Albragon, "as promised. Mastery of the Council of Twenty is no small boon. I deem that yours, if you bring them around and all goes well. More rewards I can bestow, to my faithful liege-man, in time."

"You honor me, I think, beyond my worth," said Thocratis, with a nod of his bald pate, "though I bask in your estimation of my value. Be easy in mind, however, when I tell you, Lord, that your plan marches apace, and toward a destination certain. Your token of respect to the Princess has by now achieved its purpose, limited only by the soundness of your craft, which we both know to be unlimited. So that is done. I have insinuated certain ideas into the Council: the extreme importance of Riena's views, the absolute necessity of new, lively blood for an old, tired line. As you can imagine, I found no need to fabricate these concerns. The Council is primed. We need merely lead them, with the Princess's aid, into an unexpected channel, at the bottom of which lies a treacherous marsh, in which they and all shall be thoroughly mired before they regain wits to back out."

Albragon roared with laughter. "A joyous image!" he shouted happily. "It gladdens me to deal with a man whose heart matches my own. I say this cloudy burg needs a shaking up. Mark my words, it will get one."

On this day the Princess Riena would wed the King of Dyrezan. The many avenues converging on the Central Plaza thronged with merry citizenry, bedecked in their finest attire. The noblemen of the city and their ladies trooped in large processions of family, honored friends, gaggles of servants. At each intersection stood guardsmen in armor, their swords sheathed but ready, their expected function that of maintaining order and squashing boisterous disturbances; light duty certainly, but that seldom called for in a metropolis of calm heads and fearless. The King and his people waited in the Receiving Hall of the palace, where the ceremonies would be completed once the Princess arrived.

She came. Surrounded by her train of Vasgarran advisors, guards, and maid servants she strode barefoot through the streets, according to custom, dressed in a gown of white dripping with scintillating jewels, woven with threads of gold, and bordered with frills of platinum, her head held high, her gaze fixed ahead. The ecstatic crowds went crazy at her passing, restrained from hurling themselves at her feet only by the dour guards who efficiently shielded her, gently but firmly. A commonly accepted feeling reigned in the city, a clear sense rarely spoken aloud yet shared by most, deeming her presence there necessary, holding that her union with the might and majesty of Dyrezan was critical to the health of the body politic. Something, they thought (if they carried the idea so far as reason), was not right in Dyrezan—the times grew tired and lackluster, perhaps—but she would put it right. Maybe she exemplified something the city had lost. If so, in her essence it had been found again.

At the huge double doors to the palace Morca stood guard with his handful of subordinates, his task to ensure that only those invited to the wedding entered therein. He nodded formally and greeted politely with few words the Princess as she mounted the steps and passed the doors. She acknowledged him pleasantly, then was gone. Portian risked craning his neck for a final glimpse, to spy her return glance if it transpired. It did not, which he assumed was the way of royalty; not always an easy life, he gathered. Morca curtly nodded, with sober countenance, to each great Lord of Dyrezan as he entered: the graybeard Lantonias, head of the Council of Twenty, and the other nineteen ancients of that body, including the subtle Thocratis; the grandly complacent Albragon, who came today dressed himself as a king; and the several other wise and worldly noblemen and mages of the best and oldest families, among them Harmon the Seer who dreamed extravagant truths, Nantrech the Explorer who had adventured to the corners of the earth in decades past, Falcro of the Seven Mysteries who read olden books in forgotten languages and knew by heart their unfathomable secrets.

In the skies above the palace strange signs appeared, weird twinkling lights or bright, swooping streamers like stars and comets torn from the fabric of night, and hazy forms like wispy clouds that molded themselves into unusual geometrical shapes; signs the result of the many conjurings undertaken throughout Dyrezan to mark the day and to peel back the pages of the future that destiny might be ascertained. Not all of the signs predicted good, but then they never could—the virtues of the future were never monolithic—and the vast majority undoubtedly did betoken great tidings, amazing events, bountiful possibilities. Any educated and practiced sorcerer could see that much, to discern meaning as he chose.

The selected guests took their places in the hall, from which the chairs had been removed so that all stood to attention in honor of the bride, all save the King, Skyrax, Supreme Lord of Dyrezan, who sat in full robes of office upon his gigantic throne of solid gold with its spiraling patterns of inlaid emeralds and rubies. A tall golden crown he wore on his small head, a crown that seemed to dwarf the man yet render him invincible, for it signified all the power in the world.

At the nonchalant flick of his fingers the holy priests of Xenophor came forth to invoke His favor on the day's proceedings, while the Princess commenced her solemn march up the aisle between the host of guests. When she stood before the King, the High Priest intoned his blessing in Great Xenophor's name, and that of Erinaellas. The King, too, spoke these words, according to custom, then doffed his crown, rendering himself, for this instant, man rather than ruler. The High Priest asked of him, "Have you chosen?" and he replied gravely, "I choose this woman as my consort." The High Priest asked of Riena, "Have you chosen?" and she replied, proudly and loudly, in a voice of steel, "I have. I choose as my mate Albragon, most high and lordly, he best suited to reign henceforth as glorious King of Dyrezan."

From the front of the audience, near where stood Albragon and Thocratis, there appeared a patch of curious darkness, a black cloud in the air of the room. No, a hole; a gap in being, an emptiness that expanded swiftly, swallowing up the scene, blanking out all image of form and substance. The strange mirage of darkness passed, and the gathering of noble wedding guests bethought themselves and clapped and bowed in formal obligation to the moment, for the priests were bowing and nodding and backing away, and the King sat on his throne, with his crown on his head, and the hand of his new wife and Queen in his. Only the King was Albragon, who straightened his crown with one hand, while holding tightly in his other fist the hand of Riena, who stared blandly with pale face across the hall.

The King guaranteed perpetual safety and comfort to his

predecessor, then dismissed the guests to their merriment, and they filed from the room, vaguely wondering to themselves what had just transpired. With satisfactory clarity they remembered events thusly: at Riena's shocking announcement Skyrax had stood and tossed his crown to the floor, saying, "As I mete justice to others in their circumstances, so I mete it to myself in mine, for the sake of my people. Princess Riena, the Queen to be, speaks wisely. No longer am I fit for this office. With these words I renounce the throne, conferring its majesty upon my superior, Albragon, who shall rule with better wisdom and goodness. Grant unto him all loyalty and the strictest devotion, gainsaying nothing he may do for all his future years. Honor him, honor the decisions of this day. Such is my final command." And Skyrax stepped away from the throne, strode away without further word to a side door of the hall, walking with high head and firm countenance into the corridor where he passed from view.

This they remembered, recollections supported by subsequent proclamations from the palace, shouting the news that by favor of the Gods and the will of the people, as expressed by their former overlord, a new master sat on the throne, he who men had called Albragon, though now, in deference to tradition, he assumed the style himself of Skyrax. A new Skyrax reigned, with a new and lovely Queen, the incomparable Riena. All was well in Dyrezan!

The Council of Twenty consented to the startling change, a fact shortly confirmed by no less than Lantonias, who stood in the center of the Central Plaza at the base of the Spire of Xenophor to proclaim the deeds of the day. The Council approved; the Gods approved; the former King granted, and the new accepted. Every aspect of the transition was proper, right, and just. It was, it had to be. So it was decreed.

Yet beneath the surface, within the minds of certain great men, in the solitude of their chambers away from public avenues and crowds, there lurked disquiet. Good Morca, for one—among many—wrestled with his memories of the happening. He recalled, with small imperfections, all that has been related, but he struggled as well with a competing set of memories, much more hazy, almost dream-like in quality, as of a tale told of another's life, or one read in a book long ago. This set of memories presented a different, less wholesome picture, one not entirely in accord with the tidings spread throughout the city. At odd moments the scene came to him this way: that of a sudden Lord Albragon had stood forth from his place at the head of the audience, in the company of the Councilor Thocratis, barked grim commands at which armored, beweaponed men had dashed at the throne and, ignoring the person of the chosen Queen, had laid hands on the dumbfounded King, Skyrax of the interminable line of Skyraxes. That eminent one had writhed and twisted feebly in their grasp, demanding of them explanations for their conduct, screeching in weak anger as they wrestled him down. Then Albragon and Thocratis advanced, the latter tearing the crown from the King's head, bestowing it with supercilious smirk upon the head of the great nobleman. "By what right do you this?" screamed the King. "By what right do you dare?" "By the right," thundered Albragon, "of unchecked power, and that of unquenchable desire. Here ends your day, here begins mine. Men, take him below. Until I decide how to deal with him, do not let him feel lonely." And forthwith Albragon's brutes manhandled the whimpering, cringing Skyrax from the hall, their master dropping heavily into the golden throne of the eternal Kings of Dyrezan.

So Morca saw, at whiles, this monstrous alternative to the reality he understood. He asked himself why he imagined such things, which convinced him not, for they conveyed no sense of genuineness to his mind, yet still they troubled and fretted him. Regardless, he knew where duty lay. Morca served a new King.

For a new King truly ruled in Dyrezan. Albragon, who now called himself Skyrax, lounged in the Royal Pleasure Chamber with its baths, its luxurious cushions, its garish frescoes and fantastic murals on walls and arched ceiling, surrounded by comely serving girls and athletic serving boys who fetched for him the sweetmeats and pasties for which he called. His beautiful Queen Riena stood by at his beck, still clothed in her bridal finery, her smile wide and her eyes dull. Thocratis, too, was there, and the King motioned him to an adjoining divan. "Stay by me," said Albragon, then, to the Queen, "Retire, my dear, to your royal amusements. I will call you presently." When she had departed without word, merely a fawning nod, he said to the Councilor, "As I promised, so will it be. I must have you as leader of the body. Lantonias will prove meddlesome should I retain him. Best that he be removed."

"Surely the delectable fruits of your sorcery," said Thocratis, "have satisfied them all. Such power to cloud the minds of men I did not know existed in the mortal sphere. You have gulled them thoroughly, to the extent that you need not fear an uprising of opposition. Even the Queen—a good mind there, for an outlander—even she drools at your feet, she whose heart she freely gave to another. Rest content, my Lord."

"Fall not into the doltish trap," sneered Albragon, "of complacency. Even such great magic as mine runs its course. As I calculate it, I have only days in which to anchor the foundations of my rule. Meanwhile there will, by degrees, develop chinks in the wall that I have thrown up around me. Queries will suppurate and bubble forth, for which we must have answers. Our people will ask after the old King, of the primacy of certain memories. The lowly folk of Vasgarra will inquire after their Princess. One spell, however mighty, can not subordinate the world. We should be prepared for further action. Those who question overmuch must be taken off. Ponder the matter, wise Thocratis, and make me a list."

"Great pleasure will it give me," replied the man. "I wear your harness, a weight I gratefully bear, one that rests easily on my shoulders. Given what you say, there are several we must dread in this city of big minds and stout hearts. I especially indicate to you Morca,, a devoutly trained and clever fellow who, once he insinuates annoying ideas, is unlikely to hold from intrusive activity." But at this Albragon laughed, saying, "Be he more, by comparison with me, than an apprentice at enchantery? I feared only his muscled arm. Besides, he is bound to my throne by his office. I can subvert him. Still, take note, Thocratis, and watch for any who raise their heads or hands to me."

In a crowded tavern that evening, near their quarters on the outskirts of the soldier's district, Portian said loudly over his ale to the brooding Morca, "It has been a day for the books. Little did I guess, when I arose this morning, that this would be an occasion for surprise as well as pomp. One King throws down his crown, another steps in on cue to take it up. And the Queen; shifting her presumed allegiance so unexpectedly. I did not truly read that in the cards. I must say, were she swooning for a second choice, I thought at whiles she dreamed of a chap both lesser and greater, if you get my meaning."

Morca scowled, ignored the unintentionally painful jibe, muttered under his breath, "I thought more, and better, of her. I too can dream." Portian could not hear over raucous shouts, begged Morca to repeat his words. "It is nothing. Tell me, my friend, have you misgivings of this day? Was there naught of happenings to chill your heart and disquiet your mind?" Portian began a jocular answer, thought somewhat, paused as if grappling with a dilemma, shook his head.

Morca sighed, said, "My meaning is opaque to you. Perhaps that is well. Surely there is nothing. A man can be stricken by fancies, when such suit his passions. I will indulge myself in another tankard."

So Morca frowned and mumbled to himself, feeling—without honestly believing—that something was wrong. He did not act then. Rather it was Lantonias, master of the Council of Twenty, who sought to clarify matters, and this the very next day, after a night of troubling visions, and a morning spent dealing with the suddenly haughty Thocratis, who deigned to put on airs and regard himself as an equal to his superior, and in meeting hinted at a larger role still for himself. Indeed, much of what Thocratis had to say at that session, in which recent events were bruited and affirmed, riled his fellow Councilors. "The new Skyrax," he announced, "desires a rearrangement of the epicenters of power. I have his word in this, and, I tell you frankly, I have his ear, so speak I with certain knowledge. He fashions a scale of influence differing from the old, with new highs and lows, new boons and obligations. I attend to his goals and whims. I urge you all to do so, without delay, without wasteful questioning."

"I, I, I, I!" growled ancient Lantonias, who rose abruptly from his honored seat in the Hall of Councilors and pounded with his bony fist the great table about which he and his nineteen compatriots were ranked. "You choke me with your 'I's, Thocratis. Know you something? Then tell all. Ah, no answer you give. Your snide allusions count for nothing with me. I dominate this Council, and I determine your place within it."

"Your King formulates his own views," snapped Thocratis. "Attune yours to his, for the betterment and safety of all."

"I could take that as a threat," rejoined Lantonias. "My King? Who is that? Repellent dreams assail me. Are they visions born of rank meat and overdone sauce, or be they portents and glimmers of secrets actual? Is there another here at table mortified by conflicting memories?" Lantonias paused, glaring at his colleagues, who squirmed uncomfortably but said nothing, though several seemed on the verge of response. "I see, and understand. Too much doubt, too little surety; I know that, too. Lacking confidence, nevertheless unease plagues me. I must speak with this King. I will satisfy myself that all is well, and report to the full Council in one passing of the sun. By then I hope to allay the concern that festers, at least in my own mind."

Next morning came the public proclamation of a reshaping of the Council of Twenty. Elderly Lantonias had retired from his lofty office, having grown weary of the strenuous duties he had performed so ably through long years. In stepping aside to make way for fresh blood he stated (via the King's mouthpiece) that he chose to withdraw entirely from public life, intending to journey to his estates without the city, in the valley far below, for a lengthy rest. So he was gone. It was customary at such times for a convention of Council to appoint a new leader, but due to the suddenness of the vacancy King Albragon, styled Skyrax, deemed it necessary to hasten the process, and by his will the election was carried by royal fiat. In short, he appointed Thocratis to the post, requiring the Council merely to acclaim him. This they did.

The first motion of Thocratis called for unique oaths from all the worthies of Dyrezan, oaths of special submission to the will of the new King. Political vows were common enough, in a society of headstrong intellects, but now the age old phraseology had changed; "reverence to the King who serves the eternal welfare of the city" vanished from the cant, to be replaced with "loyalty to the will of the King in all things." The oaths were administered, and accepted by all relevant parties, for it was the King's right, but accepted with dark thoughts and certain choice oaths of a different sort. For in Dyrezan these formalities were backed by magic, and it was not a little thing to sever a tie which one had sworn to in grave fashion. Nevertheless the officials of state bowed and raised their hands to swear. Morca led the way, ever dutiful, enunciating his lines clearly, without hesitation, in the Hall of Receival of the palace, standing before the King who eyed him avidly. It was Thocratis who recited the phrases that Morca repeated., and who then administered them to all who came after. This was his solemn task as master of the Council of Twenty.

"We have defanged them," whispered Thocratis to his Lord. "When Morca crumbles, they all do. His lead is decisive."

Then, in the King's name—Skyrax the name given—Thocratis set forth a series of commands in the form of a manifesto. No magic could be instigated against the King; a typical precaution, yet this law contained queer clauses, forbidding any sorcery that might be employed to foretell the King's future, or to read into the secrets of his recent past. A rule required that captives taken in wars against the barbarians (meaning anyone not of the city) must be examined, and that all desirable lasses and lads must be handed over to the King for his pleasure. The Dyrezanians were not prudes, and in their safe perch among the clouds were inclined to doing as they pleased, but such a demand grated, not only because it might limit their own fondly regarded antics, but because the reputation of the man formerly called Albragon went before him and carried over to the throne, and far too many stories concerning his private means of satiation reeked foul and disgusting. The folk of Dyrezan tended to elevate lofty their rulers in every way, so it distressed them to wonder whether the new Skyrax's behavior would bear a painful similarity to his previous ways.

Unfortunately it did, and it soon became common knowledge that the palace dungeons, nearly abandoned for countless reigns, were newly glutted with unfortunate victims who perished horribly without just cause or, even worse, lingered endlessly in unspeakable conditions, solely for their captor's amusement. It was said that Thocratis knew of the King's games, willingly took part in them, curried favor by suggesting monstrously inhuman frolics of his own. More dreadful still, it was bruited quietly that Thocratis urged his Lord, when the supply of barbarians ran short, to make do with lesser inhabitants of the city; lesser, but still citizens, supposedly protected in full from the horrors of degrading whim, however royal. The people noted that in the lower sectors of Dyrezan goodly maidens and handsome boys began to live in terror of masked gangs of men who snatched them by night, roving thugs that no authority could or would confront.

On this last point it was Morca who finally lost patience and insisted upon proper action. "When they fall within our purview," he told Portian, "arrest them; break them physically if need be, but find out who they are." Time passed, nothing happened, the Captain of the Guard called his friend and subordinate to him again, this time speaking not as a friend. "You did not act when I commanded," accused he. "Why did you not?" "I can not." "Why can you not?" "I fear to do so." "Why do you fear?" "When I sought to lay hands on the hooligans," explained Portian, "they bragged of serving in the King's name." "It is a lie." "No lie, for a retainer of the Council, addressing me personally, verified the crazy claim." "Unbelievable!" cried Morca. "Why did not you come to me?" "He told me you were privy," Portian replied, "that you spoke merely for show, desiring no true effort on my part, and that I should be punished if I persevered."

"It is the last straw," said Morca. "All is not well in the city. In fact, nothing is. Strange memories torment me more. I would conjure a spell, if I dared, to peel away the masking layers and see reality."

"That is sure death," warned Portian.

"Then I must receive audience of the King. He can explain matters to me, episode by episode, until I am convinced that I serve wisely and honestly. Without that, I question too much." Though he would not say so, the heart of Morca also broke each time the fair Riena appeared on the arm of Albragon, quietly smiling, never speaking, and with nary a nod for the Captain. If possible, he would have explanation for this, too. "I will speak with our Lord immediately. And, dear Portian, believe it not if you hear that I retired and went away without word. During this forthcoming conversation I will ask also after Lantonias."

He went to the Royal Palace as evening fell, an occasion little marked, for in his position comings and goings were routine. The guards admitted him at the door without incident, upon his plea of making official rounds, as had been his way for years, although one distinction now rankled him further: not all of the men guarding the King's house were Morca's own. These days many were Albragon's hirelings, another curious change, by itself trifling, but of a piece with late developments. Once inside Morca could wander the halls still with relative ease, for his office carried weight. It was a simple matter to wend his path to the throne room where he might ask audience. He did not do this with his intended promptness. Another idea struck him. He deviated from the way, detouring by side passages into the chambers reserved for the Queen. There he begged of her women a private meeting. Shortly this came about.

Riena entered, he stood, she motioned him back to his seat and settled herself across from her. "You honor me, Captain," she said easily, "with this visit. What is the purpose? If there are arrangements which require my approval, consider it done, and fulfill your tasks."

"I have nothing like that in mind," Morca replied earnestly. "I came to verify that you are well."

"Indeed. Is that your place? Then rest assured." Morca cared not for her glibness, her vacant complacence. Lovely she was as ever, but he missed an attribute, a factor of personality that once had beamed readily from her eyes, her voice. This Riena was a stranger, who treated him as one. She said, after a long silent moment, "Get to the point, Captain."

"I suffer from misgivings," said Morca, "as to how our singular histories have fallen out in this unconventional period. There was a time, not far in the past, when I felt I knew your heart. I was there, you know, through all, and we spoke a deal with one another. With some genuine regret I conveyed you hither to my Lord Skyrax, yet I did so, for whatever else might be, that must be. Thus I acquiesced. I joshed myself with notions that you balanced desire with duty also. Your present circumstances, however, appear wholly another matter. Not for an instant can I guile myself with the conviction that you accept this man Albragon. I know him some, know of him more. Long have I heard stories. Lately—nay, I do not repeat these tales to you—but my heart groans with dismay for your situation."

Riena emitted, as if on cue, a fey laugh. "Really, Captain, I find our closeted twosome awkward. I reign as Queen of Dyrezan, the ultimate honor, by the side of the great Skyrax, Lord of Dyrezan, as was intended. All is as was meant to be."

"Albragon!" Morca shouted hoarsely, "not Skyrax. There is wickedness afoot. You, I know, can not be part of it, therefore a baleful influence is at work to blind you. I lay that to Albragon and his minions."

"This is folly," Riena scoffed, "dangerous folly. You dare come to me, blathering slander of my husband?"

"I do," Morca shot back, "for I see now that you are charmed. It is there, in your eyes, the curious limpness of your limbs." Riena rose, crying, "Your head rolls for this!" But Morca leaped to his feet, pushed her back into her velvety chair, held her down with both hands, saying, "Gaze upon me, from the depths of your soul, and speak truth to my soul. Are you ensorcelled? Do you act freely, innately, without interference of black powers?" And Riena ceased her struggles, burst into tears. Whispered Morca, "As I thought. You can not help yourself, a sweet-minded outlander thrust into the machinations of a city of magicians. It need not have been, but so it came about. This atrocity I shall correct."

Riena sobbed meekly, with head bowed, "I can not speak. When I try, another tongue frames words for me."

"I will speak for you," said Morca with reassuring determination. "I go to Albragon now. At the very least, I may insist upon adjustments to your state. Who knows what may follow? I am bent on justice all around. Until I see you again, keep yourself safe, and carry this as my token." Morca removed from his finger a ring of gold, a ring intricately fashioned and chased with engravings of fabulous creatures. On the inside of the golden circle were cut the words, "I dwell here, awaiting the call of my master." He placed it on her finger. "Wear this always," he urged, his voice breaking, "with my love, until a happier day dawns. Now I go." He dared to plant lightly a kiss in her golden hair, then sped away, fighting to control his emotions.

SCIENCE AND SORCERY II

From Albragon's henchmen, guarding the Receiving Hall with their spears and their surly looks, he demanded admission and audience. In remarkably quick time he was ushered in, the doors closing behind him, two guards remaining inside. Albragon awaited him, sagging lopsidedly on his throne, grinning evilly, Thocratis lurking behind by Albragon's ear. Said the King, "Captain Most High, your duties consist solely of protecting my person against any threats. If you have identified such, state them; if not, justify your presence away from your post." "My duty," Morca retorted, "lies in guarding the personage of the King. I serve faithfully, now, forever, and always." "Then go to your business." "I am here," said the Captain, "to inquire after the health of Skyrax, lately my King. Promises were made at his abdication. I would know that they have been fulfilled."

"That is the King's charge," Thocratis said waspishly. "He does not justify himself to you. For your information, that one lives at ease within the palace, free of want and care."

"Indeed," chuckled Albragon, "he is happier without the burden of the crown grinding him down."

"Skyrax has not been seen," Morca pointed out, "since the day. I would appreciate an appearance. Also, I ask after Lantonias, who has vanished from our midst. I have dealings with him—" here Morca stretched the truth, with what he hoped was a disarming smile—"not yet complete. I seek contact."

"That is nothing to me," said Albragon coolly. "Track him down as it pleases you."

The King seemed serene, but Morca noted that Thocratis blanched. This fueled the Captain's dismay, and he began to feel anger. "That I will," said he. "Oh King, know you that armed ruffians haunt the city, preying upon the simpler folk in your name? I ask for the authority, which surely I need not ask, to squelch this blight."

Now Albragon grew visibly angry. His meaty face reddened, and he tugged harshly at his mustachios as he bellowed, "You assume too much. Morca, your demands pain me. It is not meet that I stoop as your supplicant. You exist at my whim, not I at yours. You do not fool me. I have watched you, observed your frowns, the mounting indications of insubordinancy. You ready yourself to defy me. Already I have taken off enemies, but there are more, for the list is long, and I will not sleep safe until each name has been stricken. It suits me that you came here, for you place yourself in my power."

Morca instinctively gripped the hilt of his sword and spat out the words, "I shun the croaking of toads, but fear them not. I know not the exact plan, nor the precise actualities of your rise, but I am convinced now that you are a false King, having acquired by black esoteric arts what you could not have openly in broad day. Appease me, or I act. Firstly, release Queen Riena from her spell."

"Enough!" roared Albragon. "You know so little, yet too much. These treasonous conceptions of yours must never leave the Hall. Men, cut him down."

Albragon's pair of swordsmen, waiting by the doors, drew their blades and came at Morca. He whirled at the hiss of steel and, whipping out his sword, began the fray by charging into their midst. Metal rang on metal, blades slashed the air, bit into flesh. The two henchmen gave up their spirits with animalistic groans, hit the floor hard. Morca stood unscathed, turned again to face the throne. Albragon, unabashed, said, "Thocratis, strike him."

The Councilor advanced before the throne, reciting olden words of power, locking eyes with the Captain and commencing the real battle. A sickly yellow light flared forth from the eyes of Thocratis, and Morca felt the first surge of death-dealing energy. Waves of force pounded his flesh, searing blasts meant to scald his bones. Morca boomed a hearty laugh, twitched his nose and clenched his teeth, thought to himself an oddly mannered phrase of yesteryear, hurled the magic heat back at his attacker. Thocratis cried out, staggered, stumbled and fell backward onto the gleaming tiles, writhing like an upturned crab.

Albragon lunged to his feet, calling out the hateful names of Antrodemus and Bolkkor, the twin demigods of pure evil. This constituted an entirely different and dangerous mode of attack. At the utterance of those nasty words two misty forms appeared in the chamber above Albragon's head. They coalesced into vile images, black-faced travesties of sanity. Wide, yellow-fanged mouths worked silently, and from those drooling maws gushed sludgy streams of killing force. Morca recoiled at the double blasts, felt the brains jellying in his skull. He thrashed wildly, went down on one knee, struggled to rise like a punch drunk fighter of the gaming arena. Albragon could not believe that any man could sustain a defense against that blow, yet somehow the Captain rallied, threatened with his head, clutched his arms to his chest and pulled himself tightly erect. Morca, for the moment, weathered the storm.

Yet his rebuff of the assault proved temporary. Barely holding on, he realized, with an emotion verging on panic, that he had divested himself of an important weapon prior to this battle, one he sorely lacked now. While he avoided defeat for the moment, he could not fire back at his opponent with any great power, and meanwhile Thocratis had recovered, shaken himself, rejoined the fray. Murderous waves of magic struck Morca again and again, grinding down his artful defiance, and soon it was all he could do to ward off destruction. Albragon and Thocratis advanced, stepping down from the dais of the throne to the floor of the hall, mentally battering their victim into submission. Came the inevitable: with a great, soul-rending cry Morca twisted, spun around as if physically struck, then, screaming a ferocious curse that reverberated and echoed from the walls, crashed to the tiles in a motionless heap.

The new King and his lackey stood over the debris of the man, they pale, panting and gasping. With the termination of the battle Thocratis sagged to the floor, utterly spent, quivering uncontrollably. Albragon stepped backward sluggishly, stumbled on the dais steps, sat down heavily on the lowest tier, where for a time he did nothing but mop his sweaty face with an embroidered sleeve and endeavor to master his breathing. Presently he said, in a husky, quavering voice, "Call more guards. Have them haul that carrion out of here." Thocratis crawled and dragged himself to Morca's side, felt at his limbs and throat. "He still lives," groaned the Councilor. "I will fetch me a knife, Oh Lord, and bury it in his breast." Albragon cackled oddly, like a man deprived of his wits. "I will call them, then," said he. He heaved himself from the step, painfully climbed to the dais, yanked the bell-pull in the alcove behind the throne. A solemn gong tolled three times. Armed men threw open the doors of the Receiving Hall, froze in stupefaction at what they beheld.

"Take this one," demanded Albragon, motioning to the still body of the Captain. "Convey him to the city walls, lift him up and cast him from Dyrezan. Do you here me? Fling him alive to the jagged rocks below. Watch him fall, this traitor, and report to me what you saw. Say nothing to anyone else, on your lives. That is all. Take him and get out."

His men obeyed, roughly removing the broken soldier from the hall, his scabbarded sword clattering on the stones of the corridor. Wearily Albragon plopped himself back onto his throne, fastidiously adjusted his crown. Thocratis remained where he was, managing merely to seat himself upright on the floor. Said the King, "That, maybe, was our worst enemy and chief threat, now to be discarded like so much trash from the skyey walls of my city. I pray to the Olden Gods that he wakes as he drops. Now, Thocratis, we need fear no one. The sheep think my hand rests heavy on their necks? Dyrezan is mine, to do with and use as I please."

In another part of the vast palace, oblivious to the events thus recounted, Queen Riena waged a mighty battle of her own, a desperate campaign against the dark fog and ruling phantasms within her mind. The potent words of Morca had awakened her, yet it was long before she could see clearly and come to understand the horrors that had been visited upon her since arriving in Dyrezan. Now she knew what Albragon had done to her, and guessed what her role in his planned madness had meant to her, her betrothed, and perhaps countless others, especially Morca who, though she dared not say so, she nevertheless dared to love.

Out of duty to her people she had offered herself to the true Skyrax, out of delusion given herself to the false, but it was the magnificent Captain of the Royal Guard who had captivated her, that warrior, nobleman, and mage. Her brains drifted further back into health as she thought of him, wondered fearfully about his fateful mission to Albragon. As she brooded over this matter she fondled the gold ring he had given her, which hung loosely on her finger.

Doing so, she sensed a warmth creeping into her room, noticed a darkening of the lamps. Their flames flickered in the absence of wind. Then icy cold assailed her, and before she could rise to wrap herself in wools something appeared in the air, a hideous apparition of a face in no wise less terrifying than the twin specters that Morca had lately confronted. This one was ghostly pale, with luminous fishy eyes and lumpish snout and uneven pointed teeth protruding from a thin red mouth curled in a sneer. The glassy eyes rotated independently of one another, scanning the chamber, then locked on and glared at Riena, who squeaked in dismay and fell back onto her divan. The baleful face grinned without mirth.

"A pretty mess," it said, in a harsh, grating voice. "So the heroic Captain has tossed you his precious bauble for your protection. That is not of the pact. I have a good mind to dispense with you all, and leave you to your fate. That might amuse me."

"Who are you?" cried Riena. "What do you want of me? I am surfeited with spirits and magic. Be gone, to torment another."

"Spirits?" the thing gruffly exclaimed. "There be no spirits here. You may seek them in their accustomed haunts. I came at the bidding of the ring, Morca's ring, as I believed. I find you wearing it; you, who know nothing of its attributes.

"I am the demon Altrazgeval, of the Third Circle, who dwells in lightless realms of cosmic frenzy beyond the paltry world and universe you know. Years ago this Morca entreated me through his esoteric arts, begging me to aid him and deliver him from the powers of enemies. He dreamed that he mastered me—so like a sorcerer!—and bound me to his will, little realizing that I serve only Great Xenophor, the Creator and the Destroyer, Ruler of All Space and Time. He of the Thousand Eyes I serve, and at His beck and whim I act. For His own purpose, or His amusement, or His lack of purpose, as He deems fit, I rode upon the multi-dimensioned angles of infinity, intruding into the meaningless, insignificant spaces that are the totality you can conceive. Thus I lurk to this hour between the vibrating chords of the Earth, interrupting the natural pattern of events when I choose. Is this such a moment? I see all; I know what has transpired; trivial concerns, as they apply to the unvalued individual, yet critical, perhaps, to the grand scheme, the endless sweep of fate."

"I do not understand," said Riena. "You speak words I recognize, but your meaning is impenetrable."

"May be that your skull is overly dense," snapped Altrazgeval. The demon assumed greater clarity of form. An ambiguously changing body of sorts—never remotely resembling the human—spread below the pointed chin, coiling in serpentine fashion across the rugs. "In times past your Morca bound himself to me with mighty oaths of unshakable power; in return I invested a pittance of my substance into his ring, which granted unto him intellectual strength, arcane wisdom, and protection from subtle harm. This I freely did, and long has he used the ring wisely. But now, at the incomprehensible tugging of his heart strings, he throws away his shield at the fateful moment when he confronts cruel and rabid opponents, men of renown eager to murder him. That he did, and he has paid for it. I tell you, in case it interests you, that Albragon has crushed Morca, beaten him into abject submission, and now, realistically speaking, no sane hope for your Captain remains."

"It can not be!" Riena wailed. "That noble man could not lose to that filthy monster. I refuse to accept it. There is high justice, the mercy of the Gods."

"There is chaos," replied Altrazgeval, "and doom, and fate, and naught else. That is the way of your world. Fate, however, is a tricky business, and what is written by the Old Ones and Their Lord is often composed for reasons that far transcend the needs and desires of mortal lice. At the beginning of things He, Himself, decreed that proud Dyrezan should sail the skies so long as the formal line of Skyrax endured. Dyrezan will die in the end, as all things die—yes, even eternal Dyrezan—but this is not the designated time. Therefore, I conclude, a certain degree of minor meddling is currently in order." Added Altrazgeval, "Already it begins. The power of the ring proved instrumental in liberating your mind. Morca's loving thoughts, I fear, would not have sufficed. That being the case, I deduce an advantage in starting with you.

"Princess Riena—which I call you instead of Queen, for you are not legitimately tied to Albragon, nor sits he legitimately on the throne—Princess, I free your soul, and therefore needs be your body. If I remove you from this building, with its circles of guardians hostile to you, whither will you fly?"

"To Vasgarra, naturally."

"You would never make it," said the demon, "nor would that serve. Your place is here forevermore, whatever destiny holds in store. That I see. Released into the city this night, what will you do?" "Seek friends and allies," stated Riena, "in order to protect myself, and rescue, if possible, Morca and Skyrax from the tyrant." "First you must act to kindle opposition," advised Altrazgeval, "to Albragon. Do that, and the rest may fall into place, if the Gods so decree. Are you ready?"

"But my heart sobs for Morca!" she cried.

"Without the ring, he is at risk," observed the demon. "I will intervene once on his behalf—call it charity if you wish—and only that once, until the time (if it ever comes) when you restore the ring to him. I decide, it is done. Now, are you ready?"

"I am. Lead me."

"Take my hand," commanded Altrazgeval, extending a frightful grayish appendage that in no way resembled a hand. Riena quailed, drove herself to comply, with infinite misgivings seized the offered paw. It felt damp and unclean as it enfolded her small white hand. At the touch an electric shock surged into her, and on the instant she, though fully aware, could see nothing but stark blackness like that of the interior of the grave.

At the iron parapet atop the granite wall of the city two men, henchmen of Albragon, wrestled with a weighty burden enclosed in a coarse canvas bag. With knives they slit the fabric, pulling forth the large limp body of Morca, still motionless save for the uneven heaving of his chest. Beyond the wall, in the remote distance, loomed the pointed peaks and picturesque crags of the rocky mountains that surrounded the valley below, their tops scarcely surmounting the rim of the hovering city. Far below, a dizzying distance, spread the circular floor of the misty valley. The two goons kicked idly at the inert form. Sneered the first, "In my day this one has risen high." Chortled the other, "In your time this one will drop far." They laughed, hefted the body, without hesitation cast it over the parapet. It plunged like a stone out of sight.

Dyrezan had come to know fear and misery; now its fair citizens learned outrage and terror. Too much had happened too fast: the changing of the Kings, the new and unwelcome regulations, the predators scouring the city by night, the disappearance of worthy men. The vanishing of Lantonias and Morca produced an effect within discerning minds that elicited growling disapproval, consternation, muted calls for retribution. In Morca's case too a story was sent forth by proclamation, but this time no one believed, and in due course the case of the missing Chief Councilor necessitated reexamination. Rumors spread, details leaked, unwise boasts were overheard. Indeed, Lantonias had been murdered for daring reproach the King, this Albragon who pretended to the name of Skyrax; overcome by subtle magic and killed with clubs and swords when taken unawares by minions of Thocratis, who craved to replace him. This became known, and the worst facts pertaining to Morca's end were also shortly common knowledge. If such grand men were doomed to die, was not every decent man destined to the same end?

Circulated other rumors, too, which certain men in the know might credit more than others. It was said that Queen Riena, she whose beautiful countenance and kindly ways had lent luster to Albragon's brutish reign, had broken with her Lord, absconding with her person into the hidden recesses of the city, where she preached opposition to the ogre squatting on the throne and marshaled forces against him. Many prayed that it were true, others refused to believe. Prognostications woven from furtive spells gave obscure results, from which wise men concluded that Albragon and his tame wizard Thocratis canted spells and scattered charms of their own to disturb the aether and render true reading a chancy matter. This further inflamed anger, and hope, for men wondered what the King sought to hide, and why.

Albragon's paid mouths derided these claims, while his armed hirelings arrested or made away with identified troublemakers. Nevertheless unrest grew, spread, passing from one to another individual, until a mass of frustrated opposition existed. Throngs took to the streets, always chased bloodily home again, not before they had cried, "Where is Riena? Where is the Skyrax of old? What of Lantonias and Morca? If they live, show them to us!" One day a mob of the lower classes, a surprisingly well organized and vocal bunch, surged toward the Royal Palace, as they had attempted repeatedly in recent weeks, only to be broken up and dispersed before. This time they were allowed to approach, and soon a massed, packed crowd filled the Central Plaza. Fronting the doors of the palace stood smug Albragon with his crowned head, a sight which infuriated the masses and drew from them disrespectful shouts; bald Thocratis at his side, his surly frown scanning to and fro about the throng; and a score of armed, savage looking soldiers in the livery of the Royal Guard, yet surely private liege-men of their Lord. Nevertheless, at their head stood Portian, appointed Captain of the Guard in place of Morca since the latter departed from public view. Portian looked the part, yet his face was set in unreadable stone, the face of a man performing, as best he can, an unpleasant or despised duty.

"I regret," boomed Albragon, at which the boisterous crowd subsided, "regret the spurious tales and damnable lies fostered by the enemies of the people and foes of sound governance. Today I put paid to their foul falsehoods. They say that I am bereft of my loved ones or, more grotesquely, that I pass the hours by eliminating those who should be friends of the King. I tell you no; but, perhaps, you care not to believe me, so, is there another you would believe? Will you doubt the plain and open speech of your former monarch, once my Lord and still my friend: Skyrax who ruled where I rule now, Skyrax of the olden, honored, and glorious House of Skyrax?"

The crowd fell silent, following scattered shouts of disbelief. Skyrax emerged from the palace, assumed a place near Albragon. Slight of stature, dressed in a common robe, he boasted little of kingly attributes, made little impression next to the current monarch, yet it was he, alive and smiling as he gazed vaguely over his audience. "Citizens," he cried, "all is well in Dyrezan. "Believe not the lies of those who would foster discontent. Evil men seek to drive mad the good with ill reports, to inflame the uninformed that they may descend into mischief. Harken to me, not to them. You see that I live, a refutation of spurious midnight tales. Indeed I live, dwelling here in my lifelong home as a guest rather than master, but meeting with respect and wholesome consideration at every turn. This is as I have chosen, and it is no man's place to deny me this. Here I am, not murdered, rather hale and hearty. Thank the new Skyrax for that. Frequently I dine with my friend, he once called Albragon, and his lovely Queen Riena, with whom I chatted amiably only moments ago. Dear Riena, currently taken with a mild sickness of the season, chooses to withdraw from view until health recovers. That is all. In good time she will graciously bless you with her beauty again. And our great men live to savor the bounties of life. Even the best, like Lantonias, must retire when the years knock, and stout men, like Morca, have been known to undertake long journeys at the will of their Lords. So stands the matter. See you in any of this cause for concern? Our streets are safe, the persons of our citizens respected. Ignore calculated whispers, reject the stirrings of dirty pots, as you love me."

Thus spake the former Skyrax. He rambled in a singsong voice, pausing oddly between sentences, but this was not so entirely different from his known manner of speaking as to excite wholly unfavorable comment. Too, Portian the new Captain reacted visibly to certain statements uttered by Skyrax, as if he restrained amazement, but there were many ways to read that; Skyrax had often flabbergasted those who heard him speak. The old King had spoken, and his words served to reassure those who craved reassurance, and there was nothing of merit to say in response. There were a few jibes and cutting barbs flung out from the immense gathering, but in short order the crowd sullenly dispersed.

Albragon laughed over his wine and roasted meat, slapped a beefy hand to the table and said, "I must grant, Thocratis, that you were right. I concede the correctness of retaining that oaf alive. With his mind firmly in my grasp, he gulled them thoroughly." "I believe it was your idea, my Lord," said the oily Thocratis, "which I merely seconded." "Was it? Of course it was. I appreciate that, Councilor. Have you stuffed Skyrax back into his hole?" "He is no longer at liberty," came the amused reply.

Said Albragon, "I think I will sit on him a while longer. He may prove useful again, if the stew of riffraff continues to simmer. It is a pity, for I would relish digging my hooks into his pasty flesh. Never mind; I hear that you provide entertainment this night."

"Three youngsters of noble family this time," said Thocratis, "two deliciously maturing girls and a lad not yet with beard. Surely they will scream to your satisfaction."

Albragon's reprieve from annoying dissent did not last long, ending in a manner most distressing to him. The very next day, in a public marketplace far from the palace, surrounded by armed followers and a handful of well known dignitaries, the Queen made an appearance before the people, in which Riena herself offered startling rebuttal to the soothing speech of Skyrax. It was Albragon the false King, she declared, and his henchmen who twisted the truth, who distorted reality with black magic to fabricate an illusion of normality. "Do not trust the usurper!" she cried. "I have broken with him, having seen through the malicious clouds of mental oppression which forced me to act as his tool. The true King, the genuine Skyrax, is held still by chains of induced madness. Albragon may trot him out when it serves him, but he dare not release the King, who would swiftly lead the citizens of Dyrezan in overthrowing the despot. It is our duty to save Skyrax and the city. Good people, will you obey me?" Those who heard cheered, agreeing to a man to the Queen's charge that they spread the word and prepare for action. "This is the time for battle!" she concluded. Albragon's swordsmen stormed into the area shortly thereafter, wreaking havoc among those who tarried, but the dove had flown. So did her words, on wings of whispers.

Albragon was furious, and when anger fired him someone inevitably died. So it happened in this case. In his private chambers, where servants laved his massive bulk with perfumed oils, he ordered the beheading of the master of arms in charge of the squad sent to arrest the Queen, then rounded on his Captain of the Guard. "I do not tolerate failure!" he screamed, "nor treason. Portian, I elevated you to the heights of command, showered you with Royal largesse. In return, I demand fealty in all matters." "I serve," Portian replied stonily, "according to my abilities, and as my sense of justice dictates. What would you of me?" "Seek the Queen!" snarled Albragon, "track her down, and when you find her, kill her. It is ludicrous that my rule should be stymied, my power infringed, by the machinations of this Vasgarran brat. Get her in your hands, and crush her to death." "That," said Portian, "I will never do."

"You disobey?" Albragon's voice almost gave out from choked rage.

"I have served you," said the Captain, "because I understood it as my duty. These are wondrous times, through which I have chosen my way warily, perhaps mistakenly. I accepted this post once held by a dear friend, sought to serve as he would. Morca was keen on duty, the fulfillment of oaths. I beg leave to speak with him, wherever he may be, that I may seek his counsel."

Thocratis, hovering at the King's elbow, snapped, "Out of the question."

"Follow your orders," growled Albragon.

"Failing that," Portian went on, "I will accept the advice of Lantonias. Produce him, or tell me where he may be found, and that will content me."

"These obstructions do not become you," said Albragon. "This is dangerous nonsense. Beware, man, lest your head roll."

"Then the rumors be true," cried Portian, "that they are dead. The suspicion has haunted my dreams, enfeebled my steps. Well, that is past. I will speak with Skyrax the true King, in private, where he may speak freely. Perhaps he will indicate my proper course."

"I am King!" shouted Albragon. "Approach that other, and you both die."

Said the Captain, after an intense silence, "There is a time for death, and a time for dealing death. I commend my soul to Great Xenophor, who knows all, sees all, who in my heart finds naught but love for my people and their just cause. I am not a high born wizard like some, but my mind is clear, my arm strong." So saying, Portian drew his sword, raised it on high, stepped toward his master.

It was a noble gesture, yet bound to fail. Albragon's eyes blazed green, and he blew the man apart. Sodden shreds of flesh splashed the King and those about him. "Clean me," Albragon ordered his slaves, "and you, Thocratis"—he tossed the fellow a soiled towel—"appoint a new Captain. Choose a brute this time, one wholly under my thumb. We need not cater to these dandies any longer. Pick a man who enjoys killing." The King paused, musing over his own words, called for an especially favored liege-man. He said to the hulking soldier, on his appearance, "Neral, an important vacancy lies open, to be filled by a man who loves me and hates all else. Are you ready for big doings, and boundless delights?"

Neral grinned a snaggle-toothed grin, hefted his sword proudly. Order, I obey. Go we hunting this night?"

"This is the man," said Albragon.

"It is commanded," said Thocratis, as he wiped smears of blood from his face, "and done. The Council, however, may not approve."

"Their day, too, is past," Albragon decreed. "Act as you deem necessary. Henceforth, the merest whiff of opposition carries with it an automatic death sentence."

His statement set the stage, later that same day, for what became known as "The Massacre of the Council of Twenty."

Thocratis approached the Council chambers fully prepared for difficulties, rightly suspecting that the King's latest summons must lead to heated resistance. To an extent the Council had ever been a servile body, accustomed to granting the monarch what he wished in all but the most extraordinary of circumstances. The current situation surpassed the tolerable norm. At the increasingly belligerent insistence of Thocratis those august men had supported each act of Albragon, however cruel, but their resolve to obey had wilted with the mounting disorders in the city. Speculation concerning the fate of Lantonias, then others, had lead to a condition of muted, mutinous hostility toward the King's hand-picked Chief Councilor, and Thocratis expected, at the least, a verbal explosion now, when he submitted the demand for another Captain of the Guard, presenting a name which conveyed little meaning to the Council, save that it clearly belonged to a base crony of the reigning monarch.

Said Thocratis, "Appoint Neral, and your duty be done." It would not be so simple this day. The Council, driven to the limit, unanimously rejected their King's ostensible request. "Dyrezan," they cried, "shall not be mastered by jackals, no matter with whom they drink and revel;" and "Where is Portian? Has he, too, retired to his estates, or been sent on secret mission to the far provinces? We would question him;" and "Give us the name of a man who will uphold the rights of the people, not trample upon them." Screeched Thocratis, "I speak in the King's name. Obey him, obey me. He commands the empire, I command this Council."

And the Council of Twenty balked, nineteen of them, hurling forth demands of their own. Suddenly questions of procedure, points of order, rose to the fore. "We call for an election within chambers," they announced. "This session is vacated. We must nominate a new Chief Councilor. Thocratis, stand down."

That one, ever vigilant, knowing full well when he entered the hall what was brewing and likely to transpire, unleashed his carefully laid trap. At the words "stand down" he threw up his arms, fingers outstretched, calling upon his most boisterous opponent a dreadful curse. Taken unawares, the man went down, the flesh sizzling around

211

his skull. Thocratis shrieked a command and burly swordsmen stormed into the room, with grinning Neral at their head, their weapons flashing and reflecting bright motes of lamplight. The maddened Chief Councilor blanketed the room with spells of sickness and disablement, which inhibited defense until the warriors were slashing amongst the noblest of Dyrezan. They rallied of course, those powerful men, assailing their attackers with loathsome, vindictive charms, flinging about the room morbid spells of death and putrescence, and they managed furious jabs at Thocratis as well, who they hurled breathless against the wall by the virulence of their desperate rage. His fellow Councilors would have killed him, and could have easily, save that their hands were full fighting for their own lives against the scores of Albragon's thugs pressing against them. When the fracas ended the survivors of the Council had retreated, many marked with permanent scars, leaving three of their number on the chamber floor. Thocratis recovered, lucky to escape with his life, his brain still reeling from the few magical blows that hit home. A dozen swordsmen were dead, countless others crippled or driven hopelessly insane, but that was of no account, for they were readily replaceable.

"Serves the Council right," said Albragon when Thocratis carried in the news. "I can pack another with my liege-men. Now the terror of my name goes before me. This is the finish of all organized resistance."

So far from stopping the spread of disorder, this bloody clash marked a turning point in the subversive upwelling, and the beginning of open internecine warfare in Dyrezan. The remainder of the Council withdrew to their castles and manors to lick their wounds, those who could—those still in good health and of unshaken mind—throwing in their lot with the rebel movement. They joined many of the lesser nobility who had already reacted from despair, and the Queen, who ceaselessly operated behind the scenes, moving from one safe haven to another, ever speaking, cajoling, calling to battle those who would not rest while the Ogre, as she styled Albragon, clung to his dubious throne.

Outright war erupted the morning after the attempted massacre when, at the behest of an informer's report, Neral sent a patrol, in the name of the King and at the instigation of Thocratis, to seize Riena, suspected to be hiding that day in the fortified mansion of the ex-Councilor Tiradees. In an alleyway behind the great house armed citizens set upon Albragon's men and slew them all, then tidied the scene so that only the heads of the dead were left to confound and horrify those who came after to investigate. Before nightfall a large force commanded by Neral stormed Tiradees' stronghold, an easy conquest, for they found it empty. Meanwhile other Royal patrols came under attack, suffering heavy losses. Within a span of hours big sectors of the city rejected the King's jurisdiction, raising the banner of the Queen and the true Skyrax.

Albragon blamed Thocratis for these setbacks. "Your clumsy assault on the Council stirs these rabble," he snarled, scowling upon his quaking henchman. "Their brains are addled and overheated, and too many big minds now support them. It will take more than Royal commands and a few hard knocks to quell them. I must savage their souls."

He did not delay. Albragon abandoned the Royal Palace, a carefully orchestrated strategic withdrawal, taking with him his faithful and the captive Skyrax, and in the midst of hundreds of warriors repaired to his grim onyx castle, which he set up as his fortress and seat of government. There he ensconced his folk within its many labyrinthine chambers, plunging the former King into the lowest dungeon, where that unfortunate dwelt miserably with the saddest victims of Albragon's furtive passions and joys. There, behind its massive walls of stone and barriers of fearsome magic, Albragon betook himself alone into the secret chamber in a high, windowless tower where he kept his esoteric books and rare alchemical materials. There he studied by the sputtering light of a strange red candle that gushed stinking clouds of greasy smoke, leafing carefully through crumbling scrolls and manuscripts of ancient lore. There he pondered the evil spells devised by fabulous wizards of antiquity, spells so dreadful than even the formulators had warned against their employment. There he sifted the choicest, most horrific specimens of arcane art, focusing on those which promised most, invariably those embodying the least of safeguards. There he learned, there he determined, and when he emerged from that place, he acted.

Then the magical war truly commenced. From the shunned castle of Albragon great arcs of fire shot like comets into the night sky, raining death where they came down. The first blasts fell at random, devastating a tradesmen's district, incinerating a budding mage's townhouse, destroying an arched bridge of antiquarian fame that choked with rubble a major thoroughfare. Many perished in this first wave of cosmic fires, the first of many that soared over Dyrezan at periodic intervals.

SCIENCE AND SORCERY II

Gazing into a polyhedron of scintillating crystal, Albragon sought with his keen mind the physical emanations of his enemies, located their presence, battered down their psychic defenses and sent forth beams of concentrated destruction, the harnessed essence of death. Fully prepared now, alive to his schemes, they fought back valiantly with all the arts at their command, but such was Albragon's magical strength that he overcame a few, mastering their minds and imploding the brains inside their skulls. These victories cheered him mightily, made him hungry for more. He especially sought the soul of the Queen, whom he openly termed a wanton traitoress. He found her readily enough (her soul being expansive and bright), would have tortured her magically to death from afar, with his leering visage haunting her imagination as he murdered her, but she, though lacking innate magical skills, nevertheless stood firm, surrounded by overlapping webs of protective energy thrown up by those sorcerial Lords sworn to defend her, including the combined powers of the reconstituted Council of Twenty. They rebuffed Albragon then, a momentary check he accepted with a shrug, one to be remedied soon. Meantime he cast his deadly thoughts farther afield, lashing at any who dared defy him.

The troops at his command he posted to critical locations, central points from which, in large numbers, they could wield sword and spear to deadly effect. The vicinity of their forts became battle zones, scenes of intense clashes with riotous crowds. Rebellious Guardsmen and the soldiers of enemy nobles joined the fray. Fierce fighting broke out whenever the King's men set out to maraud. Sometimes they gained their way, other times their recalcitrant opponents repelled them, but every clash was ever in doubt, and sanguine. Albragon saw to it that his men possessed the precinct of the Eyrie, the only reliable egress to and regress from Dyrezan. His foes, for all their strength, were largely cut off from the world.

The city rocked and shook with combat, the ordinary and the arcane. Riena and her makeshift army stormed the abandoned Palace, raised the banner of the true Skyrax over the highest tower, but they had not his person through which to reign, nor could they get to him. The Queen declared Albragon an outlaw, to be killed at will by any patriotic citizen, while the mages of the Council pronounced the dread sentence of doom upon him. Her supporters wove spells of grotesque attributes intended to batter down Albragon and his main citadel.. They threw fire at him, and plague, and toxic serpents, and crawling carpets of hungry creeping things, but these perils he deftly surmounted, returning the grim favors with his own vile concoctions of studied terror. The swordsmen of the Queen rushed the gates of the false King's castle, staggered back or dropped stricken in their tracks when hit by malevolent charms and clouds of arrows. An attempt to scale the walls by Riena's best troops failed disastrously when a swarm of buzzing, chitinous winged monstrosities fastened themselves upon the flesh of the attackers climbing the ladders, biting at faces and legs, scuttling beneath body armor. Streams of boiling oil cascading from the walls added to the distress of the valiant warriors. They died in droves. Albragon's men, led by the brutish Neral, suffered as well, suffered unspeakably, but they were hard men, with nothing to lose, rightly convinced that their only hope for salvation lay in the absolute victory of their Lord, so they fought on, there and elsewhere, even when driven to extremis, fought furiously and cruelly.

As the days passed, turned to weeks, Albragon assured himself that his forces were gaining the upper hand. Though they occupied little of the city, they reigned sovereign within their fortified perimeters, dealing death to all who approached, while a series of limited expeditions spread destruction and mayhem among their foes. Great manors of the nobility went up in flames, or were shaken to rubble with their foundations magically blasted. Having little to defend, Albragon focused his frightful powers on punishing those who defied him. With much to defend, they could not, like he, concentrate their powers to full effect, were forced to grant, painful as the admission might be, that this King by theft was a notable wizard, a giant of his kind, quite capable of holding on indefinitely, even—forbid the thought!—of defeating them all and resuming his vicious reign unchecked. Gloom spread among those who would, at the hazard of their lives, liberate and restore Skyrax to the throne.

As the war raged enchantments and the fruits of enchantments teemed within Dyrezan. By day a charmed dusk hung over the city, conjured eclipses obscuring the sun. In the many green parks (those not ravaged or despoiled), with their manicured trees, sculptured rocks, splashing streams and artfully crafted waterfalls, no birds sang. None were to be seen, they having been driven away by induced gloom and the endless gusts of morbid energy fields. By night unimaginable terror stalked the streets. Hideous portents walked abroad, physical manifestations of contending magic: foul, gibbering things that preyed upon the weak and the wounded; ghostly presences that hovered near, preaching doom; corpses that uprooted themselves from sealed underground vaults or that crept from mausoleums and shuffled mindlessly when they should not have walked, only rested perpetually. In the dark skies the stars were wont to vanish, though no cloud hid them, and strange new moons appeared alongside the familiar one, unknown orbs that gave off fiery vapors and glowing jets of billowing smoke, orbs that moved erratically with nervous speed through the ghastly night. Unsettling cries rent the air, accompanied by the leathery flapping of ponderous wings. The people prayed to the Gods to release them from their woes, calling upon those Great Ones to rescue the fair city, which seemed nigh in danger of tottering upon its aerial foundations and crashing down from the sky, to the ruin of utter extinction for all.

In Dyrezan the parties contended for the mastery of the world. Far, far below, at the bottom of the great circular valley ringed by inaccessible peaks, the simple villagers who supplied the magnificent Sky City through their labors knew naught of the goals, desires, and controversies that sparked the war, nor understood the stakes, nor what transpired above them in that realm, to them so like the contentions of the Gods. Those who dwelt in the shadow of the city saw distant flashes of light, puffs of black smoke, heard faint booms of faraway explosions, no more, from which they inferred what they liked. They knew Dyrezan to be a magical land, therefore accepted strange signs and mysteries as facts of life. The peasants of the valley had no say in great matters, tried not to speculate on the doings of those high lordly ones, for such thoughts were profitless. Events in Dyrezan were as remote and inexplicable as those of the heavens. It was better not to think of such things.

And yet they must wonder, for a Lord of Dyrezan had fallen from the sky.

Morca lived. Awakening at the last, he had groggily perceived that he was being cast from the ramparts of the city. Too late he realized his peril, knew that death clasped him firmly, in his enfeebled state powerless to save himself. Dumped from the bag by Albragon's men he fell, tumbling through the aether, passing out as the dark, rocky underside of the city shot past. He consigned his soul to the cold mercy of Xenophor before blanking out again, this time never expecting to wake in this world. He came to, however, lying on his back amidst clinging dampness, with unknown faces staring down at him, earnest, swarthy visages unlike those of his kin, mightily unlike those of the Gods who might deign to greet a wandering soul as it commenced its new career. Kind hands lifted him, and he beheld the place, a patchwork of banked mud flats given over to the raising of grain on the verge of a reedy marsh. Above him, so hopelessly far away, hovered the black disk of Dyrezan. Round about he saw a village nearby, with huts of unpolished stone, rough-hewn logs, and thatch.

The fact of his continued existence mystified. Such a plummet should have completely destroyed him. He granted the necessity of a magical explanation, knew not its source—the capricious whim or cunning design of his lost ring familiar Altrazgeval—knew only that he lived, that possibility remained. He felt terrible, sick unto death and aching from every joint, the effects of his magic combat and subsequent manhandling. When his rescuers released him he fell to his knees, sensed the world growing dark once more. He came to in a crude but clean bed, in a tiny wooden room of a hut, dressed in a coarse shift, his armor and sword on a board beside, with benefactors waiting to lave and feed him.

This was the house of Donai, the mayor or headman of the village called Streckis by its inhabitants. That worthy, dreading the consequences of allowing a visitor from hallowed Dyrezan to perish, took upon himself the tending and rehabilitation of the sufferer. Donai, his women, and his multitudes of children capably saw to every need, with food and rude medicines endeavored to blow hot the fires that flickered cool. Otherwise he knew not what to do. Should he report his find to the handful of soldiers who guarded the stone stockade beneath the Sky City? That place, from which notable passersby and foreign travelers were thought to ascend to Dyrezan (it was indeed the Lower Gate, which communicated mystically with the Eyrie), had never welcomed visitors, and just now seemed entirely unapproachable. Scarcely had this fellow fallen from heaven than fresh guards replaced the old, surly types who callously mocked the villagers and warned them off. Donai did not wish to confront them until he knew more. Said he to his youngest and, currently, most beloved wife, "Big things are afoot, and if I act rashly we will all be crushed as ants by elephants. Let us allow time, that time may give answers."

So he waited, while his charge grew strong again. With the passing of weeks Morca recovered full strength, walked and exercised to man himself as he convalesced. He spoke with his host, learned what was known of his arrival, heard the reports and rumors of remote doings. Morca guessed that battle raged in the sky, felt helpless for the first

217

time in his life. "I am truly a magician," said he, acknowledging what Donai freely assumed, "there being none greater, save that I am currently divest of my crucial elements. I lack books of wisdom, crystals and potions of power, lack even my magic ring, which in a fateful hour I gave away, to one who surely required protection. By the Gods, where is she now, what has become of her, how may I get to her?" Donai mentioned the guards at the stockade. Replied Morca, "You were right to shun them, my friend. I fear that my enemies have seized that stronghold."

"There is no other way to the city," Donai pointed out, "save the magic road through its gates. Either you stay here with us always, where you are welcome, or you find a means of entering and passing beyond."

For many more days Morca fretted, pacing like a caged tiger in the confines of Streckis, gazing up at his lost city, turning over in his mind one impossible scheme after another. Incredible powers possessed Morca, but without his materials and inscribed spells those abilities were but gold in the mine, waiting to be rendered coin. Restored to full physical strength, he scouted the vicinity of the Lower Gate, established that enemies held it, too numerous to defeat alone, nor could he, in good conscience, rally the folk of Streckis to his cause while the soldiers of Albragon could count on reinforcements from above. Willing they were to aid him, at Donai's command and gentle persuasion, but the Captain would not lead them to useless death. Tales picked up from the hostile warriors at the Lower Gate suggested that their side—yes, the party of abhorrent Albragon—gained on the struggling party of Riena, the Queen who stood for the true Skyrax. Terrible news to be sure, yet Morca's heart leaped with passing joy. Then Riena lived! She lay not, no longer and not yet, in the filthy power of the false King. There was still time to act. Morca cursed his helplessness, felt the insidious encroaching of despair.

The dream came to him one night as he tossed and turned in wretched, unrestful slumber. Morca bitterly dozed, and then it was as if he woke, sitting bolt upright, aware of a presence that lurked nearby, though his senses resolved nothing. He peered into darkness, strained his ears to catch a sound that might have disturbed him, felt his flesh creep from vague vibrations in the soundless night. But did he dream? Of a sudden he knew himself fully awake, tingling with suspense.

A man stood before him; no, the eidolon of a man, a pale, transparent shape that coalesced by degrees into an image he recognized. Without reasoning Morca cried out, "It is you, Lantonias, come to me in the night from far places whither you were sent. When I heard from these rude folk that your terrestrial estates lay vacant then I thought you written dead in the book of time, your wisdom, strength, and decency lost to us forevermore. Instead you live." Then he comprehended the ghostly form before him, deduced the likelihoods of the moment, shrank back instinctively. "So you are not flesh and blood," said he, "nor naught material. It is a shade that comes to me. Will you speak?"

The image of Lantonias spoke, in a grave, deep voice entirely like that of life. "Yes, Morca, it is I, Lantonias, or rather the dissipating remains of his spirit, torn asunder from the body by the foul machinations of the tyrant Albragon. Murder me he did, when I dared confront him. I suspected him of monstrous iniquities, yet never believed he would sink to striking at me by stealth. That was my tragic error. He, with the aid of his pet reptile Thocratis, burned my brain and broke my body, sent my soul squealing into the void. For that I hate him, a hatred enduring death. As I sank into oblivion—or whatever the Gods fairly decree for man—I cursed him with the final blast of my life and power, swore that I would return to raise hand against him, somehow, somewhen. I remember his laughter ringing in my dying ears. My curse bore fruit, though, for such was my insatiate fury that my soul did not pass on, but lingered to waft through the corridors of the base world, watching and waiting. I tarried for a chance, craving an instrument through which I could hit him back. That is you."

"You honor me," replied Morca, "with a task that I relish. All difficulties I will gladly overcome, only my position does not invoke envy. If you retain sense of place on earth, then you know I am trapped, shut out from the city where great matters approach culmination." Spake Lantonias, "That I know. You shall return to lead the forces marshaled against Albragon. This you will do, for not only I, but fate verily decrees." "You fill me with hope," said Morca, "O honored one of this world, and the next where goodness and faithfulness are surely rewarded; only, my hope gleams dimly. Here I am, up there my lore and materials. With all my sorcery I could propel myself to Dyrezan, clinging to the wings of Godly messengers, but without my transcripted charms my intentions are forestalled. I know not how to surmount the problem. Dyrezan lies more than a hard march from Streckis."

Lantonias smiled. "My power necessarily lacks its former intensity, but I am briefly enabled to act on your behalf. Here your body must rest for a time, while your soul joins mine in wingless flight. If you agree, I will separate one from the other, and thus sundered your soul shall rise to the lofty heights of Dyrezan. This I can do. Dare you?"

Morca pondered long. "I live, I breathe. You offer me passage through the land of death. The pleasures of the world entrance me with their variegated allures. I would not surrender them, if I need not."

"You may return to your body at the time of your choosing. That boon I may grant, no more. Morca, make your determination."

"I agree to the charge," said Morca, "and the means." And Lantonias nodded, saying, "Follow me," and Morca rose from his cot, following the awful presence into the quiet night. They walked unseen through the dirt streets of Streckis, passed over the fields beyond the last huts, traveled along a beaten path to a rocky outcrop decorated with curious inscribed symbols, withered bunches of flowers, and primitive ornaments of roughly shaped, painted stones. At the foot of the stony spires and rounded boulders lapped the dark waters of a wide round well. No light of stars reached its surface, or, if it did, the quivering liquid soaked up the faint radiance and swallowed it.

"This is the precise location," said Lantonias, "of the source of the energies, the incredible Gateway of the Gods, the remnant of a fabulous entrance into celestial realms, the residue of which fuels the magic that sustains Dyrezan. In olden epochs before history the Gods soared through such tunnels between the planes. Here this one arises from the earth, placed here at the dawn of the universe by Great Xenophor in His wisdom, or for His amusement. These peasants worship at this shrine, rightly believing it holy, little realizing its actual nature. Here we do what we must do. Are you ready, Morca?" "I am." "Then take my hand, and will yourself." Morca took the white, shimmering hand outstretched to him. He felt nothing there, but the fingers closed about his. "Jump," commanded Lantonias.

Morca held his breath, closed his eyes, and leaped. He splashed into the pool. Cold, oily liquid closed over him. He sank, and sank, never touching bottom, until his lungs must rupture. When he could stand it no more he despairingly inhaled. He heard, as from infinite distance, the voice of Lantonias saying, "Good-bye, Morca, until we meet in the awesome joy of the world to come. May the favor of the Gods sustain you."

Morca did not gag, nor did he drown. In utter darkness he felt no substance, liquid or otherwise, about him. The sensation of sinking ceased. He hung in illimitable void, sensing nothing around, nothing within, all existence negated, including his own. He feared that he was dead, perhaps the victim of a counterfeit spirit from beyond the veil, one that had maliciously lured him to destruction. He would have panicked, only there was nothing left inside him to feel emotion. Emptiness reigned.

A pinpoint of twinkling light appeared ahead, far out on the ultimate rim of the boundless void. He puzzled over this notion: there were no boundaries here, yet he saw to an edge, though he possessed no eyes with which to see. He tried to stimulate amusement at the thought. Nothing came. The light grew brighter and larger, however. Either it or he moved in vacuum, one or both approaching the other. Still brighter and larger grew the light, began to assume a distinct, oval form. Details emerged, linear images, cubic projections that fired memory. Somewhat he knew this thing. Closer it came, until he recognized the skyline of Dyrezan, seen from high above its plane, a perfect picture of the city floating in a sea of blackness. Then the scene spun, whirling around him, and he felt once more the sensation of sinking or swift descent.

He had emerged into the real world, stood upon the Avenue of Kings under the glorious starlight of Dyrezan, with the monumental statues of ancient heroes looming about him in frozen postures of pride. He felt the pavement beneath his feet, glanced down, saw the rectangle of a massive block through his misty body and clothing. So he had re-entered the world, yes, but in the guise of a spirit. He held up his hands, marveled at their transparency. He walked to the edge of the road, touched the curved bas relief on a statue's pedestal. He felt it naturally, yet he could, as he pleased, press his fingers into the substance. "I am like unto a deed-haunted ghost," he muttered. "So being, may I drift like the will-o'-the-wisp?"

He thought to himself of the geography of Dyrezan, fastened his mind on a location, was there with the thought. He stood within the roomy, ornate chambers of the lofty apartment that came with his bygone office, beheld (despite the absence of functioning lamps) a scene of wreckage. Apparently Albragon's henchmen had looted the place after disposing of him, stealing much, vandalizing the rest. The extent of his personal loss appalled him, but he had no time for useless regrets. He sought the sealed room on the second tier where he kept his books and implements of magic, a room into which enemies passed at their peril, desiring to behold his precious and powerful valuables. They were missing, removed to the last golden amulet of mystic charm or vial of dangerous elixir. He guessed that cunning Albragon had broken the spells that warded hostile intrusion.

Through the single small, round window he gazed up at the north wall of the Royal Palace. Few lights burned there. He thought himself to that place, did not move. The mysteries of unbodied travel failed him. Then he realized why: a barrier of magic wreathed the stronghold, repelling aught of arcane influence. He was that and naught else, therefore could not pass the screen. To verify this thesis he envisioned a favorite locale, the fairy Gardens of Osthrakkias, and was there. Before him ran the lovely stream with the swaying willows on its banks, the green lawns and green serpentine mounds, the quaint old sculptures of pixies and sprites, above him the spectacular marble terraces of blossoms marking the lushly overgrown steps of the Pyramid of Flowers. The Porcelain Tower, however, was broken down, its pink casing lying in big, jagged splinters athwart the path through the verdant landscape.

As he already knew, war had come to Dyrezan. It occurred to him that no citizens were abroad, even in this popular retreat, and that all was uncommonly bathed in gloom. Above him a strange opacity obscured at intervals the winking stars. Rapidly he moved about the city, taking in the tragic devastation, evidences of brutal conflict. He saw flattened castles, fallen masonry in the streets, burnt out quarters, occasional untended corpses. Where the merriment, where the revels and frolics of the happy Sky City? When he had seen enough he dwelt upon his mission, his fleshless potential, pondered the situation, betook himself to the Central Plaza.

This he could enter, though fronted by the Royal Palace. About that edifice, at guardian points, he observed soldiers of the watch standing to or making rounds, illuminated by magic fire globes that swayed and gleamed brightly in the air. These were men of the Guard, Albragon's creatures now surely, yet he sensed no menace from them, nor from any occupant of the Palace. Intrigued, he approached, chuckled to himself at the ensuing consternation. Armed and armored men shrank back in stark fear, fled or quailed at his coming. Before he reached the steps an impressive graybeard appeared from within and hailed him. "What manner of night haunt be you?" cried the man.

Morca recognized him as Zesdais, a member of the Twenty, called to him, "I am Morca, old friend, or enough of him to know you and claim hospitality. Who rules in the Palace?" "Queen Riena governs here, departed friend, in the name of the true King, Skyrax. Care hangs heavy on her soul, so I beg that yours leave now, nor trouble us more." "I am not dead," replied Morca, "merely parceled out across the land and sky. Grant me admittance, that I may enter and counsel the Queen." Zesdais did so, though with considerable reluctance, opening a hole through the fabric of the barrier that shielded the Palace. Morca climbed and passed within the doors, watched closely at every step by the bequalmed Councilor.

Morca thought himself before the throne in the Hall of Receival, and he was there, and she was there, with her advisors and guards. She rose at his appearance, astonished, uncomprehending. The guards advanced upon him, pale and nervous, yet determined in their duty, come what may. The Queen called them back. "Is it truly you?" she asked. He said, "It is I." "All, leave us," she commanded. Her retainers vacated the chamber, but stood near with the doors open.

Tears trickled down the beautiful face of Riena. She sobbed, as does a woman rather than a monarch, "My love, this is a dreadful revelation. Against hope I prayed to the Gods, those of my people, and to yours, the great Gods of Dyrezan, most powerful of all. I prayed that you would come back to me. You have done so, but from the shades. Can love do this, as the poets would have it?"

"I have no doubts," said Morca, "only their songs are not pertinent to my seeming resurrection. Know, dear one, that despite the machinations of Albragon—despite the crime perpetrated in this very chamber—I still live, my body safely stowed, I have reason to believe, at a far place. Only in feigned death could I reach you, a situation we must adjust without delay. I would make unseemly haste, that I may appear to you again in the flesh."

"The ways of Dyrezan are strange," quoth Riena.

"Never more than now. O Queen, tell me all that has happened since I left you." This she did, in elaborate detail, speaking tellingly of the murder of Portian, leading up to her accounting of the latest events and the tides of war, with Albragon seemingly invulnerable in his castle, wreaking havoc and gradually whittling down the strength of his opponents. Mused Morca, "Difficulties mount, I see. That can be remedied. You still wear my ring. Has it served?"

"The demon of the ring, Altrazgeval, saved my life and sanity," said she. "He promised as well, in a fey manner, to aid you too,

Captain."

"Which is how I survived the long drop," muttered Morca with a smile. "So much comes clear. Tell, me, to whom must I inquire as to the whereabouts of my private effects?"

"Much was destroyed by the Ogre's henchmen," said the Queen. "If you mean your esoteric charms and books of mystery, know then that they are safely ensconced here, having been liberated by friends from your protected chamber. They are kept intact below, beloved, in the dungeon, stored for use, though attempts at consulting your spells gave poor results."

"They would work for me," declared Morca, "in my body. This news cheers me greatly. With those spells Albragon could crush all opposition. With them, I am a match for him. I know what must be done.

"Darling Riena, my dear—is it not curious that we speak freely to one another when I am little more than the shadow of myself?—darling, I may not touch you now, for there is no substance to me in this place, but by the Gods' good graces I shall return as a man to you. I must make my way back into the city as a warrior and mage of sinew and bone. The risks frankly terrify, but there is only one way. Let me explain to you how it will be done." He did this, the chancy prospects awing the Queen, but she agreed to his plan without reservation. Said she, "I issue the orders this night. It will be done as you say. Your Xenophor strikes me as a cruel and capricious God, who treats His worshipers as playthings, that He fondles or breaks as He pleases. May He love you as do I, or may you amuse Him; whatever the case, so long as He defend you from evil."

Then Morca thought longingly of his untenanted body somewhere on the earth below Dyrezan. In a flash he found himself tumbling headlong into that weird darkness, the lightless expanse in which his soul seemed the only occupant. A drear eternity passed before he regained awareness of the world, lying in the bed in the rough room of Donai's cottage with the morning glow seeping through the window, coming to as from a dream. He cried out for his host, who came running.

In answer to a barrage of questions Donai replied, "We found you sleeping heavily by the Sacred Well, nor could normal means awaken you. Failing all else, I trusted nature and the Gods to bring you back to us."

Morca, on his feet and briskly pacing, said, "Donai, friend of mine in distress, you know somewhat of me, and here now I tell you all. I am Morca, Captain Most High, sorcerer of Dyrezan, of the sky-born, a great man among my people. Running afoul of tyranny I was cast down, sent into the jaws of death by the criminal usurper Albragon, yet this night, via pathways unknown to common mortals, my soul has flown upward to my city. Gigantic deeds await my performing. I must return to my home in the flesh, and it must be this day. My compatriots, who are legion, will act above. I must fulfill my part here, and for that I require your help, and that of your people. Know you aught of arms, Donai?"

"In my youth," his host informed him proudly, "I served as foot soldier under a former Skyrax, in expeditions to foreign lands at the edge of the world. I desired travel and excitement, so I fought. I have not forgotten those days."

"Grant me this boon, then, for which you will be rewarded well."

"What we can do," said Donai, "will be done. I swear it. We know of the nobleman Albragon. He is a plague to my people. Lead us against him."

"It will be a dirty business," Morca warned, "with much suffering."

"Suffering is the lot of man. I swear it."

During the long day Morca marshaled the young, hearty youth and headmen of Streckis and nearby villages, calling for volunteers in a glorious enterprise, instructing them, cheering them as only he could to feckless enthusiasm. They came by scores and hundreds, with spears and bows, knives and clubs, and dozens of hastily fashioned wooden ladders. With the creeping of dusk the Captain gathered his makeshift force, marched them to a point behind a low hillock close to the stockade about the Lower Gateway. Morca, the only man wearing armor and bearing sound weapon, inched over the crest, observed the soldiers of Albragon lazily strolling the ramparts. All appeared as usual there. He told off his men, the majority of them crouched in readiness facing the main gate, a smaller group shifting to the left, where the concealing rise curled slightly about the western wall.

High in the sky, above the dark edge of Dyrezan, three searing red balls of flame exploded into temporary brilliance. It was the agreed signal. To Donai and the leaders of the main body Morca issued the order to charge. The ragtag band swept over the hillock, waving their weapons and dragging their ladders, shouting wild, impromptu battle cries. Up and over the slope they dashed, making straight for the gate.

The armored and helmed liege-men of Albragon clustered up on the stockade wall, brandishing their terrible swords. The attackers closed the gap, threw up their ladders, shot arrows at exposed heads. The first daring lads clambered up the wall. Blades chopped at them, flung stones crushed them down, boiling oil scalded them, simple magic dazzled them. The ladders toppled.

This was according to plan. It was the designated task of the larger force, as Morca coldly determined, to ostentatiously die. Now they milled below the ramparts in chaos, a few hardy fellows retrieving the ladders and raising them again. The warriors above howled with bloodthirsty glee. Meanwhile, Morca took command of the lesser force, the pick of the best of this lot of farmers and cattle hands, also poorly armed, but equipped with as many ladders as the bigger group. Forswearing battle cries, in commanded silence they charged around the mound to the west, coming up in the space of a minute to the virtually undefended wall. The ladders shot up in unison, strong youths leaping upward on the moment. Morca wove a trivial charm that blinded the handful of swordsmen protecting this end of the bastion. A few of his troops fell, most of them reached the top. He drew his sword and came right after, joining the fray. Surely he swung his blade, two-handed strokes that scattered death around him. Then all along the wall it was man against man, spear against sword; then three against one, then five. The guards of the western wall perished, overcome by numbers. Having breached the wall the attackers ran riot, taking the defenders of the gate from behind, while those without scaled their remaining usable ladders, catching Albragon's hirelings in a deadly vise. The wounded commander of the post, a surly brute, promptly surrendered.

"The Gods blast me," he bellowed in his rage and mortification, "if I know why help did not come from above. With timely reinforcement I would have slaughtered you all. Doubt not that it will come, and you will pay for this evening's entertainment.."

"Bind them," said Morca evenly to his men, "all that still breathe, and lodge them securely. Donai—" for they came together there, just inside the now opened gate—"I thank you for your service. How goes it with your people?" "Many killed, many maimed for life," he replied, with an oddly joyous air, "but all who live shall boast a tale for their sweethearts and grandchildren. What of this threat, O Morca? Will retribution come?" "Not if my allies have succeeded in their part," Morca said. "Come with me, and bring a torch. We will investigate."

The pair crossed the littered soldier's compound, ignoring the ransacking already ongoing, to the simple orange sandstone structure behind the post commander's quarters, a perfectly square building with minimal ornamentation. Over the massively high and broad doors was carven the words "Gateway to Wonders Unimagined—Enter Here, He Who Is Bidden." This was the focus of the Lower Gateway, from which one could rise magically to Dyrezan, if the Eyrie were open to travelers, and great wizards above favored admission. Morca entered at once, Donai after a fearful, superstitious hesitation.

Within was a wide, empty space, and an alcove to one side containing peculiar instruments that must mystify a terrestrial dweller. Morca, on the other hand, knew them well. By the light of Donai's torch he operated controls, pulling levers and turning knobs, whispering all the while ancient words of strange power by rote. Multi-colored lights gleamed on crystal panels, toothed wheels revolved within. A dull humming noise emanated from the instruments, grew in volume. "Everything is fine on this end," said Morca. "Now, let me send a message to the Eyrie, that we shall see if the requisite answer returns." He whispered an arcane phrase into a silver speaking tube, waited silently. Shortly, rather to Donai's dismay, another unintelligible utterance wafted quietly from the tube.

"Great Morca, do the Gods reply in this place directly to the pleas of mortal man?" he asked.

"I would not limit Them," said Morca. "However, what you heard is a pre-arranged secret signal from my confederates, establishing that they hold the Upper Gateway." He grasped Donai by the hand. "For your aid I thank you. Succor your people, knowing that you shall henceforth live in my esteem and under my personal protection. I go now to the distant city in the sky. You must leave this chamber. Good-bye."

Alone, Morca activated the machinery which harnessed the energies of the Celestial Vortex. When power had built up sufficiently he abandoned the alcove, standing within the vacant interior of the building. Massy gears rumbled, the roof slid back, opening onto the starry sky. A grayish-white cloud formed in the chamber. Morca rose steadily into the air.

And when he stepped from the mist he trod on the firm platform of the Eyrie. The warriors of the Queen awaited him, and to his surprise that lady herself. "We staked too much," she said, responding to his open amazement. "I would not trust your code to another, lest betrayal strike us down in this weighty hour. Morca, it is indeed you, the man in flesh, armed as a soldier now, bruised and stained. You won through fairly?"

"I employed the materials at hand," he said. "They sufficed. Let us hasten to the Palace." Said Riena, "My carriage lies without. We will ride fast." So they with their bodyguard strode through the debris of ferocious battle, broken bodies in heaps, swathes of dripping gore, discarded swords and smashed fortifications. The two entered the gilded carriage, drawn by four white horses, rare beasts in Dyrezan. They took off at a gallop. In solitude, Morca embraced Riena, kissed her passionately, met no resistance. "I know," he said presently, "only that you achieved the set goal."

"I obeyed your commands to the letter," explained Riena. "My best wizards, and the bulk of my army, I brought to bear on this single spot. In order to accomplish that much I must give up all but the Royal Palace and a handful of strategic castles. Even now Albragon's creatures rampage unchecked throughout the city. He placed great importance in holding the Eyrie, but little did he dream that I would risk all to take it, or why.

"Loyal mages broke up the magic webs, and then faithful warriors charged the defenses, willed to do or die. Many did, but I tell you that most died. Again and again the troops advanced, heedless of casualties, my men falling back when the storm of battle blew ill, I rallying them for yet another attempt. The false King's pernicious magic intervened, with horrific results, but only after we had seized the initiative. By then the defenders were too few to hold the line. The soldiers of the true King, those who weathered the gusts of swordplay and the furies of murderous magic, hewed passage through the redoubt, and then our men, cruelly used and tasting blood, were overcome by a grim madness that did not release them until they had slain all who dared oppose them. There will be no survivors to bear the tale to Albragon."

"I will tell him," vowed Morca, "when I see him."

In the high, windowless conjuring chamber of his somber castle Albragon sat at the end of a long table, a mirrored trapezoidal crystal before him, sat gazing into the milky angles that, on the surface, reflected segments of his scowling face, while the pulsing interior revealed to him a caravan of obscure images. At the far end of the long table hunched Thocratis, glumly drinking in silence as his master labored.

"On balance," said Albragon, "I say the situation pleases me. Within a matter of hours I have seized most of the city. I control the main thoroughfares, so that none can move without my permission, and my enemies are reduced to islands of strength, cut off one from the other. Scarcely did I believe their collapse would come so swiftly. If that were all, I would expect to massacre the traitors by week's end."

"That is not all," cried Thocratis, sitting bolt upright and leaning forward. "There is that odd business at the Eyrie, for which we must account."

"I know," said Albragon, "I know that and more. Why did they squander the blood of their legions to destroy a single post, albeit a heavily guarded one? That hurt me, to be sure, but they paid tenfold for the privilege. Where the sense in that? Also, learn now, Thocratis, that the Lower Gateway has been raided by peasants—savages!—at the same moment. I have seen aspects of it here in visions, dimly discerned through mystic screens, but unmistakable. A pattern emerges, you see. What do you deduce from that?"

"They seek escape at any cost," came the nervously eager reply.

Albragon glared at his tame magician, shook his head in disgust. "You are a fool, Thocratis. Riena will not run. A spine of steel that one has. I did not realize. I thought to use her for a toy. I could have employed her better. No, fellow, not to flee have they seized those gates. They required egress for reinforcements, were willing to bathe in their own blood to get it. Yet to what purpose? To recruit a gaggle of inept farmers?"

"They are up to something," Thocratis said morosely. Despite the victories of his Lord, the Councilor had never regained full favor since his fateful handling of the Twenty. Having thrown in his lot he could do no other than persevere, yet he felt the situation fraught with complications, and the pertinacious resistance of the rebels dispirited him. By now he had dreamed of ruling de facto in the King's name. Instead, he was nothing. Neral, he of the strong arm and sharp blade, counted for far more. "Perhaps these constitute acts of desperation," he whined, "but our foes continue to weave webs. We can not rest, not for the space of a breath. My Lord, what bring they from without the city?"

"Hold the question," snapped Albragon, "until I claim the answer. It is a 'who,' be sure, not a 'what.' A warrior in armor led the rabble against the Lower Gateway. That I saw. One of their own, a lowly veteran of the Outland wars, or one of our people? That is the factual dilemma. If one of us, then who? Has he returned to the city? It seems probable, only I draw blank on the face. I have accounted for all the great ones—the current foaming dogs are known to me, while Lantonias died before me vomiting his rage, and too clever Morca nose-dived to perdition—yet this factor remains. This I must determine. When I know, I may prepare."

During the ensuing days the tactics of the Queen's forces altered noticeably. Their spasmodic ferocity diminished, replaced by a studied logic of military calculation that bore swift fruit. Albragon's marauders, suddenly faced with cunning snares and insidious stratagems, halted in their tracks, indeed gave back a portion of their recent conquests, realizing the need to consolidate and reorganize for what their master believed the last big push. Thocratis was now of little use, inclining to strong wine rather than powerful potions, but Neral continued keen to go forward, averring that a critical moment slipped away. "Why do we retreat?" he asked gruffly, "when we have them tied like prisoners for execution? Let us thrust once more and finish this." Albragon muttered, "Not yet. Strange wheels turn. Fear not, your turn will come. Thocratis, awaken and attend. Read the signs as I do. A hero coordinates their efforts; though not a sorcerer, I reckon, for his unique powers I would readily detect. I must identify him, before I can destroy him."

In conference with Morca and others Riena said, "Our circumstances improve. Thanks to the soldierly wisdom brought to bear by the Captain Most High of the Guard, we stand no more at the brink of defeat. How move we next?"

Zesdais replied, "Let us build upon defensive success, and carry the war to the Ogre on all fronts. Harry him at every turn, until no plot of land exists upon which he may stand, save before his own grave."

"Take no chances," advised Nantrech. "By degrees we shall beat Albragon, and send him to the hell that yawns for him. Time now works for us. Eschew haste, advance by slow stages. Little victories add up, in the fullness, to glorious triumph."

"That we may not do," announced Morca. Sitting at the right hand of the Queen, he rose to address the council of war. "I say we have tarried long enough, maybe too long. As you all know, I avoided great magic at first, that the tyrant be kept in confusion as to the powers arrayed against him. On my coming, therefore, I took mere emergency measures, out of necessity, that we might win breathing space. We have that, of a sufficiency, but little more. Albragon's forces remain strong, ever ready to strike again when he commands. His thug Neral will not wait to please us. Also, his magical abilities stand undiminished, which troubles me. Despite my strenuous efforts I have not seen into the fastness of his castle. I would know what goes on there. Within those walls he, Thocratis, and other slavish lackeys foment dole and doom for us. Furthermore, and most importantly, we know nothing of the fortunes of the true Skyrax, imprisoned somewhere within that hold. Lives he still? If so, how long before Albragon tires of him, or decides his life adds no weight to the scales? If the possibility remains, then Skyrax must be liberated, alive, to resume his sway over the city and empire of Dyrezan. That is our primary duty."

Morca grimaced, glanced at Riena. The Queen nodded, bowed her head to conceal her sorrowful expression. "It must be," she murmured.

Her Captain rubbed his hands together, said solemnly, "Tonight I lie in the nether chambers with my books of arts and arcana. I beg you, my Lords, do not disturb me. I must prepare myself for the battle to come."

And across the flaming, smoldering city Albragon was saying, "I will roll the dice once more with this deposed Skyrax of yesteryear. A slender reed he is, yet before we gained a brief advantage from showing him to the mob. Dredge him from his cell, Thocratis, feed him, make him pretty for the crowd, and display him again. Use your powers to relay his words to all who will hear. I will tip my enemies off balance ere I lash back at them." "It will not serve," replied his puppet Councilor, "for they have seen through the ruse. The gamble will further stoke their hatred. My Lord, make the most of arms and magic, forbear unfashionable tricks." Albragon blazed, "So I decree, idiot. Like all of Dyrezan, you survive at my sufferance. Obey, or be brushed aside. Take the task in charge, and succeed at peril of your life."

In the darkest depths of the Royal Palace Morca, dressed in the black robes, striped with crimson, of the master conjurer, sat sunken into a great chair once used by the true King, where the Captain studied and pondered by the flaring radiance of five greenly burning, smokeless candles arrayed in a circle. About him on a massy oaken table in the center of the granite chamber lay open his precious volumes of antique lore and his tomes of dreadful insight. In particular he perused those spells of advocation and invocation: those designed to hurl maximum strength in accordance with a stated task, such as the punishment of a foe, and those employed to call up powerful entities from mystic planes beyond the ken of the visible world. Morca checked and rechecked his calculations, weighed gains against debits, sought the narrow path between unlimited force and reasonable safety. When he must choose, he leaned toward the former, accepting certain frightful risks that he might dare big deeds. Along the walls on wooden trestles and trolleys the instruments of the sorcerer supreme stood arrayed, beakers and flasks and pots quietly steaming with strange concoctions, while the contents of a heavy black iron cauldron bubbled and moaned, sending forth acrid, glowing vapors. He had readied all this according to thoughtful plan.

Morca acted. At the appointed hours of darkness, midnight, two o'clock, and four o'clock, he recited in a hoarse whisper the requisite chants that, in combination with sagely prepared ingredients of esoteric formulation, break down the walls between the known and the unknown, releasing into the world peculiar energies and fitful gleams of mind held by no human head. At those wee hours Morca talked with things that lurked beyond the grave, or greater beings that dwelt beyond the rim of known space. To be in their presence was unpleasant, to deal with them painful. Monstrous phantasmagoria reared up before him, to demand, to deny, to negotiate, perhaps to appease. Morca did likewise, the hardy magician absorbing the brunt of their innately ferocious being, and in the stillness before dawn he found his way, marshaled the powers, willing or unwilling, that would march with him. In the end he rasped with dry throat the final spell, spoken in the coarse and olden tongue of a long dead mage, words which might fairly translate as:

> Pass at this bidding through the lightless halls
> Of corridors twined within unseen walls
> Stand ready at beck to the voice that calls
> Upholding him faithfully if he falls.

He crept from the chamber at daybreak, weak and sweaty, crying to those who found him, "I crave sleep. This day I rest. Tonight I fight." He repaired to the seclusion of a bedroom prepared on the order of the Queen. Guards ensured that no one troubled him.

Thocratis dragged forth the legitimate Skyrax from his stinking, dank, cramped, unlighted cell in the bowels of Albragon's castle. "Today you speak," demanded the Councilor, only long and cruel confinement had hardened the prisoner, who sneered with all the strength he could muster, "You, Thocratis, and your whip-master Albragon, are traitors enough. I will not betray my people. Even here, at the bottom of creation, I detect the signs of approaching vengeance. It matters not what happens to me. Kill me, if you please, for I will lose merely the joy of watching you die a thousand times." Screamed Thocratis in a madness of rage, "I do not brook argument from slaves. See my eyes, and obey," and the spell of Thocratis charmed the starved mind of Skyrax, who crawled out of the cell like an animal, necessitating the efforts of callous guards to lift him to his feet. They pulled and shoved him up the many stony flights of perpetual gloom into the agonizing sunlight of the inner court, where he cried out and fell, thence, after rough handling, to the top of the outer battlements. Below a tame crowd of near captives—the best that Thocratis could provide—waited to hear him, but not only to these would he speak.

"Recite the words I dictate to your mind," said Thocratis, "and my brain will channel them to all the great Lords and mages still living within range of my powers. Order them to stand down, as they love you. In the name of Skyrax and Dyrezan, call for their fealty, and their surrender."

So Skyrax spoke, yet he screamed as he spoke, as though wrestling with a terrible inward pain, like that of cancer eating out his vitals. And in a clear, high voice he shrieked, "Albragon the usurper is the devil incarnate, these others his soulless minions. Hunt them down, chastise them, destroy them like the mad dogs they are. With all of your might, my people, avenge me!" And he said more, speaking quickly, wildly, before the startled Thocratis recovered his poise and, bellowing an ugly word of blackness, struck down Skyrax with the frenzied claws of his mind. The King crumpled, whimpering, his body shaking from crown to toes as with ague.

With the first glimmer of starlight in a purpling sky Morca came forth from his resting place, to be greeted by the Queen and her stern advisors. Said Riena, "Know you, O Morca, that within these hours our Skyrax lived, and he called to us from across the inferno of the city. Time grows short. What will you?"

Morca replied, "It is time. Dismiss these." When she had done so Morca crushed her to himself in a brutal embrace of abandon, With his lips caressing her fair cheek he said, "If we meet never more in this world, know that my love cascades like a fiery volcano forever. If I should return, though, my dearest, in full triumph, it is a pity to be accepted that much of goodness must remain always in shadow. Can you bear this?" Said she, "As long as you live, beloved, I can be happy."

"So be it." And Morca steeled himself, stood apart from his

Queen, stretched forth his hand and with great solemnity said, "Madam, my ring, if you please." Riena removed it from her finger, where it had resided since the terrible night when she thought him lost forever, and she delivered it into his palm.

Albragon was tormenting his lackey Thocratis in the lofty main hall of his castle, with grinning henchmen for audience, spitefully snapping his fingers, which simple gestures spun round the Councilor, yanked him off his feet, hurled him against the grotesque tapestries masking the nearest rough wall. Thocratis pleaded for mercy, begging not to be killed. Sneered Albragon, "What, dog, I should allow you life? Ever you have been a blemish in my eye, and now, simpleton, your foolishness makes me a laughing stock, if it does not grieve me sore. Mighty mage, can you not even control the sickly brain of my half-dead prisoner? For the King who was I will issue orders for immediate death. He may thank me, but know you, fear my wrath. Great joy it will give me to tear out your entrails and wrap them around your skinny neck!" This deed Albragon would have committed on the spot, having ready a charm for such a purpose, only just then he froze in place, saying nothing for many long moments, the sole sound in the cavernous room being the gasping of Thocratis' breath.

Then roared Albragon, "Unbidden I feel it. Great power rears in Dyrezan. I see through swirling mist—now clearly—the scales fall from my eyes with the passing of a ring. It is he! Morca has returned. Against all possibility and fancy he comes. He, or someone privy to his secrets, invokes the font of his power; and who else knows his peculiar mysteries? I must see more. To the tower I go, where more will be revealed through cunning art. Find your feet, Thocratis, and attend me." Albragon whirled and stormed from the hall. Thocratis, moving like a bent old man, staggered after.

With the ethereal vibrations of a unique magic humming through the air, Albragon had no difficulty in locating the source of the disturbance. Staring wide-eyed into his crystal of seeing, he beheld by the light of many sparkling torches a tall, berobed, grim-faced man marching determinedly at the head of the armed hosts of the Queen. "It is he!" shouted the nobleman. "Morca comes, flanked by the wizards of Riena. Look you, Thocratis—get up, man, or the curse of Xenophor be upon your soul!—on your feet and see. There he is, the big man with the look of calm hate in his eyes. Within those orbs glows the red rays of mighty magic. He comes for blood. I must prepare a suitable counter.

SKYRAX, LORD OF DYREZAN

"Get hold of yourself, Thocratis, and do my bidding. Go forth, take charge of the defenses while I conjure. Call in all forces to this point, send out Neral with my soldiers, use your fusty magic skills, anything to buy time. Delay, while I devise."

Said Thocratis, his bald head shining a sickly yellow in the glare of the luminous crystal, "I am weary, my Lord. Send another." Said Albragon, "Go now. Do not tax me." "My Lord, I am afraid." Albragon rose swiftly, slapped his lackey mage with the back of his gloved hand. "Fear only me. Go, and this morning we will drink to the wailing souls of our enemies."

Morca, his sorcerial comrades, and the army of the Queen and true King tramped through the lanes and broad avenues of the desolate city. Clambering over rubble and skirting unchecked fires they advanced. With ease they drove through the outposts of the false King. When they neared their destination they bore the brunt of a hastily orchestrated, but determined counterattack helmed by the fierce Neral. Suddenly Albragon's swordsmen closed from two sides, surging forward in packed ranks. Morca commanded his fellow wizards to retire, while he ordered forth his warriors, he at their head. He cast off his robes, revealing his full combat armor, drew his sword and bawling a cry of battle braced to meet the oncoming enemy. The opposing legions in their thousands came together with a crash. Morca's blade flew left and right like an avenging eagle, biting deeply into its prey. Swords rang on shields, cleaving chain mail and flesh. The streets grew slick with spouting blood. Neral closed with Morca, roaring in his battle fury, "Was not one death enough for you? I give you another." They fought, sword to sword, those grim combatants, while the soldiery of both sides drew aside to behold the outcome. Neral was strong, a tough warrior, but an animal in armor, while Morca was clever and deft, a princely champion of swordplay. Neral went down, hewed in pieces. With his gory passing Albragon's battered regiments of liege-men fell back into the night.

Morca regrouped the army, advanced anew. The towers of Albragon's castle loomed dimly ahead, darkly silhouetted against distant blazes. From the left, rushing against the tail of the column, fresh forces of the Ogre struck. The noble Captain of the Guard swung reinforcements through narrow alleyways, took the assailants in the flank, routed them. Shattered skulls leaking brains, rent bloody muscles and butchered bone marked his path. The foe fled in panic. Morca turned his troops yet again, resuming the march to Albragon's citadel.

They arrived at the small plaza before the gate just as the last of the usurper's withdrawing men streamed within and slammed the iron doors with a reverberating clang. Atop the high, crenelated walls bowmen poured down a rain of arrows. A dark figure above the postern wildly waved its arms. "Thocratis," Morca observed. "So the Ogre relies on the rat. Bring up the breaching party." A company of the Queen's toughest men, accoutered with battering rams and a wide overhead shield of plate iron, advanced to the fore. Thocratis howled a charm which sent down flurries of blue fire and wisps of poisonous black fog. Morca called up his mages. "Remove that lout from my sight," said he.

Zesdais, Falcro, Nantrech, Harmon, and the rest of the surviving noble wizards of Dyrezan linked hands, murmured a sing-song chant, a low but vibrant sound. The battlements shook to the tune. Amidst the hail of fire and drifting fumes they uttered the spell which unseats the bedrock of the earth, in this case the ancient foundations of the castle wall. Loathsome shapes of terror blacker than night hovered or darted above the outlines of the castle. The wall wavered, stray stones toppling, then the mighty barrier began to crumble. Big rents appeared as upper sections of the wall fell, cascading screaming soldiers to their deaths. The iron doors of the gate bent as in the grip of gigantic hands, then twisted and fell forward to the ground, revealing the inner stockade of wood lined with armed men. Thocratis strove with all his arts to repel the weird attack, but wise Morca quietly blocked every attempt at interference. When all was done that magic need do he sent forth his select company.

With a cheer the tight lines of men stormed forward, bearing their heavy loads of assault equipment. The huge wooden logs of the rams, capped with fists of iron, were each carried by a squad of the strongest warriors. Others held up the massive sheet of iron, from which a scattering of arrows bounced harmlessly. The men charged through the broken gate, crashing with a resounding roar into the wooden wall within, which gave under the impact of the rams like so much balsa. Then swords flashed in the gleam of the torches, and the stout lads of the Queen hacked their way through the splintered remnants of the fence.

Morca came right after them, his blade held high, telling off orders to the warriors who rushed through the gap into the courtyard. The fight became one of desperate knots of men struggling furiously, with elation or despair, in the gloom. Morca met Thocratis as the latter descended the stone steps from the ruined wall.

"Slavish toad," cried the Captain, "prepare your soul for its dark destiny." Thocratis, his face stricken in a grimace of terror, commenced a complicated series of gestures with his fingers, his lips moving rapidly, but Morca swept aside this spell with a bemused glance. Thocratis cringed, cowering with his back to the wall. "Have mercy!" he screeched. "Do as you will to him, but spare me!" Morca's eyes narrowed, and he whispered something inaudible save to himself, and he thrust out two fingers toward the face of the woeful Councilor. Thocratis gasped a thin scream, then seemed to sink to the flagstones of the courtyard. It was as if he fell or sagged downward, yet he did not bend at knee or waist. An irresistible force drove him upright against the stones beneath his feet, only the stones did not give way under the pressure; rather, the man crumpled. Under Morca's blazing gaze Thocratis, wailing like the damned, was crushed into himself, the bones of his legs snapping, then his spine. Flesh ruptured, steaming blood gushed. Then the head collapsed, still screaming silently after the tongue was rendered jelly. In a twinkle naught remained of Albragon's pet mage but a lumpy puddle of gore, scarce noticed among the heaps of human debris.

As Morca's forces finished the bloody task of sweeping clear the yard of living opponents, a baleful light gleamed and poured forth from about the high, windowless conjuring tower of Albragon's keep. The very stones glowed, as if unable to contain the power mounting within. Morca handed command over to the nearest officer, saying to him, "Slay your enemies, and find the King. Liberate and protect him at all costs," then dashed into the ground floor of the mansion, which the occupiers were already engaged in ransacking. He ran past these men, through rooms of somber splendor, straight into two of Albragon's henchmen attempting to flee up the grand castle staircase. Cornered, they turned to fight, regretting for mere moments their decision. Morca cut them down with two strokes. He leaped over their sprawled bodies and raced up the stairs, found the door to the tower unguarded, made his way with greater caution up the spiraling flight of iron steps within. His boots rang on the metal, the echoes ricocheting from the circular stone walls. He reached an intermediate landing containing a hall given over to strange curios and morbid paintings, a museum of sorts suiting the tastes of the master of the castle.

There Morca received a visitation. Before the door leading to the upper and final level of the tower there coalesced a tall, lean, hideous form, like nothing he had seen before. Though wise in the ultimate secrets, never had Morca delved into the foul, bottomless hells from which this ghastly entity had been dredged. It was not a man, nor a beast, nor a spider, nor a jellyfish, but an inextricable amalgamation of all these things. It croaked in a filthy, mind-polluting voice, "Thus far, Captain, and no farther. Albragon wills it."

Morca hurled at the horror a powerful spell of saying down, without effect. "Fool I am," cried he, "to wrestle with this madness. I call now on my chief ally." So saying, he twisted the magic ring restored to his finger, uttering the frightful name of Altrazgeval. That mighty being of dread materialized, eyeing askance the fateful scene before him.

"What will you of me, Morca?" he hissed. "I see naught of interest. That is Cralefars, eater of men." Demanded Morca, "Rid me of this pest. This I order." Altrazgeval grinned—a sight to make a strong man quail—saying, "Your orders, Morca, liken to thin gusts of gentle breeze across a plain of naked stone. I do not hear them."

"Why so now, slave of the ring?"

"Fool you are, Morca, to believe that. As it concerns me, this conjured power is at liberty, and I commend you to your death. Our pact you voided when you delivered the ring to your lady love the Princess. For higher reasons I aided her, throwing in one further help to you in the bargain, otherwise you would not be here now, but smashed on the rocks below the city. Thus my kindness. However, my deeds are done, the equilibrium restored."

"Albragon lives!" cried Morca. Tensely he watched the hideous spawn of the false King, which seemed diverted by amused malevolence as it awaited the outcome of the debate. "While he lives the struggle hangs in doubt."

"No," intoned Altrazgeval. "Only your fate resides in uncertainty, a trivial matter. Albragon is finished. His army crippled, his citadel taken, with no scope left to him save personal vengeance. From here I can see him cowering in his tower chamber above our heads, the man nearly spent, living longer a while only in hopes of seeing you dead. I can see this"—he paused, rolled fishy eyes as if scanning a distant scene—"I see this, and more. Good fortune to you, old friend, for there is that remaining to be done, requiring your presence. Albragon's schemes for vengeance cost too dearly. You shall go forward after all, one more leap into the fire. The natural order of Dyrezan must be restored, as the Gods will, therefore I intervene this last time. Morca, count yourself indeed a lucky man."

Without further explanation Altrazgeval advanced to combat against Cralefars. To behold their clash was to peer over the shoulder of insanity. Surely any attempt to describe the battle would resemble mad raving. These were beings with shapes, but shapes highly malleable in circumstances of action. The unhallowed occupants of the paintings on the walls watched impassively as claws lengthened and slashed; tentacles sprouted, writhing and groping; great fangs suddenly gleamed and bit. Altrazgeval ripped a massive appendage from Cralefars, as Cralefars burrowed into the trunk of Altrazgeval. Gelatinous ooze slopped from many wounds. Fresh mouths opened to gnaw, new arms grew to rend, all this taking place without word or cry, a quiet butchery of arcane flesh. Then Cralefars was down, his substance leaking odoriferous into the air of the landing like oily smoke. Soon he was entirely gone. The remnant of Altrazgeval reconstituted, soon assuming its original form, complete and horrid.

"So much for that," said he. "Go now, Morca, continue to the top, where you must confront Albragon, by the determination of Xenophor, who it amuses to see Dyrezan intact, at least for this fleeting day and hour. Go, and do not call on me again, as you love your life. I grow weary of these meaningless human conceits." Altrazgeval was gone, just like that.

Alone, relieved of incredible sights and companions, Morca felt stirred to action, and he stormed forward up the twisting stairs to the ultimate chamber at the top of the tower. He knew that, for his former ally of the ring to have interceded once more on his behalf, the situation must be dire indeed. The truth of this he learned when he thundered into Albragon's conjuring chamber.

The man himself awaited the onslaught sitting expectantly in a chair of brass figured with designs of repellent reptiles and creeping vermin. In a corner, partially concealed behind a table piled high with unique relics of magic, half lay and half sat the King, Skyrax, the true King and Skyrax, bound and gagged, his eyes bright with helpless terror. Instantly Morca understood the cause of Altrazgeval's final intercession, a cause confirmed by Albragon's sneering boasting of his last crazed act. "I lose," he cried, "but you do not win, Morca. Here you die, and before I perish at the hands of your thralls, the King dies, too."

With a blast of focused fire Morca commenced the duel. Albragon sprang from his seat, easily turning the ball of flame which caromed into the geometrically woven wall hangings, charring to flaring ashes the heavy fabric. The man who had styled himself King, and laid all the greatness of Dyrezan under his boot, ejected hatefully from his mouth vile words of sinister antiquity, syllables fostered and nurtured in the detritus found in the tombs of dead wizards. Morca staggered back, feeling a band of icy iron about his neck choking off the air to his body. A cunningly chosen whisper threw off the unseen noose. He barked a spell, a gift of esoteric research hailing from the days of the first Skyraxes, that shot hot daggers into Albragon's brain. The man screamed like a beast in torment, then rallied to fight on.

So it went, great mage versus great mage, Morca all wise and fired with righteous passion, Albragon supremely able and driven to sorcerial heights beyond his powers by utter desperation and boundless rage. Each man lived solely for the desire to destroy his opponent, thinking nothing of his own life save that he tarry on earth long enough to beat down his foe and strangle his living essence. It was a strange battle, a continuous series of weird cries, muttered enchantments, and carefully wrought, complex gestures, punctuated by oddly colored flashes of light, bursts of discordant sound, puffs of smoke and hints of crabbed shadows stalking unembodied about the magical wrestlers. Both men responded physically at whiles to forces unseen, forces to be deduced solely by their effects: Morca crumpling against a wall, clutching with one hand at his chest, while the fingers of the other dragged down about him a tapestry depicting the execution of an olden sage of wizardry; Albragon doubling over in tearing pain, hurling himself over a tassel-fringed bench laden with jeweled vials of steaming elixirs, smashing the vials with his heaving bulk and spraying the precious contents onto the polished igneous floor. A man would go down, seemingly beaten, to pick himself up again, casting yet another spell of doom and breathing defiance, thus renewing the contest. "Xenophor wills it!" roared Morca, "His will, you traitor!" and Albragon bellowed back, "Damn you, Morca, damn you to all the eternities of black agony!"

The might of the magically enhanced mind may well be omnipotent, but there is a limit to the strength of human flesh. The doom of one of the contestants was preordained. With a horrid, vociferous cry of "Xenophor have mercy!" Albragon thrust himself from the floor one last time, then fell full on his face, blood gushing from his eyes, nose, mouth, and ears. He went still, a cooling lump of meat, the great will and power that sustained him obliterated. "It is ended," said Morca, choking out the words between ragged gasps. The hard won victory belonged to him, a victory gained when barely a breath remained to him. Presently health returned to him, his heart ceasing to hammer and his mind to reel, and he staggered toward the bound and squirming monarch in the corner. Morca gently released his master Skyrax, to resume his sway over the citizens of Dyrezan.

Thus concluded the ephemeral tyranny of Albragon, subsequent to which the natural, seemingly eternal order of the City of Burning Gold triumphed once more. The good folk of the city acknowledged the return of their true King with festivals and pageantry, stirring speeches and renewed oaths. Skyrax himself expressed gratitude for all that his people had endured on his behalf, promising to rule them, hand in hand with the fantastically popular Queen Riena, henceforth in a manner worthy of them. Having decreed this, he quickly returned to his old soft and lackadaisical ways, which behavior troubled none of his faithful subjects, all of whom were willing to accept him as he was, so long as he be Skyrax.

From that time on Morca's star burned brighter than ever. In the interests of a strong and stable kingdom Skyrax proved pathetically eager to grant his lionized Captain Most High of the Guard all of the power and delegated majesty necessary to ensure the safety of that fabulous city in the sky. Morca attained the informal, but very real, office of supreme counselor to the King, and in due time leadership of the august Council of Twenty, through which he ruled, in effect, for all of his days as a wise and steady administrator. Nor did he lack for happy companionship. With the King ever more preoccupied with his idle amusements, Morca took on the role of Protector of the Queen, a welcome duty which brought him often into her company, an association she deigned to find agreeable, and which persisted for all of their days.

Though King and Queen had little to do with one another, nevertheless in good time a son was born to Riena, at which the people rejoiced, a son immediately declared heir to the throne, the future Skyrax. The lords and ladies of the court marveled that such a King should sire such a King, for the new Skyrax grew tall and strong, intelligent and skilled in esoteric arts, under the watchful eyes of the Queen and her Protector. Indeed, Morca—who was always "Uncle" to the boy—lavished extreme care and love upon the royal child, who came to resemble him, in physique as well as interests, in so many ways. A wonderful mystery that was held to be, in that land of mystery, but none could gainsay that such a likely lad was destined to be one day a shining addition to the long and ancient line of hereditary monarchs, the true King and Skyrax, Lord of Dyrezan.

About the author:

A degreed anthropologist, wilderness enthusiast, and photographer who makes his home in Arizona, Jeffery Scott Sims is a writer of fantastic and weird fiction. He is the creator of popular characters such as Professor Vorchek, the investigator of strange mysteries; Jacob Bleek, the questing medieval wizard; and the combative and colorful heroes of ancient Dyrezan.

His publications include the dark fantasy novel, *The Journey of Jacob Bleek*; the harrowing thriller *All Expenses Paid*; *Science and Sorcery*, the companion volume to this one; and many dozen short stories of the bizarre and the macabre. A number of these tales are set in the exotic and mysterious wilds of Arizona, or in imaginary lands at the ends of the earth.

The author maintains a literary web site, *The Weird Writings of Jeffery Scott Sims*, which in addition to providing useful information on his works also offers an ever growing collection of entertaining essays devoted to unique or unusual topics related to the weird tale. This material may be freely accessed at http://jefferyscottsims.webs.com/index.html

www.ingramcontent.com/pod-product-compliance
Lightning Source LLC
Chambersburg PA
CBHW031314170626
46807CB00001B/418